FELLA ENCHANTED

S.O. Callahan

Copyright © 2022 S.O. Callahan

All rights reserved

Print ISBN: 9798407768463

Cover art by: Luisa Galstyan
Printed in the United States of America

ONE

"You may as well let her go, boyo!"

As the mare under me bucked again and twisted herself to remove me from her back, I barely heard Henry shouting and laughing at the fence where he had one foot propped, his cap in his hand. I had to do something, but letting go certainly wasn't part of my plan.

I gripped the reins tighter in my hands and pulled her head to the left to spin her into control. Instead, she bolted with several quick steps. Henry slapped his cap against the inside of the fence with a *whoop* as we passed; he was now standing on the lowest rail with a grip on the post for support. I took in the look of glee on his face as we blew past him.

The ring wasn't large enough for her to go far, so nearly as soon as she'd taken off, she jerked us back in the other direction, kicking up clods of thick dirt. The muscles in my legs and stomach clenched as I strained to stay upright. My saddle was designed for performance and maneuverability, not for keeping me secured in place, which worked to my advantage during our matches. In this scenario, it did quite the opposite. I whipped my head up and called to my friend, "Open the bloody gate!"

He hopped to the ground and reached for the latch. We barreled through the opening left behind like this had been both of our intention from the beginning. When I had agreed to take the mare off auld man Wallace and train her, I hadn't known that no one bothered to tell the wild creature that her event racing days were over. The tension in her body gave way as she realized that she was free of her confinement, and I would have liked to believe that it was my direction she was following as we tore down the path ahead of us.

I had spent the better part of three days doing groundwork with this horse since she arrived. Retired racehorses were known to make excellent polo ponies for their speed and endurance. Unfortunately, those skills were only helpful if you could actually ride them. I pushed my feet down in the stirrups and shifted in the saddle to find more stability after being tossed about. My cap had abandoned the top of my head, causing my hair to take on a mind of its own, as well. Not that I ever had much control over it to begin with. My unruly reddish-brown curls were nearly as stubborn as the chestnut beneath me.

As I turned back to see if I could spot my cap lying on the ground, I realized we'd already run so far that Henry had disappeared from sight. I lifted my eyes to the shrinking stables that stretched out in long fingers from the main barn. We had room for 60 horses comfortably across the three buildings, and several of them were peeking out over their wooden half doors, ears pricked forward with curiosity at the spectacle I'd made of myself. If this was what the mare wanted, then I supposed I may as well just give it to her after such an impressive effort. I leaned forward slightly and spurred her on with my heels at her sides.

We approached a gap in the stacked stone wall that ran along the road, and I urged the horse through with little protest, her legs swooshing through the overgrown grass and weeds that were threatening to overtake the meadow. Summertime here made everything come alive so quickly.

I swept my gaze over the lush expanse as we curved around toward the top of a small hill that allowed you to see most of our land all at once on days when the fog lifted. I briefly considered stopping for a moment since I'd not been up there for some time, but just as the thought crossed my mind, our path was intercepted by a bird we spooked out of the grass. My whole body tensed immediately, readying myself for the inevitable. *Fuck.*

The mare tossed her head and threw herself onto her hind legs as she swiveled to change direction. Somehow, I managed to hold onto the reins tight enough that I stayed seated, but rearing turned to bucking quicker than I could anticipate, and I gasped as I was tossed to the ground with a hard thud; my teeth clacked together and the air left my lungs. I rolled onto my back as I brought a hand to my chest, trying desperately to take a deep breath.

"Ow," I choked out after a few coughs, slowly opening my eyes and staring at the sky above me. As my heart started to beat at a more normal pace, I pushed myself up onto my elbows. The chestnut mare was standing a short distance away, eyeing me as she worked on catching her breath, too. We stared as each other for a few seconds, and then all I had the strength to do was flop back down into the tall, dewy grass. I closed my eyes again, pulling one leg up at the knee and resting an arm over my eyes, breathing through the ache in my chest as I felt soreness collecting in other parts of my body. Namely my wrist and my hip, both of which had taken the brunt of my fall.

Had I really just been thrown from a horse? In my whole life, I had been tossed few enough times to count on one hand. On three fingers, really. My mind was starting to tick with excuses about why I had to give the horse back to Wally when hoofbeats reached my ears. I remained still, guessing at the source, and then they slowed to a quick stop.

"Has she killed you, then?!"

I couldn't help the grin that pulled at the corners of my mouth. I had to clear my throat to speak loud enough to answer. "I don't think so."

"Aye, feckin' beast, she is! Where'd you land?" Henry called as I heard him dismounting from his own horse, a beautiful dark bay gelding. I stifled a groan as I held up the arm that I had been resting across my eyes. Henry cursed under his breath as he trudged through the thick grass that was tall enough to hide me from view. I opened one eye to look up at him when he stopped next to me. He let out a quick laugh and shook his head.

"Sorry state you're in, I'll bet. How's the lungs?" He extended his hand toward the one I was still holding up and he pulled me to my feet. Once I was standing, he held my shoulder and patted my chest, eyes searching my face since I hadn't answered his question. Henry had been my closest friend since we were young boys when his family moved to the country, and after all those years he was still just the same. Same red hair, same heavy brogue, same crooked grin.

"I'll be alright. Just sore, is all," I told him, half convincing him and half convincing myself. Henry narrowed one eye at me, taking in the look on my face to see if he really believed me. When he decided that he did, his smile returned, and he patted my chest once more.

"That was some ride! You really are a legend, Pete, really and truly." Henry laughed again and tromped through the tall grass toward the mare I had been forcibly removed from. She squealed and tossed her head a little as he grabbed the reins. He ignored her protest as he raised the leather strap forward over her head and started walking. I was relieved to see that she trailed after him. He passed me and went to grab his own horse. "Will you feel like riding back?" he asked over his shoulder with a chuckle.

"I think I'll walk," I replied flatly, finally taking a few steps in their direction as I rubbed my sore wrist. I couldn't tell if it would swell or not, but it definitely wasn't broken. I wiggled my fingers to confirm. Henry took the reins of his gentle gelding, put his boot in the stirrup, and bounced on his other foot once before he swung himself up into the saddle. We had been doing this for so long it had become second nature. He adjusted his position and turned back to look at me, the two horses swishing their tails to move the bugs that were starting to bother them.

"I'll drop her off for you and then be on me way, I'm required company with Da today." I nodded and Henry turned without another word, squeezing his legs to push his horse into motion, the mare at his side. I watched them go, waiting until they had turned the corner back onto the dirt road before I started winding my way down the sloping hill toward the open gate.

I realized now that the grass was tall enough to reach my waist, so I stepped carefully to avoid tripping over anything lurking below that I couldn't see. This meadow had been out of use for several years now. It connected to all the others with more gates in the low stone walls, some of which had also seen better days. As a child, I couldn't have pictured anything but the pristine grass, freshly painted gates, and horses or sheep dotting each available pasture. Now, we were lucky to have the business we did.

I rolled my shoulders a little to loosen them up. I was surprised how damp my clothes were from the dew. My thin wool waistcoat and shirt were soaked through on my back, as well as my riding breeches. As I looked up at the sky and the clouds that had started to gather and darken, I figured that it also could be left over from a rain shower. Such abundant greenery was hard to come by without the ever-present rain.

When I finally made it back to the low wall, I stepped onto the road and turned slightly to study my clothes. My backside and hip were a mess of wet, dirt, and a rather large smear of green. *Lovely.* At one time, I wouldn't have cared if my clothes got a rip or stain. I would've had new ones waiting for me before I could even start to worry about the old ones being ruined. But this was one of the few pairs I had left, and I felt fortunate that they still fit me.

I made a feeble attempt to wipe the dirt away, but

it was useless. I could already hear Nan's admonition. I sighed and started the walk back, but stopped shortly after. To my left was another gate, this one shut, that I had not been through for quite some time either. I reached up to rest my hand on the splintering wood and looked beyond the hill to a stand of trees that hung heavy with bright leaves. The slight breeze that was bringing in the rain clouds rustled my hair across my forehead and caused the grass and trees around me to sway.

I reached for the latch and paused only for a second before pushing the gate open. My feet carried me up the gentle slope to the edge of the tree line, where a small stone bench was resting. I rubbed my hands up and down my hips along the seams of my breeches, a nervous habit, and sat on the cold slab of a seat. My chest was feeling heavy again. I took a slow, deep breath as I let my gaze sweep across generation after generation of Walshes. My family had lived and died here for so long that some of the graves were unmarked, or time had worn the stone markers to the point of no longer being legible.

That wasn't the case for a small collection of them toward the right side, underneath one reaching branch of the giant Oak that loomed above. Richard Walshe. Catherine Walshe. Nicholas, Elizabeth, Mary. My mammy and dad. My brother and my two sisters.

How had it been so long already? Two years since I'd heard the girls all giggling in the garden together. Two years since I'd spent a whole day training with Dad. Two years since my family had been whole and healthy and happy.

I coughed a few times and wished I had brought something to lie down beneath their names. I turned around to look behind me, but the only flowers I could see were the little yellow ones that were just weeds sprinkled through the grass. That wouldn't do. Instead, I picked myself up off the bench and made my way back toward the gate, making a silent promise to myself that I would come back with a suitable bouquet. As I swung the gate closed behind me, I gave one last look up toward the Oak tree and started toward home again as the wind picked up.

* * *

The first light raindrops started to fall just as I reached the cobblestones that led to the kitchen door. I pushed it open, the hinges sounding their familiar squeak that made it impossible to come or go without announcing yourself to anyone within earshot.

"Lucy, dear?"

"It's me, Nan." I braced myself for the greeting I always got from my grandmother – a steady mix of affection, concern, and discipline.

"Oh, *Peter*," it came, my name both a coo and a reprimand. She looked me over and *tsked* my dirty clothes as I took a seat on a stool by the counter, across from where she was stationed by the sink drying dishes. I worked to unbutton my waistcoat as she milled about, gathering things to feed me before she picked the kettle up off the stove and poured steaming water into a cup.

"I'm sorry about the stains, Nan. It was an accident. I got tossed." The words left my mouth before I could think to stop them, and she whirled on me, eyes squinting and lips pressed together, making her wrinkles more pronounced.

"John Wallace. That man's going to get an earful from me." She slapped a plate of biscuits with jam in front of me, followed by the cup of tea, and then she wiped her hands briskly on a towel before picking up her skirts and swiftly exiting the kitchen, hinges protesting all the while. I turned to watch after her through the window as it settled on me that she meant auld Wally would be hearing from her *right now.* Or at least as quickly as her short legs could carry her.

Part of me felt sorry for the man, but another part of me was glad that her reaction had been what it was. All of it could have been directed at me. And for a long while, it had been.

Peter, she had scolded, *what are you thinking being on a horse again so soon? You're in no condition to be doing such exercise. The doctor has told you that your body needs more time to recover. Your lungs aren't strong enough. After all this family has been through. Please give it more time.*

As much as it vexed me, I had listened to her. I spent nearly half a year out of the saddle, and that was even after the months I was laid up in my bed. It didn't stop me from being in the stables, though. As soon as I'd been able to stand on my own and dress myself without help, I was with my horses.

I turned my attention back to the tea Nan had poured, reaching over for the honey she kept just for me. I lifted the spoon out of the thick amber syrup and plopped it down in my cup, stirring gently to prevent it from clanging around against the sides too much. I took a sip and felt the warmth spread down my throat to my chest, and then ran a hand through my hair before I slid off the stool and carried my late breakfast up the stairs to my bedroom.

Our house was large, by most standards, but it was not elaborate. Simple artwork adorned the walls, modest furniture was spread throughout, and there were enough bedrooms that none of us had to share – *a luxury when you have six kids,* Dad had always said. Now it felt too empty most days, which I didn't like, so I tried to spend as much time away as I could. I think we all did, except for Nan, who felt most comfortable in her kitchen and keeping the rest of us well cared for.

I passed by several closed doors on the long hallway upstairs before I reached my own. The door across from mine was open just a crack. I stepped across to peek inside. My baby sister, Lucy, was sitting in the middle of the floor, her dolls around her in a circle, and she was reading to them from one of her favorite books. She had given them each a seat on a pillow from her bed, and one of them toppled over. She stopped reading and reached for it.

"Lizzie, really, if you don't want to listen to my story then you can just take a nap. I won't mind!" She held the doll up to her ear and paused, then held it away again and looked her in the face. "I understand you don't like this story, but Mary does, and it was her turn to pick. Now sit and be quiet or go off to bed." I watched her prop the doll against the side of the pillow for better balance. A slight grin spread on my lips.

I crossed the few steps back to my own door and

pushed it with my foot. My window was open, allowing the fine mist of rain to blow in, so I quickly set down what I was holding to shut it. The sheer, cream-colored curtains slowed to a stop on either side with the breeze now gone, and I peered out at my view. I could see just a bit of the meadow I'd taken my spill in earlier. The stone wall surrounding it stretched far off into a web of grayish lines, separating the various pastures from areas that were just a bit too steep or rocky to make any good use of. Trees and hearty shrubs dotted the land.

Ivy grew thick on the wall closest to our house, running parallel with the path Nan was now coming back up after paying a visit to John Wallace, the man who managed our stables and lived in the small cottage just beyond them. I couldn't read her expression underneath the bonnet she had put on after her departure, but her pace told me that she was satisfied that auld Wally now knew better than he did before.

As I turned away from the window, I pulled my navy-colored waistcoat off and dropped it on the floor. Luckily, I remembered the disaster that was my rear end before I plopped down on my white sheets, and instead chose to sit on the wooden bench at the end of my bed to remove my riding boots. Normally I would have kept these at the barn, but before I made my way back down there, I was in desperate need of freshening up.

I pulled my knee-high boots off, then my socks, and then the rest of my clothes followed after I pushed myself up off the bench and made my way to the kettle sitting on the stone hearth of my small fireplace. Even though the days were pleasant this time of year, the nights could still be quite cold. I wrapped a thick cloth around the handle and lifted the kettle over to the wash basin in front of my mirror, carefully pouring the water out before I returned it to its resting place. I looked up at my reflection and studied the man staring back at me.

I had broad shoulders and strong legs, but falling sick had really done a number on my body. I was still trying to regain weight I had lost. Muscles I once had from spending tireless hours on horseback had been quickly diminished from lying in bed, coughing so much that it was impossible to eat or drink or sleep. Most of my clothes were still loose on me, but I was working to return to where I had been – *who* I had been, before.

I cupped my hands into the lukewarm water and leaned down to splash it on my face a few times. I reached for a small towel that was hanging beside the basin and wiped my face and chest with it. A few locks of my auburn hair fell damp across my forehead, and I brushed them aside with my sore wrist, which I examined next. Still no swelling, but tender. I could live with that. I turned slightly and my eyes went wide as they met the large bruise forming on my hip.

"*Ow*," I whispered in repeat of earlier as I reached to gingerly poke at my mottled skin. I decided that this might require some better attention later, but I was sure I would live as I looked back up into the mirror image of my own green eyes one last time before going in search of clean clothes. I stepped over the trail of dirty ones I'd left behind a few times before I stopped to pick them up and put them into the woven basket by the door. In the past, someone came and collected my clothes off the floor if I forgot. But now there was no "someone" other than Nan, and she didn't tolerate soiled clothes being strewn about for her to gather up *and* wash *and* put away.

I was dressed and halfway down the steps when I remembered my half-finished breakfast I'd left behind. I groaned internally and vowed to collect the dishes before Nan found them. I slid my hand down the smooth banister as I went, but had to pause at the bottom for a moment to catch my breath; I hadn't realized I was taking them so quickly. I straightened my shirt and peeked around the corner. The door to the kitchen was open and I heard Luc and Nan talking, so I took my opportunity to slip past, grateful that the front door was well-oiled and not a hinderance to my silent exit.

Once I made it outside, I shifted my riding boots to my other hand and followed the path along the ivy-coated wall toward the stables. John Wallace was busy carrying a freshly polished saddle when he spotted me. His thick brows knit together to become one under the thin brim of his cap that covered his completely bald head.

"Settin' auld Nan on me, are we? That's mighty low of you, seeing as how we made this deal fair and square just the two of us!" His attitude made me bristle.

"I'm sorry, I didn't know you were offering me a literal *wild animal!*" I followed him into the room that held our tack and set my boots next to a wooden crate that contained more of my belongings, while he nestled the saddle onto its stand like one might set a very expensive vase onto a table made of glass.

"I told you she was a feisty one, didn't I?!" He

huffed and turned to look up at me then, holding his cap to keep it from sliding off. I was a good head and shoulders taller than the middle-aged man. "She's a fine creature and has all you been lookin' for, wouldn't you say? Lightning fast, no doubt, with a great body. I don't see a problem."

"Wally, I can't get her ready soon enough for this season, and I won't have enough time to train her and the rest of my team over the summer. What do you want me to do?" The deal he had cut only partly involved me. I suspected that someone with a lot of money and pull made up the other part, which made him adamant that things worked out. This was a spot he found himself in too often, and I knew I shouldn't get mixed up in it, but secretly I had been excited for a new challenge.

I trailed him out of the tack room and down the row of stalls. Wealthy people – our neighbors – and several other polo players paid a lot of money to board their horses with us. Walshe was not just my last name, but a reputation to uphold. Something about the land, they claimed; the grass and water and air made for the highest quality care a horse could receive. Even people who were rich enough to have the most well-kept equine facilities on their own land bid and fought for a stall here when times were good.

I passed Henry's bay gelding and the three other horses that made up his team, and then came to a stop in front of the half door the chestnut mare stood behind. When she noticed me, her ears pinned back and then flicked forward, and she tossed her head twice. I leaned my forearms on the top of the door and studied her. He was right. What she lacked in manners she made up for in her strong shoulders and great bones. No doubt she could turn on a pinpoint. My sore body was proof enough of that. I took in a breath and let it out slowly, shaking my head. I didn't want to give up on her, but she wasn't anywhere near ready to ride in a match.

"Just give her a chance, eh? For your auld pal Wally?" He clapped me on the back and didn't wait for my answer as he turned another corner and disappeared through the open door. A soft nickering sound pulled my attention and I pushed off the door, turning to my own horses standing behind me.

I reached up to rub my palm flat against the tall bay mare's face, my fingers scratching the splash of white between her eyes. She was my champion. Her neighbor was my youngest, a gray who had proven herself to be an incredibly quick learner and even quicker on her feet. Last, on my other side, was my chestnut gelding who was the steadiest horse I'd ever met.

"Well, what do we think?" I asked them quietly, glancing over my shoulder. "Can we make something out of her yet, or am I a fool?" Their lack of response was expected, but entirely unhelpful. "Some friends you are, doubting me," I murmured. I scratched the mare's white patch again and then let my hand fall to my side as I made my way to the large door leading to the courtyard between the barn and the rows of stables.

TWO

As it turns out, I forgot the cup and plate in my room, and Nan gave me an earful over supper just as she had given Wally earlier that day. I promised her that I would do better. She gave my hand a squeeze with her rough, crooked fingers before turning her attention to my brother, William, and his bride, Anne.

Our families had known each other for as long as anyone could remember, and although it had not been put into words for the rest of us to hear, the two of them had been groomed for marriage since they were born. Fortunately for them, it turned out to be a union for money and for love. The wedding was to be a grand event, as weddings usually were amongst those who could afford it, especially since Anne was an only child.

Then we all got sick. And then we didn't all get better.

Fidgety William and Practical Anne decided that they didn't want a large wedding after all, so the ceremony was held at our home, where everyone in attendance fit very comfortably in our small garden. I saw Anne cry for the first and only time when Nan presented her with a dress to wear on her special day. Cream-colored with fine lace details and sleeves that came to her wrists; it had been our mother's dress. She had protested at first, saying she just couldn't, but we all insisted.

Anne was the one who had kept me alive.

When the first of us fell ill, Dad had arranged for Nan to take Mary and Lucy, the youngest two by a few years, and stay far away until it all passed. Before they could leave, Mary started showing symptoms, too. William was attending business in Dad's place in practice for taking over the estate someday, so he wasn't home, either. The six of us remained in our house, reduced to our weakest forms in a matter of days.

William had been furious with Anne for exposing herself to us, but she never got sick. Instead, she tended to us in our beds, making sure we were comfortable and hydrated and never wallowing in our sweat-soaked sheets for too long. She had seen my family through our absolute worst, and still loved us. So, the dress, the wedding, was the least we could do to show our love back.

And for a while, on that day, we were able to fill our minds and hearts with new memories of family and laughter that had been missing. William had been a nervous wreck as I stood by his side, and while I was certain I wasn't the most qualified person to be comforting him before committing his life to a wonderful woman, I tried my best. Lucy was the image of joy, wearing her favorite dress and a crown of woven wildflowers, and Nan's eyes twinkled as she watched our wilted family start to bloom again.

Her eyes were not so bright now as we sat around the table a little over a year later, and I worried for her. The stress of running our family estate had fallen to William earlier than expected, who was twenty-eight and business-minded like our dad had been, but Nan still carried much of the responsibility. She was the one who fed us and clothed us and kept us going.

She pointed her fork at him after taking a mouthful of food from it and spoke after she swallowed. "William, eat. How was your meeting today with Mr. Sullivan?" Nan watched as I finished the potatoes on my plate and promptly heaped another spoonful on the bare spot left behind. William tensed across the table, setting his own fork down and reaching for his glass to take a drink before he responded.

"That man is nothing if not stubborn. And predictable."

"Aye, no news there," Nan agreed, nodding her head and gently slapping Lucy's hand away from the gravy boat, giving her a stern look. We had become quite content crowding around the cramped, round table in the kitchen together for every meal. The formal dining room sat vacant through a door behind me.

"Anne, can we play before we read my bedtime story?" Lucy looked to her with big, hopeful green eyes that matched my own. Anne had proven that she was willing to do whatever she could to make her seven-year-old sister-in-law happy. Luc took full advantage.

"Of course. Do you want to play with your dolls some more, or shall we pretend to go on an adventure in the garden? We haven't done that in a while." Anne had a sweet lilt to her voice that made her sound younger than she was.

"How about we bring my dolls on an adventure in the garden!" my sister crowed from her seat.

"One doll in the garden, Lucy." William raised an eyebrow as he spoke, his thick mustache and neatly groomed beard making it impossible to read any expression on the rest of his face. "The last time you brought them all out, you lost one and cried for hours."

"I did not! I promise I'll keep them all close this time." Lucy looked to me with pleading eyes, and I shook my head.

"Don't you look at me. I'll have you remember I was the one who searched into the night. I don't care to do it again so soon, much as I love you, Luc." I reached across and tapped her on the nose, and she laughed and pushed my hand away. I gave her a playful wink in return.

I could see the sun setting in the window behind Anne's blonde head, and I wiped my mouth with the napkin I had draped across my lap. "May I go, Nan? The horses..." I trailed off, leaving the rest of my excuse unspoken.

"Horses, horses, always the horses," came her response. I stood and kissed her cheek, a thank-you for not arguing and for supper. I tossed my napkin into my seat, took three steps, swiveled back to push my chair into the table, and then exited the kitchen. "There's hope for him, yet," I heard Nan say behind me as the door shut.

***

The fading light didn't hinder my stroll along the dirt path. I could have done it backwards with my eyes closed after making the journey so many times, even with the various dips and grooves that had been worn into it by heavy cart wheels and rain puddles. I stuck my hand in the pocket of my loose brown trousers and pulled out the apple I had swiped from the bowl on the counter. I took a bite, savoring the sweetness on my tongue.

Growing up, our cook had a dessert prepared for us every night to wrap up our evening meal. Dessert had always been my favorite. Mammy teased that instead of one sweet tooth, I must've had at least three or four in there. I always agreed and would open my mouth wide and point to the ones I thought they were, making her laugh even though we had shared this inside joke a hundred times before.

Ever since Nan became our only cook, the desserts came few and far between. Nan did not enjoy baking. I was grateful that she at least tolerated making jams and jellies, and kept the honey pot full just for my tea. The auld bird did love me.

I took another bite of my apple as I ducked under a branch of the blooming ash tree that stood at the corner of the wall. I found Henry running a stiff bristle brush over his black mare's already glistening coat. I would dare say that Henry's horses were kept better than any I'd ever met, aside from my own. "How was she for you?" I asked, reaching out to touch her neck before I crouched beside her, running my hand down her leg to her fetlock, which had been swollen and warm the week before from an unknown injury. I couldn't feel any evidence of either under my fingers now.

"Grand, she was. Back to her normal self I'd say. Good thing, seeing as we have our first match in just a few days." He paused his brushing and stood on his toes to peer down at me over the sway of the horse's back. "The real question's if you'll be ready."

I looked up to meet his gaze for a long moment, my answer caught in my throat. I stood up and ran my hand down the smooth ebony side of the mare, stopping at her hip where her muscle twitched in response to my touch. Even though I had been cleared to return to riding, I'd sat out the last season. Nobody had questioned it. Some were even relieved. Henry and Nan, namely.

Our four-man team had been whittled down to three, nearly two if I hadn't held on the way I did. As the third position player and team captain, I felt enormous pressure to be there for my teammates, who were also my friends, and I just hadn't felt ready. So, Henry and Thomas Dougal had teamed up with two other local lads to play the season, during which they had done just fine. I was proud of them for representing our village so well, and I attended every match, doing as much as I could to help from the sidelines.

When I didn't answer, Henry came under the ropes holding his horse to the posts along the wall and reached out to grasp my shoulder as he had done earlier. After being friends for so long, he didn't need to ask many questions to read what was going on in my head.

"I miss him too." Henry squeezed once and then let go, turning to untie his mare, pulling gently to get her moving toward her stall for the night. She clopped along after him. The light was fading faster now, and I reached for the lantern that was nearest to us as we went, causing the flame inside to flicker. Our shadows danced in the aisle around us as Henry slid the door shut after delivering his horse to her stall and laid his tack across his shoulder.

I could tell he had more to say, so I matched his stride and waited for whatever it was he needed to share. Unlike his talent for knowing where my thoughts were all the time, there was never any way for me to know what would leave his mouth next.

Several horses popped their heads out over their doors as we passed by, looking for a handout even though they had all been fed. I held what was left of my apple on my flat palm toward one of Thomas's horses. She sniffed it before gobbling it up in one bite.

"Da says I'm to marry Sarah sooner rather than later. We've been courting long enough, he says. It would benefit the business, combining our families, and you know how Da feels about his business." Henry and I both knew well enough what that meant. His father, also Henry O'Connor, cared about nothing else as much as he cared about his money. Mrs. O'Connor and the children didn't suffer for anything except attention from the man who kept their lives well cushioned.

"How does Sarah feel about it?" I asked, wiping my hand that'd been coated with sticky apple juice and horse slobber dry on my trousers. Henry and Sarah had been together "alone" only a few times, chaperoned all the while of course, and I marveled at the thought of marrying someone I had only just started getting to know.

"She can't wait!" he exclaimed, tossing his hands in the air for effect and startling the horse nearest to him. "Last time we met, she couldn't stop talking about how she wants to make our home here in the country-side and start poppin' out wee ginger babes! And I sup-pose that'd be a great chat if we hadn't been sitting in front of my ma *and* her ma." The last bit he grumbled out through gritted teeth with embarrassment.

I stifled the laugh that threatened to escape my throat and held the lantern up higher as I leaned my shoulder against the doorway of the tack room. Henry chucked his expensive bridle and rope into the box by his things and heaved out a breath as he sat on the bench to remove his boots.

"Of course, I'm lookin' forward to parts of that as much as the next fella, if you know what I mean, and I know you do," he paused to waggle his red brows at me, "but I feel like it's all happening so quick." He pulled on his other boots that only came up to his ankles, like the ones I was wearing, and straightened his waistcoat as he stood. "Who knows, maybe it's just me draggin' me auld feet. You know how much I hate bein' forced into things if it's not my idea first."

"You, mate?" I quipped, earning me a jab in the ribs as we made our way out into the twilight. I returned the lantern to the hook I had taken it from after I blew it out. Henry made his departure down the path that led in the opposite direction of where I was going, and I stopped to call after him. "I'll be ready. For the match." He didn't pause his stride or even turn to look back at me, just tossed his hand up with a quick wave of his fingers in acknowledgement.

On my way back to the house, I passed Anne and Lucy playing in the garden. Luc must have worked her charm especially hard on Anne if they were still outside so late. That, and Nan must have been distracted by something to prevent her from coming out to collect them. The kitchen door's hinges announced my arrival as I glanced around to find nobody else in the room. I shut it behind me and made my way toward the short hallway that led to the stairs, but then I spotted what had kept Nan busy.

The large tub in the corner of the kitchen by the fireplace had steam rising from it, and I realized she had drawn me a bath. I returned to lock the door and shed my clothes before stepping over the high side into the water. It was bordering on too hot, but I bent my knees to fit the best I could as I sat down anyway. My feet jammed awkwardly at the end, so I crossed one ankle over the other to get more comfortable. This had been much easier as a child.

I closed my eyes and let my head rest back against the edge of the tub as the heat soaked into my sore muscles. The pain in my wrist had subsided, but my hip throbbed now that I allowed myself to pay it any attention. Bruised skin and body aches had become such an insignificant problem, though. I took a breath as deep as my damaged lungs would allow and pulled my legs up more so I could sink the rest of me below the water.

A knock on the window in the tack room made jump, and I shot a look over my shoulder to see Jamie with his nose pressed up against the glass, making a face at me. I laughed and picked up one of my gloves and threw it at him, hitting my mark but doing no harm thanks to the pane of the window separating us. He pulled away with a laugh of his own that was muffled to my ears and took off running. I knew he would come to me, so I turned back around and continued buttoning my shirt.

"Lucky shot, that!" he touted as he joined me in the room that forever smelled like fresh oil and hot leather.

Jamie climbed over the bench I was sitting on to grab my glove off the floor and thwapped it against his crisp riding breeches a few times to clear off the dust. He threw one leg back over the long piece of wood and straddled it as he sat beside me. "Your glove, my good sir," he said smoothly as he mocked a bow and held it out for me to take.

I grinned despite myself and grabbed it from him, but he didn't let go. Instead, he pulled it back, wrapping his fingers around the crook of my elbow with his other hand and pulling me along too so that we came close enough for him to press our lips together. I closed my eyes and reached up with my free hand to hold the side of his neck, my thumb resting against his jaw. He broke our kiss and leaned his forehead against mine, keeping a steady hold on my arm. I pulled on my glove again playfully and he gripped it tighter.

"You'll have to let go eventually," I said softly. "They won't let me play with just one."

"Always following the rules," he purred even quieter, releasing his grip on my elbow to run feather-light fingertips along the inside of my forearm. A small shiver hurried down my spine. "I hope someday you'll let me show you how fun it is to break 'em sometimes..."

I brought my head back above the surface, unable to fight the protesting burn of my lungs any longer and I coughed hard several times. I wiped the water off my face and blinked it out of my eyes, but my focus wasn't on anything in particular as my mind continued to replay the memory I kept tucked away.

"Feck! Warn a fella, would you?!"

I startled away as Henry loudly protested what he was seeing upon striding into the room, but I knew it was *in jest. He walked past us with an arm shielding his eyes. Jamie gave me a private smile and hopped up off the bench to finish dressing for our match that was starting soon, leaving me with the glove. I wished that I could have kept his delicate touches on my skin instead.*

"Jealous, Hen?" Jamie teased with a trill in his voice. I finished my last button and looked up to watch the reaction that would pull from our red-headed teammate.

On cue, Henry threw Jamie a look of contempt. "Ha. It's easy to joke when you're the one gettin' the ride."

"Ooh, do share with the class, James," Thomas chimed in, running a hand over his dark hair that was held in place with wax as he came to join us. He was already fully dressed, save for the helmet he had wedged under his arm. His boredom must've been the only thing that brought him looking for us. "Can't imagine which pretty girl would warm your bed when she's got the rest of us to pick from."

Jamie only needed two seconds to come up with a retort he knew would get under Thomas's skin. Not that it took much. "Didn't know you liked to cozy up to your sister, mate."

I cringed and Henry howled with laughter as Thomas started for Jamie, but he was too quick and dodged out of the way before the fist could make contact. He kept after him though, and Jamie darted out of the room with Thomas on his heels, who was sputtering over the words I was pretty sure he meant to be curses leaving his mouth.

"She is quite lovely!" Henry called after them, still laughing. He looked down at me then and shook his head, his mouth settling into the quirky grin he always wore as he slid his jacket on. "Wish it were the truth for both their

sakes, eh?"

I shrugged my shoulders in response. Thomas's sister wasn't completely unfortunate looking, but her sour personality really put the nail in the coffin. I couldn't recall a single pleasant interaction with her.

"Boys," I heard my dad call after them from wherever he was in the stables. He was a soft-spoken man. I never once heard him raise his voice in anger or frustration, even when anyone else might've said it was called for. "Boys, I need you to knock that shite off in here before you set off the feckin' horses." Cursing, however, was never off the table.

The two of them came back around the corner, with Thomas desperately trying to smooth his hair back into place after it had clearly been mussed. He eventually made a sound of disgust in the back of his throat and jammed his helmet down over it to worry about later. Henry looped an arm around his shoulders and steered him out of the room, offering an apology on everyone's behalf. Thomas was only a few years younger than the rest of us, but his short stature and round baby face made it easy to treat him like the younger brother none of us had.

I stood then to collect the rest of my things. I felt the weight of Jamie's brown eyes on me as their voices faded and silence settled around us again. The late summer heat made the room warmer than usual, but I suspected we both knew that wasn't the only reason a flush crept over my chest and up to my face.

"Speaking of rules," he started again finally, and then there was more of him on me as he wrapped his arms around my waist from behind and leaned up on his toes to kiss the side of my neck, "think there's anything against *playing with a stiffy?" I noticed the reason he was asking pressed against my backside.*

"Your own or someone else's?" I asked with a smirk. Jamie's lips curved against my skin, and he loosened his grip on me, his hands slowly sliding to my hips before letting me go. I reached to grab my helmet off its hook and walked past him to find some fresh air outside of the room that suddenly felt like a sauna.

I swallowed and realized that my hand had traveled between my legs, despite the limited space I had to work with. I closed my eyes again and gave a few more lazy pulls. Immediately, I felt my chest tighten and my stomach sink, so I let go. Water dripped off my hand onto the floor as I reached to grab the herb-scented soap sitting on the low stool nearby. I lathered it between my pruney hands, scrubbed them through my hair, and continued methodically down the rest of my body.

***

By the time I made it upstairs, Anne was tucking Lucy into her bed for the night. They must have already finished reading her story. I could hear the sleepy tone Luc had as she spoke.

"Why did they want to play so many tricks on the girl?"

"That's what they do. They are mischievous little creatures."

"Why don't they like humans?"

"It's not that they don't like humans, they just don't like the way we do things, and so they play tricks to get us to act a different way. Remember how Nan always tells you to keep your room clean, or else the fairies will sneak in at night and steal your toys or knot up your hair?" There was a long pause.

"Why do they care what my room looks like?"

Anne laughed sweetly. "Good night, love. Sleep tight." She noticed me standing in the hall then and gave Lucy's forehead a kiss after pulling her blankets up to her chin. Her fingers looped into the chamberstick's metal handle, and she lifted it from the bedside table. She brought her other hand up to shield the flame as she stepped quietly out of the room and shut the door behind her.

"I'm not sure what's scarier, the fairy bedtime stories or how many questions she asks," Anne admitted in a hushed tone with a tired smile.

"Both. She's become obsessed with them," I said. When Anne wasn't available, bedtime story was my duty, and Lucy had requested tales about fairies, and magic, and all sorts of other fanciful things for weeks. Luckily for her, our land's history was deeply tied to the myths that she was so desperate to learn more about. Every child was raised hearing about them in an attempt to scare them into good behavior. Mammy says shut the door behind you, you might do it, you might not. But Mammy says shut the door or else the fairies will come in and steal the pie that's cooling for dessert, you shut the feckin' door. That one got me every time.

"I was thinking maybe we could gather some things to make a fairy garden together," Anne whispered. "It might help her channel some of this focus into something more tangible. Busy hands make for quiet tongues. We might get a break from the questions."

"She would love that. Let me know if you need any help with the bits and bobs. I'll see what I can find."

"I will, thanks." Her eyes searched mine in the candlelight and she tilted her head slightly to the side. "Are you holding up alright?"

I looked at my feet and nodded. She reached up and placed her hand on my cheek, her fingers a cool contrast against my skin that was still warm from my bath. I raised my head to look at her again, and whatever expression I had on my face must have given me away. Her eyebrows pinched in concern. I didn't trust my voice, so I swallowed hard, but she spoke again before I could.

"You know, grief is something that nobody can write a book about. Only the person feelin' it can know what they need to get through. But time is the healer of all pain, so don't short yourself on it. If you need more time, then you keep taking it. And finally, one day, it will sit with you more like a scar than a wound. It's there, but it doesn't hurt so much. Or maybe it doesn't hurt at all."

Anne had steered me into my bedroom while she spoke and remained at the threshold, where she rested her hand that wasn't holding the candlestick on the handle of my door. She studied me for a moment longer before adding, "Rest well, Peter."

***

Of all the precious memories I kept safely in the back of my mind, there was only one that remained so ~owerful that I tried to keep it pushed down and locked ⸾s I laid in my bed, eyes fixed on the ceiling above me, I couldn't hold it back any longer. I shifted my hands ever so slightly against the sheets on either side of me, grounding myself. It was only a memory. It wasn't real. Not this time. I took a breath and closed my eyes.

My sheer curtains billowed on the gust of wind that swept up the stone side of our house. The window was open to provide me with some fresh air. I had been in this room, in this bed, for several weeks, but I could only remember a very small portion of it. I had lost count of the days between my bouts of wake and sleep that had no rhyme or reason.

Never in my twenty-one years had I felt exhaustion so overwhelming. Lifting my head to sip the broth Anne insisted I drink was a monumental task. Moving to the edge of the bed to use the chamber pot drained every bit of energy I had for hours. Anne told me that she was convinced I was in the kind of sleep you never wake up from. Some people might've been disturbed by that confession, but her honesty comforted me more than anything.

Pain racked through me as a fit of coughs came out of nowhere. The ache in my abdomen presented itself in waves, whenever the fits came, but the burn in my lungs was there with every breath. Which was very unfortunate, considering I had to keep doing it again and again. There was no escape from it other than sleep when the concoction of pain relief Anne poured down my throat would wear off, so I tried to sleep as much as I could.

I was attempting this task again when I heard a noise at my window. I forced one bleary eye open at the same time that my mattress dipped beside me from a change in weight, and I realized it was a person sitting there. A hand came up to brush my tangled hair away from my feverish forehead before sliding down to my cheek that I had begged Anne to shave clean for me when I had enough mind to think about it. That had been several days prior, so the stubble was back. I closed my eye again for a moment and then forced both of them open together, trying to focus on the face close to mine.

"Peter," he whispered. "You look like shit."

Jamie.

I blinked slowly and turned my head against the pillow to face him more directly. My throat was so raw from coughing that I didn't dare try to speak above a whisper in return – when I had tried before, I learned my voice had left me anyway.

"Thanks." It was all I could manage.

He shifted closer to me and pushed his fingers back through my hair now, trying to keep it off my face since his previous attempt hadn't worked. I didn't want him to get too close in case I started coughing. I didn't want him too close to... me. He shouldn't be here. He should be as far away from me as possible.

This realization jolted through me, and I blinked again, focusing harder.

"What are you doing here?" I got the last word out before the coughing started, and I desperately tried to keep it away from him by turning my head the other direction and pressing my mouth against the pillow as much as I could.

Jamie twisted around so that he could bring his legs up onto the bed and curled his body against me, his leg draping over one of mine and his hand coming up to rub gently across my chest. As comforting as it was, it did little to ease the feeling that someone had dumped a shovel full of hot coals into my lungs. I found the strength to move my hand to his arm.

"I came to see you, obviously." His tone was still light as he said this, his head resting in the crook of my neck like it had so many times before. Never in my bed, though. When he spoke again, his whisper was more serious. "I've missed you terribly, you know. My life is very boring without you in it."

For the time I had been awake during this whole ordeal, all I had thought about was Jamie. Anne hadn't heard from him or his family or anyone else, for that matter, other than the traveling doctor who was completely outnumbered by the ill people he needed to help. He had come to our house only once and told Anne to make us comfortable for our departure. My parents and brother and sisters were in their own beds in the rooms around me, each suffering as I was, but it was Jamie who filled my head and my heart.

Now that he was here, I still had so many questions. Was he sick? Had he already recovered? How did he get in here? He must have heard the gears turning in my brain because the next thing I knew he had turned my head back toward him with his fingertips on my jaw and he leaned up to kiss me. It was so gentle, but I lacked the vigor to lean into it, so I remained still and cherished the touch while it lasted.

I tried to not think about how dry my lips were when he finally pulled away, self-conscious despite everything.

"Are y-... Your family..." I started, and he moved his

hand back to my chest and snuggled impossibly closer.

"Shh. We're all fine." Jamie had three sisters like me, but two were older and his baby sister had died unexpectedly as an infant. I felt some relief. He was here, and that was all that mattered right then.

I moved my hand on his arm up toward his shoulder with great effort, and he made a quiet noise in the back of his throat. My chest tightened from the happiness I felt over him being in my arms, which triggered another coughing fit that lasted so long I was afraid Anne would hear and come to check on me. He sat up then, looking over my body as if to observe all the ways this illness had affected me.

"You'll get caught." I said finally, and he made a pitiful face as he nodded.

"I know. I didn't plan to stay long. I just couldn't keep away for one more minute." He moved to sit closer to my head and leaned down to kiss me again. This time he deepened it like I hoped he would, and I used every bit of energy I had left to wrap my arms weakly around him. He felt thinner, as I'm sure I did, but maybe it's just that I hadn't seen him for so long and I had forgotten how his body felt under my hands. No, that couldn't have been it. A few weeks apart couldn't possibly have been enough time to forget the body I'd spent hours exploring.

As Jamie's words sank into my sluggish mind, a sense of dread washed over me. I had missed him so much. I didn't want him to go yet.

"Stay," I pleaded on a wheeze between coughs. I didn't care if I sounded desperate. He pressed his lips together in a frown and he dipped down to rest his forehead against mine like he always did. His hands cupped my face for just a moment before he kissed the corner of my lips.

"I'll stay until you fall asleep, okay? You need your rest, so that when I come back again in a few days we can get you out of this bed."

He moved to lie beside me, his face returning to the curve of my shoulder and neck, where he planted a few gentle kisses on my collarbone. I wasn't wearing a shirt; I wasn't wearing anything at all under my blankets, actually. In another moment of time that would have thrilled both of us. The fatigue hit me then like a wall, and as I drifted to sleep, I couldn't tell which one of us coughed.

Jamie didn't return in a few days.

After a week had passed, and after worrying that the whole thing had been a fever dream, I finally couldn't stand it anymore. I had gained enough strength to sit up in my bed, with the help of some pillows tucked behind me. I stared at Anne as she came in with my soup and dry bread. She had grown increasingly quiet during her visits in my room, and I felt the tension between us. She had something she needed to tell me, but she wasn't saying it.

"Anne," I croaked. My voice was still recovering like the rest of me. She glanced at me quickly but looked away again as she came around the bed and set my meal down harder than she probably meant to, the spoon clattering off the edge of the plate onto the wooden surface of the night-stand. "Anne," I repeated myself with more effort this time, which made me cough. She stopped moving then and simply stood, her gaze finally making its way to my face. She held onto her skirts tightly with both hands.

The silence stretched out uncomfortably.

"Please tell me. The truth."

She shook her head almost imperceptibly, reaching up to swipe some of her blonde hair behind her ear, which had fallen out of the knot it was tangled up in. I let my head fall back against the pillows and squeezed my eyes shut out of frustration, brow furrowed. I had refused to let myself think of what had been happening outside of my room. Not only could I do nothing to change any of it, but I also knew that worrying would only make me feel worse.

Suddenly, Anne grabbed my hand in both of hers and went to her knees beside the bed. I lifted my head to look at her and she brought my hand to her lips; I could feel her trembling. "I'm so, so sorry," she had said. How her voice had remained so strong, I'll never know. She broke the news to me as gently as she could.

Mary and Elizabeth went first. Together. Within minutes of each other, sharing a bed and cozy in their blankets. Mammy and Dad had still been well enough to be with them when it happened. Two days later, Nicholas. Mam was too sick then to get out of bed, but Dad had been there. Another three days and Mam went. Then Dad.

A numbness spread through me as I listened to the words she was saying. The realization that nearly my whole family had slipped away while I slept felt like a sopping wet blanket had been wrapped around me. Heavy. Confining. I wasn't sure how I was supposed to process this information. My hands itched to rub atop my thighs, but I couldn't make them move.

"There's more."

I pulled my gaze back up to meet hers, and she began to list everyone in our lives who had succumb to this plague that I was quickly learning had wreaked absolute havoc on the village. The more people she mentioned, the more one name came to the front of my mind.

As if she could sense it, Anne let go of my hand and reached into the deep front pocket of the smock she wore over her dress. She looked down at the folded piece of paper as she brought it up to set on the table next to my soup that was growing cold. I turned my head to read the writing on it; my name in familiar, slanted letters. A wave of nausea splashed coldly into my stomach and up my throat.

"Jamie?" I whispered.

Anne didn't say anything.

My eyes darted to her face, to the paper, and back to her face again. My heart started to pound heavily in my chest.

"Peter, I-" she started, but stopped. My gaze fell. I didn't know where to look. I didn't know what to do. I didn't remember how to breathe. I had spent the last few weeks teaching my body how to do it again, and now I couldn't recall the first thing about how to bring air into my body. Oxygen to my brain. I couldn't.

I don't know how much time passed before Anne reached out for me. When her hand touched my arm, my body finally remembered how to function all at once. I gasped, and the pain was so severe that I thought my lungs had burst in a wet pop. A sob wrenched from my chest as Anne climbed onto the bed to wrap her arms around me. She held me tight until my cries turned into coughs so violent that I was sick on myself.

I tore my mind away from the memory and reached up with both hands to wipe at the wet trails the tears had left behind. I rolled onto my side and stared at the spot on my table where Anne had placed the folded letter. It had remained there for two days before I could bring myself to touch it. Another day passed before I could make my fingers unfold it.

Peter, my darling boy.

I am so glad life brought me to you.

Forever yours,

Jamie

Forever yours. Forever mine. I considered reaching underneath my bed to retrieve the small wooden box that held the letter inside, but I didn't need to hold it. The words were etched into my mind from reading them so many times.

There were questions I still didn't have answers to. No member of Jamie's family survived. I couldn't ask them if he had been sick when he came to see me. Nothing could make me regret those last kisses we shared, but I couldn't help but wonder what would have happened if he had stayed away just a little longer. I rubbed at the aching in my chest as I closed my eyes and waited for sleep to take me.

THREE

Nan forbade me from riding the next day because of my hip. Instead, I was volunteered to go to the village with Anne and Lucy to collect some things we needed. My brief protesting fell on deaf ears, so I found myself walking a few paces behind the two of them. They wore matching gray shawls over their shoulders, and each carried a woven basket with the handle in the crook of their elbow.

I struggled to make sense of how I was too injured to sit in a saddle but not too injured to walk as I listened to them talking ahead of me. Anne had told Lucy about the fairy garden idea. She was beside herself with excitement. She already knew exactly where she wanted to put it, and was now rattling off a list of the decorations she wanted to place around the door that absolutely must be red.

The fog and rain had cleared to give us a very pleasant late morning to enjoy on our way, at least. Birds were twittering on the limbs above our heads as we traveled my favorite part of the road that connected our house to the rest of the world. It was wide, with enough space for two horse carts to pass each other with room to spare, but the trees along each side were so tall and full that they touched in the middle. Only little bits of the blue sky overhead were visible between the leaves on the overlapping branches.

Beyond the trees, the road narrowed at a stone bridge built so long ago that the sides were mostly covered with moss. It crossed over the same river that provided the water everyone claimed was the secret to our success with the horses. Biting-cold all year long, it flowed from the nearby mountains, which Dad said provided important minerals that nobody else got since they reached our land first. But if anyone ever asked him the secret, he always chalked it up to love and a little magic.

After the bridge, the road forked in two directions. One way led to the heart of the village, where Anne said we needed to get some tea and a package from the butcher. The other item we could acquire for a much better price if we got it fresh, rather than buying it in the store. The mill was located along the other fork in the road, which followed the slope of the hill down along the water.

"I'll get the flour," I announced.

"Okay!" Anne called back over her shoulder. "We'll meet you here when you're done, if you want to wait for us. We won't be long."

I doubted that as I took careful steps down the embankment toward the low road, cutting off the corner to where it looped back around by the river. My tired leather shoes were slick in the grass, but I managed to stay upright. When the ground leveled out again, I slid my hands underneath the loose fabric of my unbuttoned wool coat into the pockets of my trousers. Ahead of me, the mill was nestled into a line of trees. On the other side of it was a wall of large rocks that dropped sharply, creating a waterfall where the river ran over them. The wheel of the mill was spinning slowly, turning as each bucket filled with water that was funneled from the top of the falls with a series of carved wooden pipes.

The mill itself was a small, two-story stone building that was covered in vines and moss like the bridge. It had been there forever, run by the same auld man and his wife since long before I was around to know them. With no children to pass it on to, they had left the mill vacant when they died. Nan had met the new fella running it the week before; said he was about my age. I had thought that twenty-three seemed awfully young to be operating the village flour mill, but I told her I would introduce myself.

Whoever he was, he had done a good bit of cleaning up around the outside. The overgrown shrubs and weeds that had gotten out of control had been trimmed back or pulled out altogether. Flowers were blooming in the small front garden and planters that had been empty for years, ever since the auld woman's fingers had grown too weak to plant anything like she once had. The windows were clean and framed by newly painted shutters.

"Impressive work," I thought to myself aloud before I knocked twice on the door and pushed it open. As I stepped inside, the smell of freshly pressed grains hit me immediately, followed by the sound of the mill stones grinding away on the far wall. With the small windows scrubbed clean, it was quite bright inside the storeroom.

"Hello?" I called out. I spun on my heel to look behind me, where shelves used to be stocked with the bags of flour ready to be purchased. That was still the same as it always had been. I reached for one on the top shelf, which only came up as high as my chest, and heaved it up onto my shoulder.

"Can I help you?" a voice came behind me as I heard footsteps on the stairs winding down from the top floor. I turned to greet the stranger.

He had tousled, dark blonde hair that was long enough to come down around his ears and across his forehead. His nose and cheeks were covered with freckles, which was not uncommon here, but I had never seen someone with so many before. Even Henry with his bright red hair only had a smattering in comparison. Stranger yet were the metal pieces on his ears, and as I took a step closer, I noticed a thin silver band hugging the edge of his nose, as well.

I forced my brain to think of something intelligent to say. We didn't get many newcomers to our village these days, and if we did, they didn't stay long.

"I'm Peter. Walshe," I offered finally. "I live just over the bridge. We're neighbors."

The man blinked his deep blue eyes and seemed to clear a thought from his mind after searching my face the way I had searched his, and then offered me a smile.

"How's it going?" He stuck his hand out across the low counter and I shifted the weight of the bag on my shoulder so I could free up my own to shake it. More delicate bands of metal adorned his thumb and two of his fingers. "Breck," he added, and it took me a moment to realize that was his name. "Your Granny mentioned you when I met her the other day. She's lovely."

"Nan's a spitfire," I retorted, a grin of my own quirking up my lips. I tilted my head toward the burlap sack I was holding. "Em, can I put this on our tab, or do you need me to pay for it now?"

"Tab works, thanks." He paused, and then his lips moved like he was going to say something else, but he settled on, "Good to meet you."

"Have a nice one." I turned to reach for the knob on the door, but I didn't realize that I'd already backed up so far, and I smacked my hand into it instead. An involuntary noise of surprise escaped my throat as I pulled the handle and slipped outside. I let out a slightly uneasy breath and coughed as I bunched my shoulder up, readjusting my grip on the heavy bag again. To nobody's surprise, the bridge was empty.

***

I delivered the flour to the kitchen and Nan asked me to sit and eat something, but I convinced her I didn't have time. The rest of the day went by quickly at the stables. Henry, Thomas, and I gave the horses their final grooming before the match the following day. We sheared their manes close to their necks, and Thomas clipped the hair on his horses' tails as short as he could, as well, because he couldn't be bothered to learn how to braid properly before wrapping them up.

Wally yelled at him about being lazy for doing this, as he had every year since we were kids. His eye roll that he thought Wally didn't see earned him a slap to the back of the head. Thomas went red in the face and threw the shears down into the bucket by his feet, which he had apparently forgotten was full of sudsy water. This caused auld Wally to scold him again. Henry and I couldn't help but laugh, and Thomas stormed off, cursing all the while. I reached down and fished the shears out of the water and dried them with a rag I had handy.

"How's it that we've been doin' this for so long and he *still* can't figure this shite out?" Henry shook his head as he spoke, returning to his task.

"That lad's lucky all he has to do is look pretty, s'all I can say," Wally responded gruffly. He took his cap off his head and wiped the sweat from his brow with the back of his forearm. "Anything else you need from me before tomorrow?"

Henry and I looked at each other at the same time, mutually confirming that the other was good, and I shook my head. "Don't think so. Maybe a strong drink or two," I joked, which pulled a *whoop* from Henry.

"I second that, boyo."

I knew my nerves would get to me as I tried to sleep that night, but in that moment, I was feeling as ready as I could possibly be. There was no more training to do, no more practice drills to run, no more ways to convince everyone else that I was fine. I just had to do it.

"Aye, we can all grab a pint *after* you win tomorrow."

***

Hushed chatter and the clanging of glass surrounded us at the table toward the back of the pub. Wally made good on his promise and bought the first round to celebrate; Thomas bought the second, and Henry the third. We had won easily, but that didn't make the rush of adrenaline from being back on the pitch any less intoxicating for me.

I was not looking forward to when it all wore off. The wave of exhaustion that came after a good match was something I experienced long before I got ill, so I knew it was bound to be even more intense now. I took another pull of my drink and set it back on the gnarled and slightly sticky wooden tabletop, quietly observing my friends as they nursed their own frothy pints and re-lived our success.

The ends of Henry's uncombed hair were still stuck to his forehead with dried sweat. We were all in various states of dress, having not bothered to change out of our riding clothes. The cap I recovered from the middle of the road a few days prior was doing its best to cover my loose curls, and I had rolled the sleeves on my buttoned, white cotton shirt up to my elbows. Nan said this was unbecoming, but I did it anyway.

Most of the patrons at the tables around us were trying to unwind from a long day of work. I took in their worn clothes and even wearier faces. These men were not wealthy, and they probably had not been before the troubles we faced a few years prior, either. They worked as colliers and cobblers and coopers. At the table by the door sat the blacksmith and his young apprentice, a boy just a few years older than Lucy. I knew them and the saddler well, who was perched on a bench by himself at the bar.

Moments like this made me realize that my work was easy, all things considered. I got paid to play well at something I loved doing. I didn't drag myself home at the end of the day dreading what tomorrow would bring. Henry reached out to squeeze my shoulder, and I brought my attention back to our table.

"Hm?" I questioned, lifting my glass to my lips and draining the rest of my beer to snap myself out of my thoughts. Some people get loud when they're drinking, others get violent. I was the type to get quiet and introspective, shamefully ready to spill my guts if you asked at the right moment.

"Have you become a lightweight again? You're driftin' off on us."

"No, sorry," I started, but I couldn't come up with an explanation for the expression I must have had on my face without killing their mood, so I changed the subject to something more agreeable. "I'll get the next round."

"Good man," Thomas said before he finished his own drink in several big gulps. The wince on his face as he set his glass loudly on the table told me he might have regretted it. Henry noticed the same thing and started in on him about not needing another drink anyway. Thomas was an unfortunate combination of the loud *and* agressive drunk. We had all learned that one the hard way a few times over since we were younger. Not much of a surprise, given his normal quick temper on a good day, but still unpleasant when it happened.

I sidled off my stool and made my way to the only empty spot at the bar, where I held up four fingers for the keep. I pulled a few coins out of my pocket and laid them on the counter in front of me and watched him pour someone else's drinks before he started on ours.

"Peter?"

I swung my head around toward the voice and was surprised to find the man from the mill standing quite close to me. He was holding a glass in his hand, drink mostly gone except for a sip or two. I hadn't noticed him there before. What was his name, again?

"Breck. How's it?" I managed, thankful for whatever part of my brain had held onto that information. Henry knew me too well. My walk from the table had been fine enough, but standing there at the bar told me three pints was more than I'd had in quite a long while. Truthfully, I couldn't say the last time I had given in and come out with my friends, despite their incessant begging. I angled my hips to lean against the bar for support, then quickly readjusted and leaned on my hand instead, pressing my lips together to stifle the quiet groan that wanted to escape after banging my tender bruised skin against the polished wood.

"Not as good as you, I'm sure, after that match today," he said as he took a seat on the stool next to where I was standing. I moved some to make more room for him, and he took that as an opportunity to angle himself toward me, his knee brushing my leg as he turned.

"Oh, you like polo?" I dodged his praise without really meaning to. Usually, the only people who came to watch us play were people who had a lot of money and free time. Certainly not someone who worked a job like the one he had. Or someone who dressed as he did. His knee-length dark brown breeches and the loose collar on his untucked shirt were nowhere near formal enough to meet the dress code, which was strict in the sense that you better wear something tasteful and expensive or risk getting whispered about for weeks.

"I like horses." My scrutinizing gaze came back up from his bare feet when he answered, and I realized he was watching me look him over. I swallowed and turned fully toward the bar now, gripping the lip with both hands to hold myself steady. "And I like watching rich people pretend to like polo, when really they just have nothing better to do," he added, echoing my own thoughts. "That doesn't mean it's not worth it for you to play the game, though. You play it for yourselves, and that's the best kind of entertainment for those of us who do watch without pretense."

"Most of the time I forget anyone else is there, to be honest." That was the truth. I certainly didn't play because I liked to have other people eyeballing me for hours at a time.

"Your animals are stunning, by the way. Did your family breed them?" Breck took the last swig of his drink but kept his hand around the empty glass after he set it back down, thumb slowly working the condensation along the outside.

"No, but I trained two of them from when they were green. My gelding is getting on in years, but his heart is still in it, so I can't deny him his fun just yet. All of 'em love the game as much as I do," I said, grinning a little. "I suppose I'm a lucky bastard for that."

"Magic," he responded after a pause. I drew my brows together and I gave him a look, perplexed. Had I heard him correctly?

"What?" I had hoped that would come out with more of a carefree tone, but my voice betrayed me. He raised his already arched eyebrows in response, seemingly pleased at my reaction. How could he possibly have known about Dad's silly theory?

He leaned a little closer to me before he spoke again, his voice low enough that it was just for my ears. Instinctively, I watched his lips move to make sure I caught all the words. "That's your secret, right? Magic?"

The barkeep plunked the first two of my pints in front of me, and I unwrapped my fingers from the edge of the counter; I hadn't realized how hard I was holding onto it until I let go. Did I want to deny what he was saying? I looked back at him then, searching his eyes. No. I didn't. I had always been curious why Dad said that. Did he really believe it? He took my silence as an answer.

"I can show you. If you want."

My other two drinks arrived, and I motioned to get Henry's attention so he could come help me carry them back to the table. He had already been looking at me when I turned around. I didn't think the buzz I had going was clouding my judgement all that much, but it must have been strong enough to convince me to shift out of my comfort zone, because I found myself agreeing before I could give it any more thought.

"Sure," I said finally. He smiled, patting the hand that wasn't holding his glass on his leg, where it had been resting.

"Grand. Come tomorrow at first light and we'll set off. Enjoy your night." With that, he got up off his stool and exited the pub swiftly, slipping out before the door could shut after the man who had just come in. Henry was beside me then, reaching around to grab two of the drinks.

"Odd lookin' fella, that," he observed offhandedly, bumping his elbow against my arm to draw my attention away from the door. "Hurry up, Wally is in the middle of telling us about the time he and his brother got lost with their flock of sheep in the middle of winter." We had heard this story a dozen times, and each time it became more harrowing and slightly less believable, but Wally's retelling of it was so passionate that you couldn't help but enjoy the tale for whatever it was. I picked up our other two drinks and gave one last look at the door before I followed Henry back to the table.

FOUR

The next morning, I woke up with an ache that spread from my head to my toes. I managed to roll from my stomach to my back, in desperate need of a piss and a glass of water. I silently hoped my friends were suffering as much as I was as I dragged myself from the bed, grateful that it was still dark outside.

After my conversation with the miller, we'd shared three more rounds, all provided by Thomas and his endless coinage and drunken generosity. Wally had left us shortly after round four because, as he loved to remind us tartly, he had a "real job" to do in the morning and couldn't stay. By the time we finally left, I was never happier to have walked somewhere instead of being on horseback. Henry and I had made our way home together, since his house was beyond mine on the same road, and he dropped me at the doorstep like a good lad.

After pulling on a pair of trousers, I made my way to the basin on the wall and splashed my face with water. I looked at my reflection with bleary eyes. This wasn't as fun as I remember it once being. I dried my face with a towel, rubbing the residual dampness over some of my less fresh areas, and sat gingerly on the bench by my bed. I turned to look out the window, my mind reeling through thoughts of the previous night and coming to rest on the plans I'd made for the morning. Who was this version of myself, agreeing to climb into the desolate mountains with someone I had just met?

I hadn't told Henry or anyone else about it. Nobody had asked about Breck back at the table, and even though Henry had somehow noticed his unique features from across the room, the unyielding attention and lack of personal space he had shown me apparently weren't a concern. To my chagrin, I realized they weren't a concern to me at the time, either.

I gripped my knees to stop my hands from rubbing along the tops of my thighs and picked myself up off the bench. I had agreed to this for a reason. I wanted to know more about my family's success, and I had always had a sneaking suspicion that there was something more to it than a little luck. Plus, as much as I loved my oldest brother, I knew William would never be willing to indulge in such a harebrained idea. He had always been the most cautious of my siblings, but he'd become so guarded after the illness that only Anne could get past his anxiousness and see the real man underneath.

I sorted through my clothes and came away with what I thought would be a suitable outfit for the task ahead of me. I opted for a dark gray vest without buttons, as opposed to my typical waistcoats, since the vest was thicker, and I wouldn't have to wear a coat with it. I tucked the tails of my shirt into my high-waisted black trousers and ran my fingers through my hair a few times before I stuck my cap on my head and went for the door.

I didn't dare try the kitchen for the drink of water I wanted, because I knew Nan would be up soon if she wasn't already, and I didn't trust myself to lie to her face about where I was going so early in the morning without riding clothes on. It would have to be an apologize later type of situation.

Making sure to step only on the rugs to silence my shoes, I made my way carefully down the stairs and through the front door. The morning fog was thick, which meant I only had to get a short distance from the house before I would be able to slip away unnoticed.

The trouble was not that I wouldn't be able to go and do whatever I wanted to do – I was an adult, after all. But my family worried about me so much that I hated to ever give them reason for concern. It was better for everyone if I didn't divulge all my secrets to them. That was something I had been practicing for many years, ever since Jamie and I decided to stop fooling ourselves.

We had been friends since we were fourteen. I'd made an impressive move against him in our first match together when he played for another club. My team had ended up winning because of it. He came right up to me after the game and shoved my arse into the dirt with both hands, despite being the shorter of the two of us. Clearly a sore loser. As he turned to leave, I stuck my leg out and tangled his feet up underneath him, causing him to fall too. Something clicked in our world then, and after a brief angry stare-off on the ground, we laughed as we picked each other up and dusted our clothes off.

Three long years passed while I silently weighed the risks and rewards of revealing how I felt. As silently as I could, anyway, with Henry pestering me until I told him which young lass from the village had me flustered. When I finally spilled the truth, he had been rendered speechless for possibly the first time in his life. He thought hard about it and then finally settled on, "I'spose if I was forced to pick one of you, it'd be Jamie."

Jamie's large, chocolate brown eyes and the dimple on his cheek when he smiled were enough to hold my interest, but to make matters worse, he was witty, and self-assured, and could draw you in without even trying. We had both just turned seventeen when I finally plucked up enough courage to kiss him for the first time.

The four of us had been at it all afternoon doing practice drills with Dad, when Thomas had finally taken as much of our prodding as he could handle for one day and left abruptly. Henry excused himself since it was time for him to get home for supper, and that left Jamie and me. We turned our horses over to auld Wally and the other stable hands at the time, changed quickly out of our riding gear, and he had asked me if I wanted to go down by the river while it was still light out.

I had agreed to go with him, of course. We walked close together and sat even closer on the crop of rocks by the edge of the water, and when I couldn't decide if I would be sick from the nerves or just pass out entirely, I had leaned over and crushed our mouths together. I'd never kissed anyone before, and I knew he had, but he never let on if I did something he didn't like. Instead, to my immense relief, he had grabbed my shirt and pulled me to him and didn't let go.

This collection of large rocks came into view now as I took the narrow, winding foot path down to the edge of the water. I crouched and cupped my hands into the crisp, clear liquid and brought them to my mouth to finally get my drink. At this part of the river, the water moved quickly and made pleasant trickling sounds as it eddied between stones and the grassy banks.

I rested my arms on my knees for a moment as I studied the place we had come many times together for a bit of peace. The land sloped upward behind the rocks, creating a spot where you couldn't see the house or the road or anything else around. Privacy had been a rare treat for us here, thanks to my large family and the people constantly coming and going from the stables.

I wiped my hands on my trousers as I stood up and followed the thin, worn line of dirt in the grass back around to the main road. The sky was starting to lighten up just a bit now, so I quickened my pace to avoid being late.

***

A few minutes later the mill came into view. The morning mist was particularly thick there around the falls, but it wasn't enough to prevent me from seeing that all the windows of the small building were dark. My stride faltered and I started to second-guess myself. Had I imagined him asking me to meet him in the morning?

To my relief, the door opened and Breck stepped out into the low light, wearing the same clothes he'd been in the night before. *Maybe he had a few drinks too many, as well,* I thought.

"Mornin'," came his greeting when he spotted me approaching, a smile on his face. Far too chipper to be hungover, then.

"Hello," I replied, my voice thick from not using it yet since waking. I cleared my throat and breathed in the damp air carefully. Sometimes mornings like this, with the heavy moisture hanging around, made my chest a little more achy than usual.

"Didn't have too much fun last night, did you?" he asked, eyes scanning from my head to my shoes. I hadn't thought I looked too rough in the mirror, but then again it had been dark in my room.

"Haven't been out like that for a while," I confessed. "I might've overdone 'er a bit."

"Are you still up for our hike?" I noticed the way his brows twitched upward in concern.

"Aye, I'll be fine," my reassurance came, though I was curious to see how right I was. My body was still sore all over, and I was starting to regret not sneaking into the kitchen for a bite of something before I left the house.

"Best be off then, don't want to get caught in the rain."

Breck joined me on the road along the river and we set out, aiming for the rolling and spiring mountains in the distance. Going this direction pointed us toward the rising sun, as well, and I was glad the early rays were going to have to work their way up and over the peaks to reach our eyes.

We walked in silence for a while, allowing the rest of the world to come to life around us at its own, gentle pace. A few deer were grazing on lush meadow grass off in the distance. Someone else's sheep were dotting the first hillside we came to; a hundred of them, white puffs with black faces moving casually from one place to another to find their breakfast.

"Tell me about your family," Breck said finally in a soft voice. His hands were in his pockets, steps matching mine. I realized we were about the same height, but his frame was thinner He had a lightness to his stride that made him look as though he didn't have a care in the world.

"What do you want to know?" The question was too broad for me to know where to begin.

"Well, start with your history with the horses, I guess."

I looked down at my feet while I thought about my response. Breck still wasn't wearing any shoes.

"My family settled on the land here hundreds of years and great-grands ago. I would assume the first horses came along with them. Big work horses to help with the heavy lifting needed to move the stones to build the houses and the walls. My grandad told me once that *his* grandad told him that when he was a young fella, the horses they had at the time were still working at over 60 years old."

Breck glanced at me again, and I caught his look of surprise in my peripheral.

"Of course, there are no real records of that being true, but I do believe that they were old. That's always been the case, even now. They drink the water and eat the grass, and their minds stay sharp. Their bodies stay beautiful. I've heard the competition griping about how the horses can stay for even a short time and you can start to see the effects, but as soon as they leave, they slow down again.

"I've wondered about it myself. They're not wrong when they say that we don't give any special treatment – at least nothing I do is something I would call special. They get the best care and all the love we can spare, but don't all the most important animals get that?"

"You'd be surprised," Breck offered.

"Well, that's a staple for the ones we look after. And the rest..." I shrugged my shoulders. It seemed he was the one who knew more about the rest than me.

"Do humans reap the same benefits, too?" he asked, lightening the mood. "Are you secretly an auld man there, Peter?" I laughed a little and pressed my lips together to contain my smile.

"No, not quite. Just twenty-three now. Though some days it feels like more."

"Your family was here for the sickness, I imagine." His response wasn't a question.

"Yes."

"Did you lose many loved ones?"

"I did."

"I'm sorry to hear that. The sickness, it didn't reach the folks where I'm from."

"Thank you," I said, squinting up at the steepening terrain ahead of us.

We fell into another silence that wasn't entirely uncomfortable as it took more effort to climb along the river. The road had ended, which forced us to fight with the grass and rocks scattered along the way. My lungs were starting to protest now, and I took deep breaths to try and hide my struggling.

Only a few minutes passed before I was breathing too loudly to mask it any longer. Breck stopped ahead of me when I didn't respond to him asking if I was alright. He turned around to find me with my hands on my knees, and quickly came to my side and gripped my arm, guiding me to a rock large enough to sit on.

"Feet flat on the ground," he instructed, and I did what he said, resting my forearms on my legs and forcing my breathing to slow down. I leaned my head forward and my cap fell by my shoes. Breck picked it up and set it on the boulder beside me.

"Sorry," I finally wheezed out, coughing a few times.

"Don't be. It's not an easy climb. That's why most never do it. It's not much farther."

I waited until the burning sensation had passed before I pushed myself back onto my feet. "When I was sick. It damaged my lungs." I hoped my choppy sentences made sense as I continued to suck in the air that was thinner here. The wind had picked up, as well, and I angled my face away from the direct blow of it to help my breathing.

"Oh," he said shortly. "You were sick with the others? And you survived?" He seemed surprised by this information. I just nodded in response, hopeful that my standing there in front of him was proof enough while it was still hard for me to talk. He studied my face carefully then, as if this was changing his opinion of me. I couldn't tell if it was for the better or worse.

I picked up my cap and put it back on, which he took as permission to start walking again. As I moved to follow him, I hoped he was right about it not being much longer to wherever he was taking me.

***

After pausing just once more to catch my breath, Breck finally halted, causing me to stop short behind him since I had been looking at my feet while we climbed. I took a step to the side, and I forgot all about the aching in my chest.

In front of us was a small pond. The clear water reflected everything around it with a crisp perfection that seemed impossible. There was nothing special surrounding it to keep it contained; the water came from the ground and pooled here until it fell into the stream trickling over the edge, which Breck explained eventually became the river by my house.

I turned around to look out at the land that spread from the mountains. In the distance were buildings and landmarks I had known my whole life, but I had never seen them from this perspective. They seemed so small.

My attention returned to the pond, and I stepped closer to it slowly. There were no bugs skimming the surface; no frogs croaking from their mud holes. In fact, there was no sound at all except for the wind whipping around us. Even with the wind, the surface of the water sat as still as glass. I knelt by the edge of the pond and stuck my hand it, turning it over so my palm was up. I almost couldn't tell which parts of my fingers were under the water and which parts were above. The wind mimicked the cold of the water, so I couldn't even judge by temperature.

"So, what do you think?" Breck was beside me then, kneeling too. He scooped some of the water in his hands and brought it to his lips, closing his eyes as he swallowed. This water felt almost too pure to drink, but the hike had left me terribly thirsty, so I copied him.

It tasted like nothing at all, but it was possibly the most perfect drink I'd ever had. My companion laughed then, presumably at whatever my reaction had been. I wiped my sleeve across my chin and looked at him, shaking my head.

"This is amazing," I remarked quietly. "What makes it taste that way?"

He tipped his head toward the pool, and we both returned our focus to the water so transparent you could see everything, even in the deepest areas. He reached out again with one hand this time and gestured with two fingers.

"Look closely. At the stones." I leaned forward then, blinking to focus on the smooth pebbles and small rocks of different shades that formed the bottom. Suddenly, though the water was still, a twinkle caught my eye. Then another. I realized the sun was just peeking over the highest points of the mountains we were in now, causing light to play off something shiny nestled into the stones. When I realized what it was, I sat back on my legs and gave Breck a questioning look.

"Gold?" I asked, and he dipped his head slightly in a nod, an impish grin on his lips.

"The story goes that the people who once lived here were mistreating their animals. All they cared about was the profit they made off them; their work, or their wool, or whatever else they could take from the poor creatures. The fairies took notice of this, and it greatly upset them. Bit by bit, they started taking money from those men. They coated the coins with spells of health and longevity and carried them here, tossing them into the water source that would reach all the animals that were drinking from the river.

"This has been happening on and off for hundreds of years, so I believe the power of the spells has ebbed and flowed some, but there's always a pull on these coins as the water passes over them into the stream." Breck's deep blue eyes met mine then, and one of his shoulders came up in a shrug. "Your animals are proof enough of that, I'd say."

I was quiet while I finished wrapping my head around what he was telling me. "My dad always said that our success with the horses is all thanks to love... and a little magic," came my slow response.

"Smart man, your dad. Must've heard the legend himself. Most don't like retelling the whole thing since it reflects poorly on people who do profit from their animals."

I nodded. Nobody likes to tell a story that sheds a negative light on something they're a part of, even if they're not the ones doing the wrong thing.

I shifted my weight to the side so I could reach into my pocket. I pulled out the coins I had with me and picked up one of the gold ones before slipping the rest back inside. I turned the coin over in my fingers a few times. Money had never been something I worried about as a young boy. It wasn't until things changed so dramatically for my family that it became a concern. Now, William was moments away from a panic attack any time the subject came up.

I knew we were fortunate to still have so many people boarding and training their horses with us, but it wasn't the same as it had been before. The people in our village and beyond had suffered as much as we had, if not more. We had empty stalls to fill not because people didn't want to come, but because they couldn't afford it. I'd been wrong the night before. My work wasn't just easy. It was a luxury.

The same could be said about my horses. They got the best of everything, even without the magic of the water. I had seen with my own eyes that others were not so fortunate, thanks to the lack of expendable money going around. Cart horses with their hips showing; plow horses unable to pull for lack of rest. Even some of the horses we had taken in over the last year were too skinny, including the chestnut mare Wally had brought on.

I squeezed the coin in my palm, the rounded edges pressing into my skin, and then I tossed it into the water. We both watched as it sank to the bottom immediately, settling at an angle against a small rock. "My contribution to the health and longevity of all our animals," I stated quietly.

Numbness was starting to tingle in my feet thanks to the position I was still sitting in, so I pushed myself up off the ground before I was unable to. Breck did the same, and we both stared out at the village in the distance. I crossed my arms across my chest against the wind. Maybe a coat wouldn't have been such a bad idea.

"Why did you want to show me this?" I asked, turning my head to look at his profile. His hair was whipping around his face, revealing more of the intricate rings and studs of fine metal along the outer edge of his ear. He had a strong jaw and a slightly upturned nose, which still had the thin band of silver wrapped around the side. Standing this close, I could see how his freckles spread from his cheeks to his neck, and there were even a few on his ears. I forced myself to stop before I could wonder if they continued to his shoulders and chest and beyond.

"I'd like to learn more about my neighbors, as the new fella around." He looked at me then, his hands finding their way into his pockets again. "I figured a good way to do that is to learn more about your family's history, and what's important to you." A grin spread on his lips, and he added, "I already learned your talents at the match, and what you do for fun last night, so I figured there wasn't a need for anymore awkward small talk."

I grinned then, too. He did have a point, as forward as it was. It dawned on me then that he had been the one asking all the questions.

"All I've learned about *you* so far is that you like horses and you don't like people who wave their money about."

He chuckled at that and said, "That's an accurate start."

"That, and you wake up far too pleasant after a

night of drinking," I added.

"Well now, I'd hardly call two pints a night of drinking." He reached up to run his fingers through his mussed hair, brushing it toward one side. The wind kicked it all right back out of place. "Rain's coming in. We should probably start back."

I looked up at the sky and spotted the darkening clouds gathering in the distance. I gave one more glance over my shoulder at the storybook scene behind me as we started our steep descent, and I hoped very hard that my lungs would be more cooperative than they had been on the way up.

***

We made it to the mill just as the first raindrops started to fall, and Breck quickly excused himself inside and said he would see me again soon. I didn't hurry my walk home.

As I reflected on our conversation down the mountain, I realized that he had been the one asking all the questions again. I told him more about my horses, and about Nan, and William, and Anne, and Lucy. I shared with him that Luc would be over the moon when I told her the new story I had learned about the fairies and the gold at the pond, and he had said he would be sure to think of some others she might not've heard before that I could tell her.

When my feet met the cobblestones outside the kitchen door, I decided that agreeing to this hike was probably the most rewarding dumb idea I'd agreed to in a long time, and I would have to do it more often. Within reason, of course.

FIVE

A few days passed until I saw Breck again. I had resumed working with Wally's mare, and I was feeling confident in the progress we'd made together. Henry had offered to work my horses for me so I could focus on the task at hand, which is where I found myself when I spotted the miller in the distance. I kept the mare moving at her steady canter around the ring, the rhythmic three-beat gait feeling comfortable for both of us. For such a spooky horse, I was glad Breck's billowy white shirt didn't set her off as he came to a stop at the outside of the fence.

"Mornin'," I called, echoing his greeting to me the other day. It wasn't exactly morning anymore, probably closer to midday now, but I saw that it made him smile all the same.

"Is this the infamous chestnut you were telling me about?" he asked, his eyes following our path around and around the small space.

"The one and only," I exclaimed with false pride. I'd shared the story of what happened with her, but thankfully he had not begged me to see the bruise it left behind like Henry had. My friend had literally screamed at the sight of the colorful aftermath, which had so pleasantly spread out along the outside and back of my upper thigh now, as well. Luckily the pain was nearly gone. I could only feel a twinge of it as I sat in the saddle.

"Looks like you've made some great progress with her, if she's really as bad as you claimed she was." I let this compliment slide past like the one he'd given me at the pub. I made the motions to slow the horse's stride to a walk, and she listened. We made two more rounds along the fence and then I pulled her to a stop in front of where Breck was standing.

"Did you need something, then? A favor from a neighbor?" I asked, hoping my words came off playfully in reference to him wanting to know his neighbors better, which in turn meant borrowing and sharing and helping when it was needed, knowing that it would be returned when the time came. Nan always said that's what neighbors were for.

"I actually came to see if I could be of any help here. The mill's not running today, and nobody has come by to see me yet, so I figured I could take the day off. Big benefit of working for yourself, I suppose," he mused. His sleeves were rolled to his elbows, revealing more freckles splashed along his forearms that were resting atop the fence between us. I looked toward the stables and reached up to rub the back of my neck with the hand not holding the reins.

"Well," I started, thinking aloud. "I suppose if you wanted, we could take my horses out for their exercise. Henry hasn't finished with his own yet, so." I looked down at him then to gauge his reaction. It wasn't often I invited other people to do my work with me.

"That'd be great," came his response. I pulled the mare around in the direction of the gate and dismounted after she came to a stop. The latch was easy to use with one hand on horseback, and normally I would have let the gate swing shut on its own behind me, but I still didn't trust the mare as far as I could throw her. Breck joined us on our walk toward the stables.

"Oh, *feck me*," I muttered under my breath as the scraggly barn cat came trotting toward us with her tail up, a crook in the end of it. My grip on the reins tightened in preparation for whatever level of a threat the mare took her as, but miraculously she didn't respond at all. The cat slammed herself against Breck, rubbing along his bare shins. He stopped to lean down and pet her, scratching a finger underneath her chin. The cat mewled loudly, and that was the moment the mare decided to jerk her head away from me. Fortunately for both of us, that was all she did.

Breck was still with the cat when we clopped onto the stone floor of the stables, which had been freshly swept clean. Henry must have heard our approach and came around from one of the stalls, his face red from being out in the sun.

"Pete, I was just about t- oh, hello there." His tone and attention shifted as he noticed I wasn't alone. I knew there was no way he wouldn't recognize the man with me, and he announced as much when he reached his hand out. "Saw you at the pub the other night, didn't I?" They shook hands and exchanged names, and I dragged the chestnut mare with me to her stall to avoid watching Henry give Breck an unabashed once-over like I knew he would.

I closed my eyes and held my tongue when Henry asked, "Is that shite in your ears all the way through your skin? That must'a hurt like mad!" I thanked the stars when Breck just laughed and explained that it

68

hadn't been so bad, except for the one at the top of his right ear that went through the thicker part of the skin, compared to the fleshier parts around the edge and the bottom.

One of the stable hands traded places with me in the mare's stall, a bucket full of brushes and other supplies in his grip. I removed my saddle from her back and carried it out to see Henry rubbing both of his earlobes between his thumbs and fingers, no doubt still wondering about the pain. He decided this was the perfect time to share the story about the time he got a fishing hook stuck in his thumb and had to pull it out himself because I was too scared to do it.

"Pete took one look at it and turned white as a sheet. There I was, with the hook clean through me skin, making sure he sat down before he passed out," he recalled.

"We were only ten, what was I supposed to do?" I laid my saddle across my bay mare's stall door and reached for a stiff brush to run across her back.

"He's the most squeamish person I've ever met when it comes to blood," he continued, thoroughly ragging me and enjoying every bit of it.

Before Henry could start on another embarrassing tale from our childhood, of which he had many, I told him we were taking my horses out for their work so he wouldn't have to. He said that was fine and helped me fetch one of the older saddles we kept as a spare in case we ever needed it. The one he brought had belonged to my dad.

We walked the horses outside, and before I could

ask if he was comfortable wearing what he had on for the ride, Breck had already swung himself up into the seat, bare feet and all. I decided to leave my helmet behind now that I was on my own trusted horse; I was riding my bay mare and Breck had my gelding. I mounted up as well and looked at Henry where he stopped at the large doorway, arms crossed loosely over his chest.

"We'll only be gone a short while, on the river pass," I told him. He glanced at Breck and then back at me, a mischievous grin on his mouth.

"Okay then," he replied, and waggled his eyebrows just enough for me to notice. "See you later."

I urged my mare into motion, deciding that I would be annoyed about that little jab later instead of now, and started for the trail I told Henry we were taking. It had a lot of elevation changes and crossed the water in two slow, shallow spots, which made for a stimulating journey for horses and riders alike. Breck was a natural in the saddle. I took the lead when the path narrowed, feeling confident that I didn't have to keep checking on him behind me. I picked up our pace after a short while to get the horses' blood pumping, and we kept on with only the sounds of their hooves hitting the ground.

I looked toward the mountains in the distance, feeling as though I knew a secret about them now. How many people had been up there before? I enjoyed being in nature as much as the next person, but it was uncommon to hear of anyone hiking that far into the mountains just because they felt like it. Mostly it was farmers being forced up into the hills to retrieve a stray sheep that had wandered too far.

When we approached the first river crossing, I knew both horses would have no reservations with the water. My mare splashed across without breaking her stride. Wet spots marked up my riding breeches where the water turned the tan fabric a darker shade. I realized, though, that Breck had slowed the gelding to a walk for their fording. I guided my horse to a walk as well and turned us back around to meet them when they made it to the other side.

"Everything alright?" I asked, looking them both over from my vantage point in the saddle, checking for signs of lameness in the gelding. Nothing seemed out of place.

"Saw a horse break its leg on a crossing once. Got caught up on a submerged root the rider didn't see. I've always been extra careful since then," he explained, and my chest tightened at the thought of that happening.

"Devastating," I agreed, thankful that he would take such caution even though it wasn't his own horse he was riding. "There's only one more spot we'll cross, and it's shallower than this with hardly any stones."

"Good to know, thanks." He paused. "Is this as hard as you want to push them today?"

I looked at him then, sensing there was more to his question. A twinkle in his eye confirmed my suspicion. I didn't give a response other than a quick smile before I threw my mare into a run. Breck did the same and we raced down the path one after the other, until it widened again, and I clicked my tongue to encourage my mare to go faster because I could see the other pair closing in on us out of the corner of my eye. The land took a rolling incline and another drop, curving back toward the river.

As it came into view, I noticed that the water was lower than it usually was in this spot, and it was silent for a few seconds as both horses vaulted the gully entirely rather than dealing with the few inches of water trickling by. Hoofbeats filled my ears again as we landed on the other side, Breck surging ahead of me. We continued our competition until we reached another road that was closer to the mill than my house. As we broke out of the grass onto the smooth dirt, we pulled our horses to a stop, their nostrils flaring as they breathed. My own heart was beating harder from adrenaline, and I laughed when Breck turned in his saddle to shoot me a grin.

"Like I said. Stunning animals you've got."

"Suppose I've got the fairies to thank for that," I countered, which caused his eyes and mouth to soften around the edges. He finger-combed his hair off his forehead.

"Care for tea?" he asked.

I pressed my legs into my mare's sides so she moved into a walk. Breck copied so we were beside each other. "I can ask Nan to make us some if you like. Although at this time of day she'll probably make us eat lunch, as well."

"I was thinking we could stop by to see a friend of mine. I've known her for a long time. She's from where I'm from," he explained. I remembered the decision I'd made about doing more unexpected yet rewarding things.

"Sure," I agreed, nodding. I looked down at my clothes. I wasn't exactly dressed for visiting in my tall boots and deep red waistcoat. Hopefully it wouldn't be too offensive, considering we were still on horseback. Breck scanned the area and then steered my gelding in another direction. I followed him, curious if meeting this friend would reveal more about the man I still didn't know much about.

***

When I was a young lad and Lizzie was just a baby in her arms, Mammy would bring us to the village with her a few times a week. My brothers were old enough to stay home and look after themselves, but she didn't trust them to look after me, too. She loved to peek inside all the shops and have a chat with everyone, catching up on the latest gossip that they could spare, adding new items to her woven basket along the way. Then, every once in a while, our last stop would be the flower shop.

It was in an entirely unassuming place, in the middle of a row of buildings all sandwiched together. The only indication of where one ended and the next began was the color of the paint on the front. This stretch of shops was located at the end of the main street, so you could see them from either sidewalk. And there, stuck between the shoemaker and the cigar shop, was the narrow, bright yellow façade with the hand-painted sign that read "Fresh Flowers" and nothing else.

The part that I remembered most was how every bit of sidewalk outside the door was covered. Bouquets of any color and size you could imagine poked out in all directions, mixed with greenery, and ribbons, and other decorative trinkets. Window boxes overflowed with planted flowers, while ferns and blooming vines hung from baskets that were suspended from the tiny awnings over the doorway and window.

As we approached a clearing in the trees along the road we were traveling on, a cottage with a thatched roof came into view, and it was the only rival I had ever seen to the flower shop in the village. It was surrounded by an explosion of colors that stood out boldly against the white walls. Bushes with purple and pink blossoms that were tall enough to reach the roof stretched out from both corners of the house. A cobbled path stretched from the road to the front door, which was also lined with flowers and low shrubs in a tasteful pattern.

"Your friend lives here?" I asked in wonder. Our horses came to a stop by a short wooden fence that we could tie them to. Breck and I dismounted together and secured the animals before he started toward the door.

"She likes plants," he said simply, as if this explained everything I needed to know. When his hand reached the knob on the bright red door, he didn't knock before pushing it open. I rubbed my palms along the outer seams of my breeches and went in after him.

The inside of the cottage was not free of foliage, but it wasn't quite as overwhelming as the outside. Large, leafy plants sat in pots of various sizes on the floor where the sunlight from the windows reached in. Worn, comfortable looking furniture took up the remaining spaces in the room. Something citrusy and delicious hung in the air, and we both turned as a woman came around the corner, wiping her hands on the smock tied at her waist.

"Breck, have you brought a friend?" she asked in a light, raspy voice. She was short with long, untamed hair that was so blonde it was almost white. I'd never seen a woman who wasn't family with her hair loose and uncovered before, but even that couldn't distract me from noticing her pale blue eyes and very fair skin. She was practically ethereal, a character from one of Lucy's storybooks.

"Finna, this is Peter. Peter, Finna." Breck introduced us, and I dipped my head as a greeting, not sure if taking her hand was appropriate. A bubbly laugh formed in her chest, and she raised an eyebrow at Breck.

"He's not what I pictured from your description," she said, propping one fist on her hip and bringing the other hand up to tap a finger on her lips thoughtfully. Her wrists were adorned with thin bands of various metals like the ones Breck wore on his fingers, which clinked and jingled as she moved her hands. I couldn't see her ears to check if they were decorated, too. "Come, I've made tea."

She spun around and returned to where she had come from, which turned out to be a tiny kitchen. I glanced at Breck before I followed her. How had me described me to this diminutive woman? And why was he describing me to her in the first place?

Long strings stretched from side to side across the windows along the wall, supporting small bundles of herbs and other plants tied together and hung upside down. Every surface was covered with jars and cannisters of various sizes, along with more plants, unlit candles with drips and puddles of dried wax around them, and fruits and vegetables.

75

Breck took a seat on a chair by the table, so I did the same opposite him. Finna moved swiftly about the space, pouring three steaming cups and cutting into a cake of some kind that she'd pulled from the windowsill. All the windows hung open, letting a gentle breeze in.

"How do you take your cup, love?" she asked, and Breck looked at me across the table.

"With honey?" I answered, though it came out as more of a question.

"A sweet tooth, then. You'll like my lemon cake. Some say I make it too sugary for their taste, and I say they can make their own confections." She winked at me as she delivered my cup and a slice of cake that was a creamy yellow with a glaze on the top. My mouth started to water. A small jar of honey came on her next pass by the table, and I stirred some into my tea before taking a sip.

Finna finally swished her skirts around her own chair and sat delicately at the end of the table between us. She brushed some of her hair back over her shoulder, and I noticed that there was a thin braid with a periwinkle-colored ribbon running through it tucked underneath the mass of waves and frizz. Her ear, I could see now, was more heavily pierced than Breck's were. Some were rings and some were tiny, sparkling stones.

I took another swig of my tea and set it down, reaching next for the fork that was lying partially in the glaze that had melted from the cake. I speared a corner off and brought it to my mouth, hoping that the warm icing wouldn't drip onto my clothes. My free hand flew to my mouth as I felt it land on my chin instead, and I wiped it off with two of my fingers, licking them clean before I could remember my manners.

"Oh... *what*..." I spoke through my full mouth as I chewed the delicacy I'd been served. "That's so good." I finally managed, looking up and finding two pairs of eyes on me. Breck smirked and drank from his cup, and Finna wiggled her shoulders a little, looking proud of herself for good reason as she sipped her tea.

"Breck tells me that you're a very talented horseman, is that right?"

I swallowed my next bite of lemony deliciousness and set my fork down. "I guess you could say that. It's something I'm very passionate about. But it's taken a lot of years and practice to get where I am now." I laughed shortly and raised my eyebrows, adding, "I got thrown the other day by a new horse I'm working with, though, so maybe I'm not as talented as you've been led to believe."

Finna's face scrunched in response, glancing down my body briefly. "Were you hurt?"

"I got a pretty nasty bruise on my hip," I confessed.

She stood from her chair and left us in the kitchen for a moment, and then returned with a small jar and set it next to my plate on the table. "Rub that on the colored areas for a few days and it'll clear up."

"Oh. Thank you," I said, picking up the jar and opening the lid. The cream inside smelled like lavender. "Thanks," I repeated myself as I put the lid back on the jar so I could eat more of my cake.

"Finna has a fix for just about everything," Breck mused. "Just don't take her up on an offer to meddle in your internal affairs. She once mixed me a drink with raw eggs to cure a sore throat and I was sick at my stomach for two days."

"Now! You're leavin' out the very important fact that you're allergic to the mallow root I put in it," she added sternly, then softened. "I didn't know that at the time."

"On the bright side, I did forget all about my sore throat," he added with a smirk.

"Wait, you had to drink *raw eggs* to fix the pain?" I shuddered at the thought. "I think I'd rather wait for it to pass on its own."

"Says the fella who got the sickness and lived to tell the tale," Breck said, causing Finna to shoot me an astonished look. It was a similar reaction to the one Breck had when he learned that, too.

"Oh, love," she started softly, reaching to put her hand on mine that was holding the fork. Her short fingers wrapped around to touch my palm. "Was it bad?"

"I was asleep for over a week. My sister-in-law Anne – she's the one who cared for me – couldn't wake me no matter how hard she tried. The doctor said my body was too weak, so it made me sleep to save all my energy for healing. When I finally did wake, it was..." I paused, looking down. I hadn't ever spoken about it like this with other people who didn't experience it, too. "The world I woke up to was not the world I left behind. Physical ailments aside, the... the people I lost was the hardest part," I finished quietly. "But sometimes I do still struggle with the effects on my body. My lungs; the coughing and such." I dug the fingers of my free hand into my leg beneath the table to stop it from moving.

Finna shook her head sadly and patted my hand a few times after she let go. I felt the intense stare coming from across the table and glanced up at Breck quickly before my gaze shifted out the window closest to me. I couldn't see the horses, but everything else was as tranquil as it had been when we arrived. A small butterfly was making its rounds at a lilac bush with pale purple blooms.

"We should get back. Peter has more work to finish, and I've already taken up a lot of his time. Thanks for the tea, Finna." Breck was on his feet then, and I got up also, pushing in my chair to make Nan proud. He stooped to kiss the petite woman on her cheek; she squeezed her hand on his upper arm and grinned at him affectionately.

"Peter, you best come back so I can have someone to eat more of my sweets. Tell me your favorite, and I'll see what I can do."

"Apples, probably," I offered. She smiled at that.

"Easy. Take care, fellas," she said as we left, the jar of the healing balm in my hand. I didn't have any pockets, so Breck offered to carry it for me. We untied the horses and pulled ourselves into the saddles, setting off down the road in the direction we had come from at a smooth pace.

"I wish it wasn't so uncomfortable every time someone asks me about being sick," I said finally. "Is it the topic or is it just me?"

"It's not you." Breck was focused on the road ahead of us. "It's only uncomfortable because it was a horrible thing that happened, and there's no easy way to talk about it. You're brave for even being willing to share your experience. I'm sorry I brought it up that way though, that wasn't my place."

"No need to be sorry," I tried to reassure him. "But I'll feel better if I don't let you win this time." Before he could respond I pushed my mare into a gallop. I heard him make a noise of objection behind me, but the pair quickly picked up speed in pursuit.

SIX

That night in my bedroom, I stood in front of my mirror with the small jar in hand. The bruise looked much worse than it felt now, but I figured it couldn't hurt to use what Finna had given me. I dipped my fingers into the cream – it was stiffer than I expected, more like a salve made thick with wax. We had used something similar on our cuts and scrapes growing up, but it never smelled as good as this.

I spread the concoction onto my skin and rubbed it in small circles. After I replaced the lid on top of the jar with the fingers I hadn't used, I rubbed my hands together, not wanting to waste any of it.

Fat raindrops tapped my window as I laid on my bed on top of the sheets in the dark, leaving my hip uncovered so the salve could soak in properly. I bunched my pillow up under my head and settled my gaze on the moonlit streaks of water making random trails down the glass. Typically, a night like this would lull me to sleep right away, but I found myself with too many thoughts running through my head.

I wasn't sure what to make of Finna. Breck had said they both came from the same place. Where was that, exactly? I was certain I'd never met Finna before, but her cottage was so covered with well-tended plants, and filled with so much stuff, that she must have lived there for some time. She looked like she could be around

Anne's age. Maybe they knew each other?

A chill came over me then, and I reached to pull my blanket up, wondering if I should've had a fire going that night after all. I closed my eyes and drew in a measured breath, filling my lungs as much as I could without making myself cough, before I let it out just as slowly. The lavender scent hanging in the air around me was very calming.

I decided that whatever Finna's story was, anyone who could make a lemon cake like the one I'd tasted was alright with me. She and Breck had both been nothing but kind. I needed to stop being so skeptical and appreciate the fact that our village was not destined for an ever-dwindling population as a result of the illness like we all feared. New people had found their way to our home, and that was something to be grateful for.

***

By the time we played our third match of the season a week and a half later, my bruise had been completely gone for days. My first instinct was to show Henry, but I decided against it. He would've asked me to explain where I got the salve from, and I wasn't sure I was ready to tell him about the peculiar little woman who had given it to me.

Unfortunately, the same could not be said about my ride with Breck. The second he'd left, Henry cornered me and demanded that I tell him more about this person who suddenly kept popping up in my life out of nowhere. I let him know it was none of his business, but the truth was that I wanted to tell him everything.

He still hadn't let up as we stood by our horses,

quickly refreshing ourselves while the well-dressed spectators wandered around the field after the second chukka, jovially kicking clumps of grass back into place and stomping on them with their expensive, polished shoes. I was halfway through an apple, while Henry and Fergus finished the water they'd ladled from our bucket. Thomas was eating his third hand pie.

"Any special friends here to watch you play today, Pete?" Henry drawled thickly, mischief on his face. I gave him a bored look from my seat on the low stone wall and didn't say anything. Luckily, Thomas was ready to jump in like always.

"Silly question, Henry. All two of his friends are right here," he chaffed. Then something dawned on him, and he added, "Ah, sorry Fergus... all *three* of his friends, I should say."

Our fourth man glanced at Thomas dismissively. He was in his mid-thirties, and we had all decided that he only agreed to play with us because we were one of the best teams that had an open spot to fill for the season. We were far from friends. He was a sound player, though, so it worked for us. Thomas barely noticed his reaction and continued talking.

"Speaking of special friends, I see *yours* is here and enjoying herself loudly."

We all looked at the group of young women in the middle of the field. The four of them were sisters, all beautiful, and cultivated, and dripping with the finest of everything. Henry's Sarah was the second oldest and the first to be promised in marriage. The massive stones set in the new ring on her finger glinted as she held her hand up to her mouth to cover a laugh dramatically. I'd seen it up close when he'd shown it to me several days prior, the night before he gave it to her. I turned my attention back to my friend, who was regarding her with what appeared to be a mix of adoration and fear. The poor fool.

Their engagement was the talk of the village. Any reason to celebrate was welcome, but an event backed by so much wealth was especially exciting because it meant that even the most common of us would be invited to several of the parties leading up to the big event. Auld Wally appeared then, scratching his fingers through the beard he was letting grow out. He'd just finished preparing our next horses for the remainder of the game.

"Oi!" he snapped, clapping his hands to draw our attention from the pretty girls. Thomas jumped with surprise at the sound, clearly the most absorbed in the distraction. "There'll be time for all that business later, lads. Focus now. Their defense is stronger this year, and you can't let up for nothin'." The team we were playing was one that we had a bit of a history with, and they were known for being brutish. "Peter, you need to send more long shots to Henry to get him some distance to work with."

I nodded and took the last bite of my apple, tossing the core behind me over the wall as I pushed my hips forward off the stones, dropping to my feet. The field had started to clear as spectators were being directed back to their various seating arrangements along the sidelines, which meant the next chukka was about to begin. As Wally shared more pointers with the rest of my team, I went to collect my gray mare. I stroked her neck before I checked the straps on my saddle.

"Incoming," Henry warned in a murmur as he came around to get his own horse. I looked at him over one shoulder, and then turned to look over the other and spotted what he was talking about. *Who* he was talking about, rather, as Breck made his way toward us with his hands in his pockets.

He tipped his chin toward me in greeting, a smile appearing on his features. I could all but feel whatever unsaid comment was burning on Henry's tongue behind me. Or maybe the burning was my own, as I bit the inside of my cheek to control the grin threatening my lips. I nodded back at him.

"Great game so far Peter, Henry," he greeted, acknowledging us both. "I hear congratulations are in order." Henry had untied his horse and walked her to the mounting block along the wall; her stubby, wrapped tail flicking behind her.

"Aye, thanks a million," he responded, sincerely enough, as he hoisted himself into his saddle, mallet in hand. His short response told me that he was already getting his head back in the game. "Enjoy the rest of the match. See you out there, Pete." His shifted in the saddle and squeezed his legs, and his black mare set off at a jog toward the field.

Breck watched the pair ride away and then turned his attention back to me. I was about to ask him how he'd been since I had seen him last, regretting that I didn't have anything more meaningful to say, but he spoke first.

"You've been using Finna's magic cream," he said observantly. For a brief, horrifying moment, I wondered if he had seen me through my window one of the past nights while I'd been applying it in all my naked glory. Memories flashed through my head as I tried to remember which part of me had been facing which direction, and what had been propped up where for easier access, but then he added, "I can smell the lavender." I managed to contain any indication of my previous thoughts and nodded in earnest.

"It's magic alright. The bruise vanished on me." I grinned sheepishly then, glancing at him before I untied my mare. "I hope she wasn't wanting me to return the rest of the jar. I'll admit I've kept using it, even though I don't really need it anymore. Helps me sleep."

"I'm sure she'll be thrilled to hear that. She loves mixing up those oils and herbs and seeing what good they can do."

"She should open a storefront in the village. The people could use her talent." Unless you had a visit to the apothecary or had a grandmother who was particularly skilled with poultices for only the most common of ailments, you didn't have many options. I could already picture the line of people stretched out the door onto the sidewalk, waiting with the aching backs and painful hands of people who worked hard, physically demanding jobs.

Breck made a thoughtful noise and then said, "But what is it they say, "*never do what you love for work, or it'll become a chore,*" or something like that?"

I laughed a little. "I think it's, "*do what you love,*

and you'll never work a day in your life," actually." I would know; I may as well have that quote branded on me. I stuck my foot in the stirrup and swung my leg over my horse, settling into a comfortable position before I reached down make sure my other boot was secure in the metal support. Breck was next to me then, holding my mallet up.

"Finna said she's nailed down a new dessert you might like. Care to come 'round with me tomorrow for another visit?" I finally met his gaze then as I took the mallet from him and shifted it to my other hand. A feeling bloomed in my chest that I couldn't put a name to, and I opened my mouth to respond but was cut off sharply.

"Peter!"

Both of us turned to see not only my teammates, but the other team's riders, the game officials, and everyone in else attendance staring at me in the distance. The field was large enough that the spectators were very small from my vantage point, but I didn't need to be close enough to see them to know that they were not pleased with being kept waiting. My face burned as I wheeled my mare around.

"Okay," I answered him quickly, risking one more look into his blue eyes as I rushed my horse onto the pitch. Henry gave me an incredulous look when I stopped beside him. I never let anything distract me during a game, and I wasn't about to start now. I tightened the strap on my helmet and cleared my thoughts.

***

It was a close second half, but our team ended

up losing. The ride back to the stables would've been silent if it hadn't been for Thomas complaining the whole way. The rest of us seemed to have too much on our minds to contribute to the one-sided conversation. I couldn't be sure what Henry and Wally were worrying about, but my mind was stuck on hoping that they weren't blaming me for our loss as hard as I was.

I thought I'd done a good job staying focused while we played. I even sent Henry one long pass that he was able to score with. But as soon as the haughty clapping began around us to congratulate both teams on a game well played, I was scanning the crowd. I attributed it to the fact that we hadn't settled our plans. I was just looking for him to confirm what time he would be coming by to collect me. Should I have the horses ready, or were we going to walk? Did "visit" imply that it would be another informal gathering, or should I dress for a meal?

"Oh, *dry it up*, would you?!" Wally's yelling at Thomas cut into my spiral of thoughts. He must've had all the complaining he could take. Thomas hushed immediately. I took a breath deeper than I meant to as I tried to calm my mind, and it made me cough several times. At least that no longer made them all look at me with concern. It was just something that happened.

We turned our horses over to the stable hands and returned our equipment to the tack room without any of us speaking. Wally didn't say anything before he walked out into the fading afternoon light. An attitude like that from him usually meant he'd fared poorly on a bet of some kind. I wondered if our loss had affected the weight of his pockets. Henry had something to say, so I remained on the bench near my things and waited for him to spit it out after Thomas left.

"I'm brickin' it, boyo," he said finally, his voice quiet and serious. I blinked and drew my eyebrows together. When he didn't continue, I picked up and moved myself across the room to sit next to him for support. He was wringing his cap in his hands.

"What is it?" I asked.

"I'm gettin' married, that's what it is. I'm gettin' married and it's all gonna be over." He sounded miserable. "I've spent me whole life playing like the rich kid, and now I gotta grow up and take all the responsibility for myself, and Sarah, and a house, and everything else!"

"I thought that was the general idea...?" I said carefully, which caused him to set his cap on his knee and push his fingers back through his short hair before he leaned back against the wall, hands dropping to his lap. His slumped posture and the frown on his features made him look young and entirely despondent. I had never seen him like this before. He was silent again for several moments.

"Were you nervous?" His words came barely above a whisper, but with a slightly curious tone. "You know... with Jamie?"

Jamie was not the person I thought Henry would bring up during this conversation. I'd been sure he wanted to scold me for the way I had behaved earlier with Breck. Not that I could blame him. "I don't know what—"

"*You know*," he repeated sternly, jaw tight, giving me a look that said he desperately did not want to elaborate, so I better fill in the gaps myself. Suddenly, I realized what he meant, and I gaped at him.

"Henry, I—"

"I'm sorry, I'm sorry," he cut me off again, leaning forward to hold his face in his hands, elbows resting on his knees. Our long friendship meant that we had shared nearly everything with each other, but this topic was something we both steered clear of, if for no other reason than to save ourselves from the uncomfortable nature of discussing such private things. It also didn't help that our interests in this matter didn't align, and I was terrified that even our close relationship couldn't withstand too many details of what went on in my head versus what went on in his when it came to intimacy.

"No," I answered softly, emotions stirring in me. He picked his head up then and looked at me like I was an auld man from the village, ready to share a bit of advice over a pint, who you'd be smart to listen to because he had seen and done it all.

I supposed that it made sense he would look at me that way. To my knowledge, Henry had only ever kissed a girl one time, and it was someone he didn't know and never saw again; a drunken, sloppy exchange with a lass dressed in barely anything at all hanging 'round the pub one night several years prior. She propositioned him and he was willing, but the rest of us stopped him before he made a decision we knew he'd deeply regret and never make sober.

"I mean," I continued then, staring at the floor between my feet, "I guess a little." I stopped again, my heart beating harder in my chest from the uncertainty I felt over sharing this with him. I sighed then, realizing that I knew better. Henry wouldn't be asking me if he didn't want to know. "Mostly I felt nervous because of the anticipation of it all. You know better than anyone else how long it took for us to even reveal how we felt, let alone act on it."

"Aye. And then you sure did *act on it*," he agreed, adding emphasis on the last part as he elbowed me in the ribs. A grin came to both of us then, and I couldn't stop myself from looking at the bench I'd moved from. His gaze followed mine to it, then suddenly snapped back to my face, expression completely different as a strained sound left his open mouth.

"What?" I asked, concerned.

"You... you didn't... *here*?!" he whispered loudly, and after a few seconds my face pinched into an apologetic look that made him groan and shake his head at me. I didn't have the heart to tell him that my bare arse had been directly where he was sitting.

Jamie had told me to meet him here one night after the moon was high and the house was asleep. It ended up being so cloudy that I couldn't see the moon or stars at all, so I waited as long as I could stand it and then snuck out toward the stables wearing the same clothes I'd come home in. It was a night with a chill in the air, which meant everything around me was silent except for my misty breath and the crunching of my shoes on the cold dirt as I walked.

When I made it inside the long, stone building, I blinked several times to adjust my eyes to the dark. "Jamie?" I'd whispered into the unlit tack room, still blinking to try and see better. I stood in the middle of the room dumbly then, not sure what to do with myself, but a sudden quick noise made me turn to find him lighting the lantern on the wall. The flickering light didn't reach the entire room, but it was enough to cast us half in a glow and half in shadow where we were standing.

Jamie blew on the match to put it out and dropped it near the doorway. There was a look on his face that told me his thoughts were up to no good, and I'd never been more glad of it, despite the nerves in my stomach. He was also wearing the same clothes I'd seen him in last. A pair of thick black trousers that met the tops of his shoes, a white shirt with the collar unbuttoned once, a black vest with large, flashy buttons, and a thick coat that was long enough in the back to reach his calves. He'd taken off his hat and puffy neckerchief.

The exposed skin on his throat is where I aimed my kiss when he came toward me, our arms wrapping around each other briefly before we pulled apart to slide our coats off our shoulders and unfasten our vests to get rid of them, too. I had his shirt unbuttoned halfway down his chest when he took my wrists in his hands and guided me backwards toward the bench by our tack boxes. I sat when the wooden edge of it met the back of my legs.

Before I could look up again, Jamie made his way onto my lap, straddling me with his legs hanging off the other side of the bench. Heat spread through my chest as he wrapped my arms around him and then let go of my wrists, his hands finding their way around my neck and into my hair at the back of my head. Then his lips were on mine, our eyes closed, and I pulled him closer to me. His shirt wasn't unbuttoned quite enough for me to wrap my fingers in the taut fabric, so I settled for holding one hand flat against his back and sliding the other to his hip. I had to hold a gasp in as he began rocking his hips torturously slow, back and forth.

He grinned against my mouth as he felt my reaction to this and kissed me again before he angled his head to the side, planting soft pecks along my jaw and neck, fingers tangling and untangling in my brown curls. He knew this was something I loved, his fingers in my hair, and I wanted to accuse him of cruelty for using it on top of everything else he was doing to me.

When I was starting to worry that I couldn't take much more, he sat up again and kissed me deeply before he removed himself from my lap. I was breathless and throbbing and must've looked a total mess, but all I could think about was getting his mouth back on me. He must have been thinking the same thing, because he reached for me as I stood up and slid his hands down my chest and stomach to the front of my trousers. We both looked down to watch his fingers unfasten them in the dim light. His hands weren't shaking, but mine definitely were.

As if he was removing his own trousers and underthings after a long day, he shoved mine down off my hips to the floor in one swoop. The drag of the fabric against my most sensitive area made me wince. Jamie looked up at me again, pulled me down by the back of my neck for a kiss, and turned me with his free hand on my hip. I shuffled my feet to avoid tripping over the clothes wrapped around my ankles.

With the same two hands that Jamie had first shoved me with all those years ago, he now pushed me down onto the bench by the boxes that belonged to Thomas and Henry. I caught myself on the way down, one hand grasping the edge of the bench and the other flat against the wall behind me. I lowered myself onto the seat, but I had no time to adjust to the foreign feeling of my bare skin against the wooden surface. Jamie was in front of me, on his knees, kissing me again. I resumed working on the trail of his shirt buttons, hopeful to see more of his olive skin exposed. I only made it through one more button, though, before Jamie's hands were on my legs and I couldn't make my fingers move any longer.

His were working quite well, fortunately for me, as they found their way up my thighs to my erection. I squeezed my eyes shut and leaned my head back against the wall, trying in desperation to remain silent in this relatively unprotected space. It was the middle of the night, but there was never any way to know for sure who would be there at any given time. Plus, I knew for a fact that you could hear Wally sneeze inside his cottage from the tack room. That could only mean other sounds would travel that distance back.

Luckily, my breathing was not strained or noisy or cough-inducing then, because panting was all I could do in response to his hand moving along my length, faster and faster. The other was placed gently on my lower stomach, holding the bunched fabric of my shirt out of the way. When he eventually leaned down to place a wet, open-mouthed kiss on the tip of me, it was all over. My muscles jerked and the feeling surged through me, leaving me weak and breathless.

I heard Jamie laugh soundlessly, air escaping his nose in a few short bursts, and I opened my eyes to him wiping his face off with the sleeve of his shirt. Embarrassment washed over me as I realized what I'd done to him, not giv-

ing any sort of warning so he could move out of the way or something. I sat forward immediately, my hands coming to his arm and elbow with a whispered apology ready on my tongue, but he just moved to grab my arms instead and pulled me off the bench to the ground with him and kissed me slowly.

"You're living it again in your head, aren't you?" Henry's dry voice broke my trance.

"What? No," I said quickly, clearing my throat and swallowing hard.

"You were, mate. I could see it on your face."

"Sorry," I offered then, feeling no desire to keep denying it. That never worked with Henry. He squeezed my shoulder and stood up to leave. I remained where I was as he wished me a good night and reassured me that we would do better at the next match. Only after I heard his footsteps fade completely did I risk standing up, to avoid presenting him with the bulge in the front of my tight riding breeches. I pulled at the fabric to attempt a readjustment and to ease the heavy feeling that had collected there, but it didn't do much good.

My body had all but stopped responding this way after Jamie died. Even on the few rare occasions when I'd felt *something*, a tightness would form in my chest, an uneasiness would settle in my stomach, and the thoughts would be washed away before I could think to act on them. Quite obviously it was a part of my grief, but I didn't know how long to allow it to happen before it was something I should be concerned about. And who would I even talk to? The last thing I needed was for the doctor to tell me it's normal to feel this way, and that soon enough the right sweet colleen would catch my eye in the village and bring all my feelings back.

***

When I made it to the house for supper, the whole family was in the kitchen, ready to console me after our first loss of the season. I told them it was fine and repeated Henry's sentiments about doing better next time, before I excused myself toward the stairs.

"The miller stopped by for you." Nan's words halted me in my tracks. I came back around the corner, playing casual.

"Oh?" I asked, not risking a look at anyone else's face but Nan's for fear of what I might see. She handed me a small envelope that was still sealed. I took it and turned it over to look at the front, but there was no writing on it.

"He said he copied down the list of grains you asked him about. Something to do with new ideas for your horses?"

"Oh, right. Thanks," I said, nodding and turning back toward the stairs. I took them two at a time and slid my finger underneath the flap of the envelope before I could shut my door behind me. I pulled out a piece of paper and an increasingly familiar mix of scents met my nose. Freshly ground flour and mint. I unfolded the parchment and read the words written on it.

> *Wheat, barley, oats.*
>
> *Come by round midday and*
>
> *we can walk together.*
>
> *B*

I read the words a few times over, unable to keep myself from smiling at the trouble he'd gone through to get this message to me. I set the letter and envelope on my nightstand and quickly washed up and changed clothes, remembering that my family was waiting for me downstairs.

Would I tell Nan that I was meeting him tomorrow to further discuss these grains in person? Or would I tell her the truth? Was the truth really so scandalous that I couldn't tell her? I wondered if having the same set of friends my whole life had made it that much more difficult for anyone – myself included – to believe that I'd made a new one? And that this friendship didn't require me to be on a horse like it always had before?

I pulled a clean shirt on over my head and slipped the two unfastened buttons at the top into their holes, ran my fingers through my hair to attempt to calm it into the sideswept part I preferred, and gave myself a final once-over in the mirror before I made my way back to the kitchen to eat.

SEVEN

I spent the next morning as I usually did, running through my list of chores with the horses. It was all made slower by the gentle rain coming down. A thick fog hung over the land, hugging the curves of the river and thinning out over the crests of the rolling hills. I decided against any training, even with Wally's mare, and turned them all out into the pasture with their rain sheets on instead. The chestnut was not yet friendly with my horses, so she stood apart from them when they finally settled on one of their favorite patches of graze.

My last task was to clean the stalls and put down fresh bedding. This normally would be something that the stable hands took care of, or even Wally himself. Recently, however, William had decided that everyone would be given a leave of work one day per week, as much as they might want to be here. So, I was by myself, except for the horses and the barn cat who kept trying to tangle herself in every step I took since there was no-body else around to entertain her.

I carried the bale of straw by the tight strings holding it together, trying to hurry from the barn to the stables during a heavier moment of rain. I knew better than to walk too quickly on the slick stone floor, but in my rush, I wasn't careful enough and my boot slipped. I dropped the bale heavily and landed at an awkward angle on my knee. The cat went skittering away.

"*Shit*," I cursed under my breath, pulling my hand free of the grip I still had on one of the bale ties. Two of my fingers had been sliced by the string. Lines of bright red were spreading from where they bent at the second joint. I got up and searched for the nearest piece of cloth I could find and held the rag tightly to the injured area. I hoped it wasn't too dirty from whatever it had been used for prior.

I pulled the fabric away after a moment and examined the cuts. Nausea bubbled in my gut from the sight of the blood, but it didn't appear that my fingers were hurt too badly. I breathed out shakily and wrapped the cloth around those fingers and tucked the loose end in at the top to keep it in place and got on with finishing my task.

By the time I was done, I was running later than I wanted to be. I quickly tried to wash the smell of horse off me at my basin and ruffled my hair with a clean towel to try and dry it some. Out of my wardrobe, I selected my long, heavy cloak with a cape covering the shoulders and a smart hat with a wide brim to better protect me from the weather during my walk. On my way out, I encountered Anne in the front sitting room. She was reading in the large chair by the fireplace, and she gently closed her fingers in the book to save her place as she smiled up at me.

"Well, don't you look nice. Plans in the village?"

"I'm having a late lunch with some friends," I told her honestly. "With Breck, and someone he knew in the village he's from. Her name is Finna. Have you met her?" Her gaze shifted away from me as she gave it some thought, but she shook her head as she decided she hadn't.

"No, not that I can remember. Might recognize her if I saw her, though. Have a good time. And take care."

"I will," I said over my shoulder as I pulled the door open and slipped outside. The rain was still coming down, a little stronger now. I pulled my cloak tight around me and stepped out into the shower.

There was no doubt that Anne would recognize Finna if she'd seen her before. She was unmistakable. I was looking forward to seeing her again. Something about her, about her whole house, left a feeling with me that I couldn't quite describe. There was a lightness, almost. Like Breck's carefree stride I'd noticed on our hike. The thatched trees above me provided some relief from the raindrops *tap-tap-tapping* on my hat as I approached the bridge. Only a few puddles formed in the road here, and there was a clear line on the ground where the precipitation fell at either end of the living tunnel.

My eyes darted to the mill as soon as I could see it, and again there were no lights in the windows or any indication that anyone was around. As I got closer, I did notice something white closed in the door. An envelope, I discovered, same as the one I'd received the day before. I peered in the window closest to the door before I pulled the envelope free. There was no writing on the outside of this one either, but I opened it anyway and read the note inside.

Had to leave early to help Finna

with something important.

You remember the way.

B

I folded the paper back up as I turned to face the road. Did I remember the way? We had been on horseback before, and we also had not left or returned from this spot. I pulled my cloak open and tucked the envelope into my breast pocket before I retraced my steps back toward the bridge. As I reached the top of the hill, I took another surveying glance and started down the other fork in the road.

***

Relief came over me as I spotted the cottage with the red door and walls made of flowers. Doors painted red were common amongst the homes surrounding the village. The stories said that it was a form of protection for the people who lived there, warding off evil and negativity. But none of the other cottages with red doors looked quite like this one.

Unlike the mill, Finna's home was pouring light from all the windows. The rain had slowed to a drizzle, but the clouds were dark and swirling with agitation above me, indicating that they were still full and ready to spill when the time was right. My squelching came to an end at the front door. I knocked three times and waited, listening to the muffled voices coming from inside, and then the approaching footsteps. When the door swung open, I was greeted with a smile and smells that made my mouth start watering immediately.

"Peter! Oh love, you're soaked. Come in, quickly now."

Finna took me by the elbow and led me inside without giving me a chance to remove my muddy shoes. I looked down to see the damage I was doing to the floor, which caused the water that had collected on top of my hat to trickle off, adding to the mess I was making.

"Oh— sorry Finna, I'm sorry." I stumbled over my words and my boots as I kicked them off. She reached up to remove my cloak, which was also dripping wet, and helped me toward a chair by the fire that was going on the hearth.

"No bother. It's not the first time my floor's been muddy, and it won't be the last."

I sat down, hopeful that the rest of me was dry, and looked around the room. It was different in this light. The plants weren't so overwhelming now. Instead, my attention was drawn to the varied collection of items that were catching the dancing light from the fireplace, making them glow. A vase sitting on a table appeared to be made of tiny pieces of mirrored glass, creating a mosaic effect. Several of the plants had tiny, sparkly trinkets sticking from the soil or tucked between their leaves. One fern hanging by the window was decorated with crystal beads on a string.

Finna returned from wherever she had gone and draped a fleecy blanket over my shoulders. I turned my head to look at her and say thank you as Breck came into the room from the kitchen. A look I couldn't read spread across his features as he noticed the state I was in, eyes scanning me head to toe.

"Mind the floor," Finna warned as she picked up my boots and spread a towel over the wet trail I'd left behind me. He sidestepped the area and came to sit across from me, leaning forward in the chair, forearms on his legs.

"You got my notes," he said, still giving me an odd look compared to the easy air about him I'd grown accustomed to.

"I did. And I remembered the way like you said. Only got turned around once," I replied, shrugging my shoulders and giving him an embarrassed grin that quirked up only one corner of my lips. I knew I must've looked like a drowned rat on my approach to the cottage, which he probably saw through one of the windows in the kitchen. I ran my fingers through my deeply parted hair self-consciously, relieved that it didn't seem to be too wet despite everything.

His eyebrows knit together, and he didn't return my smile, so I dropped mine and pulled the blanket around my shoulders a little tighter. When I did, pain stung in my fingers where I'd cut them on the bale tie earlier. I let go of the blanket to examine them and make sure I wasn't making a mess of Finna's throw, too.

"You're hurt," Breck said, as if it was a realization he'd come to. He got out of his chair and in two steps he was in my personal space, leaning down to take a closer look as he held my hand with both of his. There was no more blood, but the cuts looked angry.

"I dropped a bale of straw earlier," I explained, struggling to keep my gaze from the side of his face so close to mine. The same smell I'd experienced the night before on the letter he wrote me, the nutty flour and fresh mint, was strong enough now to overwhelm my senses. I would've held my breath to calm myself if I hadn't thought it would send me into a coughing fit.

"Finna?" he asked then, loud enough to draw her from the other room. He didn't move until she appeared beside him. He held my hand toward her, angled to the firelight so she could see better. She squinted at my fingers, then her eyes went wide. She looked up at me then.

"That needs to be cleaned, love. It'll fester soon."

Before I could say anything else about it, the pair of them had left me alone in my chair to collect various items they needed to fix me up. After Finna had dabbed the wounds with puffs of cotton grass soaked in a mystery liquid that burned a little, she applied another of her special salves and wrapped bandages around them with care.

"I'll send you home with what you need to keep them clean and covered," she said finally, gathering the items they had brought over in her arms so she could carry them to the kitchen.

"What smells so good?" I asked Breck, who was seated across from me again, trying to lighten the mood back to what I had been hoping to find here on my way over. I examined my fingers now that my hand had been released back to me. They were already starting to feel better, if that was possible.

"The important thing I had to come help with," he replied. A hint of his typical, amused tone had returned to his voice.

Just then, Finna came back in carrying a bowl with something steaming hot inside. I took it as she offered it to me, my wrapped fingers sticking out stiffly as I did, and brought it to my lap so I could see what was inside. I immediately recognized the traditional stew I'd been served, though it had a stronger smell than I was used to. I picked the spoon up with my thumb and two uninjured fingers and brought it to my mouth. Stronger smell *and* stronger flavor.

I was four or five bites in when I realized I was the only one eating.

"Did you already eat?" I asked, and Breck nodded. He had one leg crossed over the other, ankle resting on his knee, the fingers of one hand supporting his cheek and chin as he watched me. I took another mouthful of the hearty mixture of meat and vegetables in front of me, unable stop for long. I hadn't realized how hungry I was until then. Being warmed from the outside by the fire and inside by the stew was soothing after my trek through the wet weather.

A crack of thunder sliced through the calming sound of rain on the thatched roof over our heads. The miller sitting opposite from me uncrossed his leg, straightening from his comfortable position, and Finna's eyes met his as she came back around the corner. I noticed their strange reaction and set my spoon down, abandoning my next bite.

"Is something wrong?" I asked. Breck got up then, a mere second before another boom of thunder rattled nearer than before. At the same time, they both turned to look at me, and my stomach dipped with uncertainty.

"Peter," Finna started, "there's no time to explain, but everything is fine. Do you trust us?" I blinked several times, not sure where my voice had gone, so I nodded instead. "Grand," she said cheerily, though it didn't come across as entirely genuine. There was a voice on the other side of Finna's door then. No, several voices. And then the knob turned, the door opened, and I struggled to hold onto the bowl perched on my legs.

"Finna!" The first person to enter through the doorway, a massive man with an even bigger voice, greeted my host with a hug that I was afraid would snap her in half. His neatly coiffed dark brown hair and full beard were a surprising contrast to the state of his clothes. The shirt he wore was a drab green, made darker across the shoulders and chest by the rain, and he had brown pants that reached his knees and bare feet below them that were coated in mud.

"Let me get more towels," Finna said, a hint of annoyance in her voice as she turned, her skirts whirling around her legs. Behind this muscled man came two women, both stunningly beautiful and nearly as tall as I was. The first had hair the color of honey that stretched in a long braid down her back, golden skin, and bright eyes. She followed Finna around the corner after offering to help her with the towels. The other woman had the darkest black hair I'd ever seen, also in a braid, and her clothes... I think I stopped breathing for a moment when I realized she was wearing *trousers*. This was confirmed when I couldn't restrain the coughs that escaped me, which made everyone in the small room turn to look my direction.

"I thought I smelled something," the woman with black hair said to no one in particular, eyebrow arched as she crossed her arms. The man regarded me with surprise and then turned to Breck, who was giving me the most apologetic look.

"This is my friend, Peter," Breck said, his eyes still fixed on me. "Peter, this is Carrick, and Fallon."

"And Elina!" chimed the honeyed woman who returned with a stack of towels, handing one to each guest. None of them bothered to wipe the water from their faces; instead, they began drying their feet, which I realized now were all bare. "Murray should be joining us soon, you know how he is," Elina added.

"I didn't realize *all of you* were coming today," Breck said, turning then to look at Fallon, who had pulled her braid over her shoulder and was busy squeezing water out of it with a second towel she'd been given.

"I thought it was better that we all heard the story first-hand, in case one of us picked up on something the others didn't," she said plainly.

"Plus, everybody loves a good story," Carrick added, his gravelly voice laced with humor. Breck took a few steps toward the newcomers and began speaking to them in a hushed tone, though I could still hear what he said.

"I haven't asked him yet. He arrived later than we planned because of the rain." The way he spoke to them told me he knew these people well.

"Either he'll tell us, or he won't, Breck, and if he doesn't then—"

"Absolutely not." Breck cut off Fallon's leading words, and his harsh tone drained what was left of my appetite, so I set my bowl down by my feet before I could drop it.

"I'm not suggesting we force him," she said with

an attitude. "I'm just saying that we need to know what he has to say, one way or the other."

Finna came around the other side of my chair and picked up my bowl, her small hand resting on my arm for a moment until I looked at her. She was so short that I barely had to look up to meet her pale blue eyes. She tilted her head slightly then, and after a few seconds I grinned at her, reassuring her that I was alright. She returned the gesture and left me. When I turned around, the entire party was seated on various perches around the small room, all their attention on me.

"Peter," Breck started from his seat on the floor, nearest to me of everyone. I slid my sock feet closer to myself across the rug, giving him more space. He wanted to say something else, but stopped, and then he sighed and shook his head. "I have to talk with him first. This isn't fair."

"Take your time, I'm just pouring everyone some tea first anyway," Finna said from the kitchen, surely trying to create a distraction with her perfect herbal blend. The rest of the audience watched as I stood from my chair and followed Breck through a door I hadn't noticed before. After he shut it, I glanced around and realized it was Finna's bedroom.

When I looked back at Breck, he was staring at me intently. I swallowed and felt scarlet creeping across my chest and cheeks. His eyes were so blue, even in the low light coming from the window on the far wall, and the set of his jaw made his sharp, handsome features stand out even more.

"I need you to understand that this decision was

not mine. You've trusted me with a lot, me and Finna both, and the last thing I want to do is damage that. So, I hope you'll realize that I would not allow what's happening if I didn't think it was very important."

"What *is* happening?" I finally asked. Breck looked away from me then, down to his feet and out the window, before meeting my eyes again.

"They're here to ask you some questions about your sickness. About what happened to your family, and the others here in the village."

"Alright," I said, shrugging my shoulders a little. I didn't have a problem talking about it. The agonized look on his face said that maybe there was still more to it, though.

"If they ask anything you don't feel comfortable answering, say so. If you want to stop, we will."

"I will, yeah," I urged, trying to indicate that I was capable of deciding for myself how to handle this. He gave me a final, long look before he pulled the door open and let me back out into the sitting room. As the door latched behind us, the low chatter of everyone's conversation stopped and they all looked at me again. The other person they had mentioned, Murray, was now seated next to Fallon. He had long, red hair that reached his shoulders, an impressively thick beard, and was wearing nothing but a pair of loose, brown trousers.

"Have you prepared him, then?" Carrick asked through a smirk. I took a seat in my chair by the fire and wished that it wasn't quite so warm now. Breck sat on the floor beside me again, one leg pulled up at the knee and the other crossed underneath him.

"He said you have questions about my being sick two years ago," I said. Finna brought Breck and me our cups of tea; everyone else was already holding theirs.

"Yes." It was Fallon who responded. "We need to know as much as you can tell us."

I told them about how quickly my family fell ill, and how some others in the village never showed any sickness at all. I explained in as much detail as I could of what Anne had shared about our symptoms, the fever and lethargy, the body aches and chills. I noted what the doctor had told her about making us comfortable and to prepare for the inevitable.

"I always thought that part was odd," I confessed, after taking another sip of my drink. "How certain he was that none of us would survive it."

There was a heavy silence. I started to wonder if I'd said something wrong. The logs on the hearth popped and crackled as they burned, but everything and everyone else sat perfectly still. "Nothing odd about it," Fallon said then. She adjusted her scrutinizing gaze on me and then looked down at the cup nestled between her hands. "You're the only one who got sick and lived."

"That's not true," I came back quickly, eyebrows bunched together. But as I paused to think about someone else who had shared my same experience, I realized slowly that I couldn't think of anyone. I looked at Breck, but his eyes were also cast down toward the floor. "That's not true," I repeated, my voice faltering.

A chill swept through my body as this information settled.

How had I never thought of this before? Had I

been so caught up in the trauma of it all that I never stopped to see you either lived or died and there was no in between, except for me? Did Anne know this? Word spread so fast in our village that it seemed impossible for nobody to have realized it until now. My eyes darted to the faces of the people sitting around me. How did *they* know this?

"Why?" I demanded quietly, my eyes landing on Fallon, since she was the one who seemed to have the most information. "Why would I be the only one?"

"That's what we're trying to figure out, love." Finna's voice came from the kitchen doorway, the only one who would make eye contact with me in my moment of vulnerability.

"This illness," Murray started, his accent thick and even more foreign to me than the rest of them, "we fear it's not like other human illnesses."

"The symptoms mimic those of more common ailments, but underneath, we think it's something worse." Breck finally looked at me as he spoke, expression still pained.

"Worse?" I asked, my eyes searching his.

"Deadly, obviously," Fallon said, "and malicious enough to make us think that it must be something beyond what nature is capable of on her own." I felt the look of confusion on my face as I tried to understand what she meant.

"Dark magic," Carrick and Elina said at the same time, an echo of each other.

"*Magic*?" I blurted out. "You think *magic* is what

made me sick?"

"And killed your family," Fallon added plainly.

"Enough!" Breck interjected, on his feet before I even noticed he was moving. He seemed to catch himself then, brushing past Finna on his way to the kitchen and out of sight, abandoning his teacup and me by the fire.

"Peter," Elina said, tucking a stray blonde tendril behind her ear, which was decorated like Breck and Finna's were. "We're curious... if this *was* magic... what effect it may have had. We cannot know with the ones who perished, for that would be very rude of us to disturb them." She paused, considering her words carefully. "If we could know more about how it affected you, we could possibly figure out where it came from. And how to stop it from happening again."

Her words filtered in through my ears, but my brain was a scrambled mess. Magic. Dark magic. That meant bad. Someone bad was using magic to make us sick? To kill us? To kill *me*?

"Someone wanted to kill my family?" I asked numbly. Breck appeared beside me again. He grabbed my arm and pulled me to my feet, dragging me toward the door as Finna's thick blanket fell from my shoulders to the ground.

"That's enough of this," he said darkly, addressing the room. He collected my hat and cloak and placed my shoes near my feet so I could put them on. I braced myself with a hand on the wall as I slid one foot inside, my head in a fog. After repeating the task with my other shoe, I glanced back at the group of strangers. None of them were looking at me now.

I felt as though I was the only one left out of an inside joke. Like they all knew something I didn't, and it was pathetic how ignorant I was to my own situation. Breck all but pushed me out the front door and into the humid air. The rain had stopped, but the gloom remained. He said something to the others still inside and shut the door behind him. When he began walking, I forced my legs to join him. He carried my things, along with the sack of items Finna had promised for my fingers, and we did not speak a word until we reached the stone bridge.

I stopped cold at the fork, my gaze stretching down the road to my house.

"I don't think I want to go home yet," I said weakly. I looked at him, and he tilted his head in the direction of the mill, a silent offer.

***

Inside, he hung my coat and hat by the door, and I followed him up the staircase to the second story of the mill, which also served as his home. It was furnished simply; a basic kitchen in one corner and a bed at the other end. There was a stove along the far wall with the black pipe stretching straight up through the ceiling. A table with two chairs stood in the middle of the room.

I sat in one of the chairs after he pulled it out for me, and he got busy with something near the stove. I looked out the giant window above the bed, through which you could see the top of the wooden wheel of the mill and the waterfall beyond. The water was pouring over the rocks heavily thanks to all the rain. I watched for a long while before I spoke.

"Too bad the bed is facing the wrong direction for the view," I observed.

"Says who?" The amused tone to his voice was there again.

"The—" I paused, realizing that his bed didn't have a headboard. "The pillows are arranged that way. With your head near the window."

"They fall off the end if I don't keep them against the wall," he explained, coming to join me at the table with a tray carrying two cups of tea and a small jar of honey. "I've tried it before." I watched him as he sat down, a small grin on his face, though it didn't seem to reach his eyes. He looked about as tortured as I felt after my encounter at Finna's cottage. I reached for the cup closest to me and stirred a spoonful of honey into it before I took a sip. The strong mint flavor washed through my nose and over my tongue to my stomach.

Another silence stretched between us, neither one ready to talk about what had just happened, despite the hundreds of questions that were knocking around inside my skull. Finally, after the herbaceous tea had time to work on the ache in my head and the gurgling in my stomach, I allowed myself to start asking.

"Did someone really want to kill us?" I queried, my eyes searching his face. He didn't respond right away, taking another pull from his tea first.

"We aren't sure, to be honest. It's one of the things that has confused us the most. Some families were not affected, some only lost a few, and others..." He didn't need to finish. "So far we've discovered no viable reasons for why some got sick and some didn't."

"How many have you talked to about it?" I wondered how many others had this bucket of information dumped on their heads before me. Breck looked at me then.

"Including you? One," was his reply. "We've been trying to figure this out without involving any of the families, for fear of it being too painful still. But, unfortunately, our search for information has been stalled for enough time that we couldn't put it off any longer."

"Well, if you want a little advice, maybe next time you should forget to invite Fallon."

Breck laughed at that, and a grin pulled at my lips.

"I didn't want *any* of them to come. It was supposed to just be Finna and me. Then Fallon said she would send Carrick or Elina, and then it was everyone." He shook his head in defeat. The uneasy feeling in my stomach came back, and I decided to ask what I suspected was making me feel the worst of all.

"Is this the only reason you've been talking to me? To get me to trust you enough to answer your questions?" It was silly how small asking that made me feel.

"Of course not." He seemed surprised that I would think that. "I've enjoyed getting to know you very much, Peter. Life can't be all about work, after all. Despite the saying I still can't remember correctly."

"Do what you love, and you'll never work a day in your life," I reminded him.

"That's the one," he confirmed, wagging a pointed finger in my direction. My eye caught the glint of the thin band wrapped around it, and I risked looking at the rest of the metal on his fingers, along his ears, and at the edge of his nose. I allowed my eyes to dip lower, tracing the line of his lips, before I looked away.

"I just have one more question," I lied. He nodded, encouraging me to ask it. "All of you kept referring to it as the "human illness" at Finna's. What does that mean, exactly? Are animals getting sick now, too?" This was the worst thing I could possibly think of. If my horses were at risk, I would let them do whatever they needed to do to me to stop it.

Breck took an awfully long time to respond.

"Magic," he began, "is not used by humans, as I'm sure you're well aware. And since we're concerned that this may have been a result of magic, we're also concerned that this was done *to* humans. By other beings who do use magic."

My gaze shifted out the window behind him as I tried to decipher his words. Other beings? Like the magical creatures in Lucy's bedtime stories? The ones we were warned about as children? The ones who played tricks and did naughty things when nobody was looking?

"What, like fairies?" I asked, my eyes meeting his across the table.

"Yes," he said. "Fairies who are not friendly with humans and wish to do harm rather than good." I balled my hand into a fist on my thigh, stopping it in its place. "Something tells me you don't believe what I'm saying," he guessed, reaching to place my cup on the tray with his as he began clearing the table.

"Can you blame me?" I turned in the chair as he walked to the kitchen, placing the tray on the counter that was barely large enough to hold it. "I've never seen a fairy, and I've certainly never seen magic. Mam had us scared to death of what the fairies would do if we didn't act right, but that only lasts so long before you grow up, and you realize it's all just made-up stories that are easier to dish out than a good spanking."

"You didn't seem so skeptical when I told you the story about the gold in the river." He leaned his hips back against the counter, crossing his arms and studying my face. I realized he was right.

"That was different," I started, but stopped when I couldn't think of what else to say to support my argument.

"Was it?" he asked, looking at his feet, one crossed over the other in his casual position. I drew in a breath when my lungs told me I wasn't bringing in enough air, and I coughed twice.

"I haven't had a reason to believe any of it for years," I said then. "I used to. When I was a child. But when I got older, I realized that it didn't make any sense."

"Most stop believing as they get older. Fairy tales lose their luster when life gets hard. The adult mind has a way of seeking out reason over the unknown." He returned to his seat across from me at the table, and I narrowed my eyes, considering his words. He leaned toward me then, his forearms on the tabletop supporting his weight. "Just because you don't think about something anymore, that doesn't mean it stopped being real."

His words hit me in a way I didn't expect. It made me think about my family. About Jamie. For so long, I worried about what would happen if I *did* stop thinking about them. Thoughts of them swirled in my head endlessly during the months after I woke up. I was desperate to hold onto them. Slowly, though, I realized that I had to let those memories settle so that I could get on with my life. And they didn't disappear. The most important memories were still with me, always, and I could draw on them whenever I needed to.

"You really believe magic is real? Dark magic," I corrected, "that could hurt people and do terrible things?"

"I know it is." He reclined against the back of the chair, tousling his thick hair to the side to get it off his forehead. I was able to see for the first time that his golden freckles scattered all the way to his hairline.

"And... fairies?" I asked cautiously. A grin spread on his mouth, and he looked down for a moment before his eyes met mine again.

"More common than you might think," he confirmed.

EIGHT

Breck sent me home with my coat, hat, and the bag of supplies. As I opened the sack in my room after supper, through which I'd been mostly silent thanks to all the information I was still processing, I realized there was something else inside. I pulled out the thick bundle of parchment tied with twine and sat on the bench at the end of my bed. I unwrapped it carefully, having no idea what I was about to find, when a sweet smell reached my nose.

It was a square of flat, dense cake with a layer of crumbles on top. I held the parchment up with my injured hand and brought it close enough to take a bite off the corner. There were tiny pieces of soft apples baked inside, and I was sure that I tasted honey, along with cinnamon, and sugar, and I moaned without meaning to as I swallowed my second bite.

I decided to save the rest for later and wrapped it back up the best I could. After dressing my fingers with new bandages and removing my clothes, I collapsed into my bed. I stared at the ceiling above me. I'd long since memorized every dip and notch in it after sleeping in the same spot every night of my life. A few coughs were pressed from my lungs, which happened sometimes when I laid on my back for too long, but I couldn't bring myself to move. *What a feckin' day.*

Somehow, hearing that my loved ones might've

been killed rather than dying of natural causes was not the most jarring part of what I'd learned. Maybe because this information didn't change the fact that they were gone. My life had been spared, and the guilt I felt for that still hung with me every day, even though everyone had reassured me that I shouldn't feel that way. How could I not? Especially knowing now that it had been some-thing – some*one* – who had decided that I lived when the others didn't.

I wished I had applied some of the lavender salve to help me fall asleep. The one I'd slathered on my cuts didn't have a strong smell. I picked up my hand and looked at my wrapped fingers in the moonlight. Why had Breck's reaction been so strange? I wasn't exactly the most graceful person. I found myself with bumps and scrapes all the time. He wouldn't have known that, though.

Maybe worrying about the impending conversa-tion was what made him act out of character. My thoughts shifted to the rest of the people I'd met at Finna's house. What a strange group they were. Strange, but gorgeous. Enough to have made me forget all about the clothes they wore – and didn't wear. I was as guilty as the next fella about not wanting to dress up all the time like we were expected to, with vests and coats and hats and the rest, but this was a level of casual that would've sent some into shock.

A realization hit me then. I knew where I had seen clothes like theirs before. I sat up, brow furrowed, and paused for a moment before I threw my blankets off and reached for my own clothes I'd just removed.

As silently as I could manage, I crept across the

hall to Lucy's door. She was asleep in her bed, a nest of pillows surrounding her and her dolls. I pushed the door open just enough for me to slip inside and stepped toward her bookshelf along the wall. I squinted at the row of spines and carefully pulled one with swirling, golden details from the collection. I glanced at my sister again to make sure I hadn't disturbed her, then quickly made my way back to my own bedroom.

I struck a match against my bedside table and lit the candle there, which cast a gentle light over the corner of my room. I sat on the edge of the bed and opened the book atop my legs, flipping pages until I found what I'd been searching for. I scanned the words on the paper briefly, but my focus was on the illustrations.

My eyes settled on the face of the creature on the page. She was exquisite in every way, from her flowing hair to her gauzy, billowing dress that revealed her thin frame. But that was where her human similarities ended. The text indicated that she was tiny, no bigger than a robin, and intricate wings sprouted from her back that were the same color as her frock.

I returned my attention to the words, framed with a square of golden vines, reading them in more detail. Fairies, it explained, were mythical creatures who lived anywhere you could find nature and animals in abundance. For the most part, they were kind, peaceful beings, unless you did something to offend them. It didn't go into detail on what they found offensive.

After turning to the next page, I was greeted with more drawings of multiple fae creatures. The males were wearing brown trousers and nothing else. One had long hair, the other had shorter, but they both had features as lovely as the females. I leaned down closer to the page, studying the flowers and ribbons tangled in their hair, the decorations in their pointed ears, and on their fingers and wrists.

The words on this page revealed that fairies loved to eat sweet foods the best. They enjoyed being helpful to humans and could be rewarded with baked treats or fruit. It said they're also attracted by objects that sparkle or catch the eye with bright colors. I shut the book and stared out my window at nothing.

***

I dove into my work over the next few days, distracting myself from sunrise to sunset. Though I later regretted it, I never ate the rest of what Finna had baked for me. I didn't have the appetite for anything at all. My grumbling stomach and Henry whipping his cap against the back of my head were the only things that forced me to finally stop and eat something mid-afternoon. I chewed a bite of my bread with jam while Henry groomed his horse after their workout.

"The date's been set now, and invitations have been sent. There's a big thing planned for this weekend. A party to celebrate an even bigger party. How's that for excessive?"

"I guess you've got to do something with all that money both of your fathers work so hard for," I said blandly, which made him groan.

"I'm supposed to ask you to come. And I was supposed to have already asked you to be me best man, but I might've forgotten." He looked at me expectantly, and I grinned, nodding my head loosely as though my answer was obvious.

"Sure, Hen, I'll be your best man and come to your engagement party."

"Grand," he said, relieved, and then added, "bring somebody, if you like. Preferably someone who eats a lot. They've ordered enough to feed our village and the next." I sensed the implication in his words. I knew he could see through my act I'd been putting on, working to avoid my problems, but he hadn't said anything about it.

"I'll have enough trouble finding something fancy enough to wear by that time." I thought about what I had available in my wardrobe and made a mental note to try some of the items on that evening. Maybe William had something I could borrow, if nothing else. I finished my bread and wiped my hands together to get rid of the crumbs. The cuts on my fingers had healed in record time. The lines of new, pink skin were the only evidence left behind.

"Aye, I'll be wearing something they measured me for last week. I'm sure it'll still be uncomfortable and itchy." He dropped his brush into the bucket near me and untied his horse from the wall. I stood up from my seat on another bucket I'd turned over and I reached down to flip it right-side up when a scream pierced the air.

Henry and I looked at each other instantly, and I took off running as he yelled for a hand to come grab his horse. He was behind me in moments, and despite the burning I already felt in my lungs, I kept going in the direction I thought the sound had come from.

Another, shorter cry had us veering toward the river. Henry passed me as the pain in my chest became too much. After a gasp, I started coughing as I forced my legs to keep moving. As soon as the mass of dark yellow fabric came into view, Henry splashed into the river and scooped my sister into his arms.

"Lucy?!" Anne was coming from the house in a rush, panic in her voice. "Lucy!"

"I've got her!" Henry called back, though he was struggling to lift her out with both of their drenched clothes weighing them down. I caught up to them finally and took Luc from him. She wrapped her arms tight around my neck and cried against my chest, her shoulders shaking. I held her close to me, one hand on the back of her wet head and the other arm supporting her weight. When she reached us, Anne grabbed for Lucy's face with both hands and pried it away from my shirt so she could look at her. Her brown curls were plastered to her neck and around her cheeks, and she was pale from the chill of the water.

"I was looking for s—stones for my fairy ga—arden," Lucy managed through her sobs.

The three of us sighed collectively and exchanged glances, relieved but irritated that her search had put her in such danger. Lucy was not a good swimmer and had been warned time and time again to never go near the river alone.

"Come here," Anne said as she took Luc from my arms and held her in a tight embrace against her hip, turning to carry her back toward the house, even though Lucy was nearly as tall as she was. I leaned forward and put my hands on my knees, still struggling.

"Thank you," I said on an exhale. Henry patted me on the back a few times.

"Couldn't expect the littlest Walshe to be any less accident prone than her brother," he replied, crooked grin on his lips. I stood up, finally able to breathe somewhat normally, and pushed my fingers through my hair. "Better go check on me horse, I just left her standing there," he said with a laugh, and we trudged back up the hill together.

I gave Henry a sidelong glance and smoothed my hands down the front of my damp waistcoat. "Do you remember the stories they told us as kids? About doing as we were told, or else the fairies would come out?"

"Of course," Henry responded easily. "I remember once I left me shoes outside overnight after Ma asked me to bring them in for the hundredth time, and the next morning I found them full to the top with little rocks." He laughed again, quieter this time. "I don't think Ma would've wasted her time doing that just to teach me a lesson." He was probably right. Mrs. O'Connor was not known for her sense of humor.

"So... you believed they were true, then? The stories?"

"Sure, why not? No reason not to believe them." We walked into the stables and found that someone had collected Henry's horse for him and returned her to her stall. When she noticed us approaching, she stepped forward and stretched her long neck over the half door. Henry rubbed a hand down her face, then looked at me. "Some things just can't be explained otherwise."

"Coincidences, you mean?"

"Aye. I never thought that made any sense. Things gotta happen for a reason. Even if we don't know the reason ourselves."

"Even when the illness came?" I asked, searching his face. He drew a deep breath through his nose and sighed, scratching the top of his head for a moment before his hand slid down to hold the side of his neck.

"That one I'm not so sure about, Pete. What's this all about, anyway? Worried Lucy's little garden will bring some mischief to your house?"

I gave him a small grin for his effort to lighten the mood. "You never know," I replied with a shrug.

"Well, I'll see you tomorrow. Being soaked to the skin is where I draw the line on pushing through for one day of work, I think." Henry reached up to squeeze my shoulder as he walked past me on his way out. I looked down at my own clothes that were still drying and decided that he had the right idea. Plus, there was something else that I needed to do.

***

The chestnut mare behaved herself on our ride past the village and out toward where the trees grew taller. I slowed her to a walk as the thatched roof of Finna's cottage came into view, still taken aback by the sight of so many flowers in one place. As we approached, I noticed there were a handful of bees and butterflies visiting the blooms.

I dismounted after we came to a stop and tied the horse up, praising her for a job well done with a few pats on the shoulder. I adjusted the strap of the worn satchel I'd brought with me and approached the front door. It felt different than it had when I'd left a few days prior. The cloudless sky helped, no doubt. I knocked a few times and waited, but there was no sound coming from inside. The wind rustled the plants around me, leaves swaying gently, and I heard a sweet, tinkling melody from somewhere not too far away. My curiosity got the best of me, so I followed the path around the side of the house to the back garden. I couldn't stop my eyes from going wide at what I found.

Rows of bright, leafy vegetable plants and herbs were carefully arranged in raised beds, which I counted at least a dozen of. Paths of finely crushed stones weaved throughout the beds and around an impressively large birdbath located in the middle of everything. Trellises along the back wall supported more climbing flowers and vines. I spotted the chimes I'd heard, hanging from the lowest beams of the roof, still playing their delicate songs.

Finna had her back to me as she knelt in front of one of the immaculate beds. A small stack of discolored leaves was beside her on the ground. She plucked another one from the plants and added it to the rest of the pile before she brushed her long, unruly hair away from her face with the back of her wrist.

"Do you like cabbage?" she asked before I could announce myself.

"Em... yes," I replied, caught off-guard. Finna turned to look at me over her shoulder and smiled.

"Hello, love. Glad you didn't get scared away forever." She got to her feet and dusted her skirts off with her hands, though it appeared she's been kneeling on a folded towel. After retrieving a small basket off her potting bench in the shade of the cottage, she bent to place the leaves she'd collected inside and motioned for me to join her.

I pushed open the gate that had stopped me to begin with and followed a few steps behind her, studying what was growing on either side of me. Some of them I could recognize as things that grew easily in our own garden, but others I wasn't sure I had ever seen before. If I had, they were probably already ingredients in something I was eating. We exited through another gate under an arbor thick with vines, which revealed a small orchard of fruit trees and berry bushes.

"I didn't realize you had all this back here," I said, trying to contain my bewilderment.

"It makes it much easier to have my own fresh supply of everything I need," she explained, tipping her basket upside down over a large pile of discarded organic matter. The leaves and petals and other items inside fell out in a clump but broke apart upon landing. She shook the basket a few times for good measure. "Are you hungry?"

"Thanks for the apple cake," I offered in a rush, feeling bad that I hadn't said it before now. She giggled and slid the handle of her basket to the crook of her arm. The sleeves of her dress were long, but I couldn't see the rest of it behind the smock she always wore.

"I don't have any more of that, but I can make you something else. Oh, I might have some blackberry scones left if Breck didn't take the rest." Before I allowed myself to start fantasizing about the scones, I shook my head and tried to focus.

"I just came to ask you something, if that's alright?"

"Of course. Come inside and we can talk."

We retraced our steps toward the cottage and went inside through a back door, which led to the kitchen. A plate with a few of the scones she had mentioned made their way to the table before I could as Finna rushed ahead of me to place them there. I lifted the satchel strap over my head as I sat down but kept it in my lap. I couldn't resist taking one of the pastries.

"Let me just fix you a cuppa," Finna said from her stove after she washed her hands quickly in the basin and dried them on a towel. I decided to not waste my time saying no thank you. We both knew I wanted some of her delicious tea. I enjoyed every crumb of my scone while she fiddled, the music from the chimes making its way in through the open window, and soon she delivered my cup and the honey jar.

"Go on, then," she said, urging me with raised eyebrows as she took a sip of her tea from her seat at the end of the table. I studied her for a moment, going over what I'd planned in my head, and then set my satchel by my feet as I opened the flap. I lifted the book out by the spine and laid it between us so we could both see. Finna's eyes scanned the title, the golden font flowing in elegant letters, before her eyes found mine again.

"This is my sister's book," I started. I reached to open the cover, turning page by page until I found the ones I'd stared at for several nights in a row. I pressed on the seam where the pages met to keep them flat before I brought my hand back to my lap. "Lately, she's been consumed by magic. She only wants to read stories about fairies before bed. She's made an impressive fairy garden at our home. She's begged my Nan to make her a pair of wings to wear."

Finna grinned at my words as she studied the images. "She sounds like a sweet girl."

"She's under the impression, thanks to books like this one, that fairies are sweet, too. That unless you do something terribly objectionable, they've no reason to do any harm to humans." Finna didn't say anything. Instead, she kept looking at the illustrations and reading over the text as if it all genuinely interested her. "Breck told me it could be fairies who used the magic that made everyone sick. Why... what could we have done that was so terrible to make the fairies think we deserved that?"

Finna looked down at her cup that she was holding with both hands. I couldn't read the expression on her pale face. "I think that's a question for the others."

I had hoped she would lead the conversation in this direction. "The others. Breck. You. Why are the lot of you doing this work?"

She took another sip and swallowed it down, her eyes scanning over the drawings of the fairies in front of her again, before she looked up at me. With her soft beauty and the ribbons braided into her long hair, she could've stepped right off the open page between us.

"What's the real question you wanted to ask me, Peter?" Her tone was patient.

"Are you… a fairy?" I asked quietly. I could've sworn she blushed, with her coy smile and the way her long eyelashes fluttered against her cheeks as she giggled, though no color appeared on them.

"No, love. I'm not a fairy." She drained the last of her tea. "But the others are."

NINE

Her words came so casually that it took a moment for me to realize the weight of them. "Okay," I finally said, lifting my cup to my lips so I could gulp down the rest of my tea. I had been hopeful that she would tell me the truth, but I was unprepared for her to confirm my suspicions so easily. I felt as though I could've just asked her outright and received the same answer.

Finna brushed her hair back over her shoulder and reached across to put her hand on my arm, her stack of bracelets clanking against the table. I forced my gaze up to meet hers. Her pastel eyes searched mine before she offered a small, comforting grin.

"There's nothing to be afraid of. Like you said, fair folk are generally kind and want to help humans," she explained. "Breck and the others have been asked to search for answers about the sickness to do just that. They have it on good authority that members of the Unseelie court might've been the ones responsible."

"Dark magic?" I asked, bringing the only words I knew on the subject into the conversation.

"Aye, dark magic. The Unseelie are the fairies who wish to harm humans, sometimes for no good reason at all. This was far beyond what anyone would consider a nasty prank, though. Some of them think it's a trick gone too far, but Fallon thinks it was done on purpose."

My eyes sank to the book that was still open between us. "How can they know if it was those fairies just by talking to me?"

"That's a question they'll have to answer. If I'm able to help, I will, but only they know what they need to hear from you." She pulled her hand away from my arm and got up to clear our cups and the honey from the table.

I looked beyond Finna's empty chair to the sitting room where I'd talked with all of them. My gaze settled on the spot I'd been sitting in by the fireplace, and then on the place Breck had occupied by me on the floor. He could've sat anywhere, but he chose to sit there. Protecting me from the harsh words of his friends. Were they his friends? He didn't act the same with them as he did with Finna.

"I want to talk to them again," I started, turning to look at her. "I want to help." Finna seemed relieved by my decision and nodded.

"We can all meet here again in a few days," she said. "Whenever you're able to come."

There was one more thing I'd brought in my bag. I closed the book sitting on the table and put it back inside, trading it for an envelope with no writing on it. I held it out for Finna to take. "Can you give this to Breck for me, when you see him?"

She reached for the envelope and took it gently between her thumb and forefinger. As soon as she touched it, she blinked and her eyebrows went up again, her smile reaching her eyes as she slipped it inside the pocket of her smock.

"Of course, love."

***

The night of Henry and Sarah's engagement party came after our fourth match of the season, which we'd won. I was always glad for a good game, but it was especially nice to have everyone already in high spirits going into an evening of celebration.

Henry had all but begged me to arrive early, so I'd rushed home to put on my least favorite outfit in my wardrobe. The navy suit made of thick wool had a matching waistcoat, but I switched it for a dark blue plaid one instead because it fit me better. The uncomfortable high collar on my white shirt underneath it was barely visible thanks to the wide tie I also had around my neck. Shiny black shoes and a hat atop my head completed the look. As I'd stared at myself in the mirror, I decided I looked like a taller, less-hairy version of William. I hoped with everything I had that I would never have to dress up like that for work as he did.

I found Henry in the kitchen just as his hand was swatted away from a plate of food by one of the cooks. As soon as she turned her back, he quickly stole the piece he'd been after and gave me a mischievous grin as he popped it in his mouth and came to join me. "What did I tell you about the food?" He swept an arm out around the room, which was covered with dishes of meats and fruits and cheeses. "This isn't even half of it."

"Glad I brought my second stomach along," I said, patting my gut for emphasis. Henry laughed and crossed his arms over his chest, which was clad in the new outfit he'd mentioned. It looked like several others he owned, except this one featured a low-cut waistcoat made of deep emerald silk with golden buttons that was tailored to a perfect fit. Expensive just for the sake of being expensive, but he looked nice in it.

"Speaking of, did you decide to bring anything else?" he pried jokingly.

"I didn't know I had to bring a gift," I grinned. Henry rolled his eyes and reached up to flick my hat off my head. "*Hey,*" I complained with a laugh as I leaned to pick it up off the floor. By the time I was setting it back where it'd been, Henry had walked down the long hallway toward one of the rooms in the manor that had been set for the event. People were bustling about, still preparing for guests to arrive.

"Sarah said I'm not to see her until her grand entrance after everyone's gathered in the foyer," he huffed as he fell heavily onto a couch with precariously thin legs. "I told her I thought this was *our* engagement party, and she said it is, but that if I walk down the stairs with her, I'll take too much room away from her *dress*." I sat in the chair next to him and leaned against the tall back, amusement tugging at my lips. "So I said, well what if I walk behind you, and she said I'd better just stand with everyone else and watch. Can you believe that?!" He shook his head and tossed his hands up theatrically. "I swear, Pete, sometimes I think she thinks I'm simple."

"She doesn't," I reassured him, although this wasn't the first time in their months of serious courtship that she'd said something that would make a man question himself.

"I'll be the first to admit me own sisters are as spoiled as sour milk, but I never met another lass who thinks so highly of herself. At least not so loudly."

I would've worried more about Henry's impending marriage if it weren't for the fact that he was far from simple. He was quite smart, in fact, and nobody could push him around unless he allowed it. Suddenly I had the image of Thomas being thoroughly lambasted by a strong woman in my head, and I couldn't stop the laugh that escaped me.

"What's so funny?" Henry turned his attention to me, and I shook my head.

"Just picturing Thomas in your situation," I shared. "He wouldn't stand a chance." Henry cackled and rubbed his face with his hand, clearly agreeing with me.

"Oh, you're so right dear, wouldn't want to get in the way and mess up your gown!" he mocked in Thomas' posh accent. "Better yet, I'll just wait outside and come running when you're ready for me!" We both laughed again. Where Henry had little experience with women intimately, Thomas had little experience with them altogether. Something about his grating personality made them steer clear, but on the few occasions he'd managed to corner a girl long enough to hold a conversation, he was terribly awkward.

"Maybe tonight will give him a chance to practice," I said. "Nothing like a fancy event with lots of alcohol and wedding talk to lower your standards."

***

A few hours later, the sunlight had been traded for a star-lit sky, and the bugs were noisily serenading guests from the grass surrounding the large patio some of us were gathered on. Sets of double doors were thrown open, making it easy to pass from inside to outside and back again. Guests were wearing their fine dresses and top hats, but it wasn't quite a white tie event.

I recognized most of them as spectators of our matches. Many made a point to catch my arm and praise us for our success in the season so far. I politely thanked them, making small talk when I had to, and nursed my second fizzing drink in a crystal glass with a stem so thin I worried it would break between my fingers. I gave the bubbles most of the credit for the uneasy feeling in my stomach. I realized I hadn't eaten much, despite what was available, so I wandered back inside toward the tables laid out with ample food.

I passed by the grand staircase that Sarah had presented herself on. She wore a dress made of fabric the same emerald color as the waistcoat Henry was wearing. It hadn't been a lie when she said it would take up all the space available around her on the steps. The skirts puffed out in all directions as she'd sauntered her way toward the crowd, looking like royalty. I'd glanced at my friend's face as he watched her descent. There was no denying the look of tenderness he wore for her.

My stomach grumbled as I approached a spread in the room Henry and I had been sitting in earlier. I placed a piece of cheese on a thin, savory biscuit and put the whole thing in my mouth, preferring that to the crumbs from taking a bite. While I chewed, I scanned the crowd for familiar faces.

Anne and William had found me earlier when they arrived. William hated parties, but this was an opportunity to mingle amongst the men he worked with, so he'd allowed Anne to dress him up and haul him down the road. I spotted them again now. William was standing stiffly at Anne's side while she spoke with another couple; a friend of Anne's from the village and her husband.

Not far away, Thomas was indeed practicing his swagger on a group of young women who were trying to ignore him. It was hard to notice if you didn't know him, but I could tell his chest was puffed and his shoulders squared, hands gripping tightly to the lapels of his suit jacket. The lot of them laughed, though I couldn't tell if it was at something he'd said, or just at him in general. I stuck another square of cheese into my mouth as I grinned at his ignorant confidence. Henry was beside me then, reaching across to steal a handful of stuffed olives.

"Having fun?" he asked me with his mouth full. I looked at him and he smiled widely, clearly a little tipsy.

"Loads," I responded with forced enthusiasm, flashing my eyebrows.

"Aww, come on, Pete. Go talk to somebody. Even Thomas has found an audience." He thrust his open hand toward our teammate for emphasis. "Don't be the weird lad standing by the snack table alone all night long."

"Well, when you put it that way…" I snorted out a laugh and picked up a pinch of thinly sliced cured meat to drop onto my tongue. The saltiness had me reaching for my glass I'd set on the edge of the table, and I took a swig to wash it down.

"At least come back outside with us. Work your charm on Sarah and her sisters so they'll stop talking about the feckin' wedding for five minutes."

"Henry, it's an *engagement* party," I reminded him as I trailed him back to the patio, dodging people in the crowd as we went. "That's the whole point." He groaned and cleared a path for us to rejoin his betrothed.

The skirts of her dark green dress appeared pillowy and soft, but the top half was a stiff corset that held her tightly, except for the revealing dip at the front; scandalous amongst this crowd and surely already being gossiped about. Long white gloves reached her elbows, and she was decorated with jewelry, including the ring Henry had given her. A strong but pleasant perfume hung in the air around her. She was thoroughly overwhelming.

She offered me her hand and I took her fingers gently in mine, touching my lips to them. "So glad you could come to the party, Peter. I know Henny relies on you to keep his head about him when he's stressed." Henry's eyes bulged at the use of the nickname, and I pressed my lips together to fight a smirk.

"We've had a lot of years to learn how to help each other through stressful times," I agreed.

"There's something to be said for a man who can be counted on during hard times, especially in this day and age," Sarah mused, her voice hinting at being suggestive. There was a soft chorus of agreement from around her, and I realized that all three of her sisters were staring at me with big eyes and soft grins. I drained the rest of my champagne and wished for another.

"You looked great out on the field today," one of the sisters said sweetly. I couldn't remember her name, but she was the youngest. All four of them had matching strawberry blonde hair and bright green eyes.

"Had to recover from last week," I said with a shrug.

"Henry tells us that you have a new horse in training. Will we see her play soon?" The second-youngest sister bounced a little as she asked about the chestnut mare. Now this was a topic of conversation I could get behind.

"I hope so. Maybe in a few more weeks. She's improved a lot faster than I thought she would. I could barely ride her when I took her on. Gave me a good toss and a few headaches so far, but it's nothing I can't handle." The two of them gasped, and the youngest reached out and put her hand on my arm, genuine concern on her youthful face.

"Oh my! Was it terribly painful?" she asked, and I took the opportunity to pull my arm away from her as I held up my wrist and rotated my hand, studying it to indicate it was one of the places I'd been hurt.

"No, I was only sore for a few days." The girls made sounds of relief. As a server presented us with a tray full of more flutes, I took one and replaced it with the empty in my other hand. The bubbles tickled my nose as I took a sip. The sisters giggled over the rims of their own drinks and glanced at me before whispering something to each other. Where was Thomas when I needed him?

Henry looked up from whatever he was saying to Sarah and the oldest sister to tap my shoe with his. I met his gaze, hopeful that he would say literally anything to remove me from this conversation, and he tipped his glass slightly toward something behind me.

I spun around as casually as my champagne buzz would allow and searched the crowd for whoever Henry had seen. Maybe Anne was coming to tell me they were leaving. A few people moved near the double doors, creating room for someone to pass by, and my heart leapt.

I left Henry and the sisters without excusing myself. I stepped toward the middle of the patio where Breck met me, hands in his pockets. His tousled blond hair was parted to one side and swept back from his face with wax. The rings and studs in his ears had all been removed, but the thin loop of metal at the edge of his nose remained. His worn, comfortable clothes had been traded for a sharp three-piece suit that fit him well. Black shoes completed his look.

I cleared my throat and brought my eyes back up to meet his. "You got my note," I said, unable to stop my grin.

"Finna handed it to me so quickly when I arrived that I nearly got a paper cut," he returned with a charming smile. "She told me there was a lot of energy folded up in the paper, and I had to open it right away."

"Energy?" I asked, taking a sip of the drink I remembered I was holding.

"Another talent of hers. I'm not sure what she's shared with you already..." His eyes searched mine for a moment. A small part of my brain told me I should still be confused by everything she *had* told me, but the part that was floating on bubbles told me to worry about it later.

"Not much, but there's time for that. Do you want a drink?" I asked, turning to search for another server with a tray. "Let's go look inside." I stepped around him toward the open doors, taking a deep breath and regretting it when my cough gave me away. We found a table that was set out with rows of the tall crystal glasses. He took one, swirling it twice before he took a pull of it. He scrunched his nose a couple times after and drew his eyebrows together briefly before he took another sip.

"You saved me from a very uncomfortable chat with two of Henry's soon-to-be sisters."

He glanced back in the direction we had come from and nodded. "They appear very upset." I didn't dare look. "What was so uncomfortable about it? I've seen them at your matches laughing and carrying on together. They seem nice enough. The shortest one talks about you all the time."

"She's only *sixteen*," I whispered loudly, reaching with my free hand to rub my forehead beneath the brim of my hat. Then the words he'd said settled more and I dropped my hand back to my side. "Do you come to all of our matches?"

"Yes."

"Oh," I said, and took another large drink out of my fancy glass.

"It's a great place to hear people's conversations when you need information," he explained. "They get caught up in watching the game and forget who might be around to listen." He also took another sip and seemed to struggle it down. "But I also like to watch you play."

"I'm sure I don't want to know what she says about me," I said, steering the conversation.

"I suppose that depends on if you want to know what she'd do to you behind closed doors," he said with a sly grin. I gaped at him and came dangerously close to dropping the fine crystal flute in my grip.

"You're lying," I accused him, draining my glass so I could set it down safely on a table.

"I'm not," he said earnestly. "Is her age the only issue you have with it? She's pretty."

There were about twenty good reasons I had to never begin a courtship with her. "Her family is incredibly wealthy. So is Henry's family," I said, gesturing vaguely to everything around us. "I would have nothing to offer her after we were married. Her father wouldn't ever consider it. It wouldn't be advantageous to anyone. She would be very unhappy stuck with someone like me for a lifetime." I realized I was rambling and forced my mouth shut, but only briefly. "I need to eat something," I told him as a cool wave washed through my body, finding I'd still neglected to fill my stomach to help soak up the alcohol.

I made my way toward a table covered mostly with cooked meats and bread. Breck paused a short distance behind me as I chose a small, plump roll and tore half of it off to put in my mouth. I noticed the look on his face and swallowed it down. "Are you alright?"

"All this," he shook his head, looking down at his

shoes.

I turned back around to look at the spread. He was right. The surplus of food available seemed nearly untouched, and I guessed there was more waiting in the kitchen if it was needed. I avoided looking at the face of the whole roasted pig lying in the middle of the table that served as decoration more than anything else, from the look of it.

"We should go back outside." I grabbed another roll and walked the opposite direction of the patio, familiar enough with the place that I knew where we might be able to find some privacy. I located the door I was looking for after climbing the stairs and pushed it open, revealing a small balcony that looked over the back garden. This one was nothing like Finna's. It was purely for decoration. Breck followed me out and shut the door behind himself. I leaned my hip against the railing and ate another bite of bread.

"I don't eat meat," Breck said, gazing out over the moonlit garden and the well-groomed grounds beyond. As I realized what he was telling me, the bread in my stomach settled like rocks.

"I'm so sorry. I didn't know. I—I just made you stand there and look at that—"

"I'm just apologizing for my reaction, is all," he said gently. I took that as him wanting to drop the topic there, so I nodded and forced myself to eat more to ease the sloshing happening inside me. "Is it rude of me to attend this party and not speak to either person being celebrated?" he asked, and I laughed a little.

"No," I said over my mouthful. "Henry saw you

come in, that's plenty. He knew you'd be here."

"Did he?" Breck looked at me then, arched eyebrows raised slightly. I swallowed and looked out at the garden below. I hadn't even known if he would come as I'd written the invitation for him hastily in my bedroom before my visit with Finna, but Henry had seemed confident enough in his persuasion that I trusted him.

"He's the one who told me to ask you to come, actually," I confessed. "I think he still worries about me more than he wants to admit."

"I'm sure he does. It had to be difficult for him to watch you go through being sick, and then have such a long recovery." Breck took another quick sip of his drink.

"At least he doesn't give me a look every time I cough anymore."

"Was it worse than it is now?" he asked, watching as I took a bite directly off my roll.

"It would take my breath away. Sometimes it would double me over and I'd have to sit down where I was to keep from falling on my face," I said lightly, even though it had been frightening when it was actually happening. I realized I was rubbing a hand across my chest at the memory when I noticed Breck watching me do it. I stilled my hand and shoved the last of my bread in my mouth.

"How does it feel now? The cough?" he asked, and I realized he'd come closer to me than he was before, his own hip resting against the railing, his body a reflection of mine. I swallowed forcefully to get my food down past the tightness that had appeared in my throat.

"It, em… it's fine?" I said with a question, my buzz and his closeness suddenly blurring my thoughts together. Breck grinned to himself and looked back out at the garden, hand gripping the outside edge of the railing. I noticed his rings were gone, too.

"Why did you take off all your jewelry?" I asked, somehow managing to keep my hands to myself, despite my urge to reach and touch his naked fingers, or his ear, or the sharp line of his jaw. My eyes went wide at my thoughts, and I took a step backwards, turning fully to face the garden. The height of the balcony made the swimming in my head more intense as I looked over the edge, so I closed my eyes instead and held tightly to the railing with both hands.

"Peter?" Breck asked, concern in his voice, and then his hand was on my back, and I struggled to take slow breaths of the night air.

"I'm alright. Just… just wrecked," I said helplessly, admitting my own drunkenness.

"Do you want to leave?"

I nodded, eyes still closed. His other hand came to my arm, his drink abandoned somewhere, and he steered me back inside. We somehow managed the stairs and exited through the front door. We made it just far enough that I couldn't hear any music or talking coming from the party anymore before I veered to the edge of the road, tripped over my own feet, which sent me ungracefully to my knees, and heaved. I moaned out a weak *ugh* from my position on the ground. I'd never wished to disappear more than I did in that moment.

"I hate champagne," Breck admitted as he bent to

FELLA ENCHANTED

pick up my hat from where it had fallen. I looked up at him, and he reached a hand out for me. I took it and let him help me back up to my feet.

"You didn't have to drink any," I said, taking my hat and putting it back on my head.

"I struggle to fit in enough as it is," he replied, straightening it for me. "I needed a little something to help me blend with the rest of you."

"The suit helped with that. And the hair," I said, glancing at him as we walked slowly toward my house again. The churning in my stomach had calmed, which I was grateful for.

"That's why I hid my jewelry," he added, answering my question from before.

"Hid?" I asked, looking at him again. Moonlight caught the metal that had appeared back in his ear. I couldn't see his fingers because they were in his pockets again, but I could only assume his rings were back, too. He caught my gaze and winked at me, which caused heat to spread through my chest and across my face.

"I want to ask you about... about what Finna told me. But I don't think I'll remember your answers tomorrow if you tell me now."

"Ask me now, ask me tomorrow. I'll answer as many times as you need me to."

TEN

I ended up not asking any questions, but I did throw up again, leaving me thoroughly ashamed of myself. The rest of the night was a blur of Breck guiding me to my house, crawling upstairs to my bedroom, washing my mouth out, and removing some articles of clothing.

I woke the next morning, face down on top of my blankets, with one shoe still on. A feeling I thought was nausea coursed through me, and I moved quickly to avoid making a mess of the bed, but as I made it to my feet, I stopped. I blinked a few times, bringing one hand to hold my head and the other to hold my stomach.

I felt... fine.

The items on my bedside table caught my eye. A steaming cup of tea was sitting on top of an envelope with no writing on it. I lifted the cup and brought it up to my nose. Mint. I sat on the bed as I took a long pull of the drink and exchanged it for the envelope, opening it swiftly.

Wishing you a pleasant morning.

B

My eyes carefully traced each word in the note again as I reached for the cup. I remained sitting on the edge of the bed until the tea was gone. After the last sip, I realized that my cheeks hurt from grinning so hard. I didn't think too much about what sort of trick had cured my hangover as I took off the rest of my clothes and dressed in something more practical for the day.

Nothing shook me from my fog until I arrived at the stables and Henry greeted me with an enthusiastic, "Where the *feck* did you disappear to last night, boyo?!" He sounded a little rough.

"*Quiet!*" a voice hissed from nearby. It was Thomas. He looked how I had expected to feel. Maybe worse.

I gave Henry a look as I passed by him to collect the grains for my horses. Had we really disappeared? It probably seemed that way. After Breck had arrived, I'd only spent time with him, and then we'd left without a word. It dawned on me what Henry might imply from that. On my way back toward the stalls, I walked behind him and leaned close to avoid anyone overhearing.

"Nothing happened," I whispered, and he shot a grin at me over his shoulder.

"Sure, it didn't," he whispered back.

"I mean it," I insisted, reaching over the half doors to dump the grains into my horses' buckets. All their heads dipped out of sight as they leaned down to eat their breakfast. The soft noises of them chewing filled the air.

"You just seem awful cheery for a lad who drank so much bubbly, is all. Poor auld Thomas is sufferin' something wicked, aren't you Thomas?" Henry called, raising his voice at the end for emphasis. Thomas held his head with both hands at the noise and glared at us angrily. We both chuckled and went about our morning chores in silence.

***

After turning my horses out for the day, I'd gone by the house to tell Nan I would be back by our evening meal. She'd missed the engagement party to stay home with Lucy, so when she asked how it went, I stayed to tell her about some parts of it, like the live music, and the food, and the guests who were there.

"Well, it'll never be as grand as that, but I hope in my lifetime we get to celebrate you and Lucy that way," she said, no subtlety in her words.

"I know, Nan," I said, feeling the pang of guilt she'd successfully delivered.

"The offer still stands for you to meet Bette. She's such a gentle lass," Nan said, referring to her friend's granddaughter I'd already met several times over the years, though it was never anything formal.

"Nan, she doesn't *talk*," I said carefully, not wanting to upset her. The girl had spoken maybe three words to me that weren't hello or goodbye.

"She's shy, Peter. You have to give her some time to warm to the conversation. Just think about it, would you?"

"I will, yeah," I promised, even though I certainly would not.

My walk to Finna's was faster now that I was confident in where I was going. I'd also figured out the shortcut Breck had taken us on the first time, which trimmed a lot of time off, too. I looked at the sky, where clouds had started gathering, and I wondered if I would regret not bringing a coat along. The red door of the cottage opened before I could get close enough to knock, and Finna waved me inside.

"Come in, everyone's here," she said, and I looked behind her at the sitting room. Breck was the only one looking at me from his spot on the floor. There was no flame on the hearth today. He nodded his head my direction and I made my way to the chair beside him, sitting gingerly.

"Thank you for meeting with us again," Elina said, her golden hair loose and flowing around her shoulders. Fallon still wore hers in a tight braid. Carrick and Murray looked the same as I remembered them, too. Armed with the knowledge I now had, so much about them made more sense.

"You figured us out," Carrick said, grinning behind his thick beard. "Are you surprised?"

"I was at first," I admitted. "But I had decided some things on my own before I came to ask Finna for the truth."

"Smart lad," Elina said, giving Fallon a hopeful look that wasn't returned.

As Elina turned her head, I noticed the earrings she wore, and my eyes trailed them up to the delicate point at the tip of her ear. I looked at Fallon, then Carrick, then Murray; they all had ears like the fairies in Lucy's books. I glanced at Breck, and somehow, I was still surprised to find that his ears looked the same.

"Can we answer any questions before you answer ours?" Elina asked, her hands clasped in her lap as she leaned toward me from her seat. I considered this for a moment. Yes, I had a million questions, but which ones were important enough to ask right now? Could I admit to them that everything I knew came from a child's storybook?

"Can all of you do magic?" I asked, feeling confident that this was the most stereotypically human question I could've thought up.

"Yes. But we can't all do the same kinds of magic," Elina explained. "All fairies can disappear at will. Our senses are heightened above those of humans, which I guess isn't really magic." She paused then, thinking. "Some can fly. Some can communicate with animals."

I nodded slowly, listening. I looked at all of them in a sweeping glance. "I thought fairies were... small," I said quietly, holding up my thumb and forefinger a short distance apart to emphasize my words. Carrick burst out laughing.

"Only when the water's too cold, eh Breck?" he said with his gravelly voice. Breck was hugging one leg close to his chest, the other folded underneath him. He smirked and pressed his face against his bent knee, avoiding the look I gave him.

"Many are, but we come in all shapes and sizes," Elina spoke again, ignoring Carrick. "We—" she started, but stopped, uncertain.

"Go on, Elina. He deserves the whole truth," Finna said from the chair she'd pulled over from the table in the kitchen. I noticed her feet didn't reach the floor.

Elina looked back at me and took a deep breath, and suddenly her body appeared as though it was illuminated by candles, glowing with a warm light. I squinted my eyes and had to look away from her as the light became stronger.

"We are designated as the keepers and protectors of this land, chosen by Eabha herself. Our magic reflects the responsibilities we have been given."

"Light, as you can see, is Elina's specialty," Finna added from her chair. As Elina's glow faded, she continued. "Carrick is guardian of the land; Murray, the ocean; Fallon, the air." She paused for a moment, and I waited breathlessly to hear confirmation of how powerful the man beside me was. "Breck sees after the river." I looked at him then, his cheek still resting against his knee, and he gave me a gentle grin.

They weren't just *any* fairies. A series of coughs forced their way from my lungs to make me breathe again. I gasped a little and coughed more, leaning against the back of my chair with my hand on my chest. "Sorry," I managed.

"Peter told me that his cough used to be much worse than it is now." Breck addressed the group, sharing what I'd told him.

"Did it start before or after you slept for many days?" Fallon asked.

"After," I said. "Anne told me that it was the first indication she had that I was coming back around. The cough started, and then I woke up a few hours later."

"Nothing could ease it?" Elina asked, her brows pinched with concern.

"No. It was sometimes worse at night, but mostly it was persistent through any hour of the day." I let my hand fall to the armrest and watched as the group exchanged looks and whispers.

"Have you ever made any deals with a stranger, Peter?" Murray asked, his accent so thick that I wasn't entirely sure I'd understood him. Fallon rolled her eyes but remained silent, waiting for my answer.

"I don't think so?" I said with uncertainty. "Wally likes to make bets with people over sports. He's our stable manager, and he manages our team, too." He was the only one I could think of who did things like that.

"How many of your team got sick?" Fallon's stare was so intense that I couldn't look at her.

"Me, and Jamie," I told her, his name feeling heavy as it left me. I didn't want them to question Jamie in all of this.

"He perished," Fallon said, not a question, but I responded like it was.

"Yes."

"And the others?"

"Henry never got sick. Neither did Thomas. None of their family members, either."

"And your manager?"

"No."

"*Fallon,*" Breck said, cutting her off before she could ask another rapid-fire question. She shut her mouth and got up off the low sofa, stalking toward the kitchen.

"Tea, anyone?" Finna asked, hopping off her chair to join her. I sighed and released the grip I had on the arms of my chair. We sat silently for a moment, and then I remembered something I wanted to tell them when I saw them again.

"My friend Henry. He and I had a chat a few days ago." I waited a moment, and Fallon reappeared around the corner, leaning against the frame of the doorway to the kitchen, arms crossed over her chest.

"Yes?" Elina urged me to continue.

"He told me that he believes in fairies."

Carrick laughed heavily again, stroking his beard with a large hand as his shoulders shook. Elina shot him a look to quiet him.

"He told me he's *always* believed in fairies. It was after I told him that I'd stopped believing the stories we were told as children. I told Breck the same thing," I added, looking at him quickly, recalling our conversation at his home above the mill. Breck seemed to catch on to the direction I was going and sat up straighter.

"I told you that most people stop believing as they get older," he said, and I nodded.

"Do you think that could have anything to do with who got sick and who didn't?" I asked.

"Many children died, too. Even your own wee sisters," Murray said.

"How do you prove that you believe?" I searched their faces. They all seemed to consider this, before Fallon spoke again as she returned to her spot on the sofa.

"It's not something you have to prove. You just do or you don't. Fairies in the Unseelie court have no qualms about reading a human's mind to find something like that out."

"They can read minds?" I questioned.

"Many of us can," Carrick said casually. He was looking at Breck. My heart thudded a little harder in my chest as I turned to look at him, too.

"Only when I need to," Breck reasoned.

"So, when you told me you go to the matches to *listen to conversations...*"

"Humans have a very complex internal dialogue," he explained. I pushed my fingers through my hair and looked away, head spinning at the idea of him knowing some of the things I'd thought about over the weeks since I met him. Finna served us all tea and we drank in silence for a while.

Before the conversation could ever pick back up, Murray excused himself, claiming that he had to get back to something important. The others took this as their opportunity to leave, too, and Breck and I did the same. We opted for the road instead of the shortcut.

"I'm sorry for last night," I started finally.

"It was a party. People drink at parties. Fairies drink at parties." He shrugged.

"Well, usually I don't allow myself to slip that far away." What I really wanted to apologize for were my thoughts the night before, but that was even more uncomfortable to say. I gave him a sidelong glance and he grinned, though he was still looking at the road ahead of us.

"I'm not reading your thoughts," he said quietly.

"But you have before?" I pushed.

"Yes, I have before."

"Has it been something terrible? Because I can explain—"

"None of it has been terrible," he reassured me. I exhaled with a cough and rubbed my forehead with my fingers before I looked at him again, still flustered by my own worries. He studied my face and added, "Fairies cannot lie to humans. So, you can trust what I'm saying as the truth. Alright?"

"Okay," I said, still conflicted.

"What're you doing the rest of the day?" he asked then.

"I don't know. I thought we would be at Finna's longer," I said, looking for where the sun was in the cloudy sky. He also looked up at the gloom hanging over us and shook his head.

"*Fallon.*" He said her name like it was a swear. I blinked up at the clouds.

"Is she also responsible for the weather?" I asked, remembering what Finna had said.

"Not really. She can't create it, but she can manipulate it. This is her fault," he said, gesturing to the dark sky. I considered the power her magic must have to be able to do something like that. We continued toward the fork in the road, and again I found myself not wanting to return home.

"Thanks for whatever you did this morning, to help with... you know," I said vaguely. The thought of him seeing me in the state I'd passed out in was *almost* as embarrassing as the notion that he could've seen me how I normally slept, in nothing but the bedsheets.

"I figured you would need a little help. Don't ask me what Finna did. I just provided the refreshments." I wasn't sure if Finna's involvement made it better or worse.

"And the note," I added. He grinned and nodded.

"Would you care for some more tea?" he offered, and it was my turn to give him a nod.

ELEVEN

He led the way up the staircase inside the mill, and I nearly tripped over the last step as the room came into view. It looked nothing like it had the last time I'd seen it.

That wasn't true. The kitchen and table and bed were still in the same places. But the floor was now covered with thick, earthy colored rugs, and folds of sheer curtains framed the picture window behind the bed. Vines with large, dark green leaves crept up the walls toward the roof and curved around shelves, which supported plants in pots, books, and a few other trinkets. Orbs of soft light rested on two of the wooden shelves, but they didn't come from a candle. I gave Breck a confused look, and he glanced around the room before he returned his focus to the kettle on the stove.

"It was like this before. I just didn't show you," he explained.

"You hid all of this from me? How?" I took a seat in the chair I'd used last time, my eyes still wandering.

"Same as how I hid my ears."

"I noticed that," I said, turning to look at him. "The earrings last night, but also the..." I stopped, rubbing the pads of my fingers over the tip of my own ear. My eyes traced the curve of his that I could see, which was partially hidden by his hair.

"I knew you would figure it out soon enough," he said, his back still turned to me.

"Why didn't you just tell me? I got to play the fool instead."

"We aren't supposed to announce ourselves to humans. But if they figure us out on their own, that's different."

I didn't respond. I was caught up with watching the water falling over the rocks outside again. I wasn't sure how I could ever leave my bed if that was the view from my window.

"I sweetened it already," Breck said as he set a cup in front of me. I tore my focus from the falls and looked down as I grasped the handle and brought it to my lips. He'd added the perfect amount of honey.

"Do all of you know how to make tea so well? I wouldn't even know where to start," I admitted, taking another sip. The kitchen was foreign to me, best left to the experts.

"Just lots of practice, I guess," he reasoned. "Living alone will do that for you."

"Are fairies solitary creatures, then?"

"Not necessarily. Many find mates and start families like humans do. But others enjoy the peace of living a more secluded life. There's no societal pressure to wed and have children like in your world."

"Are any of the others— do any of you have them? Mates?" I asked, the word feeling strange as it left my mouth. His lips quirked at the corners as he sipped his tea.

"Only Carrick. His mate is lovely."

"How long have they been married?" I hadn't thought Carrick was much older than me. Maybe William's age.

"We don't marry like humans do. But they were joined in a ceremony before Eabha about sixty years ago, I think." I looked at him in disbelief, and he raised his eyebrows.

"*Sixty*?" I asked. "How old is he?"

"He's seen over a hundred years, I'm sure. You'd have to ask him for the exact number."

"How old are *you*?" The question spilled out of me, and Breck chuckled.

"Fairies age as humans do for the first twenty-one years, and then it goes slower after that. Much slower." He considered his next words before he said them. "We're able to stay youthful by helping humans. The more acts of kindness we perform, the longer we can live – to a certain point."

"What about the mischief?"

"Some fairies see playing tricks as a way to deceive humans into being helped, which in turn helps them. For example, a fairy might fool a human into thinking they were lost in nature, but then leave a trail of acorns or mushrooms to help guide them back home."

"That doesn't seem fair," I said.

"It's not. These acts count as only a fraction of what true kindness does."

"What if fairies don't help humans?"

Breck looked down at his cup and remained quiet for a moment. "There's only one other way. The life— the life has to be stolen," he said softly.

"Stealing as in killing? Killing humans?" My voice was equally as quiet now, and Breck nodded solemnly. We sat in silence and finished our tea.

"You never answered my question," I said finally. His eyes met mine across the table.

"I'll turn twenty-one on the winter solstice," he said, voice still low. His response sparked several thoughts in my head, but the one I decided to put into words was purely to relieve the seriousness that had settled over us.

"Imagine Nan's face when I tell her the fella running the mill is younger than I am." His lips tugged into a smile, and then we both laughed. I took the opportunity to appreciate his dappled nose and cheeks. "When Finna told me about all of you, she also told me she's not a fairy," I said, changing the subject. Given that she was the one who looked most like the illustrations in Lucy's book, I found that hard to believe.

"She's a witch," he said plainly, standing to take our cups from the table.

"*Wow*," I said on an exhale before I could stop myself. "That actually explains a lot."

"But don't ask her how old she is," he warned. "She won't tell any of us, and it makes her angry if you push her about it."

"I'll remember that," I said. "I've seen my Nan

angry, and they're about the same size, so I can only imagine what Finna looks like when she's mad." Breck laughed again, quieter this time, and I rubbed my palms up and down my thighs a few times. He'd told me so much, and I had the feeling it wasn't just because of his inability to be dishonest. Something inside me was pushing to tell him more, too, but another question came out instead. "Am I allowed to ask about your magic?"

"What do you want to know?" came his response as he walked past the small table and chose to sit on a particularly plush rug on the floor, resting his back against the end of his bed. He crossed his legs and placed his hands in his lap.

"The river," I began. "How does that work?" He thought for a moment. I guessed he probably didn't have to explain it very often.

"It's like… it's like a connection of sorts. I can feel it rise and fall. I know it's flowing the same as I know the blood is moving through my body."

"What does it feel like?"

"It's not painful or anything. It's more of a sense I have. Especially if something is wrong," he explained. "I felt when Lucy fell in the other day. I felt it, and then I could see it briefly in my mind. But all of you were there, and Henry had her in his arms, so I didn't think I needed to go help."

"Sometimes you do help, though?"

"Yes. If an animal is struggling to get out, or if a human is alone." He paused then, looking down at his hands. "The first time I saw you after I came here, it was this way." I frowned as I tried to remember what he could have seen. I couldn't recall falling in the river lately. "It was because you held your breath under the water," he continued, answering my question as if I'd asked it aloud. "You were bathing. I think the pain in your lungs triggered it to reach me."

The water would've been drawn from the river. I felt the blood drain from my face as I remembered what he was talking about. The bath I'd taken the night before we met. I'd held my breath and come up coughing. I'd been thinking about Jamie. I'd been doing more than that.

"Exactly how much did you see?" I asked cautiously. The look on his face told me everything. I folded my arms against the table and laid my forehead down on them, squeezing my eyes shut. My bent posture made me cough twice. I'd been wrong the night before. *This* was the moment I wished I could disappear.

I felt a touch on my arm, and I picked my head up enough to find Breck's face close to mine as he crouched near the table. My pulse quickened and I searched his eyes. "Don't hide," he said, voice gentle.

Before I could respond, he stood swiftly and shifted his attention as the door downstairs opened. He took the steps down and greeted the person who had come inside. I listened as they carried a conversation about whether it was going to rain or not, which was customary in the village. If you didn't have anything to say, just complain about the weather. Breck helped the man with his purchase of several bags of flour. After they wished each other a good afternoon and the door had closed, I made my way down the stairs. Breck turned to glance at me from where he was standing at the counter, sorting through the coins the man had given him as payment.

"I should go," I told him. "I didn't know you had work to do."

"I'm always working unless I lock the door. And sometimes even when I do, they still bang on it until I open up," he said lightheartedly.

"That's awful," I said, though I wasn't entirely surprised. "How do you ever get any privacy?"

"I find a way." He grinned at me and dropped the coins into a bag with a drawstring that he'd pulled from somewhere. The rounded shape of the small sack told me that he collected quite a lot of those coins for his wares. Nan had commented that the flour seemed to be finer than it had ever been before.

I stepped past him toward the door and plucked my cap off the hook I'd hung it on when I arrived. I combed my hair back with my fingers and flopped it down onto my head.

"Well," I said, reaching for the knob on the door as I turned to look at him.

"Well," he repeated, one eyebrow arched more than the other. He'd stowed the drawstring bag and was leaning forward casually on both hands against the countertop. My complex human internal dialogue was desperate to beat me over the head with one of the burlap sacks along the wall, and I was just as desperate to ignore it.

Despite my inability to stop drinking when I

should, or my penchant for injuring myself, I wasn't an eejit. This man with deep blue eyes and storybook features was offering himself to me – *had been* offering himself to me – for weeks, and I was too damned broken to take him.

"I'll see you later, then." The door cracked open as I pulled on the knob, and as it did, an icy sensation curled around my hand, up my arm, and around my throat. Chills spread across my body. I swallowed, the snap of fresh mint tingling in my nose and on my tongue.

"Come back to me when it storms," came a whisper against my ear. As soon as it had happened, it was over, and I was outside with the door shut behind me.

***

I'd never felt so conflicted about the weather in my life.

It didn't rain at all for several days. I was completely useless at everything I tried to do, including my work, which is how Henry found me after I'd spilled a full bucket of grains across the floor in the storeroom. My curse hadn't been as quiet as I'd thought, and he came around the corner, eyes landing on my mess as I scooped it up with my hands back into the bucket. He knelt across from me and started doing the same.

"I bumped it when I turned around," I explained, glancing at him again. He didn't say anything at first, and that's what I had been afraid of.

"Tell me what's goin' on."

"Nothing's going on. You know how I am," I said,

trying to sound casual about it.

"I know you've been acting strange. Listen here, you tell me, or I'll assume the worst and report to your Nan," he threatened. I glared at him and kept scooping.

How was I supposed to tell him that I'd been meeting with a bunch of powerful, magical creatures at a witch's cottage to discuss the possibility that our families and friends had been murdered by other magical creatures? And that, despite all of that, I was still so helplessly attracted to one of them that I could barely get through menial tasks without fumbling around.

As I threw another handful into the bucket, I sighed and slid sideways off my knees into a sitting position on the ground, rubbing my forehead with my hand that was dusty from the grains. Henry stopped, too, and waited for me to say something.

"It's the miller, isn't it?" he guessed when I still didn't speak. "What's he done to you?"

"*Nothing*," I said, with a little more of a whinge than I intended. "Nothing. It's not—"

"He's not done anything to you?"

"No, he—"

"But you want him to," he pressed quickly.

"*Yes*," I said, and my hand flew to my mouth as I realized what I'd done. Henry gave me a look of delighted surprise before he laughed. I went scarlet and collapsed to my back on the floor, covering my face with both hands. "Henry, it's not funny," I moaned.

"Sorry, sorry, I didn't mean to laugh. I just don't normally get you that easily," he boasted. He wiped his hands on his breeches and moved his legs from beneath him so he could sit. "What's the problem then, lad? He came to the feckin' party and you still didn't make your move. I can't help you more than that." I brought my hands to rest on my stomach and knit my brows as I stared up at him.

"You tried to set us up," I accused.

"Of course, I did! Isn't that what friends are for? You haven't looked at anyone like that—you haven't looked at anyone at all since Jamie died." His tone softened as he spoke, and I looked away.

"You know it was different with Jamie. We were friends for so long before it became something else."

"And even with all the time you had, you never got to tell him how you really felt. I can't watch you do that to yourself again." Henry was right. I spent years feeling so much for Jamie, and even though we did express it, I never actually said the words. Neither of us did. I looked at him again.

"Do you love Sarah?"

"I'm not *in love* with her. That'll take time away from her feckin' sisters and chaperones," he grumbled. "You're a lucky bastard that you don't have to parade your relationships around for the whole village like I do. Every bleedin' person I know has a piece of paper dated with the night I'll lie with her!" I couldn't help but laugh a little at that. I took a breath and let it out slowly, bracing myself.

"The night of the party, Breck held my hat while I got sick in the bushes. Twice."

"Oh, *feck me*, Pete. Are you serious? That's how you repay me efforts?" Henry shook his head and pinched the bridge of his nose, though I could tell he was playing up his aggravation.

"Why are you making such an effort?" I asked.

He gave me a look that said it should be obvious. "Because you deserve to be happy again."

"I am happy," I protested weakly. Wasn't I happy? I had a great job that I was good at, I had a family that loved me, I had friends. I didn't want for anything, really.

"Your dad would say you need to get this shite sorted before it affects your game. I don't want to lose again on account of your head bein' up in the clouds."

"What do you mean *again*?" I asked as I pushed myself up onto my elbows.

Henry barked out a laugh and got to his feet, brushing the dust off his clothes. "Do I need to remind you about holding the whole game while you chatted him up?"

"I didn't—" I started, but I knew there was no denying that one. He raised his eyebrows at me and pressed his lips together.

"Uh-huh," he said, and I rolled up onto my hands and knees, making it to my feet slowly. I looked down at Henry and he clapped his hand against my shoulder before he turned to go back to his chores. I bent and picked up the bucket. My horses were impatiently waiting for me; I could hear them nickering at me from their stalls.

"I'm coming, I'm coming," I said under my breath.

***

That afternoon, clouds had gathered, and it was drizzling just enough to send everyone inside. Nan was busy in the kitchen preparing supper. I'd heard Lucy talking her ear off when I passed by on my way in from the stables. The sitting room was empty, and there was no fire burning. Instead of going up the stairs, I turned and continued down the hallway toward the study and the bedroom my parents had once shared. Now it belonged to William and Anne.

I knocked my knuckles lightly against the door to the study and listened for William's voice, but it didn't come, so I pushed the door open and stepped inside. It smelled exactly as it had when my dad occupied it. Old books and wood polish. There were stacks of paper piled on the large desk at the far end of the room. I didn't pretend to be interested in what was written on them. Instead, I came around the desk to one of the bookshelves that stretched to the ceiling and regarded the photographs sitting in frames.

My family looked back at me stoically in monochrome. I recalled the trouble we'd gone through to get the one of all of us together. Dressed in our best clothes, hair washed and coiffed, we'd been instructed to remain still for an impossibly long time. Next to it sat a photo of my parents. Dad was sitting in a chair and Mammy was behind him, her hands on his shoulders. A small grin spread on my lips.

"Dad always joked that if anyone wondered if he loved his wife, they should just ask his six children," William said from behind me, and I turned to look at him as he closed the door. He crossed the room and sat stiffly in the chair behind the desk. I copied him in one of the other, less stately chairs that sat below the window. I watched my brother as he shuffled through some of the parchment in front of him. He was dressed for business like always. I couldn't think of the last time I'd seen him without his getup.

"More love than most," I agreed. Large families were fairly common in the village, regardless of social status or wealth, but a family with as many children as ours was above the average. "Henry is afraid he and Sarah will have only daughters. Since they both have three sisters."

William didn't look up from his work. "Certainly a concern for someone who needs to carry on a family name." I shifted in my chair to gaze out the window. The mist and fog made it impossible to see much. I exhaled against the glass, creating a patch of haze, and brought a finger up to draw several lines through it. Each line I made created a small, dull squeaking noise. "Can you not?" William asked tersely. I shot him a look and wiped my arm across the spot to erase it with my sleeve.

"What if you hadn't wanted to take all of this over from Dad?" I asked. "Even if he hadn't died when he did. Why are you responsible for it all just because you're his son?"

William stopped what he was doing then and stared at me. "We wouldn't have anything if it weren't for his efforts. Dad worked incredibly hard for what we have, and to carry on what his fathers before him created here."

"I'm not saying he didn't. I just don't understand

—"

"You wouldn't, would you?" He returned his focus to his papers and picked his pen up to write something down. I unfolded myself from the chair and nearly had a grip on the door handle when he sighed and said, "That's not how I meant that to sound."

"Sure, it wasn't," I said coolly. William and I had never been particularly close, but the tension between us was worst whenever our work came up. I thought he shouldn't be so obsessed with his because it kept him from his family, and he thought I shouldn't be so obsessed with mine because it wasn't going to take me anywhere in life. I pulled the door open, and he got to his feet so fast the legs of his chair scraped against the floor.

"Anne is in a delicate way," he said, his whole body tense enough that it reflected in his voice. "And I'm quite out of sorts. Forgive me for my behavior." I'd stopped in my tracks at his announcement.

"Is everything alright, then?" I shut the door again and kept my voice low, stepping closer to him.

"The doctor says yes but has advised that we should be careful." I could see the conflicting emotions on his face, even behind his thick beard and moustache. It wasn't the first time I'd been told this news.

"Is she well?" I asked as more questions flooded my mind.

"She is. She's very excited. We both are."

I searched his face for a moment before I came around the desk to wrap him in a short embrace. He patted my back lightly a few times with one hand and didn't meet my eyes as we pulled apart.

"I'm happy for you," I said, and he nodded once before he reached for his chair and pulled it back toward the desk as he lowered himself into it, immediately reaching for more papers. I watched him for a moment longer and then left him to his work.

I stood in the hallway outside the study and gazed at the door to their bedroom. I rubbed my palms along the stitched seams on my hips. Anne was only a handful of years older than I was, but after she'd helped me through the illness and taken on such an important role in our family, I couldn't help but feel protective of her like she was my own mother. Before I spoke to her, though, I decided I needed to let my own emotions about it settle. I went to join Nan and Lucy in the kitchen, instead.

Luc was perched on a stool by the counter, reading. Nan was stirring something in a large pot on the stove. She brought the wooden spoon to her lips, her other hand underneath it to catch any drips, and she tasted whatever she was making.

"What's this word, Peter?" I peered over Lucy's shoulder to where her small finger was pointing on the page.

"Enchanting," I said, already guessing what this tale was about. "That's a big word for a children's story." I sat next to her on the other stool. I didn't recognize this book as one from her collection.

"What does it mean?"

"Em. It means something catches your attention

in a way that's very charming. In a way you can't ignore because it's so nice." This answer seemed to satisfy her, and she went back to reading, her finger sliding along to each word as she mouthed them silently.

"She and Anne collected some new books at the library. She's read all hers so many times that they weren't challenging her any longer," Nan said, her back still to us, a hint of pride in her tone.

"All those books and you still picked one about fairy tales, Luc?" I teased.

"It was the only way she'd calm down over misplacing her favorite one," Nan added.

"The one with the gold letters," Lucy said sadly. My stomach sank when I realized I'd never put it back on her shelf after I'd taken it to Finna's. It was still in my bag underneath my bed.

"I'm sure it'll turn up," I tried to reassure her. "I'll help you look for it."

"Okay," she agreed, her eyes still on the page of her story. I looked over at the illustration of the beautiful little creature hiding underneath the petals of a pink rose bloom. Her ears were pointed, her lips plump and fashioned in a sweet smile. Her big green eyes seemed to hold a secret. *You and me both*, I thought.

"Go wash up for supper," Nan instructed us. I slid off my stool as Lucy closed her book, and I let her go ahead of me up the steps as we went to our bedrooms. My eyes shot to the strap of my satchel where I'd abandoned it. I braced myself with one hand on the bed and leaned down to grab it. I opened the flap and pulled the book out, eyes tracing the gold letters Lucy had mentioned.

"*Sorry, Luc,*" I whispered as I threw the bag back under the bed and set the book on my blanket. Outside my window, it had stopped raining, but the fog made it seem later than it was. I looked up toward the sky, studying the clouds. The horses weren't out grazing in their favorite spots anymore, which told me that Wally thought it was going to rain again and had brought them in for the night early. My heartbeat quickened and I ran my fingers through my hair, gripping the back of my neck with both hands as I paced toward my basin to splash some water on my face.

Had Breck known it wouldn't storm for so long, and told me that to keep me away? What did he do during the week other than running the mill? What was he doing right now? I reached for my towel and dried my damp skin, staring at my reflection. Henry was right. If I didn't do something about this, it was going to mess up my game.

Lucy's door finally shut with a bang across the hall. I reached for the book and went to return it to her shelf. It occurred to me that a book going missing and then returning without anyone knowing what happened to it sounded a lot like a trick a fairy might play. I wasn't sure if that made me feel bad, or excited to see her reaction when she found it. I slipped the book in with the others and quietly left her room.

TWELVE

I woke to a roll of thunder outside.

My eyes opened, and I blinked a few times as I turned my head toward the window. A heavy rain was falling against the roof. I drew in a deep breath and pressed my face into my pillow to silence my coughs before I rolled onto my back. As my sleep left me, new emotions streamed in that made my chest tighten a little. Was it from excitement? Anticipation? Uncertainty? *Yes, yes, and yes*, I decided as I threw my blankets away and brought my legs over the edge of the bed, resting my bare feet on the floor.

A flash of lightning lit up my room, and by the time I'd made it to my basin on the wall, another deep rumble spread through the sky. I'd already washed my entire body before I'd gone to sleep. Some places I'd gone over twice for good measure. I reached up to rub my cheek, watching my hand move in the mirror. It was smooth enough after taking the time to shave before bed, too. I rolled my eyes at myself as I reached for my clothes and shoes. Inside my wardrobe, I found my heavy cloak, and I shrugged it on as a gust of wind blew a sheet of rain against my window. I decided that a hat would probably be more trouble than it was worth.

My door latched behind me, and I stepped silently toward the stairs. Another whip of lightning illuminated them as I went down. My eyes shot to the sitting room before I crept by. It wasn't unheard of for someone to be up reading or gazing out the windows on a stormy, sleepless night in our house. It was Anne's favorite place to be. Thankfully, it was empty, and the front door opened and shut without announcing my departure.

I wrapped my cloak tighter around me as I set off into the rain. The wind immediately whipped the long fabric hard against my legs, and I realized this storm was a little stronger than I'd thought from the safety of my bedroom. Knowing that it would make my lungs angry, I picked up my pace so that I was jogging by the time I reached the road.

I held one arm in front of my forehead to keep the droplets blowing sideways out of my eyes. My foot splashed into a puddle I hadn't noticed in the dark, sending water all over my trousers and thoroughly soaking my shoe all the way to my sock. At that point, I decided I would arrive a sopping mess no matter how hard I tried to avoid it, so I ran.

My chest was burning by the time I crossed the bridge over the river. For the first time, though, I saw light coming from Breck's windows. This sent a thrill through my body, and I slowed to a walk as I navigated down the hill toward the road along the river, breathing heavily and coughing into the night air.

As I approached the door, I realized I wasn't sure how to do this. Any of this, really, but I had to start with the door. Should I knock? Was I supposed to let myself in? My chest was still heaving as I brought my hand up to do something, but I didn't have to because Breck opened it for me. He was holding a chamberstick, which was the only light in the mill aside from what was spilling from upstairs.

Our eyes met across the threshold before his gaze fell as he stepped aside so I could come in. I coughed a few times as I slid one arm out of my cloak, then the other, and I hung it on one of the hooks along the wall. I ran my fingers through my hair it to get it off my forehead as I turned, and then kept turning as I realized Breck and his candle were gone.

I quickly kicked my muddy shoes off and walked across the room to the staircase, trying to get my breathing back to normal. When I reached the top of the steps, I found there were a few more candles burning around the room. The peculiar, soft orbs of light were still resting on the shelves, and more of them appeared to be suspended as they hung at various heights above the bed. When one of them started to move, however, I realized they weren't hanging. They were floating.

I looked at Breck and he shrugged a little, grinning. "Magic," he explained.

Now that I could see him better, I studied his face in the gentle light. He was standing on the plush rug in front of his bed, hands in his pockets. Thunder shook the sky above us and I glanced down at my clothes. The legs of my trousers were soaked with rainwater and mud, my socks were wet, and my hair was plastered to my head. I was about to apologize for all of it when he spoke.

"Tea?" he asked casually. I looked back up at him, wiping my wet hands on the seat of my trousers. I shook my head, sending some droplets of water from my hair to my shoulders and the floor around me.

"I'm fine, thanks," I said. I found some confidence to take a step closer to him, and he shifted his weight. Wind threw the rain against the side of the mill.

"Something to eat, then?" he offered, and my heart thudded in my chest at the smirk that had appeared on his lips.

"No," I said on a breath. I took another small step forward, and the icy sensation I'd felt days before crept around me again, feeling even colder on the damp skin around my wrists and neck. I shivered and pulled a shallow breath of minty air into my lungs. It was strangely soothing.

"How about—"

I closed the distance between us in a few strides. His hands came from his pockets to grab my sides as I put a hand on the back of his neck and pressed my mouth to his. There was no hesitation on his part as he pulled me close, palm flat on my lower back, and angled his head to deepen the kiss. We broke apart and I was already short on air again, breathing through my mouth as we stared at each other.

The next thing I knew, he'd pulled us down to the rug on our knees. I couldn't look away from his face as he worked on the buttons of my waistcoat. He pushed it off my shoulders, and I kissed him again a little rougher than I meant to, off balance because my arms were behind me. When I got them both free, I tossed the waistcoat aside and reached for the hem of his shirt; he raised his arms and I pulled it off in one swoop. My eyes trailed over his chest and shoulders and the freckles I had known would be there. I looked back up at him as I wrapped my fingers behind one of his thighs and pulled. He leaned back on his hands as he moved his legs out from underneath him, and as he settled onto his back on the rug, I climbed over him, still on my knees.

I sat with my hips above his, straddling him, and we both reached for my shirt to pull it off. As it came over my head, my wet hair flopped back against my forehead. Breck blinked and flinched a little at the drops of water that fell onto his face.

"Sorry," I said as I went to wipe them off. My hand stopped and my brows furrowed as I noticed that several of the drops had darkened against his skin. I leaned closer and realized it wasn't the rainwater that had changed color. In addition to the freckles he always wore across his face, these small flecks of a sparkling silver-blue were now on his skin. My eyes went to his. I realized by the look on his face that he knew this would happen. He'd been waiting for it to happen.

I brushed my thumb across his cheekbone, and as the wetness from the raindrops spread across his skin, more speckles appeared. He moved his head against the rug and they caught the light, glittering. I sat up and searched his face for an explanation, but his hips moving under mine forced me back into the moment. He would tell me later if I asked.

Our kissing on the rug turned into kissing on the bed, but not before the rest of our clothes were crumpled on the floor. My body was humming at the newness of this. All times I'd been with Jamie had been stolen, secret moments, alone for metered time in the stables, the hay loft in the barn, deep in the trees. We didn't have time or privacy enough to be so bold – or so naked.

It was my turn on my back. I was silently begging my lungs to behave as my pulse hammered. However, as soon as Breck's touch grazed something even more sensitive, I realized my lungs weren't the ones I needed to be speaking with. A startled cough escaped me as I looked down at his teasing fingers, and then our eyes met as he gave me a slightly concerned look. His lips were swollen, and a few sparkles remained across his cheeks.

"I haven't—" I took a breath. "I haven't in a while," I told him. His look softened briefly before it shifted to something more devious.

"If you come too fast, we'll just make up for it later," was his response, and then he wrapped his fingers the rest of the way around me. I could feel some of the thin bands of metal on them as his hand began to move. The sky was still bucketing around us as he worked a different kind of magic, and I couldn't do anything but lie there until I was stricken with my release. I panted as I came back from it, barely aware of where his hands or mouth were until I realized his tongue was sliding across the skin on my stomach. Jamie had never done that before.

"Alright?" he asked as he settled on his side, arm propped on the pillow next to the one my head was on. He had many of them, I realized. I brought my hand to my chest and rubbed it slowly.

"A little sore, if I'm honest." There was a dull ache, but it was something I'd grown used to. "I ran here, so. That probably didn't help," I confessed with a rueful grin.

Breck laughed at this and arched a brow. "Were you that excited to see me?"

I laughed a little too and met his gaze again. "Well, I did spend the first part of the week checking for clouds every five minutes."

"I wanted you to see," he explained, the side of his pointer finger grazing his cheek. "It happens when my skin gets wet in the human world."

"Like how Elina's skin was glowing at Finna's," I remembered, and he nodded. I reached up and cupped his face with my hand, sliding my thumb against his cheekbone again. "*Beautiful*," I whispered. He chuckled and pushed my hand away gently.

I sat up and pushed him in return, against his shoulder so he rolled onto his back. He didn't lose the impish grin on his face as I pulled him toward me while I moved backwards, slipping off the edge of the bed onto my knees. His head settled back against the sheets, and he raised one arm above him to grip the edge of the mattress. I let my mind wander to which other parts of him could sparkle as I took him in my mouth. He moaned softly and adjusted his hips on the bed. I gripped the rest of him in my hand, working him slowly. Carrick hadn't been wrong when he'd joked at Breck's expense.

He lasted longer than I did, but not by much. I felt my own face flush as I watched him finish, mostly because of the sounds he made as he did. It was so raw and uninhibited that it pulled a twitch from between my legs. I released a shaky breath and let go of him as I stood to find something to clean up with. When I came back, he was watching me, arm still above his head, chest rising and falling evenly. He held his other hand out for the towel; I tossed it to him after I wiped my fingers with it. My trousers were still dirty but somewhat dry as I pulled them back on.

"That's mine," Breck said as I picked up what I thought was my shirt. I stopped, holding it out to look at it before I tossed it onto the bed and picked up the other one next to the rug. My waistcoat was wrapped around a leg of one of the chairs by the table. I laughed to myself as I untangled it. Breck came to help me with the buttons, still in the nip, and I shamelessly reached up to touch his bottom lip with the tip of my thumb. His mouth tugged into the smallest grin, and he looked at me under hooded eyelids as his fingers worked.

"I'm going to Finna's in the morning to help her prepare for Lughnasa. You're welcome to join us if you're free," he offered. I nodded and smoothed my hands over the front of my waistcoat after he finished.

"Sure. I'll meet you there," I said.

"She's going to know. About this," he added, not needing to explain what he meant.

"You're going to tell her?" I asked, my eyebrows going up, nerves prickling.

"I won't have to. She'll just know."

I considered this as he picked up his trousers and laid them with his shirt across the back of a chair at the table. "Has she known the whole time?" I asked, even though I was sure I already knew the answer.

He stepped closer to me and hooked a finger in my waistband, tugging me gently as he closed the gap between us. Our noses touched as he spoke quietly against my lips. "We both have." A mix of embarrassment and arousal washed through my body as he released me, and I turned to watch him as he went to his small stove. He put some water on to heat. "Tea?" he asked over his shoulder.

"I have to get home. I've barely slept," I confessed, remembering that it was still the middle of the night. The storm seemed to have calmed some outside.

"I'll see you at Finna's," he said then.

I found my things where I'd left them by the door. I stooped to put my shoes on and shoved my arms into my coat as I pulled the door open. The rain had slowed considerably, but it was still coming down. Only a distant rumble of thunder broke in the sky now as my steps squished through the mud left behind on the road.

After I was across the bridge and safely beyond the tunnel of trees, I reached up with my fingertips to touch my lips. They were still tingling. I allowed myself to unleash the grin I'd been repressing. Back in my own bed, I fell asleep quickly with his smell on my skin and mint on my tongue.

***

When I woke again, it was light in my room. I rubbed my eyes, squinting at the window.

"*Shit,*" I cursed under my breath as I shot up out of my bed, stumbling as my foot got caught in the sheet. It had to be mid-morning already. I put my clothes on as fast as I could and took the steps two at a time, and for some reason I decided the kitchen was the smartest route to the stables.

"Peter Walshe, you stop right there."

I skidded to a stop and swallowed hard. "Em, good morning," I said, meeting Anne's gaze where she was sitting at the table. Her mouth was set in a hard line.

"Are you sick?" she asked, her tone softening already. She looked tired.

"No. I just didn't sleep very well last night. The storm woke me up," I explained, leaving out some other details.

"You never sleep this late. You haven't since you were so ill." She looked away as her voice broke on the last bit. I pulled out my chair and sat across from her in the spot I occupied for supper every night. I resisted the urge to look out the window behind her. I was so late.

"I'm fine, I promise," I urged. When she looked back at me, her eyes were wetter than they had been before. She never cried. "Anne?"

"William said that he told you our news," she said, her voice still weak.

"He did," I confirmed. "It's wonderful." We sat in silence for several moments.

"I can't bear to lose another," she whispered, and a tear escaped down her cheek. She reached up to wipe it away with the base of her thumb. I pushed out of my chair, moving around the table to wrap my arms around her. I struggled to keep away the memory of when she'd held me this way, fighting to keep all my shattered pieces together when I couldn't do it for myself.

"You won't, alright? You won't. This time will be different," I told her in the most encouraging way I could manage. I held her shoulders in my hands and squeezed them gently, looking up at her from where I was crouched by her chair. "You just take care of yourself, and nature will do the rest."

She finally met my gaze again. She looked so sad, but she nodded. Her eyes shifted to my hair, which was an absolute disaster from the night before underneath my cap, and I stood up before the conversation could turn back to me. "Get to your chores," she said, waving me away after she wiped under her eyes again. I gave her an apologetic look, and she shook her head. "Go. I'll see you at supper."

I all but ran down to the stables, where I found Henry and Thomas nearing the end of their morning routines. Henry was already removing his saddle from his horse's back.

"Well, look who decided to join us," Thomas announced when he noticed me first.

"Overslept," I explained quickly as I whisked past them, avoiding Henry's eyes. "The weather last night was wild."

"Aye," Henry agreed. "We got to the river this morning and had to turn around, it's so high." My eyebrows went up and I looked at him finally.

"It's never so high that you can't cross at all," I said skeptically.

"That's what I thought too, but it's runnin' mad quick, as well. Too dangerous."

I had thought about riding to Finna's after I was done, but now I was second-guessing that idea. My gray mare whinnied at me, letting me know I was late with their breakfast. I no longer felt weighed down by my anticipation of meeting Breck. Instead, I was feeling like I'd had the best night of sleep I'd had in ages. Memories of the night before sent a shiver through me, directly to my groin. I grinned to myself as I dumped food into my horses' buckets.

Out of nowhere, I was pegged in the back with something. I turned to see a bristle brush next to my feet. I leaned to pick it up and looked at Henry, who glanced at Thomas, before he gave me a suggestive smirk. I also shot a look at Thomas, who was paying us no attention, and threw the brush back at him, hitting him on the hip as he turned to protect himself.

"*Feck off*," I mouthed at him, and his crooked smile spread wider. He inclined his head toward me even more, eyebrows waggling, and I sighed and couldn't help but grin again. I looked down, nodding subtly in response to his unspoken question. He dramatically mimed wiping his forehead in relief and proceeded to engage in some hip-heavy victory dance moves in my honor just as Thomas finally turned around.

"What are you doing?" he asked Henry, giving him a confused look. I laughed and turned away. I couldn't help but fear that Henry was far too invested in my personal life.

"Mind your own, Thomas," Henry warned him as he reached to pick up his brush.

***

As I passed over the bridge for the third time that

day, I got to see what Henry had been talking about. The water was nearly touching the keystone, and it was running faster than ever. We didn't get a lot of storms like the one that'd passed through the night before, but even when we did, it never had this much of an impact on the river. I glanced at the mill and noticed that the wheel had been stopped.

It was an effort to avoid muddy patches in the road on the way to the cottage. I was glad when the dirt became more solid and grassy as I went up the slight hill. The windows were open, and I could already smell whatever it was they were making inside. I let myself in and removed my boots by the door. I hadn't bothered to change out of my riding clothes, mostly because I didn't want to run into anyone else in my house and risk getting caught in another emotional conversation.

"We're in here, love!" Finna called from the kitchen. When I turned the corner, I was not prepared for what I found.

Any available surface was covered with ingredients, finished loaves of bread, and every step in between. Finna's pale hair was gathered up on top of her head in a massive bundle, with many curly pieces falling around her face and down the back of her neck. There was a smear of flour on her cheek. She smiled and spread her arms wide as if to present all of this to me.

"Happy Harvest," she said in a cheery, forced way, before she went back to the dough on the counter in front of her. My eyes shifted to Breck, who was sitting comfortably in a chair at the table. He offered me a gentle smile as I sat across from him.

"Happy Harvest?" I repeated in question.

"Lughnasa is the celebration of the harvest and the end of summer. As you can see, we honor it by eating ridiculous amounts of bread and dancing the night away," he explained casually as he watched Finna work.

"You're going to eat all of this?" I asked incredulously.

"The fair folk and other magical creatures," he added. "And anyone else who wishes to join."

"Oh," I said, nodding. "When?"

"This evening after sunset, into tomorrow."

Finna plopped some of her dough into a pan and wiped her hands on her smock, then brushed her hair back with her forearm. "I need more eggs," she said as she got off her stepstool and walked out the open door that led to the garden.

"What's going on with the river?" I asked quietly as soon as I couldn't hear her footsteps crunching on the gravel anymore. Breck turned to look at me.

"The river?" he echoed, studying my face.

"It's never like this, even after a hard rain," I said. His eyes shifted down, and his fingers drummed the tabletop lightly as he seemed to formulate his response.

"It responds to me in many ways. It has a little to do with the storms, but a lot more to do with last night," he explained.

"Last night..." I returned with uncertainty. He met my eyes again, a smirk growing on his lips.

"You do remember last night, don't you?" he

asked playfully.

"Yes," I responded, quicker than I meant to. "Yes, I remember." He shifted in his chair and leaned closer to me across the table.

"When I feel strong emotions that I cannot control, such as pain or pleasure, the river responds in kind. It's something that I'm still working on."

I sat silently and let this information sink in, realizing that what we'd done, and what he'd felt as a result, was the cause of the abnormally large surge in the river. Before I could think of anything to say, Finna returned with an armful of eggs, retrieved from chickens I wasn't aware she had.

"Can I help?" I asked her. I didn't know the first thing about making bread, but she seemed a little frazzled.

"No, love, that's alright. Your company's help enough. Always glad to have you here," she said. "Breck, why don't you put on some tea?" We looked at each other across the table and shared a private smile before he got up. "Are you going to join us tonight?" she asked as she cracked one of the fresh eggs into a bowl and discarded the light brown shell into another.

"Me?" I asked dumbly.

"Everyone should experience Lughnasa at least once in their life," she said, looking up at me briefly. "It's one of the most important events of the year."

"He's still getting used to all of this, Finna," Breck said, his back still to us.

"What's a few hundred more fair folk?" she said,

waving her hand nonchalantly, causing some crumbles of drying dough to fly off her fingers.

"A few *hundred*?" I choked out.

"What? Weren't there at least that many people at the last party you went to?" she reasoned.

"I guess so..." She had a point. But where were all these creatures coming from? At least I knew roughly where most of the guests at Henry's party lived in the village.

"Breck, invite the lad so he'll say yes," Finna pushed. I wasn't sure if I should be offended by the fact that she thought that's all it would take for me to agree to it, but as he turned and came back toward the table with our cups in his hands, I already knew she was right.

He placed my tea down and returned to the chair opposite me, taking a sip of his and setting it on the table before he said, "Would you like to come to the harvest celebration with us tonight?"

"*Oi!*" Finna cut in sharply. "That's no way to do it! Remember how his invitation for you was so personal and sweet? Be a gentleman about it, then." Heat crept across my face. I hadn't realized what I'd written was any of those things.

"Peter," he began after a pause, and I met his blue eyes across the table. "I would be honored if you would attend the harvest celebration with me tonight."

I caught Finna's satisfied grin as she began whisking the eggs in her bowl, her hair bouncing a little atop her head as her arm worked. Breck's eyes were still on me, and I took a long pull of my tea to give myself a moment to think before I responded. If I wanted to, I could come up with several excuses for why I couldn't go. If I wanted to, I could lie and say I just didn't want to go. If I wanted to.

"Do I have to dress up?" I asked finally.

"You can wear anything you'd like," Breck said.

"Some choose to wear their most favorite outfits, and others wear no clothes at all. Nothin' you haven't seen before," Finna added.

"So... something in between those would be appropriate?" I queried, hopeful that I didn't look too horrified at the last bit of what Finna said, and Breck nodded. I stilled my hands on my thighs and patted my knees instead, indicating that my decision was made. "Alright."

THIRTEEN

I'd returned home just long enough to put some food in my stomach at supper. Anne seemed to have recovered from earlier, though I noticed she didn't eat very much. Nan and William noticed the same thing, and both made comments about it. I was secretly glad to not have this directed at me for once. I excused myself to check on the horses one last time for the night. Thomas was just finishing up when I arrived.

"Going for a ride so late?" he asked. I was still dressed in my riding breeches and boots.

"Never changed from earlier today," I told him as I walked past.

"You've been quite busy lately. Haven't seen you around much."

I paused then, giving him a sidelong glance from where I peered over the chestnut mare's half door. Henry and I had often thought of Thomas as more of an annoyance than a friend over the years, mostly due to his quick temper and immaturity. I sometimes forgot that he was capable of carrying on a real conversation.

"I guess that's true," I agreed, not offering him any details. Suddenly, something dawned on me. "When is your birthday, Thomas?"

He looked at me suspiciously. "The sixth of December. Why?"

"How old are you now?"

"I'll be twenty-one," he said, his arrogant tone returning for some reason I couldn't guess. How could he and Breck possibly be so close in age? My gaze shifted down over Thomas's body. In my head, he remained the portly little lad who put too much wax in his hair. While his short, dark hairstyle remained unchanged, he'd grown taller at some point. His figure had slimmed a bit, though his cheeks were still round and soft.

"Did you hear me?" he asked, sounding annoyed that he had to repeat himself.

"No, sorry," I said, moving along to the rest of my horses.

"I asked if you really intend to court Emma Clare after Henry's wedding."

"*What*?" I gave him a look, and then I realized I didn't even know that name. "Who?"

"Emma Clare. Sarah's sister...?" he said in a leading way, as if this detail would make it obvious who he was talking about. I blinked a few times, an apologetic look growing on my face, and he rolled his eyes dramatically. "The youngest one," he added finally, and I had to stop myself from reacting in a way he might notice.

"Why would you think that?" I asked.

"That's what she's been telling everyone. That you're being respectful of Henry and Sarah, but as soon as their wedding is over, your courtship will be announced."

"That's a bloody joke, right?" My eyebrows couldn't get any closer together.

"Not at all," he started. Where Henry was known for his wisecracks, Thomas was known for the opposite. He really wasn't joking. "She's the most beautiful of all the sisters, and nearly the most talented with her singing voice and domestic training. It's a wonder Henry didn't pick her for himself. But you're the most eligible bachelor in the village now, so it only made sense when I heard it. I was just going to offer my early congratulations—"

"Hold your whist!" I blurted without thinking, my hands squeezing into temporary fists at my sides. "Where is all of this even coming from?!" He looked startled, and I instantly felt bad for my reaction.

"I don't know, it's what everyone is saying," he replied quickly.

I went to respond but started coughing instead. When the fit didn't end as fast as it normally did, I reached for a half door and sat down against it, resting my head on the rough wood, keeping my back straight. I closed my eyes and focused on breathing.

"Should I get Wally?" Thomas asked in a slight panic. I shook my head without lifting it. I stretched my legs out in front of me and rubbed my palm along my thigh with the hand not covering my mouth, calming myself the best way I knew how. Slowly, I was able to regain my composure, and the coughing subsided. When I opened my eyes, Thomas was standing closer to me, but still at a safe distance, face pale and eyes wide.

"Sorry," I wheezed on an exhale. A lasting fit like that hadn't happened in a long time. I got up, one hand braced on the top of the half door behind me, and brushed myself off. "I'm sorry," I repeated, meeting his worried gaze.

"It—it's quite alright," he said, though it wasn't very convincing. He seemed conflicted for a moment as he turned his back to me and then faced me again right after. "So... you're not courting Emma Clare?" he asked.

"No," I said, my voice a little hoarse. "I have no intention of it."

"Somebody should probably tell her that," he concluded, and a small laugh escaped me.

"Be my guest," I told him.

***

When I spotted Breck on the bridge over the river, he was gazing down at the water that had calmed since the morning. He was wearing what he always wore, which was good since I'd still managed to forget to change out of my riding clothes. My encounter with Thomas had messed with my head and my lungs more than I wanted to admit. Breck turned to me easily, hands in his pockets, and the look on his face shifted a bit.

"Are you alright?" he asked. I nodded, out of breath from my walk, and he studied me carefully in the light that was left from the setting sun. I prepared myself for more questions, but unlike Henry he didn't press the issue, which I was grateful for. He tipped his head toward the road, and I followed him down the hill. As we passed the mill, I let my gaze wander up to the window above the bed upstairs. The flush that spread across my chest made me cough several times.

"It is not unheard of for humans to attend a harvest celebration, but many folk are still cautious when it comes to being seen by people. It may be difficult, but if you can help it, try not to stare."

"Will anyone be upset I'm there?" I asked, already worried about standing out too much.

"Maybe Fallon, but she's always irritated about something, so don't pay her any mind," he said.

When we approached where the trees got especially thick along the road past the mill, Breck motioned for me to follow him again. I was grateful to still be wearing my high boots as we stepped through the thick grass into some rougher brush that grew around the base of the trees.

The silence of the road behind us gave way to bugs singing their twilight songs. Somewhere nearby there must've sat a small pond, because a few frogs were also making themselves heard. I looked down at Breck's bare feet as he carved a path for us. Surely, he had to be feeling some pricks and snags against the exposed skin below his knees where the fabric of his trousers collected. If he was, he didn't let on.

When the canopy became too thick to see any more sunset light, the tangled undergrowth gave way to blankets of moss draped across stones, tree roots, and dark soil that was pulpy with moisture under my feet. I couldn't recall ever seeing this place, even though I had thought based on the location that it was very close to the edge of our land. Only after I released a few coughs that I couldn't hold back any longer did I realize that my breathing was the only sound I could hear now. Near-darkness had surrounded us, and as Breck turned to look at me, I spotted a faint glowing ahead of us in the trees.

"Ready?" Breck's voice was hushed, apparently swept up in the silence and not wanting to disturb it. I nodded again, and he looked down between us. I followed his gaze and realized he was holding his hand out for me to take. Despite the intimacy we'd shared the night before, my heart still did a funny little something in my chest as I slid my hand into his. He closed his fingers and gave a gentle squeeze before he turned and continued in the direction of the glow.

"Close your eyes," he whispered a moment later, and I did. I recognized the icy sensation as it crept around the wrist of the hand Breck was holding, up my arm, and eventually around my whole body, enveloping me as a chill spread over my skin. I rubbed at the gooseflesh that prickled on my forearms with my free hand, stepping along blindly as I was led through the darkness.

I breathed in a slow, deep breath just as Breck stopped walking. I bumped into him and coughed out the precious, minty air I'd pulled in. Light danced on the other side of my closed eyelids. New sounds met my ears. "You can open them now," Breck encouraged. When I did, the scene before me was nearly overwhelming.

A massive fire was burning in the center of a clearing in the trees. There were more of the glowing orbs I recognized from Breck's floating aimlessly through the air, their slowness highlighted by other tiny balls of light zipping by. As one passed closer to me,

I realized that it wasn't just a ball of light. It was... "A fairy," Breck confirmed.

My eyes shifted from the sky down to the crowd in front of me. Creatures of all shapes and sizes and colors were spread across the clearing, reclining against gnarled roots and perched on mossy rocks, eating and drinking and dancing. I couldn't see the source of the music being played, but it was jaunty and soothing all at once. Finna had been right about their clothes. Some were wearing items of the finest materials, similar to what Henry was often forced to wear. Others were as naked as the day they were born. One thing was certain, however. I was the only one wearing a waistcoat and riding breeches.

A small girl passing nearby seemed to notice this at the same time I did, and she gasped, grabbing up the ample skirts of her dress and skipping over to us, dipping in a rushed curtsy. She stood no taller than my waist. With a bright smile, she said something in words I didn't understand, though it was difficult to hear her quiet voice over the festivities to begin with. Some of the closest partygoers did hear her, though, and they stopped to regard me. To my relief, it seemed to be more with curiosity than fear or anger.

In my effort to not look at any of them too long, I swept my gaze across the clearing again and spotted Finna offering her homemade bread to a small crowd gathered around where she appeared to have set up shop for the evening. She was wearing a gown of dark purple, with flowing sleeves that showed off all her bracelets and rings. Her long hair was down her back and over her shoulders, decorated with plaits and ribbons and topped with a headpiece of braided wheat spikes.

My attention was drawn back as a small group of fairies approached us carrying another woven wreath. This one was more elaborate; there were red and yellow flowers twined with the golden spikes. In a tick of horror, I thought they were about to present it to me, but instead I watched as Breck dipped low enough for them to place it on his tousled blond hair.

I realized several things then. One, our hands were still clasped between us, because he used his other hand to steady the headpiece as he righted himself. I withdrew my hand as Breck thanked the other fairies for what they had given him. Two, his cheeks and nose were thoroughly dusted with the silver-blue flecks now, which glittered wildly as he moved in the firelight. And three, I desperately needed a drink, because four was that I had never wanted someone so badly in my whole life as I did in that moment.

I tried not to stick to him like a foal to its mother, but parties already weren't in my comfort zone, let alone a party like this. As we went, the folk greeted Breck warmly, occasionally reaching to touch his arm, or leg, or cheek, depending on how tall they were. Then their focus would shift to me, and they offered a greeting less warm but not at all rude. Just uncertain.

"Peter!" Finna called my name from her post, and I glanced at Breck before I zig-zagged my way over to her, nearly tripping on several of the shorter fairies around me. "What did I tell you? Quite a party, eh?" She handed me a piece of bread without asking if I wanted any. I took a bite of it, chewing slowly as my eyes scanned the crowd, landing on Breck as he greeted Elina with kisses on her cheeks, a headpiece like Breck's resting on her golden hair. Her skin had an extra glow to it in the firelight.

"Thirsty?" A small voice asked, and I turned toward the sound. One of the fairies with wings was hovering near my face. It was as if one of the illustrations from my sister's books had sprung off the page into life. She backed up slightly and waved her hand for me to follow her. I did, and she led me to a long, cut slab of wood balanced on top of two stumps still rooted into the ground. The makeshift table held stacks of mismatched cups and bowls that appeared to have been collected from various places. I couldn't see any two that were the same. As I approached, other flying fairies swished into action.

"For the human!" called one of them, his voice deeper than the others but still small, and several joined him behind one of the stacks to grab a clear glass with a long, fine stem. I was already having flashbacks of Henry's engagement party as they worked together to fill it with a rich, golden liquid for me. I reached for the stem of the flute where they held it in the air for me to take, and I brought it to my lips for a taste. The sweetness of the drink along with the heady rush of the alcohol made my eyes go a little wide.

"What is this?" I asked, looking from fairy to fairy as they hovered and darted around me, trying to find the one who had invited me over.

"Honey wine with juice from sweet apples," one of them said, and I nearly chuckled. Certainly, there wasn't a drink made more specifically for me than that.

I took another sip and turned back toward the roaring fire.

Lucy would never forgive me if I told her I had seen something like this without her. The illustrations in her stories were accurate enough, but in reality, all of them were too stunning to ever capture in a drawing. I thought back on the word she'd needed help with in her borrowed book. *Enchanting.* Yes, that was appropriate, no doubt.

I remembered the bread I was holding and enjoyed the rest of it, glad to be getting some padding in my stomach for the drink I was about to finish, too. I still couldn't see where the music was coming from, but the song had changed to something even quicker, and everywhere I looked, there was dancing happening.

As the heat from the flames in front of me became too intense on an already warm night, I wandered in the direction I thought Breck had gone, taking in what was happening around me. A group of child-sized fairies were holding hands, winding through the crowd on skipping feet, their dresses flitting this way and that. Some others had settled beneath the low branches of a tree, sharing from a tray overflowing with fruits and berries.

There were probably a hundred folk in and around the clearing, as Finna had said there would be, but many of them were so small that it didn't seem nearly as crowded as I had imagined. I couldn't help but compare them to the people from the village I usually saw at parties, standing stiffly in their fancy clothes as they shared their most recent business successes or grand accomplishments.

I had known for years that I didn't fit in with them, but as two fairies ran past me in the nude, laughing as they waved long ribbons out behind them, I wasn't sure how well I fit in here, either. I drained my honey wine and wished that I hadn't strayed so far from the table where it was being served.

A sweet giggle caught my attention, and I turned to find a lass with short, dark hair and brilliant green eyes staring down at me from a branch in the tree I was standing under. Wings unfurled from her back in a snap of shimmering dust, and she fluttered them a few times.

"Humans think so loudly," she mused, and I felt a warmth around my hand that was holding the empty glass as the velvety scent of rose petals tickled my nose and tongue. I looked down at the cup, and quickly raised it in front of my eyes as I realized it was full again.

I took a careful sip and found it tasted the same as my previous drink. When I looked back up at the limb she'd been perched on, the girl was gone. As I reminded myself to be careful of what I was thinking, several of the folk passed by me on foot and by wing, and I looked in the direction they were going. The fire had been abandoned as they made their way toward another clearing, so I followed.

I spotted Finna's wild hair in the crowd and caught up to her. "Be careful with the mead, love. It'll hit you like a mule kick," she warned after eyeing my drink, and then wrapped her tiny hand around the crook of my elbow.

"Where is everyone going?" I questioned, but she

didn't respond. Instead, she gestured with a tilt of her head toward what I now could see was a semi-circle of impressive chairs with high backs fashioned from woven sticks, vines, and more stalks of golden wheat. My eyes settled on the woman sitting in the middle seat, her long black braid resting over her shoulder. It was Fallon. To her left was Murray, and beside him was Carrick, who appeared to be draining his own hearty cup of mead. They all wore the braided wreaths on their heads. On Fallon's other side was Elina, and I swallowed as my eyes came to the final seat.

Breck sat with the same calm, confident air he always did, legs crossed beneath him on the chair. Elina leaned over and said something to him, and they shared a genuine laugh.

I coughed and quickly gulped down the rest of my sweet drink. Finna raised her eyebrows at me as I ignored her advice. Her slim shoulders shook as she chuckled to herself. I watched as Fallon silenced the crowd gathered there on the ground and in the trees with nothing more than her standing up. The smaller fire their seats were arranged around flickered light across her face.

"Tonight, we celebrate another year of hard work and care that has been put into this land. Tomorrow, we will reap the benefits of the efforts made by the folk and humans alike. We will aid in the harvesting, bring luck where we can, and ensure that the land has not been stripped too badly as to prevent success next season." As she paused, the crackling of the fires surrounded us. "Remember now, and always, that our efforts are rewarded most when we help the humans with genuine kindness."

Fallon held her hand up in the air, and a shiny chalice appeared with a gleam. The others sitting behind her did the same, raising cups they were already holding, and the folk around me copied them. I raised my glass even though it was empty.

"Happy Harvest," Fallon said without much emotion, and the crowd cheered before taking a collective pull from their hodgepodge of containers. I lowered mine and watched Breck drink from the gilded cup in his hand, holding his wheat crown in place with the other, his cheeks and nose sparkling in the low light. The music began again almost immediately, and everyone returned to their celebrating, including Finna, who had quickly disappeared from my side. I decided to find the fairies serving the mead again so I could try to tame my loud thoughts a little better.

Fresh drink in hand, I located a spot to sit on a rock near the edge of the clearing. I brushed at it with my hand before I sat to protect the light fabric of my riding breeches. Unfortunately, my quiet seat away from the festivities allowed my mind to start working on other, more troubling things.

Anne and William were expecting a baby. I was apparently now the most eligible single man in the village, and Henry's sister-in-law-to-be was spreading false information about us to enough people that even Thomas had managed to hear about it. I pushed my fingers back through my hair and took a long drink of my honey wine.

Something made a sound in the darkness behind

me, and I turned to find a couple wrapped in nothing but their long hair embracing each other against a rather large tree trunk. Before I could look away, I realized there were actually three of them sharing kisses and touches there in the heavy night air. I got to my feet quicker than I needed to and stumbled a little as I searched for a new place to sit that wasn't quite so private. As I worked my way around the largest fire, which was still burning strong and high, someone grabbed my wrist. I trailed my eyes down my arm and up to find it was Elina who had stopped me.

"You seem like you have a lot troubling you tonight," she said airily. "This is a night for forgetting all of your troubles." She released me and spun around, her gauzy dress skirts brushing against my boots. Her arms came up loosely around her head and shoulders as she began to sway with the music. I watched her for a moment, took another sip of my drink, and could all but guarantee that I looked as uncomfortable as I felt as I tried to follow her lead.

The music grew louder in my ears. I closed my eyes briefly, but I realized in a hurry that I didn't have the balance for that. I couldn't think of many things that would be worse than surviving the illness, only to die after going headlong into a giant fire.

When my eyes opened again, most things around me were a blur of warm colors. Elina was still there, smiling at me. There were others around us dancing, too, and I turned to see them. Their hair and wings and flowy clothes all started to meld together. The girl who'd filled my glass before was there. She laughed as she guided my cup to my lips, encouraging me to drink more. I swallowed the last of it and wiped my mouth with the back of my hand.

Rose petals danced around me as more of the amber liquid filled my glass, and I tried to bring it to my mouth, but someone took it from me. I blinked hard to clear my vision and realized it was Breck. He drained it himself and handed it to the girl, who was still hovering near me.

"No more," he told her, and she must've taken that as a dismissal, because she was gone in seconds. I turned my attention back to him, swaying a little. He reached to steady me at the same moment I reached for him in search of some balance. Warmth spread across my chest and up my neck and I grinned at him, a laugh escaping me for some reason.

"I don't know how to dance," I confessed to him.

"Could've fooled me," he said lightly. I couldn't quite read the look on his face. My eyes went to the crown resting on his head.

"You didn't tell me you're... em..." I managed. I pointed to my own head and drew a lazy circle in the air with my finger a few times, my words not coming to me as easily as I wanted them to.

"The folk view us as deities because of the responsibilities we have with the nature here. They look to us to guide them in their roles both in the human world and our own."

"So, they view you as deities because you *are* deities," I emphasized, one eye squinting as I tried to clarify what he was telling me. I studied his face as he shrugged and nodded. His answer was sobering in its own way, but not enough to keep me from tightening my grip on his shoulders and kissing him.

His hands loosened on my arms, one coming to hold the back of my neck and the other wrapping in my hair. Our bodies pressed together, and the radiance from the fire at my back and my own heat from whatever dancing I'd managed to do worked together to threaten me with beads of sweat. I think it was my lips that parted first, allowing our tongues to touch once, twice.

Breck groaned against my mouth and pulled away then. I forced my heavy eyes open, breathing hard as my lungs shared their displeasure with me. His fingers stroked the back of my head beneath my curls, and he kissed me again before he leaned toward my ear and murmured, "We'll never last all night if you keep this up."

I was suddenly aware of the music and everyone else around us again, still dancing and drinking. He kissed my neck gently and let me go. Part of me wanted to protest and share that there were plenty of places around for us to get busy *not* lasting all night, but I decided that I was equally as happy over the simple fact that he'd found me again in the crowd.

He didn't leave me alone the rest of the night. I wasn't certain if it was more because he wanted to make sure I didn't drink too much, or because he wanted to be with me, but I didn't question it. He fed me honey cakes and cheese and introduced me to some of the fairies I learned were older and more comfortable conversing with humans. Some of them had been around long enough to have known my grandparents, and even my great-grandparents.

The pinnacle of the celebration arrived unexpectedly to me, when the crowd again seemed to flow in one direction toward where Breck and the others had been seated for Fallon's speech. I was glad to have him with me to describe what was happening. Finna had been no help at all before.

"Eabha has arrived for the joining ceremony. This is a most special night for it to happen. Carrick and his mate were joined on Lughnasa all those years ago," he explained. I was listening, but also distracted by how close he was leaning toward me as he spoke. When we got near enough to see what was going on, it appeared that the ceremony was already in progress. Couples were kneeling on the ground, facing each other, with their hands clasped together. Fallon and Elina were busy wrapping ribbons around their hands. Elina was smiling; Fallon had no expression on her face.

I put my mouth near Breck's ear and asked, "Why are Fallon and Elina the ones doing that part? Because they're women?"

"Because they're the oldest," he said. I kept watching closely. When they finished wrapping their hands, the couples bowed toward each other until their heads were touching, and then their joined hands served as a cushion between their heads and the ground. They remained like this until the last of the three couples was joined by Elina. A hush swept over the crowd.

My eyes jumped toward the seat Fallon had occupied before when someone moved on it. Slowly, gracefully, a woman stood from the throne. She had skin the color of cinnamon, and her hair reminded me of Finna's, but it was darker and much curlier. She was stunning.

Breck whispered a simplified translation of her words to me as she started talking over the couples. His hand found its way to my back as he spoke, and that combined with the lines about commitment, and partnership, and pleasure eventually had my pulse thumping in my chest and… other places.

When it was over, I expected the couples to kiss, but they didn't. They got to their feet with their hands still bound together, and then the ribbons faded away to dust that glittered as it fell to the ground. Like it had before, the music and festivities started again immediately. The crowd pushed forward to encircle the newly joined couples, congratulating them and offering hugs, and cheek kisses, and cheers with mismatched cups.

"Peter Walshe," a velvet voice said, and I turned to find Eabha standing in front of me. Breck had backed up to give her space, and I looked at him quickly, feeling unsure of how I was supposed to behave. I decided to handle it the way I would handle an interaction with one of the fine ladies during the social events at Henry's.

I put an arm behind my back and bowed my head neatly. "Hello." Eabha studied me for a moment, her face unreadable, and then she grinned softly and nodded back at me. I let my hand fall back to my side as Breck stepped forward cautiously to stand next to me again.

"You are our very special case," she said. Her voice was so smooth, despite the thickness of her accent. "May I?" She raised her hand between us, palm up and fingers relaxed, gesturing slightly toward me. I nodded. She closed her dark eyes, and I felt her magic wrap around me right away. It was more powerful than Breck's; strong and purposeful. It smelled like the roots of a plant freshly plucked from the ground.

There was a fullness in my lungs. It got heavier as I watched her face change slightly, and then it was almost painful, before it left me completely and her eyes opened. I brought my hand up to cover my mouth as I gasped in a breath and coughed deeply several times.

"What is it?" Fallon had appeared on my other side, and then I realized the others were there, too. Eabha said something foreign, looking me over with a new, more critical expression. "*I knew it*," Fallon whispered, as if this was great news. It was the most positive sounding thing I'd ever heard her say.

"Dark magic?" I asked, turning to Breck. His brows were furrowed, arms crossed.

"Yes. Here," Eabha said, reaching her hand out to rest flat against the middle of my chest. I looked down at her hand, and then back up at her face.

"It's inside of me?"

"Resting deeply. Delivered by someone very powerful. Or by someone who felt very strongly about you," she explained.

"Someone wanted him dead," Carrick guessed, his gravelly voice breaking in.

"Could you tell whose it is?" Breck asked then. Eabha responded to him, looking away from me finally. The others made various small sounds and reactions of disappointment. "No smell or other discernible factors.

It was done this way to avoid being traced," Breck said, translating for me again. I had so many questions.

"We will keep searching for the answer." Eabha moved her hand from my chest to my cheek, comforting me briefly, before she dipped her head again and left us. I believed her.

***

I had no idea what time of night it was when Breck told me we were leaving. All I knew was that I hadn't felt that exhausted since I was bedridden. The drinking and dancing had given way to more of what I'd seen at the edge of the clearing, and as we walked past the dwindling fires, all I could see were fairies across the forest floor, their sated and languished bodies tangled together. Some of them watched us with lazy smiles. Others were still too busy with their night pleasures to notice us at all.

"They don't mind being seen?" I asked in a low voice, curiosity getting the better of me.

"It's not viewed the same as in your world," Breck explained as we stepped carefully in the direction we'd arrived from. "Pleasure is something to be enjoyed by anyone who wants it, as long as all parties involved are willing."

"They all seem to be very willing, indeed," I noted, and Breck gave me a sidelong smile. I couldn't let go of my human shame around the subject as I continued. "And, there are no reservations about... gender?" Many of the fairies I'd seen together that night didn't seem to notice who they were with one way or the other. One of the couples joined in the ceremony had been two women.

"There are preferences," he reasoned with a small shrug, but he didn't elaborate further. I felt another trait I guessed was entirely human bubbling up in my chest, and undirected jealousy reared its ugly head as I wondered about Breck. What did he prefer?

I looked at him then, studying his profile as we walked past the biggest fire one last time, which had simmered mostly to low licks of flame and hot embers. His harvest crown was still nestled in his hair, resting against the pointed tips of his decorated ears. The sparkles on his skin hadn't faded like they had when I'd wet them with my thumb. I rubbed my fingers slowly against that thumb now, and I had to look away to keep myself from reaching out to touch his cheek, or his lips, or anywhere else.

FOURTEEN

"It'll be morning soon," Breck said, looking toward the sky. "Would you like me to help you before we leave?"

"Help me?" I repeated, feeling something coil low in my stomach. He stopped walking, and I turned back to face him.

"Unless you want to go home still drunk?" he asked, levity in his tone.

"Oh," I said, understanding what he meant then.

Mint overpowered my senses and I shivered as his magic came around me. I closed my eyes against the prickling in my nose. It was so strong that it made me sneeze. When it reached my lungs, however, it was a cooling relief that I wished could stay longer every time. When I opened my eyes again, the last of the chill was leaving me. There was an emptiness behind us where the party had been. Now it was just quiet trees. I also felt an emptiness inside me; the effects of the mead and dancing and fatigue had left me completely.

"How do you do that?" I asked, following him as he started walking again like this task had been as simple for him as breathing.

"Your body is made mostly from water," he explained. Of course. That made sense. My mind went back to the events of the night and everything I'd seen. Everything I'd learned. Everything I'd done. I'd kissed

Breck, and I hadn't even cared who was there to see it. Maybe nobody noticed us, but they'd been all around us.

I looked up at him as he removed the crown from his head and ran his fingers through his hair, ruffling it to bring it back to life after being mashed down all night. I briefly wondered if that's what it looked like when he first woke up in the morning, too.

"It suits you," I said as I looked down again to step over some of the thickest undergrowth at the edge of the trees.

"What does?" he asked as he reached up to hang the woven circle on a branch before we emerged into the first light of the day. The sun wouldn't be up over the mountains for a while yet, and it looked like clouds might keep it hidden anyway.

"Wearing a crown."

He laughed and quirked an eyebrow at me as we reached the road. "I'm not used to it still," he said quietly, his hands finding his pockets. "The others have been doing this for a long time. They know how to handle themselves in these situations. I like the work, and the responsibility, but having everyone fawning over me is a little unsettling."

"Well, you don't let on. You're a natural." I recalled the image of him sitting on his chair, his *throne*, with poise, and self-assurance, and those glittering freckles. I swallowed hard.

"Your breathing seems strained already, like yesterday. It's worse than usual," he noted.

"Em, it's not all that," I mumbled, reaching up to

rub the back of my neck and wordlessly swearing at my lungs for giving me away so easily. "Yesterday I was a little flustered when we met."

"Did something happen?"

I was waiting to unload everything I'd been told on Henry, and I knew I probably still would, but I figured it wouldn't hurt to tell Breck, too.

"Anne shared some precious news with me yesterday. She's not had any luck starting their family since they got married, despite their best efforts," I said. I didn't like to think of those efforts going on so near to where I slept every night, but I supposed it had to happen somehow. Breck nodded thoughtfully.

"We should talk to Finna. Maybe she has some concoction that will help. You know that's her favorite thing to do," he said.

I glanced at him, eyebrows raised. "Really? There's something for that?"

He shrugged. "Couldn't hurt to ask." I hadn't expected him to have advice on the matter, but this lifted my spirits about the situation immediately. If Finna could make something for Anne like she'd done for me, then surely, they would get to keep this baby.

"I also ran into Thomas right before we met. I haven't got a clue where he heard it from, but he's too dense to have made it up just to annoy me, I think. Apparently, it's being said that I'm due to court Emma Clare, the lass we talked about at the engagement party."

"The sister who talks about you all the time," he added, and I nodded. "That's not surprising."

"Why not?" I asked, more defensive than I meant it to be. Breck looked at his feet for a moment and then back ahead of him on the road, grinning. Birds were starting to twitter in the trees around us. I wished they wouldn't. It was nice to have that time with just the two of us and nobody else.

"She's not the only one whose lips your name is on. I'm sure she's just got more pull than all the other maidens who wish to catch your eye at your matches."

My mouth fell open as I turned to look at him. Was Thomas really telling the truth? Why hadn't Henry told me any of this? Maybe he didn't know either. The fact that Breck knew made me feel even worse. I had no idea what to say, so I just groaned and rubbed my eyes with my thumb and forefinger.

"Is it really so bad?" Breck asked. "Do you not wish to get married and have children? I've learned that's what most humans want." I had to force my face to stay neutral. Was I about to explain why I would never get married or have children to the fella I'd *sucked off* the day before? I'd never had to talk about this so openly. Not even with Henry. If too many details started coming out, he got weird, and we changed the subject. I didn't blame him for it.

"I—" I started, pausing. "I like lads," I said, my face heating. I'd never said it so bluntly before, maybe even to myself.

"Okay," Breck said, as if that part was obvious. At least we were on the same page there.

"*Only* lads," I added. This seemed to register as his expression changed slightly.

"Okay," he repeated, this time with a little more understanding. "I guess I could see the problem, then." A nervous laugh got caught in my throat. "I'm not sure Finna can make you something for that."

"Too bad," I said. Then I realized I wasn't sure if he meant something to strip the girls of their feelings for me, or something for my attraction to the same sex, so I clarified with, "I just hate feeling like a fraud. Emma Clare – and I guess the others – are just doing what feels right to them, all because I can't be truthful."

"I can imagine that would be very difficult for you," Breck said as the mill came into view. "If only humans could hear thoughts or feel emotions like I can. That would make it much easier."

I cut my eyes to him. "Feel emotions?" He met my gaze and nodded, an apologetic look growing on his features. I was starting to realize something about fairy magic. It might seem cool in a storybook, but damn if it wasn't continually embarrassing to experience in real life.

"I wouldn't be able to do my work if I couldn't. Even Carrick must have a sense on how the flora is feeling. Otherwise, how would he know to bring Elina or Fallon to make sure they have what they need to grow? How could Murray and I take care of the creatures in our waters if we couldn't feel them responding to their environment?"

As we reached the worn, wooden door to the mill, my mind was juggling this information. Breck must've felt this, too, because he reached out to touch my arm. My eyes shifted to his. Deep blue. Wise. Powerful. Beautiful. *Enchanting.*

"Are you really only twenty?" I asked. He nodded, his mouth twisting a little at the corner like he was thinking of something to say. I didn't give him the chance; I grabbed his face in my hands and kissed him. His hands came to my elbows, then slid to the backs of my shoulders.

"Come inside," he whispered against my lips, and we broke apart just long enough to stumble in and shut the door behind us. Breck's back ended up against the wall, and he shifted us over some so his head was in between the hooks hanging there. It was darker inside the mill with its few, small windows letting in the early morning light. The powdery smell of fresh grains surrounded us as I pressed my hips against his and kissed his cheek and jaw. It was nice being the same height. I knew where everything was because it was a reflection of myself, though his shoulders and hips were narrower than mine.

"You know what I'm feeling all the time?" I asked in between my lips finding new places to touch his skin. He nodded again as he leaned his head to the side, giving me more room to kiss his neck.

"I can't block it out like I can with your thoughts. It's just—" he paused to exhale sharply as I sucked on the freckled skin by his collarbone, "it's all around you. Like the air."

"What am I feeling now?" My thoughts were fuzzy in my head. Breck let out a breathy laugh and swallowed against my lips that had returned to his neck.

"That one's easy. I can feel it pressed against my hip." My riding breeches didn't leave much for interpretation down there, usually to my dismay. I pressed harder against him, enough to earn one of his small moans, and he pulled my head up and kissed me deeply.

I was just about to reach for something, any piece of clothing I came to first, to start removing it, when Breck brought his hands to my shoulders abruptly and pushed me away. Our eyes met and he looked sorry.

"*Go upstairs. Quick,*" he whispered in a rush. He stood up away from the wall as soon as I moved, and I did as he told me. I tried not to let my boots clack on the steps too hard as I bolted up them. I stopped in the middle of his room and put both hands over my mouth to hopefully muffle some of my panting. There was silence for a few seconds, and then I heard the door click open. "Mornin'," Breck said to whomever came inside.

"Hello, Breck, good morning." My eyes went wide, and I dropped to a crouch where I stood, as if getting lower would hide me better. My hands remained over my mouth. It was Anne.

"How can I help you today? One bag enough?" My heart pounded in my chest as I listened. I wondered if he was hiding his tented trousers behind the counter, or if the shock of being interrupted had helped it fade.

"I actually came to ask if you'd seen Peter since yesterday." I swallowed hard and pushed my fingers into my hair, my elbows on my knees. "He never came home last night, and that's not like him." I could picture the expression on her face just by the tone of her voice. Slightly concerned and slightly cross. She'd picked that up from Nan.

"Yes, I've seen him," Breck said, not giving away any hints in his words or his voice. "There was a party."

"Hm. Maybe he stayed the night with Henry." There was a pause that told me she wasn't quite sure she could believe him, but she wasn't going to argue it. I imagined she was giving the storeroom a subtle once-over to make sure I wasn't hiding anywhere. "Thank you for your help. We have a bit of flour left, I believe, but you know I'll be back soon."

"I'll be here," Breck said, as friendly as ever. The door opened and shut, and I let out a massive sigh as I stood up, which made me cough. I looked toward the steps as Breck appeared on them.

"That was close," I said, one hand on my forehead and the other on my hip. "I'm sorry. I'm glad you didn't have to lie."

"I couldn't have lied," he reminded me, stopping a short distance away. "Sometimes I have to stretch the truth, though. Avoid the question. It's a skill you pick up quickly." He stepped closer and reached out to hook a finger in the front of my waistband, tugging me toward him. There wasn't much extra room to do that in my riding breeches. "You look good in these," he said, his voice low.

"I should probably go. If she finds Henry before I do..." I let the end of my sentence hang, and he kept his eyes trained on his hands at my waistband, waiting. Henry could lie for me all he wanted. He was pretty good at it, too, charming as he was. "But a few more minutes probably won't change anything," I added.

Breck's mouth spread into a grin as he unfastened my breeches with deft fingers.

He kissed me slowly and pushed me back until I was against the wall by his stove, which sat cold. I opened my eyes and watched him as he sank to his knees. He attempted to peel down my breeches, working them side by side off my thighs, but they weren't coming down fast enough for him. Instead, he pulled me out through the fly and directly into his mouth.

I was desperate to hold onto something. One hand went out to grip the stove; the other wrapped into his hair. He ran his tongue flat against the length of me, from bollocks to tip, his hand taking over as he looked up. "I'm going to be gone for a few days with the others. We're meeting with Eabha. I'm sorry I'll miss your next game."

I almost asked him what game he was talking about. Then I remembered. *That's right, I play polo,* I thought through the fog. I nodded, struggling to keep my eyes open and my legs sturdy beneath me. I loosened my fingers in his hair when I realized how tightly I has holding onto it. Keeping still was torture, but his other hand was pressed into my hip, holding me firm against the wall. He was stronger than he looked.

I leaned my head back, breathing hard. His mouth was on me again. His tongue, teasing. His lips, squeezing. I could feel the sting of mint, the same way I could feel it in my mouth when we kissed. Typically, a cold sensation there wasn't pleasant, but this was enough to push me toward and over the edge in near-record time. He didn't lean away from me until I was completely spent, taking everything I gave.

He stood up before I let go of his hair, and our eyes met. I pushed my fingers through it to the back of his neck as he fixed my breeches for me. "You have chores to get to. I'll see you when I return," he said quietly. I leaned forward and pulled him closer to me at the same time. Our lips met for a short kiss, and then I left him.

I spent the whole day training. Thomas was right. I'd been busy, and my horses were suffering for it. Wally also made sure to keep both eyes on me as we worked, shouting critiques one after the other. I probably deserved it. Even after several rough hours in the saddle, though, I realized nothing was going to bring me down from the cloud I was on.

***

We won our game the next day. I ate supper with my family. I watched Anne and William closely at the table, searching for any signs that something was wrong. There were none. I read Lucy her story for bed that night with a fresh perspective. Her hair was getting so long; tendrils of it tickled my arm that was around her where we reclined against the ample pillows on her bed. When I was done, she asked if we could read it again. I said we could, but only if she read it to me. She agreed.

Several days passed this way. It was almost as if my life had returned to normal. I allowed myself to think about Breck only when it didn't interfere with my work. The chestnut mare was quickly approaching a place where I might be able to trust her during a match. I was riding her, and Henry was beside me on his own horse, as we looped over a hill on our favorite trail at a walking pace. We'd already run them on it twice.

"I told Sarah to tell her sister, *all* her sisters, that they better leave you the feck alone," he said. I laughed shortly and glanced at him. "I love you like a brother, and you know I do, but I can't share sisters with you."

"I'm not sure that's how that works, actually," I told him. We both grimaced at the thought.

"Well, never mind that, I need to keep somebody on the outside that I can talk to. Just imagine if we both had to live with all that drama every day! I'm truly taking one for the team. And so are you for listening to me complain. You know it's not really that bad. Sarah is grand."

"I know." Their wedding was approaching quickly. Henry floundered daily, sometimes hourly, between feeling confident and nervous about it. I tried to tell him that he was putting too much pressure on himself. He said it was Sarah doing all the pressuring, along with his own sisters and mammy.

"How's your miller?" he asked then, catching me off-guard. I let the words settle. I listened to the sounds of the horses' hooves beating into the ground with each rhythmic stride. Henry had known my secret for years, nearly as long as I had, but it still surprised me when he spoke about it so casually when we were alone.

"He's away, working," I told him.

"Lots of faraway meetings to be had in the flour business?" he joked, and I grinned at him, shaking my head. He laughed and tipped his chin up toward the trail ahead of us. "Best two outta three?" He didn't need a response, and I didn't give one. Our horses took off under our command. I'd been able to develop the chestnut mare's agility on the field, and get her nervous energy under better control when we were right up against another horse, but when it came to a full out sprint, she was my girl. I'd never ridden another horse who could run like her. She truly lived for it.

I leaned into her as we overtook Henry on our approach to the river. It had rained the day before, so the water was running swiftly on all our other passes, which didn't thrill the mare. I began to brace myself mentally, just in case she decided to respond differently this time. When I could finally see the spot where the trail took us across, I felt her energy shift under me. Winning wasn't worth the risk of getting thrown into the river; I let up on her so we could slow down. This wasn't enough to please her, though, and she tossed her head and squealed in protest. Then I realized what was upsetting her.

I pulled her back and we veered off the trail into the grass so Henry and his horse wouldn't slam into us from behind. They went around us at full speed, and he shouted something at me as I turned the mare in a tight circle, whipping my head around to look at the river. Or rather, the bed of the river.

"What the feck—" Henry had stopped his horse right at the bank. He turned to look at me, and our eyes met briefly as I moved the mare over next to his horse. There was barely a trickle of water moving along where a healthy flow had been on our last pass on the trail. We blinked down into the gully, both trying to process what we were seeing. "Do you think it's dammed up somewhere?"

"I don't know," I said seriously, looking in the direction the water should've been coming from. I directed the mare onto the riverbed, and she listened, moving carefully forward into the shallow mud. I could still feel the nervousness in her muscles beneath me, her steps slightly prancy and uncertain in the muck.

"Should we follow it down to see where it's blocked?" Henry asked, already moving his horse in that direction with a pull of the reins and a squeeze of his legs. I watched him go for a moment before I moved the mare back up onto the grass on the opposite side of the riverbed. We took up a quicker pace and looked as far down the land as we could see. The only time I'd ever seen the water this low was when Breck—

Suddenly, his words came at me like a slap to the back of the head. *When I feel strong emotions that I cannot control, such as pain or pleasure, the river responds in kind.* If pleasure was what had sent the river surging, then having it all but dry up must mean...

"Ride ahead and check that way," I called to Henry. I didn't wait for him to say anything before I whirled the mare around and kicked into her sides. I was never more grateful to be riding a bullet. We tore across the land, abandoning the trail as I directed us toward the shortcut to Finna's. I couldn't explain why, but something was telling me to go there first.

The ride gave me just enough time to work myself into a state. My heart and head were racing with thoughts of what could be going on. Maybe I was completely wrong, and I was just overreacting, but my gut told me that I should trust a lifetime of knowing this river. Even during the times of year when it didn't rain as often, it took days to see a significant change in the water. This had happened too suddenly to be nature's doing.

When we made it to the cottage, I dismounted in one swift motion and tied the mare up with shaking fingers. I took a few slow, deep breaths, coughed them out, and rubbed my palms hard against the seams on my breeches. The door opened as I approached it, and Elina peered out at me.

"Peter," she said. For someone who could quite literally glow, her face looked awfully pale. She reached for me and hugged me around my arms so I couldn't return the gesture.

"What happened? What's wrong?" I asked as she ushered me inside. I looked toward the sitting room. Carrick was there, on the chair by the fireplace, and Fallon was glaring at the sleeping hearth, her arms crossed tightly across her chest. They both looked a little worn and disheveled like Elina. They turned their heads to look at me, and Fallon made a disgusted noise in the back of her throat.

"Oh good. Come to cause more problems for us?" she demanded. I gave her a confused look and she rolled her eyes, brushing past me on her way out the door I'd just come through.

"She doesn't always handle her emotions well during trying times," Carrick said from his chair. "Don't worry about her."

"Where's Breck?" I asked, looking from him to Elina. I hadn't seen Finna yet, either.

"Finna is with him. He's resting. He—" Elina stopped, considering her words as her tired, honey-brown eyes searched mine.

"He made a reckless mistake," Carrick finished for her. Elina shot him a look as if to say he could've said it a little more gently than that.

"Is he hurt?" I asked, swallowing at the sour feeling in my stomach. I already knew the answer, thanks to the looks on their faces and the state of the river, but I had to ask anyway. I needed someone to tell me what was happening.

"Murray is trying his best to return the river levels to normal before the hu— before anyone becomes concerned," Elina explained. "You're very observant."

"Anyone could see that the river is *dried up*," I returned, getting agitated with the avoidance in her reply. "Tell me the truth," I said, quieter.

"He's hurt," she confirmed, looking down at her bare toes that peeked out from underneath her skirts.

"Hello, love." I turned at the sound of Finna's sweet, raspy voice. She looked just as wrung out as the rest of them. I went to her and stooped to give her a hug. She wrapped her arms around me and kissed my cheek. "He's asked for you," she said, looking toward her bedroom door. "I'll put on some tea."

I closed the door behind me as quietly as I could. The smell of the room clobbered my senses. It was so strong, and such a strange mix, that my lungs betrayed me. I coughed into the crook of my elbow, trying to mask the volume of it.

"It's their magic," Breck spoke weakly. His eyes were still closed.

"I'm sorry?" I said, coming closer.

"The smell. It's their magic. To help me recover," he explained. That must've been why they all looked so exhausted. They had put all their magic into him.

"Are you alright?" I asked, deciding to sit next to his hip. Finna's bed was small, only big enough for one person, and the ropes under the mattress sagged heavily with my added weight.

"Better now," he said, his lips forming a small grin.

"I'm being serious," I said. This scene brought back enough bad memories to have me on edge. Breck finally opened his eyes, looking at me. I had to admit I missed those blue eyes, even though he'd only been gone for a few days. I'd thought about them, and those freckles, the curve of his nose, and the arch of his lips.

"As am I." He blinked a few times, sleepily. I coughed again and decided to be bold, reaching up to comb my fingers through his hair to the side the way he liked to wear it. His eyes closed again, and he breathed slowly, his lips slightly parted.

"I'll let you rest," I told him quietly. He was already asleep.

I eased myself off the bed and went to rejoin the others in the sitting room. Finna put a cup of tea in my hands the moment I sat down next to Elina on the sofa. I wished it was mint as I took a sip. Elina glanced at me, and a faint smile came to her mouth as she looked back down at her own cup. She was reading something about me. Thoughts or emotions, I wasn't sure, but I tried to shut them down to avoid embarrassing myself.

"Henry and I have been crossing the river all day training. The water just changed. When did this happen?" I asked.

"We've just arrived back." Carrick cleared his throat, and I got the sense he was preparing to tell me more, when Fallon came back inside and shut the door louder than she needed to. They all looked at her, but my gaze fell to the floor as I took another sip of my tea. I didn't want to make her any angrier than I already had just by being there.

Fallon said something to the others in their words I didn't know, but her spitting tone was all I needed to hear to understand how she felt. I went to get up and excuse myself from the situation, but she shot me a look. "Sit down," she barked, and so I stayed where I was. Breck had said she and Elina were the oldest. Maybe she was like Nan. Old enough that she didn't give two shites what anyone else thought of her and what she said or did.

Elina spoke back to Fallon, and she touched my arm as she did. I listened carefully to the words she said, trying to pick out anything familiar, but I couldn't. When I finally looked up, Fallon was glowering at me, arms crossed again. She looked as drained as the rest of them. Whatever it was that had happened, Breck must've been near death if it took that much effort to bring him back.

Fallon sat swiftly in one of the other chairs, her back straight and arms still tight across her body. I glanced out the window as heavy raindrops started to fall against it. Dark clouds had gathered in the sky above the small cottage. Fallon must've done that to help Murray fill the river back up.

"We were away to meet with Eabha," Carrick finally continued. "There are many important things to discuss this time of year."

"Breck got it in his head to be a *hero* and took his chance to sneak off to meet with the Unseelie," Fallon cut in, spilling what I guessed Carrick was working toward.

"As such a young fairy, he doesn't have the strength to face them in their realm for long. Breck is very powerful, but not enough to go there alone," Elina explained.

"Why would he do that?" I asked. Part of me felt a tug to protect him against their harsh criticism. They were speaking about him the way I might talk about Lucy. Just a child. To them, though, he was.

"Your influence on him has been incorrigible," Fallon said coldly. "No matter how much warning we give, no matter how much trouble our young ones get into, humans are irresistible. Until they get hurt. Until they learn the hard way that humans cannot be trusted. Not as friends, not as *lovers*." I felt my cheeks flush at her implications.

"Peter, when we learned what had happened to you, we knew that we had to get closer to you if we ever wanted to uncover the truth about this human sickness." Elina's hand was still on my arm. The place where her palm and fingers were touching had grown warm. Her magic must've been returning. "Soon, Breck will come of age, and he must prove himself to Eabha – to all of us – that he's committed to helping humans," she continued. "We gave him this task... well, we gave him *you*."

"And then he went and nearly got himself killed trying to find answers," Carrick said.

"Because he's let his emotions and desires get in the way of his responsibilities." Fallon stood again, shooting out of the chair and stalking to the window to stare out at the weather.

"Nothing has gotten in the way of my responsibilities." All of us turned in unison to look where Breck was leaning against the frame of the bedroom door. Finna rushed to his side from where she'd been sitting silently during all of this.

"You need to rest, love," she told him, but helped him forward anyway. He eased himself onto the spot on the sofa that Elina and I made for him between us. I studied his profile as he had to move with some effort to pull his legs up to cross under him. His thigh rested against mine, and I resisted the urge to offer a comforting touch. He looked so tired.

"You can be angry with me all you like, Fallon. But I went there to get answers that I knew I could get."

"You're a fool," she said plainly. She came back over from the window and said more to Breck in unfamiliar words. He responded back, and I had to fight incredibly hard to not think about how attractive his voice was speaking those foreign sounds and inflections. *Not the time*, I told myself. They argued back and forth, Fallon cutting him off several times, before Carrick and Elina's attention perked at something he said. He seemed to be relieved by getting whatever he'd said off his chest, and his head dropped against the back of the sofa, his eyes closing. Immediately after, all their eyes shifted to me.

"What?" I blurted out, nervous. Had he told them something about me? Something we'd done together? Breck swallowed, his throat working with his head bent back, and he breathed in deeply before he spoke.

"I realized that we had been looking at it all wrong," he started. I stared at him, uncertainty filling me up over the fact that he might have actually learned something important, despite his risky behavior. Without thinking, I reached and grabbed his hand in mine, waiting.

"Tell us," Finna encouraged him gently from her chair.

"We were so focused on it being malicious." He paused, licking his lips and picking his head back up. His eyes remained closed. "We discovered the presence of dark magic and assumed the worst, fearing that the Unseelie had a hand in killing these people."

"How could we not? All the evidence pointed to it," Elina said. I felt a twinge in my chest, thinking about the dark magic that lived inside my lungs now.

"He's the only one, Elina." Breck opened his eyes then and looked down at his lap. He turned over the hand I wasn't holding and opened his fingers, revealing two crumpled silk ribbons. Elina drew in a slow gasp and reached for the strips of fabric. She took them from him and cupped her hands around them, closing her eyes and tilting her head like she was trying to listen to something. A glow bloomed from her slowly, filling the space with her warm light.

"*Oh*," she whispered, her eyes opening. She looked at Breck, then at me. I couldn't read the look on her face. It was something between sadness and hope. "Fallon, look," she said, her voice still quiet. Fallon sighed impatiently and grabbed the ribbons from her hands, copying what Elina had done.

The dampness and smell of fresh rain swirled around me, and I realized that was the first time I'd felt her magic. Slowly, the tightness in her face eased. Her shoulders relaxed a little. Then a frown formed on her lips, her eyebrows came together, and she opened her eyes. She all but threw the ribbons back into Elina's hands and marched outside into the rain.

"Someday she's going to break that door off its hinges," Carrick chuckled, standing up to take the ribbons from Elina. He repeated their actions, hands clasped and eyes closed, and the earthy smell of tilled peat filled the room. His eyebrows went up and he nodded slightly before his eyes opened quicker than Fallon or Elina's had, apparently learning all he needed to in just a few seconds. "Well done, lad," he said, placing his large hand on Breck's head before he went around the sofa and left us to join Fallon.

"Come on, then, you two. Share with those of us who can't see," Finna said, hands on her hips behind us. "Peter looks as if he'll be sick if you don't stop filling this room with magic, anyway." They focused on me, and I realized she was right. My head felt light and dizzy. I took my last sip of tea and blinked hard a few times. Breck let his head rest back against the sofa again, and Elina gave me a new look of wonder. She reached across

Breck to hold the ribbons out for me. Finna took my cup so I could take them. They just felt like normal strips of silk in my hands. Nothing special at all.

"What are they?" I asked.

"They're wishes," Elina said, smiling. My eyes narrowed in confusion, and I felt Breck's thumb start to rub against my fingers. Again, our hands together felt so natural that I'd forgotten about them.

"Oh, my word," Finna gasped, her hand coming to her mouth. "*Breckabhainn*, you took from the *Wishing Tree*?"

"I didn't remove them, Finna. They had already been taken down."

"Wishes?" I queried, looking at the ribbons in my hand again. There was nothing written on them. Nothing attached to them. The threads looked a little loose on the ends where they'd been cut at an angle, and one of them was a little dirty like it'd been lying on the ground, but that was it.

"The Wishing Tree is a very special place. Sacred to the fair folk, and one of the only places where our two worlds overlap with any regularity," Elina said. "Only those who believe in our kind can find it, and even then, it's quite difficult. You take a ribbon to the Wishing Tree, speak your wish into it, and then tie it onto one of Her many branches. It must be tied tightly."

"If your ribbon falls on its own, your wish is granted with Eabha's blessing," Breck added.

"But your wish can also be chosen," Elina continued, excitement lacing her words. She was eyeing the ribbons like they were the most magical thing she'd ever seen, despite the fact that her whole body was made of the stuff. "If this happens, a fairy unties the ribbon and uses their magic to grant the wish. Only the strongest, most powerful fairies are able to do this, so many wishes remain tied in place for a very long time – sometimes forever."

"Members of both courts can choose wishes. Humans don't realize that their wish might be granted by a fairy with ill intentions. They'll demand something in return." Breck turned his head against the sofa and searched my eyes with his before he continued. "Often, they seek out wishes with the most desperate voices, because they know the person is willing to give up more to get their wish."

I looked down at the ribbons in my hand again. "Whose are these? Whose wishes?" Breck and Elina exchanged a glance, and Elina gave him a disapproving look.

"I don't know if—" she started, but Breck sat up and cut her off.

"I'm fine. Help me," he told her. She hesitated for a moment, but relented as she took his hand. They both looked at me then; Elina was holding her other hand out for mine.

"Hold the ribbons between our hands," she instructed. I extended my hand, and she took it, clasping our fingers together over the strips of silk. They both closed their eyes, so I closed mine, too. The silence of Finna's sitting room gradually gave way to a confusing blend of voices echoing in my ears. I tried to differentiate them, focusing hard on what I was hearing.

"*Please— everything— never forgive me— lost— I won't—*"

My hands were a split of fire and ice as Breck's magic curled up the hand he was still holding, and Elina's heat crept up the other. Crying mixed with the voices now. I felt a surge up both arms as they held my hands tighter. Then, one voice became clearer over the other.

"*I can't lose him. He's got to pull through this. Please. Please save him,*" a woman spoke, sounding echoey and far away, pleading through her sobs. "*William will never forgive me if his whole family is lost on my watch. I'll give anything.*"

William? As in... my *brother* William? The crying faded, and the other voice got louder.

"*I love you. I love you. I love you, Peter. You're every-thing good in my life. I can't live without you. I won't—*"

I yanked my hands back and got up, taking a few steps toward the hearth. There was no stopping the tears that burned at my eyes. My hands came up to clutch at my shirt and the ache in my chest as a pair of arms wrapped around my middle. It was Finna.

"I—" was all I could manage before the coughing began. At least, it started as coughing, before it dissolved into a mix of coughing and trying not to cry. More arms came around me then, and I was guided into the chair by the fireplace. "*Anne? And Jamie?*" I whispered, eyes searching Elina's as she looked into mine. She nodded slowly. I looked at Breck, who was still on the sofa. He looked like he'd just witnessed an assault.

Maybe he had, if the wounded, whumping muscle in my chest counted for anything.

He knew. He knew I would hear their voices, his voice, and that it would break my heart all over again. I looked away from him then, wiping angrily at my eyes before the tears could fall. Their pleading voices were still echoing in my head. He'd loved me. I knew that. I knew for a long time. But we'd never said it. I'd never heard him say it to me. I'd wanted to tell him so badly that I loved him. So many times, the words had been at the tip of my tongue. I'd been too afraid.

He'd loved me enough to make a wish on my life being spared. He and Anne both had.

"The dark magic isn't what made me sick," I said finally, my voice unsteady as the truth settled in my head. "It's what made me live."

"You must've been so ill, Peter," Finna said grievously, her own voice breaking with emotion as she stroked my hair. I noticed that Fallon and Carrick had come back at some point and tried harder to pull myself together.

"Your mate gave up his life for yours," Fallon mumbled, her eyes unfocused and cast down, like she was talking to herself out loud.

"We don't know that," I said defensively, drawing her attention. "His whole family died from the illness." I paused, my tone softening. "He came to see me, when I was sick. I always blamed myself for it. I thought I gave it to him."

"Maybe he would've been better off that way."

"Fallon!" Elina whirled on her. "How could you say that?"

Fallon scowled back. "You know *exactly* how I could say that," she said tightly. Nobody else spoke. Finna fussed over me silently, wiping at my face with the soft sleeve of her dress, still petting my hair and cheeks like I was a newborn baby who needed tending to.

"I need to check on my horse," I said finally. I got to my feet and walked out, sending out as much *leave me alone* energy I could possibly muster. It must've worked, because nobody came after me. I apologized to the mare for leaving her out in the rain as I untied her, and we rode off into the weather without looking back.

FIFTEEN

I couldn't bring myself to get out of bed the next morning.

Nan came to check on me and bring me some tea and toast. Midday, Lucy and Anne took their turns making sure I was alright. I didn't make eye contact with Anne as she spoke to me. They swapped my uneaten breakfast for another plate of food that I didn't touch. None of them came at supper time.

After sleeping for most of the day, I was wide awake as the light faded outside. I didn't feel sick, exactly, but there was a weight on my chest that I couldn't shake. I probably would've felt better if I had gotten up and gone to work, but I'd had no willpower to do it. Eventually, I dragged myself out from under my blankets to splash some water on my face. My gaze stayed low to avoid my reflection in the mirror; I didn't want to look at the man whose life had been spared at the expense of someone else's.

Had Jamie known what he was doing when he spoke his wish into that ribbon? Did he understand that he was risking his own life by trying to save mine? He loved me. I loved him, and he loved me, and I would've done the same thing for him, given the chance. I crawled back under my covers and pulled them up over my head. I'd just settled into a comfortable position when my door opened, and little feet came across the wood floor.

"Can we read in your bed instead of mine tonight?"

I moved my blankets down and nearly jumped when I realized Lucy's face was right in front of me. "Sure, Luc." I held the covers up for her to get under them with me. Fortunately for both of us, I'd been too unmotivated to even remove my clothes like I normally would have before bed. Lucy set her candle on the table and climbed in next to me, resting her head on the pillow beside mine. She opened her book to the beginning and started on the first line. I listened to the slight inflections in her voice as she said the words I'd read to her a hundred times before. After a few pages, I closed my eyes. She didn't need my help with this story.

"You're not looking at the pictures," she complained, and I opened my eyes again.

"I can see them in my mind," I told her. At that point I probably could've drawn them from memory, but I took the opportunity to compliment her instead. "You do such a good job painting the pictures with your words that I don't even need to look."

"Well, look anyway," she said, before returning to where she'd left off. I nodded and put my eyes back on the page, reading silently along with her. A breeze came through my open window and lifted my curtains gently; the flame on the candle flickered. I glanced up at the moment I felt a slight chill come over me. The faintest minty sensation filled my lungs on my next breath. The day before, I would've been leaning out my window in seconds, looking for the source. Instead, I exhaled deep and slow to rid my lungs of the crispness and looked back down at Lucy's storybook.

***

If riding horses my whole life had taught me anything, it was that problems had to be faced, not avoided. That was the only reason the chestnut mare had come so far. I hadn't let her behavior scare me away or control the situation. She'd learned to trust me only because I'd given her situations that demanded her trust. I'd learned to trust her the same way.

This was my mentation as we returned to the stables after winning our match. We were all tired after a very competitive game. Even Thomas was riding in silence. A light, misting rain was falling as we arrived, and we turned our teams over to the hands who rushed to meet us. Wally was busy giving them instructions as the three of us wandered into the tack room to put our equipment away.

"The chestnut looked grand out there, Pete. You've really done a lot with her," Henry said, praising my efforts. I scrubbed my fingers through my hair, scratching my scalp after finally removing my helmet for the first time since that morning.

"Thanks." I had critiques on her performance at the ready, but I decided to just let it settle for the night. There was plenty of time to work on those tomorrow and the next day. I hadn't been doing anything except working, sleeping, and eating when someone put food in front of me.

Why was it so much easier to face problems with my animals than it was to face them with people? Was it because I understood horses better? I could judge the flick of an ear or the twitch of a muscle and know what my horse was thinking. I could be two steps ahead of her and brace for a reaction to something, if I was lucky enough to see it coming.

People were unpredictable. They had thoughts and emotions and experiences that influenced each action and reaction in a way that made them impossible to foresee. Even Henry could still surprise me sometimes with how he responded to things. I sighed and slid my feet out of my riding boots and removed my thick leather knee guards, not bothering to sit down. I was afraid if I did, I might not have the energy to get back up again. I also wanted to hurry up and leave before Henry could question my short reply. I hoped that he was too tired to talk like I was.

"See you tomorrow, fellas," was all he said as he bumped the side of his fist against my shoulder on his way out.

I reached down to guide my other boots on and trailed after him a few moments later. "Thomas," I said with little enthusiasm. He grunted at me in response. I stepped out into the gentle rain, squinting my eyes up at the clouds, and took my time on the walk up to the house.

I still hadn't talked with Anne about what I'd learned. I wasn't sure how to broach the subject. The sound of her crying pleas kept replaying in my head. I didn't know for certain, but I could only imagine that the tears were fueled by the trauma of watching the rest of my family take their last breaths. She'd known I was going to die, too, and had made the wish on that ribbon as a last attempt to save my life. It was terribly unsettling knowing that I had been so close to never waking up again.

I pushed our loud kitchen door open. Nan turned to look at me briefly before she went back to cutting something with her tired fingers. "I can't tell if your game went well or not by the look on your face," she said.

"We won, but barely. I put the new mare in for the first time." I contemplated sitting on one of the stools by the counter, but I really just wanted to go lie on my bed.

"John Wallace is lucky that you're such a talented horseman. I'm still not happy that you took her on, but I'm proud of you for sticking with it and making something of her."

"Thank you, Nan. I'm going to go wash up." I excused myself and climbed the stairs, legs heavy and muscles sore from the hours of keeping myself anchored in the saddle. My shirt was unbuttoned by the time I shut my door behind me. I stopped short when I noticed what was on the table beside my bed.

My eyes remained on the teacup and white envelope as I removed my shirt and kicked off my shoes. I stepped around the corner of my bed and slid the cup to the side, battling with myself over how much I wanted to drink the tea; to let the mint and honey wash through me and soothe all the places that ached. I picked up the envelope and pulled out the folded parchment inside, opening it slowly.

When you're ready.

B

Was I ready to talk? What was I going to say? Thanks for crumbling two years of recovery in a single moment? Thanks for making my confliction over my feelings for you even more complicated?

No. I didn't need to say those things. I didn't need to say them, because I wasn't as weak as I felt sometimes. As it happened, yes, I felt like my world was completely shaken. But now, after giving it some time to settle, I realized that nothing had changed. I just had more information than I did before.

I put the paper back inside the envelope and set it down so I could remove the rest of my clothes. I wiped away the dirt and sweat from my skin with a wet rag, washed my face, and dressed for supper. I looked at the table again – at the cup of tea that was still steaming – and sighed as I gave in, reaching for it to take one sip before I went back downstairs.

***

The soft rain persisted into the night, having grown a little heavier after the sun disappeared behind the hills. I pushed my hand back through my damp curls as I stood at the door of the old mill. I hadn't knocked yet. There was no light in the upstairs windows, but I'd still walked myself across the bridge and down the hill to stand there, waiting. I wasn't sure what I was waiting for.

Breck knew, somehow, when others were approaching. He must've known I was there. Maybe he was the one waiting for me. I raised my hand and rapped my knuckles against the thick wood a few times. There was no response. I took a few steps backward to look up at the windows again, blinking up into the precipitation. They were still dark. I turned then, deciding that he wasn't home. Perhaps Finna had demanded that he stay at the cottage longer so she could continue helping him gain his strength back. I'd been tossing and turning in bed for several hours before I convinced myself to get up, but I was too tired to walk all the way to Finna's. I'd only made it a few steps back toward the road when I heard something behind me.

"Wait," his voice came, and I turned to find Breck in the doorway, chamberstick in hand.

"I didn't know if you were home," I told him quietly. Judging by his disheveled hair and the tired expression on his face, he had been sleeping, though maybe as restlessly as I had been.

"You got my note," he said, giving me a sleepy grin. When I didn't return it, as much as I wanted to, his face fell a little and he shifted his weight, looking at his feet for a moment. I closed the distance between us and stared up at him. He was slightly taller standing on the step of the entryway.

I had so much to say. I'd been thinking nonstop about everything that I'd learned. I would've never known any of it if Breck hadn't done what he did. He was sent to me specifically to uncover more about what I'd gone through. He'd been assigned a task, and he'd completed it successfully. How could I be upset with him for doing his job?

"Do you want to come in out of the rain?" he tried again, looking up at the gloomy night sky above me. My eyes immediately went to the exposed skin of his throat, and then his mouth, before our eyes met again. I wasn't trying to make this moment uncomfortable, but none of my words were willing to come out. I found myself wishing that I hadn't told him to not listen to my thoughts.

I wanted to know more. I wanted to hear every detail of what he'd learned on his visit with the dark fairies who did this to me. What had they told him? Did he speak directly with the one who put this magic inside my lungs? Was I going to be stuck with this cough for the rest of my life? What about Jamie? Had his fate been sealed by his wish? Had he known he was going to die before it happened? Did he even know that I lived?

"He knew," Breck said, pulling my attention back from wherever it had gone. I studied the pained look on his face. He knew. *He knew.* I hadn't considered if that was better or worse.

"I told you not to do that," was all I could force out. It was such a petty thing to say, especially when I was the one who'd just wanted to ask him to do it. I sighed and closed my eyes, bringing my hand to hold my forehead. "I'm sorry."

"I want to help you," he said earnestly. A gust of wind blew from behind me, strong enough to rustle my wet hair. I opened my eyes and felt something in my chest at the few glittering flecks that had appeared on Breck's cheeks and nose from the drops of rain that reached them. The flame of the candle guttering between us brought me back to our night in the woods all over again.

"Is that all you want?" I asked, my voice low. His

eyebrows went up slightly as he seemed to consider my words. I struggled to keep my thoughts quiet in my head to give him time to answer without my influence. His lips parted as he went to say something, but then he paused and closed them again. I hoped this wouldn't be a time when he used his word trickery to avoid the truth. Finally, he tilted his head to the side a bit as he shook it slowly.

Heat bloomed in my chest as I reached up for his face and pulled it down to me so our lips could meet. Breck stumbled forward off the step, but he caught himself as his arms came around me. His chamberstick fell to the wet ground by our feet and the flame blinked out.

I crooked my fingers under his chin, tipping his head back as I pulled away from him. He kept his eyes closed against the raindrops falling onto his face, and I watched as more speckles appeared, catching the scant light around us. He swallowed and held me tighter, his eyebrows furrowing briefly before he breathed, "*I want you, Peter.*"

My hand fell and he opened his eyes, lifting his head back up to look at me. We stared at each other, droplets of rain rolling down our faces and dripping from our hair, soaking into our clothes. I knew he didn't have to ask me if I felt the same way. It had to be emanating from me like the heat from a fire. It probably had been for some time.

Again, my words seemed to be caught inside me, so all I could do was nod. Breck's grip on my hips tightened and he closed the small gap between us, pressing his mouth against mine for another kiss. Before I could reciprocate, he turned and pushed me past him toward the door that was still hanging open. As I lifted my foot to step inside, I felt his cold magic wrap around me in a rush, sliding over every bit of my skin like a silk sheet. I shivered violently and turned just in time to watch a whirling fog slip out the door before Breck closed it.

"What was that?" I asked. I couldn't see his expression in the dark, but I did watch his silhouette as he made sure to secure the lock on the door.

"Wet clothes are much harder to remove in a hurry," was all he said before he walked past me. I looked down and brought my hands to my chest, patting my shirt. I tried it again on my thighs. Everything was dry. I touched my hair next, finding my loose curls were no longer sopping, either. "Come on, then," he called, and I turned to find him waiting for me. I chased him up the stairs, which made him laugh playfully. I felt myself grin for the first time in a while.

"Can't you do that with our clothes, too?" I asked when I finally caught up to him, coughing a handful of times. I grabbed his hips and pulled him back against me, ducking my head to kiss the side of his neck. His clothes and hair were also free of any evidence of our time out in the rain.

"Where's the fun in that?" he responded. I could hear the smile in his voice, too.

We made quick work of the task. At some point I became aware of the glowing orbs on the shelves along the wall, lighting the room just enough to see. As Breck crawled across his bed, I took in the tossed bedclothes and pillows that he'd been sleeping in not long before. If I had been the slightest bit tired, it would've looked very inviting.

I climbed onto the bed after him, taking my time as my eyes trailed over his body, the low light creating dramatic shadows across his lithe figure. He kept his gaze trained on my face the whole time, silently beckoning me closer as he settled onto his back. I braced my arms on either side of his head and leaned down to kiss him.

"I would've liked this to stay," I said quietly, placing gentle kisses on his cheeks and nose that were now dry and no longer sparkling. His eyes opened with heavy lids, a soft smile on his lips. His hand came up to my arm to guide me onto my back; I let him take the position I'd been in, straddling my hips. Then, he reached above us to the large window and unhooked the latch, pushing one side of it open just slightly. The unmistakable roar of the falls outside returned to my ears, but my sense of touch overwhelmed all the others as Breck's lower body moved against mine while he worked on the window.

He took me by the wrist of the hand I had on his hip and held it up near the crack in the window. I felt his magic cool my fingers and palm. When he released his grip, I studied my hand and found it wet. Our eyes met again, and his lips curved into a smirk. I brought my fingertips up and swiped them delicately across one cheek, over his nose, and to the other cheek. Instantly, his skin glittered.

I let my touch continue down to his jaw, along his neck, and across his chest. My eyes trailed the path, and I was admittedly delighted when the last bit of moisture on my hand called out a few flecks of blue and silver with the freckles he had in those places, too.

His hips moved against me again, and I closed my eyes as his lips found my neck. He made a trail of gentle kisses down my chest before his mouth came to mine. Then he was moving again, leaning over the edge of the bed. I brought my hands up to brace his precarious position so he didn't fall off like I was sure I would have. When he sat back up, there was a tiny jar in his grip. It looked like the one Finna had given me with the healing salve inside. He carefully removed the lid and set it down on the narrow sill of the window. He must've felt my question as it formed in my head.

"Finna's creation," he explained, though it didn't help with my confusion. I watched as he dipped two of his fingers into the jar. When he removed them, the viscous liquid ran down toward his cupped palm, and he quickly set the jar down next to the lid and rubbed his hands together. It smelled nice enough, whatever it was made of. Breck leaned down to kiss me quickly before he shuffled backward on his knees.

I realized all at once what this concoction was for when he took me in his hands, coating me with the warm liquid. A shaky breath escaped me, and my hands came up, fingers knotting in my hair. I didn't know which view was more arousing – Breck's face focused on his task or his hands working on me. I decided to watch both, my eyes shifting up and down several times.

Breck reached up again to put his fingers in the jar, and he rubbed his hands together before he braced himself with one slick hand on my shoulder, the other disappearing behind him. He kissed me deeply, making a small sound against my mouth, and I let go of my hair to touch him wherever I could reach first. My pulse was already hammering. When he sat up again, I felt his grip return to me, and I was so distracted by the last remaining sparkles on his cheeks shimmering in the light that I didn't realize what was coming until it was happening. He let out a low moan as he lowered himself onto me slowly.

"Oh, *fuck*," I said under my breath, though it escaped me as more of a groan. Breck glanced up at me with a grin.

"So, he's not a mute lover after all," he quipped gently. I couldn't help but chuckle at that, even though my nerves were rattling around enough to make my hands shake. Both of us let our eyes fall to where we were now joined. After Breck had settled on me, he started to move, one hand still on my shoulder and the other on himself between us. I slid my hands to his thighs, kissed him when I could reach his mouth, and breathed. It was all my brain and lungs could manage at once.

When I told him I was close, we switched positions so that I was sitting over him again. He pushed one hand back through his hair, moving it to the side off his forehead, and his focus came back to where we were both working to finish ourselves. I watched as his face changed slightly, his eyebrows pinching closer together, and then he sighed heavily with a tiny whimper as he came.

A few more feverish strokes and I was hit with my own release. Our foreheads met as I tried to regain my composure and calm my lungs without coughing. His hand came to the back of my neck, and we remained like that until I could finally bring myself to move. Breck said something on an exhale in his words I didn't know, his eyes still closed.

"Sorry?" I asked. He opened one eye to peek at me before he closed it again, grinning.

"Mmm..." he paused, thinking. "There's not a good word for it in the human language." I found a towel and brought it to him. He wiped it across his chest and stomach before he dropped it on the ground by the bed.

"Well, hopefully it was something nice, at least," I said, and he laughed warmly. "You're not calling me a dirty bastard, are you?" I leaned down to sort through the pile of clothes we'd abandoned on the floor.

"Only if you feck me and leave me," he murmured. I stood up then and looked at him, holding a pair of trousers.

"You... want me to stay?" I asked, my confidence wavering.

"It's still early in the night. You can be home before morning."

"That's not what I asked," I countered. His grin grew, and mine did, too.

"I want you to stay." He pulled one leg up at the knee and swayed it side to side, giving me a show of what I'd be leaving. I dropped the trousers back to the floor. His hands came to the sides of my face as I joined him on the bed again, and he kissed me with that impish grin still on his lips. "*Dirty bastard,*" he whispered against my mouth.

In unison, the lights along the wall went out. I blinked into the darkness; Breck let me go and reached for the blankets bunched near our feet. I moved to help him pull them up over us, and I was surprised to discover how soft they were. He barely had any belongings in the tiny room, but I doubted even Henry slept in bedclothes so fine. And if he did, he certainly wasn't in bed with a beautiful creature curled up against his side underneath them like I was.

"I'll try to overlook the fact that you're thinking about someone else while you hold me," Breck said into the crook of my neck.

I choked on a laugh that was more like a scoff and moved my hand to the sway of his lower back, learning how to lie with someone in that very moment. It was better than I'd always imagined. "I figured jealousy was a human affliction."

Breck picked his head up to look at me. I could see him better now that my eyes were used to the low light again. "Fairies can be incredibly jealous when it comes to things we care about. Passion isn't a word saved for the bedroom. Fae will fight and defend and protect just as passionately as we love." As the words settled, his expression fell to something more serious, and he put his forehead against my cheek. "*Sé aiteall*," he said quietly, repeating what he'd said before. "It's like… the calm in the weather between two storms." It made sense for our circumstances. A brief, enjoyable pause in the difficult situation we had both been thrust into.

I circled my fingertips against his back, trying to comfort him. "I'm sorry that they forced you into this. I would've never wished for anyone else to have to be involved with it."

"I'm not sorry. At least, not about being a part of figuring out your case. I'm just sorry that what I've found has been so painful for you." I moved my free arm to wrap around him, and he pressed closer against my side, his bent knee coming up over me.

"Will you tell me what you learned?" I asked after a short stretch of silence.

"I'll tell you everything. But not tonight. The next storm can wait until tomorrow."

I nodded, which felt a lot like nuzzling my face against his hair, and closed my eyes. I breathed slowly, finally feeling exhaustion beginning to creep in. The smell of whatever had been in the jar was in Breck's hair from when he ran his fingers through it. I could still feel it on me between my legs, too.

"Was that the intended purpose of the contents of that jar?"

He practically giggled and propped himself up on his elbow, reaching to put the lid back on the forgotten glass container. My hand moved to his waist as I watched him, waiting for his response that he seemed to be stalling on. When he finally looked at me, it was the closest thing to bashful I'd ever seen on his features. "Finna said you would like it," he offered with a shrug.

"How long have you had it?" I pressed, not sure if I should be amused or mortified. I decided feeling both was acceptable for the situation. He brought his hand to my jaw and kissed me, his lips lingering on mine.

"Will the answer change your opinion of me?" His

fingers trailed down to my chest and beyond, coming to rest on my lower stomach. I shook my head. "She gave it to me the night of the party at Henry's," he confessed.

I laughed and then groaned, bringing my free hand to cover my eyes. "I really fecked that one up, didn't I?" Breck settled himself along my side again and laughed too, quietly against my chest.

"It doesn't matter now," he said.

SIXTEEN

Breck woke me up at first light with a cup of tea. We'd spent only a small part of the night sleeping. We made plans to meet at Finna's later that day. The rain had stopped, but clouds still hung low in the air. I decided to avoid the main road and took an alternative route after I'd crossed the bridge, following one of the horse trails that skirted the house but still took a relatively direct path to the stables.

I'd noted the way the river surged, and it brought a smile to my face.

When I was younger, sneaking around after a night out gave me a rush of adrenaline that was almost as enjoyable as the events of the evening. Whether I'd been out drinking with my friends, or secretly meeting Jamie somewhere private, it was the innocent fun of a boy learning how to navigate the world of rewards and punishments.

I no longer felt that way. The excitement had been replaced by resentment. I didn't know how to balance the feeling of not wanting to hide who I was anymore with the uncertainty of telling the truth. I'd spent my whole life trying to be the best version of myself for my family, which included hiding the parts of me that would upset them. When would I be ready to stop doing things just to protect them? Would I ever be ready?

I yawned as the stables came into view, and I realized I hadn't stopped to look at myself. Did Breck even have a mirror? I reached up to smooth my hair down and examined my clothes that he'd sorted through and hung on the back of a chair for me while I was still sleeping. Good enough.

I was already done with my morning chores and had my gray mare saddled when Henry finally appeared. "Shit, Pete. How'd your worm taste this morning?" he joked.

"It was delicious," I told him with a grin as I swung myself up onto the mare's back. We only had one match left in the season before the championship trophy would be awarded. I hoped my mare was prepared for an easy ride, however, because I was too tired for anything adventurous. "Do you want me to wait for you?"

"Sure, yeah," he answered from inside the stables. Wally was approaching from his small cottage, scratching his beard and looking as crotchety as always.

"Mornin', Wally," I called to him, causing my horse's ears to flick. He looked over at me and tipped his head in acknowledgement. It was his day to rest, but William was away for business, so nobody would come and tell him to stop working.

A short time later, Henry walked his horse out and over to the mounting block that was built into the fence of the round pen. He saddled up in one graceful movement and wheeled the mare around. I recalled what Breck had said about me thinking of Henry in bed the night before, and I stifled a laugh with a smirk that hurt my cheeks. I looked down to try and hide it as I urged my horse forward with gentle pressure from my legs, but I wasn't quick enough.

"Ahh, boyo. Back to your auld self again, I see. Do I dare ask what's brought you back around?"

"Better for both of us if you don't," I warned him. He pulled his horse right up against my mare, leaning to bump his shoulder into mine and flashing his signature crooked smile.

"Only two more weeks until I wake up with that cocky grin on me face, too."

"Still bracing myself for that one, lad," I said, and he laughed.

"Don't worry. I'll be gentle," he crooned. I gaped at him, and he winked back at me. I laughed then, too, shaking my head.

"You're wrong for that one." We pushed our horses faster as we reached the trail, and I let Henry take the lead.

***

I managed to keep my distance from my family for the rest of the morning, successfully avoiding any admonishment for my night out. I felt a little guilty for not checking on them since William was away, too, but I tried to push it aside. Unfortunately, being out of the house all day meant I also hadn't eaten anything. I was starving by the time I reached Finna's cottage. My rear end had barely met the chair at her table before I was being served a whole meal, complete with a dessert of spiced fig cake. I tried my best to be polite as I shoveled the food into my mouth.

"Thank you for being so kind to me," I said. "It's been difficult having to keep all of this from my family. It's nice to know I have at least one other person I can confide in." Finna smiled at me over the rim of her teacup, which she was holding in both of her petite hands.

"Of course, love. I always thought I'd like to have children of my own, but I've found it's just as enjoyable taking care of ye wains who aren't mine."

I felt a twinge in my chest as I thought of my mammy. I'd never considered myself to be a child who had lost his mother, since I was already grown when she died. But that didn't stop me from missing her. I recalled what Breck had said about not asking Finna how old she was. For her to have already settled for a childfree life made it sound like that window of time had come and gone long ago, despite her youthful appearance.

"You never found someone to build your life with?" I asked, taking another bite of food.

"Oh, I've had plenty of lovers. But at some point, I discovered that I didn't need a fella to help build my life. I was perfectly capable of that on my own." She chuckled sweetly and shook her head to herself. "I suppose they were just perks along the way."

The door opened around the corner, and we both looked up at Breck as he came in. I couldn't help the grin that appeared on my lips. He leaned to kiss Finna's cheek and then, to my surprise, did the same to me before he took his seat. I quickly glanced at Finna, but she had no reaction other than slipping out of her chair to go prepare another plate of food. Our eyes met across the table, and Breck glanced at my mouth before he looked up again, a quirk of a smile tugging at the corner of his lips.

Dirty bastard, I thought. He looked down and fully smiled then, and I decided maybe it wasn't so bad that he could hear what I was thinking after all.

"Something tells me I'm here to play mediator for a tough conversation," Finna said with her back to us still.

"As long as Peter's ready," Breck told her.

I was ready. As ready as I could be. I nodded and watched as Finna returned with Breck's meal. "Eat first," she told him. "You'll need your strength." I took the opportunity to finish the rest of what she'd served me, too. The spice cake was magic on my tongue. I tried to focus on that to avoid the nerves that were starting to settle uneasily in my stomach. I wanted to hear anything that Breck could tell me, as painful as it might be.

When we were done with our food, Finna told us to go to the sitting room and she would join us there. We sat together on the sofa, and Breck crossed his legs underneath him, his thigh resting comfortably against mine. The tiny woman joined us moments later.

"Chilly in here," she muttered. She reached into the pocket of her smock and pulled out a handful of something. She clenched her fist tightly and blew on it, then forcefully tossed what looked like flour into the hearth. A flash of fire came to life on the stones. My eyes went wide, and I blinked at the flames that quickly settled into a well-cultivated burn. She brushed her hands together and climbed up onto the chair by the hearth. "Right then. Let's hear it, love."

I turned my head to look at Breck, who appeared to find what had just happened completely normal. He looked at his hands that were resting in his lap, and then his eyes met mine, searching briefly before he looked away. I realized this must've been hard for him, too. I brought my hand up to rest on his leg. *It's alright*, I thought for him.

"I sought out the Unseelie because I knew they were the only ones who would have the answers we needed. They're no strangers to death, but it's still taken seriously enough that I thought I could ask them about a specific case." As he spoke, I studied his profile. "I had already started to form a new theory in my mind about your situation, but I couldn't prove it without their help." He drew in a breath before he continued. His eyes were trained on the flames dancing across the room.

"When it was my turn to stand before them, I simply asked if they knew your name. They did not. That was the first indication that we might've been wrong about everything. Surely, they couldn't have killed hundreds of humans and left one alive without knowing who you were. I showed you to them from my memory. One of the court members recognized you then, and said he remembered your case."

Breck shifted his weight against me and reached into his pocket. He pulled out the two silk ribbons he'd shown me before. The wishes. He looked down at them in his hand.

"He threw these onto the ground at my feet and said how this one in particular had been screaming so loudly in his ears that he had no choice but to take it." He laid the teal ribbon on his knee. "Apparently, as he untied this one from the branch, another called to him." He laid the yellow ribbon next to the first one. I moved my hand from his thigh to pick them up.

"It makes sense that a high member of the court was responsible. It would take a very powerful creature to come away from the Wishing Tree with two ribbons," Finna said from her chair. I studied the strips of silk in my hand, smoothing over them with my thumb.

"When I asked him to tell me more, the entire court laughed at me. They said I had no right to ask for that information." He paused, and I could tell he was choosing his words carefully. "I told them I had wished you to be mine before the sickness, and I needed an explanation." I looked up at him quickly then, my heart jumping at his words, but his eyes were fixed on the ribbons in my hand.

"Dark and light magic cannot mix," Finna explained. "If dark magic exists inside someone – inside you – then you cannot be taken by someone of the Seelie court." Something cold washed through me as I began to understand. Now wasn't the time to be worrying about what that meant.

"It was the only thing I could say to get the answers I needed."

"Did they tell you?" I asked.

"Anne's wish was specifically for you to stay alive long enough for William to return home. But Jamie..." Breck stopped, closing his eyes as if he was trying to see and not see something at the same time. "Jamie delivered the magic to you himself. As the fae demanded. And then his life was taken, a trade for yours."

My mind shot to the last memory I had of us together. "But when he came to see me, I was awake. We —" I paused, catching myself before I shared too many details. "He told me he would come back in a few days to check on me."

Breck swallowed hard before he said, "He went to you twice. Once before you'd woken up, to carry out the magic. And once to say goodbye." Finna made an anguished sound from her chair. I looked up to see her wiping tears away from her eyes. My whole body was quivering, and I realized then that I could feel the chill of Breck's magic spilling across me and around me. Protecting me. I wasn't sure he even knew he was doing it, judging by how distracted he still looked by his own thoughts.

"Jamie's life was his trade. What... what did they take from Anne?" I asked. Breck's eyes finally met mine again. The ribbons were now gripped tightly in my hand. I needed something to hold onto.

"A child. For each day that passed, until your brother returned home."

My grief quickly shifted to anger. My fists came up to press against my forehead as I leaned back against the sofa. "*No,*" I whispered. Anne was so desperate for a child. "Does she know this?"

"She doesn't. The fae never contacted her, because it wasn't her life being traded."

"Can it be reversed? Her wish isn't the one that saved me. It was temporary."

"That's very dangerous territory," Finna said. "Magic doesn't like to be tampered with."

"What if I meet with the Unseelie? Plead my case, and ask for them to change it?" I felt my emotions growing inside me, urging me to do something. I looked between Finna and Breck, seeking a response of some kind.

"It's not that simple," he told me. A frustrated sigh and a few coughs were pushed from my lungs as I leaned forward and placed my elbows on my knees and my head in my hands. Breck sat up more to give me space. His magic finally withdrew, causing me to shiver again.

The conversation I needed to have with Anne had just gotten so much more complicated. How was I supposed to tell her that her wish to save me had taken away her greatest wish of all?

"I don't know how long William was gone," I said miserably. "And I don't know how many she's lost." Breck's hand came to my back. "She'll never forgive me if she finds out the truth." I picked my head up then, turning to look at him. "William will kill me himself. He believes his greatest accomplishment in life will be to pass his legacy to his son." I got up then, pacing toward the hearth, hands working hard on the seams of my trousers. I'd ruined my family's future. The Walshes would end, and it was all my fault.

"Hey," Breck said softly, standing in my way to stop my pacing. His arms came around me, one hand on the back of my head, and he hugged me close. I pressed my face against his shoulder. "It's not your fault."

"We'll help you, Peter. We'll figure something out," Finna reassured me. I recalled what Breck had said about asking her for help with Anne's situation. I pulled away from him, and he let me go.

"Is there anything you can make, Finna? Something that will help her?" Her many bracelets clanged together as she brought her fingertips to her lips, tapping gently as she considered the question.

"Normally I would say yes, but this is a very unique situation, indeed. I don't have a lot of practice fighting magic with magic. Especially not magic that's been cast by a high member of the Unseelie court." She pushed herself up out of the chair and walked past us toward a bookshelf that was cluttered with all sorts of things. She braced the knuckles of one hand against her hip as she studied the items on the shelves, her finger tracing the spine of each book as she came to it.

"I can get you whatever you need," Breck offered, joining her by the shelves and leaning closer to read the titles of the books that were higher up.

"Give me that one," she said, pointing to a large, red spine that was out of her reach. Breck slid it from its place and held it for her to take. She nestled it in her arm and reached for another, and then another. She carried them to the table in the kitchen and laid them out carefully. They looked incredibly old and fragile. We watched over her shoulders as she flipped them open to various pages. I couldn't recognize any of the writing. Breck seemed confused too, but then his arched brows twitched up as he read something, and he looked at me with mild distress. *What is it?* I thought. He just shook his head and started to mouth something at me, but Finna's words cut him off.

"So, it's not an issue of conception, is it? They're able to successfully—"

"No!" I blurted out. "No. It's not that," I added quickly. Finna laughed and looked up at me over her shoulder.

"It's alright, love. No need to get jumpy about it." I was perfectly happy with my limited but satisfactory knowledge of how all of that worked. I didn't feel the need to learn more. "Give me time to do some reading. I'll let you both know what I come up with."

"Thank you," we both said at the same time.

Finna closed the books and moved the stack of them to a small table in the sitting room and instructed us to sit for tea. We returned to our spots on the sofa, Breck even closer to me than before. "Here," I said, holding my hand open, the ribbons resting across my palm.

He shook his head. "You keep them."

I looked at them again before I moved them to my other hand and angled my hips a bit to push them into the pocket of my trousers. I wasn't sure I wanted them, either. Finna returned with our tea on a tray. We each picked up the cup that was nearest to us.

As we all sat in silence, except for the crackling of the fire, I couldn't help but wonder if this moment would ever be possible in my life outside of this new, magical one I'd found myself in. Could I be in a room with my family and confidently, comfortably sit with a man at my side? Finna swung her feet gently in her chair as she gazed at the fire, before she turned to look at us.

"So, how did the lubricant suit you?"

I choked on the sip of tea I was in the middle of, spraying some of it from the sides of my cup as I coughed. I brought my hand up to cover my mouth and shot a look at Breck, who chuckled and wiped at the side of his face. A few specks glittered with the freckles on his cheek in the firelight, and I had to look away, drawn dangerously close to thinking about the previous night.

"It was very... helpful," Breck said carefully, grinning at me.

Finna's shoulders went up in a happy shrug. "Lovely."

SEVENTEEN

It was mid-week before Breck came with news that Finna had discovered something in her books. We were in the middle of a mock match on the field we used for practice. I'd just sent a pass to Henry when I noticed Breck standing along the stone wall by the road. A little voice in my head told me to sit up straighter, but the years of perfect posture I'd had drilled into me made that impossible. Instead, I decided to show off for our spectator.

I charged my horse across the field, calling to Henry for him to send it back to me. Thomas was hot on my trail. I swept my mallet out and captured the ball, knocking it away from his attempt to steal it from me. Wally barked at Thomas from his own horse as he rode alongside us, but I was too quick to allow him to do what our manager had suggested. Instead, I kept the ball right where I wanted it, safely within my reach. Our horses' hooves pounded into the turf, and I felt Thomas beside me, his mare tossing her head in my peripheral. Before he could make the reach I knew he would try, I hooked my mallet and flung the ball through the goal.

Henry let out a *whoop* from his spot on the field while Thomas cursed me. Wally laid into him about letting me go, even though he really hadn't, as he hit the ball back onto the field. Henry took my place, and I used the opportunity to trot my horse over to where Breck was standing. I *woah*ed my mare up in front of him and used one hand to shield my eyes from the sun that was starting to sink in the sky.

"Was that one for my benefit?" he asked, gazing up at me. He was leaning on his forearms against the top of the low wall. "If so, it was very effective and much appreciated."

"I don't know what you mean," I replied, feigning innocence. "I'm just very talented."

"Indeed, you are," came his response. I was glad nobody else was around to hear the suggestive undertone of it, or to see the way his eyes were moving over my body. I shifted in my saddle and glanced back at my teammates as Wally shouted something else at them. Sometimes I missed that about my dad. He never had to yell to get his point across when we were training.

"Did you just come by to ogle us, then?" I asked, turning my horse around. Her impatient steps told me she wanted to rejoin the game.

"Finna thinks she might've found something. Can you come?"

"To the cottage?"

"Yes, to the cottage," Breck confirmed. "You can come later at mine if you feel like it, though." I squinted an eye at him and wrinkled my nose at his play on words before we both grinned.

"Later," I promised him, before I gave in to the mare and we rode back out onto the field. I wasn't sure how long Breck stayed to watch after that, but I practiced hard for the rest of the match.

I remembered this feeling. This feeling inside me

that I couldn't tamp down. It was like a bucket of water that just kept filling, spilling over the top everywhere at once and pooling on the ground. Jamie had given me my first and only taste of it until now, though I was starting to wonder if it was somehow different this time.

Jamie and I had spent plenty of time fooling around and making lewd remarks when nobody was near enough to hear them. But I had never found myself longing for him. Maybe it was because I saw him all the time. We trained and competed together nearly every day for years. I hardly had the chance to miss him. I would think about him at night, or in the morning when I would wake, but I never found myself so compelled to see him that I would have to force myself to stay put as I did now. The want was constant. The thought of being near him was endlessly tempting.

I knew it was dangerous. I had begged myself not to think of what Finna said about dark and light magic mixing. I couldn't think about that. It would be too painful to face it when I had all these other emotions coursing through me that I didn't want to push away. Not yet.

Besides, I had much more important things to be worrying about. I still had to talk to Anne. I had to make sure my best friend survived his wedding. We had a championship to win. Figuring out what I was doing with this lad would have to wait.

**

I arrived at Finna's with an empty stomach after telling Nan that I would be out for the evening. I could tell she was unhappy with me for not sitting with the family for our meal, but she let me go. To my good fortune but no surprise, I was greeted at the cottage with a steaming bowl of stew, bread with butter, and soft oat biscuits. I felt a stitch of guilt over how much I enjoyed it instead of Nan's supper.

"Finna, tell us what you've found." Breck seemed very interested in moving past the eating portion of the evening and getting on with the research part. He did have books on his shelves at the mill. They were just about the only things he had that could be deemed non-essential. I wondered if they were books like the ones here, full of information, or if they held stories like the ones Lucy could never put down. The thought of Breck in bed reading a storybook about fairies made me bite back a chuckle.

Finna drew in a deep breath and exhaled in a puff, looking at both of us. "As I said before, normally this would be something that I could help with easily. I've brought many healthy babes into the world in my time, be it from a distance or not." She got out of her chair and collected our empty dishes; I grabbed one last biscuit before she turned away from the table.

"That's when there's no magic working against you," Breck said as he watched me take a bite, his gaze lingering on my mouth, before he turned his attention back to our host.

"Precisely. I wouldn't be opposed to offering Anne some of my most successful remedies, but the fact of the matter is that our efforts won't make any difference until the magic is satisfied."

"So, you're saying there's nothing we can do until

this prophecy unfolds in its entirety." Finna met Breck's gaze, and her mouth twisted into a frown as she nodded in response. Breck's fingers came to his forehead, rubbing slowly.

"There was one other thought I had. But..." Finna stopped, wiping her wet hands on a rag after she'd cleaned the dishes in soapy water that had filled the room with the smell of citrus.

"But what?" I asked, wanting to hear anything she could offer. She stepped down off her stool and came back around to join us. Her small kitchen was ablaze with flickering candles that were tucked in and around her many jars and baskets and containers. Her pale blue eyes appeared nearly silver in this light as she looked at me pointedly.

"I don't see a way to make it possible without telling her."

"Oh." That was the last thing I wanted to do. I knew I needed to tell her *something* about what I'd learned, but now it had shifted to become so much bigger than it had been before. My anger over her risking her life for mine had now become an intense guilt over what I'd taken from her. From my family.

"If she knew, then what could we do?" Breck had let his hand fall back to his lap.

"Well," Finna began, pulling herself back into her chair at the end of the table. "You said it was one child for each day that William was gone from the day the wish was granted. If we knew the number of days, and if we knew the number of losses—"

"All we have to do is get past the number," Breck

finished for her. "Once the magic is satisfied, it will be over." He looked at me then, expectantly. I was still trying to process what they were saying. "Peter, she will have a child."

"But... not *this* child," I guessed. Finna reached out to put her hand on my arm. "How...?" I didn't know the best way to word such a sensitive question.

"She will lose them. Until she doesn't."

"Can we speed up the process?" Breck asked quickly. I shot him a look, eyebrows furrowed.

"I suppose it would be possible to encourage—"

"No," I said firmly. They both looked at me. "Absolutely not. Those are her *children*. You haven't seen how she grieves for them as I have." My voice began to waver, and I swallowed it away.

"Maybe if she understood what is to come, it would help with the pain?" Finna reasoned.

I considered this. I was fairly confident that the others before this one had been lost very early. But this time, it was different. I thought of how her hand never left the swell that had recently appeared beneath her dress and shut my eyes, sighing. "What if this one is the one that will be alright?" I asked.

"We would have to know the specifics," she said, her voice gentle.

There would be no easy way to do this. I'd secretly hoped that Finna would produce a simple salve or capsule to give Anne, and everything would be fixed. I should've known better. This wasn't a scrape or bruise or sour stomach. This was dark magic. Even my paltry knowledge of what that truly meant told me it couldn't possibly be that simple.

"I'll talk to her," I said finally, though I sounded more defeated than I meant to.

"She loves you very much. She wouldn't have done this if she didn't. Remember that." Finna patted my hand that was resting on the table. I moved to stand, and Breck did, too.

"Will you be alright?" he asked, and I looked at him across the table once more.

"I'll let you know tomorrow."

***

The house was dark by the time I returned. I climbed the steps as silently as I could, listening. I heard Anne and Lucy talking in her bedroom. Anne was busy fielding the last questions Luc could squeeze in for the day. I waited as they said their last goodbyes for the evening, my stomach in knots.

"Anne?" I asked just as she closed the door behind her. She gasped and turned quickly, one hand on her chest and the other holding her chamberstick high to see better in the dark.

"You startled me. I didn't know you'd come back," she said, her face relaxing.

"I'm sorry." I hated this. I hated every part of it. "Em, can we talk for a bit?"

Her eyebrows went down as she studied my face, and finally she nodded. "Of course."

I followed her down the steps, and she started

for our sitting room. "Do you think... could we walk?" Maybe if she wasn't sitting and staring at me, this wouldn't be so uncomfortable. She turned to look at me, and I could tell her suspicion was growing. My hands itched at my sides. I stretched my fingers out a few times before I made fists, trying to calm my nerves.

"Let me get my shawl," is all she said.

We fell into stride along the road. Her hair was tucked under her bonnet, and she wrapped her thick wool shawl tightly around her shoulders against the cool night air. I briefly wondered if she should be out in her condition, but then I remembered it was possible that I knew more about her condition in that moment than she did.

"Shall I go first?" I gave her a sidelong glance. I hadn't realized she might have something to say, too. She continued before I could respond. "Nan is worried sick about you. I am too, if I'm honest. You're never home anymore. You barely touch your food. Lucy asked me tonight if you were going to leave us. You can imagine the unease that created."

"I'm not leaving," I started, but she had more to say.

"What's up with you?" I felt her eyes on me. If only she knew what a loaded question that was. When I didn't say something fast enough, she sighed and touched her fingers to her forehead before she tossed them toward the stars in the sky. "If I didn't know any better, Peter, I'd think you *were* going to leave us. And sometimes I wonder why you haven't already."

"What?" My lungs felt the squeeze of my worry

and I coughed a few times.

"Don't think I haven't noticed you sneaking back home early in the morning. You don't eat here, but you haven't lost any weight. I'd wager that you've even gained some lately." I glanced down at myself. Had I? Anne stopped abruptly, and I turned to face her. "Is there… someone?"

I felt my face flush and I looked away then, up at the sky before I stared at my feet. She reached for my hand with the one that wasn't holding her wrap and squeezed it. Her eyes scrutinized me in the moonlight. I thought of the overflowing bucket inside me. I thought of the repercussions of allowing it to spill now. I wasn't sure I could come up with enough lies to cover all of this at once. I felt the words coming up my throat like bile. *Oh no, oh no.*

"Yes," was all I could manage, barely above a whisper. My heart was thudding in my chest. I felt her staring at me for a moment longer before she let go of my hand and started walking again. I took a few extended steps to catch up with her.

"I have more questions. But now it's your turn."

I'd tossed around all the possible ways to do this in my head. I decided the gentle approach was the only one I felt comfortable with.

"How are you?" I asked finally. Anne laughed beside me.

"That's what you wanted to talk about?" She laughed again, quieter. "I'm fine."

"And the baby?" I imagined that her hand was on

her belly underneath the shawl.

"Fine, too." She had a gentle smile on her face now.

"Are you... feeling anything?" I continued, dying on the inside. She glanced up at me before she looked ahead of us again.

"Feeling anything?" she queried, clearly skeptical. "I suppose I—" she started, but then she gasped loudly and turned to me again, her eyes wide.

"What?" I asked quickly, worried that something was wrong with her. Her hand flew to her mouth but then she moved it lower so she could speak.

"Peter! Have you gotten a lass *pregnant*?! Is that it?"

"What? No!" I flinched as I pushed a hand back through my hair and looked over my shoulder at the house, certain that I'd just accidentally woken everyone up with my startled response. "*No*," I said again in a harsh whisper.

"Are you certain?" she urged, tilting her head toward me with an arched brow.

"*Undoubtedly*," I forced out. I silently cursed the fact that there was nowhere to sit down to relieve my legs, which had gone wobbly. "Anne, this isn't about me at all." It was, actually, but I was desperate to take the focus off myself.

"Then what is it about?"

My nerves were pulled as tightly as they could possibly be inside me as my eyes searched hers. This was too complicated to skirt around any longer. I jammed my hand into the pocket of my trousers. My eyes shifted to the silk ribbons as I pulled them out. I grabbed the golden yellow one with my other hand and held it out to her.

"What is this?" she asked, taking it from me. She looked at it the same way I had when I saw it the first time. Like it meant nothing at all.

"It's yours," I said. My hands were shaking.

"I don't recognize it," she continued, holding it back out to return to me. I didn't take it.

"It was yours when you tied it on the Wishing Tree," I said quietly.

She said nothing. I watched her look at me, then the ribbon, and then back at me. I could see the realization crashing down on her as it happened. Finally, she made a quiet *huh* sound, and then she swayed on her feet. I reached for her as fast as I could and gently guided her to a sitting position on the dirt. She gripped my arms tightly. I sat in front of her on my knees.

"Who gave this to you?" she asked weakly, not looking at me. I couldn't answer her questions now. It wouldn't make the story any easier to tell.

"The wish you made on my life was granted. But it was granted by a fairy who has dark magic." I paused, bracing myself. "In exchange for my life, something was taken from you." She was still silent. I couldn't decide if that was better or worse. All I could do was continue. "Anne... I have to ask you something. Can you hear me?" She nodded. "How many? How many have you lost?" Her shoulders jumped with a sob, and her hands came to cover her face. She shook her head and didn't answer for a long time.

"F—five," she finally said, tearfully. My heart broke for her. I didn't know how to comfort this kind of sadness. I wasn't sure if this was the right time to ask the other part of the question, but she spoke again before I had to continue. "The doctors keep saying there's nothing wrong with me. They can't explain it."

"It's a curse," I told her. "It's not you. It's the magic. I have to tell you more." She made another sad sound but moved her hands so she could look at me. Her cheeks glistened with tears. "Do you remember how long William was gone after you made your wish?"

Her forehead wrinkled at the question, but she looked down, thinking. She shook her head again. "I don't know. It was all such a blur of terrible days. It felt like an eternity."

"Okay. Okay. That's alright," I told her, pulling her into a hug against my chest. "We're going to fix this, I promise." She never asked me her other questions that night. I brought her back to the house and helped her into bed. I didn't know if she slept, but I hoped she did. I hoped even more than William had returned on the sixth day.

***

I struggled to make it through my work the next morning. My head was pounding from lack of sleep and the spinning of my mind all night. I had my palm pressed to my temple when Henry returned from the paddock.

"Alright there?" he asked, and I opened one eye to look at him.

"Bleedin' headache," I told him. In truth, my whole body was exhausted, and my chest was particularly sore, but the headache was the most pressing issue. He made a pained noise out of sympathy.

"Can I help you finish up?" he offered.

"I'm nearly done, thanks." What I really wanted to do was tell him everything that was causing the headache in the first place. I knew he'd listen if I told him I needed to talk. I just didn't think I had the energy to do it after what'd happened the night before.

He left me for the tack room, and I walked my bay mare out of her stall. I knew I was in no shape to ride, as hard as that was for me to admit, so turning the horses out would have to be enough for the day. She was the last one to go. I guided her out into the morning light, wishing that there were at least a few clouds to shield my eyes from the sun. I brought my hand up to cover them until I had to unlatch the gate. The mare followed me through the opening in the wall, and I sent her on her way to join the rest of the horses. The chestnut mare picked her head up from the dewy grass and pricked her ears toward me. *That's a good lass*, I thought. She'd come so far.

I closed the gate behind me and laid the rope across my shoulder. I didn't feel like going back to bed, but I wasn't sure what else would help my headache. Finna probably would've had something. That meant a trek to her cottage, though, and I knew my aching lungs wouldn't appreciate that.

I walked through the door to the stables and mindlessly steered my steps toward the tack room to put away the rope and change out of my riding boots. My hand returned to rub at my forehead. I heard Henry come around the corner ahead of me, and I decided maybe I should talk to him for a while, even if I didn't share everything. I started to speak, but when I dropped my hand and raised my eyes to look at him, I was hit with a wave of dizziness that blurred my vision.

"Peter," he said. His voice sounded strange. I reached out for one of the half doors to catch myself before I fell. The last thought I had was that Henry hadn't called me Peter since the day we met.

EIGHTEEN

My headache had gone from throbbing to splitting. I tried to bring my hand up to hold it against the pain, but I found my arms were caught behind me. I blinked my eyes several times to clear away the last of the dizzy spell. I'd never fainted before. As my vision cleared, my confusion shifted to unease. I was no longer in the stables. I was on the ground, encircled by dense forest. The canopy above allowed only narrow shafts of light to reach the earth around me. It was unnaturally quiet; I couldn't hear the sounds of any birds or bugs.

A groan escaped me as I shifted up to a sitting position. I pulled on my arms again. When I peered back over my shoulder, I realized that my wrists were bound. I'd been restrained with my own rope. That's when I allowed myself to worry. I turned my head slowly to take in my surroundings. I didn't recognize anything, but that didn't mean much. This could've been any part of the forest that bordered our land. I coughed a few times when my lungs protested the hunched position I was sitting in.

"Apologies about your head. You bashed it quite hard when you fell." That explained the new pain. I turned toward the voice, and that's when I allowed myself to panic.

"What do you want?" I asked, my voice coming out strained as it had been when I was ill, coughing relentlessly. The person who had spoken to me made a sound of disapproval. All I could see was their silhouette in between the thick trunks of two trees.

"Asking the hard questions straight away. That leaves little time for conversation."

"Who are you?" I quickly took in whomever – *whatever* – stepped out of the shadows. Their skin was pale, and their hair was as white as Nan's, falling long enough to reach their shoulders. The pointed tips of their ears jutted from beneath the thin strands that hung around their face. "Fairy," I concluded, mostly to myself.

"That's all you need to know about me," they confirmed. I couldn't tell if they were male or female. They wore a long, crimson cloak that reached the ground. As they came closer, their hair caught some of the light peeking through the trees, and it glinted like silver.

"What do you want?" I repeated myself.

"You've been trying to meddle with my magic," they said.

"I haven't done anything." The creature came to a stop a short distance from where I was sitting and crouched, arms resting on their knees. The cloak parted, revealing black trousers and a bare torso. Suddenly, a sharp pain seared deep in my chest. It brought back memories that I thought I'd blocked out forever.

"*Ah,*" I hissed, doubling over and landing on my side where I'd started. When the sensation eased, I breathed in deeply, which started a coughing fit.

"Definitely mine." He stood and remained staring

at me. I panted and looked up at him again, this time with more understanding.

"You're the one who granted Jamie's wish on my life. You put this dark magic in my lungs. You killed him," I accused, my voice unable to raise as loud as I wanted it to.

"It was a fair trade. The human asked for it to be done, and so it was." He crossed his arms beneath the cloak and tilted his head back slightly. "This is not my concern. You are trying to interfere with the other one who begged for your life to be spared."

I found the strength to sit up again and wiped the side of my face against my shoulder, trying to remove the dirt and dead leaves that I could feel sticking to my cheek. When I pulled away, I saw the smear of blood on my shirt. Nausea began to gurgle low in my stomach. I swallowed hard and closed my eyes.

"Nothing can be done. We know that now." There was no point in lying. He already knew the truth. There was a long pause, and I wanted to ask more questions. If anyone could tell us how much longer this would go on for Anne, it was him. What repercussions would I face for asking, though?

"What would you do to change it?"

I glanced up at him then. The faintest hint of a smirk was playing on his features. His lips were gray, edging toward the purplish color of a body that had met the cessation of life. This was the look of someone living on a stolen existence. "What do you mean?" I asked. Something told me it was dangerous to entertain this offer, but it was too late. I'd already opened my mouth.

"What would you trade in exchange for her curse being lifted?"

"What do you want?" I asked for a third time.

"I cannot make suggestions," he snapped, though it seemed to be more out of irritation than anger, as if he found it ridiculous that I would've asked. "I can simply agree to take the trade, or not. It is up to you what you offer, if you decide to offer anything at all."

"I... I don't know," I fumbled over my words, sounding more desperate than I intended. How could I decide something like that with no time to think?

"Consider it. I do love to barter." With that, the world spun around me again, and I was gone.

***

The sharp stab of cold made me gasp, which was a terrible mistake. I knew right away that I'd been thrust into the frigid water of the river. My eyes shot open, and I struggled to right myself as my head slipped under. My hands were still fixed behind my back. I kicked my legs hard against the current as much as I could, unable to reach the silty bottom, but the chill and my sodden clothes were already slowing me down.

I couldn't be sure how much time passed before there was a commotion beside me in the water, and then I was above the surface. I gasped again and coughed hard, expelling some water as I was placed on my side in the grass along the bank. Someone was talking, but I couldn't understand the words. I felt the release of my hands being untied; I continued to cough and rolled forward, bringing my arm in front of me to help support my weight.

Hands found my face. I forced my eyes open. *Breck.*

"Wake up. Wake up, come on." His clothes were soaked through, and his hair was dark and dripping. His freckles were gleaming brightly in the sunlight. "What *happened* to you?!" He sounded scared. I realized I probably should be, too. All I felt was cold. My whole body was shivering. I tried to speak, but I couldn't stop coughing long enough to form any words.

Something was pressed against my forehead. I winced at the discomfort it caused. I felt more hands on me then, and more voices were talking over me, but I closed my eyes and let myself slip away once more.

***

When I woke up again, I sat up too fast and immediately regretted it. The pain in my head was still lingering. I reached up to touch the side of my face, remembering the blood I'd seen on my shirt. I glanced down at my shoulder. There was no evidence of it now. My fingertips slid to my temple. Someone had placed a thick bandage there.

I was in a bed, but it wasn't my own. My eyes swept around the room. There were no windows. The only light came from a few orbs glowing along the walls, which appeared to be made of stone, and a small hearth set into the wall where a fire was burning. I had no idea where I was. Again. This sent a streak of fear through me, and I tried to get to my feet, but a hand caught my shoulder.

"Hold it," came a voice from behind me. Fallon. I pulled away from her and made another attempt to get out from under the bedclothes, but she reached for me again and captured my wrist in her hand. "Stop. You're not allowed to get up yet." She sounded as agitated as she always did.

"Why not?" I demanded.

"Because I said so." I turned again to look toward another familiar voice. Seeing Finna brought a small amount of relief. I stopped struggling against Fallon's grip, and she let me go, practically throwing my own hand back at me.

"Where am I?" Finna was beside me then, guiding me back down against the pillow behind my head. She pulled the blankets up to my shoulders, one at a time, from where they'd collected on my lap. There were five or six of them, at least. No wonder I felt so hot.

"My home," Fallon said flatly. I hadn't ever given any thought to what her living situation would look like, but somehow *dank cave* seemed extreme, even for her.

Finna ignored her. "Do you remember anything, love?" I nodded faintly and told her what I could recall, beginning at the stables and ending with being pulled from the water. It sounded more like a nightmare than reality as the words came out of my mouth. Could it have all been a bad dream? Was I still dreaming?

"I spoke with Anne last night. He knew that, somehow, and accused me of trying to meddle with his magic. I guess he wasn't wrong," I said, half telling them more and half thinking out loud. I brought my hand up over my closed eyes briefly, before I pushed my fingers back through my hair and gave Finna a worried look.

"What time is it? How long have I been here?" *Where's Breck?*

"You've been asleep the whole day. We had to bring you here because it was the closest to where we found you, and we needed to get you warm. Unfortunately, Elina isn't here, otherwise we could've had her help with that. We had to heat you up the old-fashioned way." Finna patted my chest through the thick layers of blankets on top of me, her bracelets tinkling together on her wrist. "Care for tea?" She didn't wait for my answer as she disappeared from the side of the bed.

An uncomfortable silence spread over the two of us remaining in the light of the small hearth near the bed. I turned my head slightly and found Fallon glowering at nothing. "Sorry," I muttered, returning my gaze to the ceiling. She probably had many reasons to be angry with me. I was in her home, in her *bed*, which I imagined was quite unpleasant, considering how much she already disliked me. And then there was everything else, of course.

"Humans use that term too lightly," she said, her voice neutral. "You apologize for things to placate others, but you don't always truly mean it." I expected her to make her usual dramatic exit, but she remained sitting beside me until Finna returned with a cup. I pushed myself up, slower this time, and took it from her. The flavor was stronger than any tea I'd ever tasted before. I almost couldn't manage to drink any more of it.

"I added some herbs to speed your healing," she explained, tapping a fingertip to her own temple to indicate what she was talking about. As I took another sip, I realized I would have to tell my family something about how I got hurt. They knew that I was prone to injury, but I also usually went limping home needing care, not already patched up and on the mend.

I glanced at my sore wrists. "Why would he tie my hands? Surely he wasn't afraid of me fighting back." He could've killed me in an instant if he'd really wanted to.

"Probably just to scare you. Or for added effect. Fae love a good performance," Finna said wearily. The bed was just tall enough that she had to pull herself up onto it to sit beside my legs. Her expression changed to something more serious as she smoothed her hands down her skirts to tame them. "We're worried this is going to happen again if we keep at it. I think it's best if we just let the magic run its course for Anne."

Emotion rose inside me. "I can't give up now, Finna. I have to fix this for her. She doesn't deserve it."

"You're right, but in the end, she made the wish and got what she asked for. That's how things work with magic. Sometimes adding new magic can create a new outcome, but we cannot change what has already happened."

"But—"

"Your actions brought the Unseelie within a stone's throw of your loved ones," Fallon cut in. "By trying to fix one problem, you are creating more, and they are problems that I have to deal with." I closed my mouth as her words settled on me. She was right. He was there for me in the stables, but my family had been just up the hill. I thought of Lucy playing in the garden, or Nan in the kitchen, and the horror of them encountering the dark fae instead of me. Despite the heavy blankets and the warm drink in my hands, a chill ran through my body – and not the kind I'd grown fond of. I sighed and looked down into the cup, nodding.

"Protecting this land and the humans who live here is my purpose. My responsibility. You know more than you should, and you see the problems it has created. Our worlds shouldn't overlap." With that, Fallon made the exit I'd been expecting before. I watched her go, and then looked at Finna. She gave me a sad smile.

"I know this is difficult for you. Sometimes, though, things just cannot be changed. That was a hard lesson for me to learn, too." She placed her hand on my knee, which I could barely feel through the covers. "You should get some rest. You'll feel better when you wake up."

Without any other warning, I felt the crash of exhaustion hit me. Finna took the cup from my hands after she got off the bed and set it down swiftly before she helped guide me to the pillow once more. I got the distinct feeling that something in her tea was responsible for the wave of fatigue. I barely had time to close my eyes before I was asleep.

***

Finna was right. Physically, I felt better, but I'd been plagued with terrible dreams as I slept. I couldn't make sense of most of it, even in the moments right after I woke up when it was fresh in my mind. I decided not to fight it and let the images slide away. I was still underneath the mountain of blankets, curled up on my side. I pushed the covers off my head slowly and breathed some cool air into my lungs.

The fire was still going on the hearth. Without windows, it was impossible to know what time it was. I needed to go home before everyone started to worry about me. I pushed the blankets back more, and since I didn't have Fallon sitting sentry anymore, I got to my feet.

"Your shoes are outside. They smelled terrible," she said from somewhere. I turned to find her sitting in a different chair, this one plusher than the wooden one beside the bed. Her long, dark hair was unbraided and hanging over her shoulder in loose waves. She had the look of someone who had been awake for too long.

"Is it morning?" I asked, my voice rough from sleep. The floor of the room was also made of stone. I took a small step closer to the fire, glad to find the heat had spread across the ground, too. Fallon nodded, still not looking at me. She must've sat in that chair all night, waiting for me to leave. I was never going to get in her good graces.

"I'll show you out when you're ready," she said. It came across as less demanding than I'd expected. I would need her help. I didn't know where I was. I couldn't even see the door to leave on my own if I'd wanted to. I gestured that I would let her lead the way, and she stood gracefully from her chair.

"Fallon, I really am sorry." I decided I had to take my opportunity while I had it. There was no influence coming from the others. Nobody to step in and try to protect me from whatever she needed to say to me. "I was thinking about this selfishly. I wanted to help Anne, but really I wanted to help myself so I wouldn't feel guilty about what happened." She remained a few steps ahead of me, walking us toward an area that was too dark for my eyes. As if on cue, tiny orbs of cool light zipped up to join us in what I could now see well enough to call a tunnel. My feet progressively got colder as we walked, the chill bleeding up through my socks.

"Anne made her choice. You shouldn't feel guilty about a decision she made, even if it had repercussions that she wasn't prepared for. That's the danger of our worlds mixing." Her voice echoed off the walls as she spoke, the orbs dancing around her as if she was their energy source. Maybe she was. As I watched this scene unfold in front of me, I started to comprehend Fallon's actuality. She was the one all the fairies in the woods stopped and listened to just because she stood up. She was their leader. She was the guardian of two worlds. She was divine.

I rubbed my palms hard against the seams of my breeches and tried to squelch the nerves that had lit up inside me. When Breck spoke about meeting with the Unseelie, I had pictured a formal gathering where he stood alone before the members of the court. I hadn't stopped to think that this image I had in my head wasn't drawn from my own imagination. I'd seen it before, the night in the clearing when they all sat on their thrones with woven crowns on their heads.

Fallon and the others were the high Seelie here.

My distracted thoughts caused me to trip and stumble over a dip in the stone floor. I caught myself, but it caused Fallon to turn and look at me. Her features sharpened and softened as the orbs circled her in random patterns. I realized I was breathing hard over the epiphany I'd just had, and Fallon seemed to realize it, too. She arched an eyebrow at me and dipped her head in a small acknowledgement before she turned and continued walking.

I couldn't bring myself to speak any more words, so we walked the rest of the way in silence. Finally, my suspicions were confirmed as we approached the mouth of the cave. The early morning light was still enough to make me blink several times after emerging from the darkness. I spotted my boots and stooped to put them on. When I stood up and faced the world outside, I nearly had to reach for something to hold onto.

Wind whipped our hair and clothes as I stared down at the craggy, grassy side of a steep mountain. We were high enough to be above the thick fog blanketing the rolling hills and trees below. The fog also made it impossible for me to check my surroundings and discern where I was. I shot Fallon a look, and for the first time, she didn't look unhappy. There was even the slightest hint of a grin on her lips. When she gazed at something over my shoulder, I turned to see what it was. Breck was standing atop a large stone with his back to us, hands in his pockets.

"I'm nothing if not true to my word, Peter. We're here to help you."

Breck heard her speak and turned quickly to look at me. His hands came from his pockets as he took a swift step down off the rock. He put one hand on my shoulder when he reached me and used the other to push my hair off my forehead so he could examine my temple. The thick bandage I'd felt before was gone, replaced with a smaller one. I figured that had to be good news. I watched his eyes scan my head and face thoroughly before his gaze met mine, and then he looked at the woman beside us.

"Thank you, Fallon. This won't happen again," he assured her. I could still hear the worry in his voice. Fallon didn't say anything, she just turned and started back into the darkness of the tunnel. As soon as we couldn't see her anymore, Breck took me by the wrist and started guiding me down through the rocks and swaths of crushed stone and dirt streaked through the grass. I tried to keep up the best I could, but his guidance quickly became him dragging me downhill, which was a recipe for disaster.

When we made it to a spot that was flatter and somewhat protected from the wind blowing around us, I wrenched my arm from his grip. I held my wrist in my other hand and pressed it protectively against my chest in case he tried to grab it again.

"What are you doing?" I asked, not trying to mask my irritation. This was nothing like the fond memory I had of our last hike in the mountains. When he turned back toward me, my emotions swung in the other direction as I realized how troubled he was. My own face softened as I stepped closer to him. A few specks glinted on his cheek in the growing light, and he reached up to briskly wipe away the wet trail a tear had left behind. "Breck?" I urged, and that made him look at me finally. His eyes were brimming with more tears when they met mine.

"This was all my fault. I'm so sorry." His normally smooth voice broke on the last bit, and my heart strained in my chest. It was my turn to reach for him now. I pulled him into a tight embrace, my hand on his head so I could press the side of his face against mine, my other arm around his shoulders.

"I'm okay," I tried to reassure him. "I'm standing here talking to you, aren't I? I'm fine." What had happened was my fault as much as it was his. He didn't force me to talk to Anne. It had been my choice to tell her as much as I did. He simply had the idea. He was trying to help. "I was a little worried when I woke up and you weren't there," I admitted, speaking just loud enough by his ear to be heard over the wind. He still didn't move his hands to touch me, but I felt him sigh as his chest depressed against mine.

"Fallon doesn't let anyone inside her home except for Finna. I'm lucky I even know where she lives," he explained apologetically. I leaned away from him slightly to do a quick sweep of our surroundings, glad that at least one of us knew where we were. Then I came to a dreadful realization, and I pushed him away so I could look at his face.

"Did you stay out here all night?" My eyes jumped to his hair, his clothes, the faint shadows under his eyes. My eyebrows drew together as I shook his shoulders in my hands once, trying to get my answer. "Did you?"

"I didn't want to be far away until I knew you were alright," he said, his eyes cast down.

I squeezed my eyes shut and put my forehead against his with a pained groan. "Don't do that," I scolded him gingerly.

"Do what?" he asked.

"Don't worry about me so much." Those are the words that came out of my mouth. In my head, I wasn't able to stop the other words as they threaded through my thoughts. *Don't love me.*

NINETEEN

The rest of our journey down the mountainside went at a slower pace. The wind and cold air aggravated my lungs and made me cough, which in turn made my head hurt. I pushed through the pain so we could talk about how to explain myself to my family.

We decided it would be possible to style my hair over my injury well enough to hide it for a brief encounter. Finna had left Breck with another salve to give me to speed the healing. She'd told him there was a deep but small cut and a bruise; she put two sutures in to keep the wound closed. I was grateful to have been unconscious for that. I felt my stomach roil as I tried to stop thinking about it. I wasn't sure if it was queasiness from the thought of the blood or from being hungry. One cup of strong tea wasn't enough to hold me over for that long.

By the time we reached the base of the mountain, some of the morning fog had lifted, and I was surprised to see that we were on the far end of the village. My head was hurting too much to think about how I'd been transported so far away from the stables without my volition.

"Do you want to get some breakfast?" Breck asked. I gave him a quizzical look.

"What, in the village?" My stomach decided to answer for me and made a loud gurgling sound. Breck chuckled and raised an eyebrow.

"I guess that's a yes."

I was glad that the remainder of our walk had given him time to clear his head. His hands had returned to his pockets, and he was strolling beside me with his shoulders back, though he did still look tired. My guess was that his emotions ran high because he'd held vigil at the mouth of a cave all night. I would've been exhausted and ready to cry, too.

"I don't have any money with me," I realized then. The only thing I'd had with me the morning prior was my rope, and I'd lost that, too. I would've patted my empty pockets to emphasize my predicament, but my riding breeches didn't have any to begin with.

"No bother," he said easily, bumping my arm with his elbow, hand still in his pocket. "I've got a job too, remember."

I decided to stop making excuses and allow myself to accept his offer. The first buildings of the village came into view as we rounded a curve in the road. It was early yet, but I knew people would already be bustling about, tossing their doors and windows open to welcome the morning that was turning out to be sunny and mild. That meant everyone would be in a fantastic mood.

When we approached the main stretch of road after navigating the side alley, my eyes were drawn to the yellow façade of the flower shop. The paint wasn't as vibrant as it had been when I was a child, but the flowers blooming out front were as bright as ever. I smiled as I thought of how happy Mam would've been to pick out a bouquet to take home. It'd been a long time since I'd spent a morning in the village. Most of my visits had become a stop at our favorite pub after a match. Anything after that was mostly a blur.

We walked silently as we watched our neighbors going about their morning routines. The owner of the general store was busy taking crates from the tea merchant, who brought goods on his cart pulled by a massive mule. As I had predicted, the bakery's windows were propped wide to allow the smell of fresh bread to waft out into the street and draw in hungry customers. The tailor and the man who owned the store where Nan liked to buy her salt and sugar were having a spirited discussion. They paused to wish us a good morning before they went back to their conversation.

I sent a quick glance in Breck's direction when he'd greeted them just as warmly. It was amusing to me that he would be so friendly with the man who was his direct competition in the business of selling flour, but then again, Breck didn't *need* to run the mill. He did it so he could blend in with the rest of us.

I wondered if it ever bothered him, having to put up a front of being someone he wasn't just to earn a spot in our world. I noticed that the tips of his ears were rounded like mine now. The metal bands and studs were hidden, too. His charade wasn't just about acting like a human. He had to physically change himself and hide things, even if they were subtle, so that nobody would question him. He had even created a whole career for himself to make it more believable that a young, single man would've moved to our village of all places to start a new life.

It dawned on me then that he probably understood me better than anyone else. We both had to play this game, in our own way. Hiding something about ourselves for the sake of others. Keeping up appearances and giving all the right answers to avoid suspicion. I felt a tug of empathy inside me, laced with something else that felt more personal. More intimate, just for the two of us.

Across from the sorry excuse for an apothecary was the pub that also served the best food. Breck must've learned this, too, as he pulled the door open and let me inside. Most of the tables were empty. I picked one along the wall, and Breck placed an order for us at the bar. I didn't care what he got me, as long as it was hot. My riding clothes had provided little protection from the chill of the mountains.

"I still think Finna could change peoples' lives if she opened a storefront here in the village. There are so many who could benefit from her talents," I mused as Breck joined me at the table.

"Are you saying my flour isn't life-changing?" he asked, grinning at me. I laughed and gave him a sorry shrug.

"Nan thinks so, but I'm not sure she'll live longer because of it."

"I put a lot of time and care into my product, believe it or not. I'm in the business of helping people, after all. Selling mediocre goods would go against everything I stand for."

We'd barely had time to settle into a comfortable chat when we were served tea with milk. I didn't prefer it this way like most others did, so I left the delicate porcelain creamer full of milk for Breck and raised the cup to my lips.

"Mm-mm," he shook his head, eyeing my tea. "It's very hot." I lowered it back to the table and watched as he added a bit of milk to his cup and stirred with the spoon it'd been served with. His long fingers made the delicate silver utensil look even smaller. I noticed then that his rings were missing, too. When he finished, he placed the spoon gently on the saucer. My eyes followed as he drank his first sip.

Instinct told me to copy him, and I brought my cup back up for a swallow. I quickly realized my distracted mistake as the tea scalded my mouth on the way down. I set the cup down with a clatter and exhaled more dramatically than I meant to, mouth open. Breck chuckled and shook his head, his gaze falling to the table after watching my antics. "Told you," he offered quietly.

We had to move our drinks out of the way as the food arrived. My eyes went wide as I realized what I was being served. The plate was overflowing with fried eggs, beans, thick bacon, black *and* white pudding, buttered mushrooms, tomatoes, and diced potatoes, all on a bed of soda bread. I looked across to Breck's meal, which was a simple bowl of oat porridge with a swirl of honey and bread with dark jam.

"Consider it my apology," he said as he picked up a piece of his toast and bit off the corner. I tentatively picked up my fork and began eating the feast he'd ordered for me. It was delicious. I kept expecting Breck to react or say something as I ate certain parts of my food, but he never did. Twice, though, he caught me looking at him. The first time was over the rim of my tea, which had finally cooled enough to drink. The second time, I was unabashedly admiring his profile as he watched more people file into the pub to eat their own late morning meals. When his eyes caught mine, all I could do was grin as I chewed my mouthful of fried potatoes.

"What?" he asked, reaching up to wipe his mouth as if I was staring at a smear of blackberry jam on his chin.

"What was it you said the other night? The calm between the storms?" Breck made a sound of acknowledgement before he put another spoonful of porridge in his mouth, nodding. He glanced around us and then back at me, and I realized he probably didn't want to speak the words that would sound foreign to the other people sitting nearby, too, and risk drawing their attention. "I think this is another of those moments," I concluded softly.

"It's lucky to be able to recognize them when they're happening," he added.

When I'd sufficiently stuffed myself, I leaned back in my chair and breathed deeply, which surprisingly didn't make me cough. The rest of my reality, however, had started to creep in. This was the last stop before I had to step back into my world of responsibilities with my family and my work. I should've been in the saddle all morning, training with my teammates and preparing for our match the next day. I should've been home to check on Anne and Lucy. I was still worried about what I was going to say to explain where I'd been.

It was my turn to catch Breck staring at me from across the table. The look on his face was that of someone who was listening closely. I knew then that he must've been following my thoughts. That explained the stress that also laced his features. He blinked and tilted his head toward the door.

***

"Is it possible to make someone forget everything you told them?" I asked as we stepped out into the daylight. The street was crowded and louder than it had been before, with children running and laughing around the various carts peddling everything from fresh vegetables to woven baskets.

"It's possible, but not advisable," he told me. "Taking away those memories could create other gaps. If it happens right away, it's not as risky, but a lot of time has passed now."

"I think I need to go back to the pub for some liquid courage," I joked, though it didn't seem like the worst idea. Breck kept his expression neutral as we made our way through the crowd.

"Peter!" Someone called my name from a distance in a sing-song way, and I turned to see who it was. A whole new layer of dread washed over me as I found the source. Sarah and her gaggle of sisters were making their way toward us across the square that was connected to the wide main street we'd been walking down. I looked back at Breck, desperate for an excuse, but he didn't provide one. Instead, he just grinned and peered behind me at the drama that was headed in our direction.

"Peter," she repeated breathlessly, as if they'd run instead of sauntered. "What a surprise to see you here. Henny convinced me that the whole team would be training from daybreak to nightfall until your last match. Which is terribly inconvenient, considering our wedding is just one short week away." Her sisters tittered behind her, clearly unable to contain their excitement over the impending celebrations. I couldn't help but glance down at Emma Clare. The look she was giving me was unmistakably sultry. I took a polite step back to put a little more distance between us.

"We've just come from the final meeting with the seamstress! You lads are in for a real treat when you see what she's come up with for us," the other younger sister teased, swishing her skirts to mime the fancier dress she was going to be wearing.

"I'm sure you're right," Breck spoke up, finally coming to my rescue as he moved to stand beside me. "But fair maidens don't need special clothes to impress, as is evident." He said it innocently enough, but the words hit their mark as the two younger girls blushed and excused themselves.

"So, the question still stands. Was my beloved telling lies?" Sarah eyed me carefully. I scrambled to come up with a good excuse for myself. In truth, I was the one who wasn't where I should've been. There was no doubt in my mind that Henry was exactly where he'd told her he would be.

"I'm here to buy flowers for my sister." I glanced back over my shoulder toward the yellow storefront and the rainbow of blooms spilling out into the street. When I turned back to Sarah, I saw how her expression had softened considerably, and her hand was over her heart. She poked out her bottom lip before she spoke again.

"That's the sweetest. Nobody has ever bought *me* flowers. Maybe I would've liked having a brother instead of all these sisters," she chaffed. That earned her a light slap on the arm from her oldest sibling. She sighed loudly and dipped her head at us. "Well, good luck with your shopping. Give Hen my love when you see him." With that, both sisters turned and walked back in the direction they'd come from, their strawberry blonde hair bright in the sun where it fell in perfect curls down their backs.

"Looks like the disguise worked," Breck said as soon as they couldn't hear us.

"If anyone was going to make a big deal about it, it would've been them," I agreed, reaching up to pat the hair down over my forehead. I recalled the reaction they'd had to me being tossed from the chestnut mare at the party. Something like this probably would've earned me more than a delicate touch on the arm.

"Are we buying for Anne or Lucy?"

I turned to look at Breck. He was serious. "I still don't have any money. I just made it up," I started, but he was already walking back toward the flowers. I stepped quickly to catch his stride.

"You can pay me back," was his only response. He led the way to the tiny shop, and we took longer than we should have as we admired the selection available. Breck lingered over certain areas as he searched, holding his relaxed, open hand over the blooms, but never touching them. When he found ones he liked, he plucked them gently by the stems. I had no idea what he was doing, but soon enough both my arms were full of the ones he fancied best. The florist gave us a surprised look when Breck asked to buy everything I was holding. When it became evident that calculating the cost would be overwhelming, he overpaid without a second thought. The florist helped us arrange his selections into several large bouquets.

"I'm going to keep one to give to Finna. The rest are for you," he told me as we finally put the village behind us. There were five total. I looked at the three I was carrying.

"What do I do with all of them?" I asked. He didn't give me an answer. When we arrived at the bridge, Breck handed me the fourth bouquet and started in the direction of Finna's cottage. I wanted to tell him he should go home and get some sleep, but I didn't. I wanted to kiss him goodbye, too, but I didn't do that either. Instead, I turned and crossed over the river, steeling myself already for whatever reaction I might get when I arrived home.

I stared down at the flowers as I walked. He'd taken such care to pick each one. He even pulled some from mixed bouquets that had already been put together. I thought these looked better than any of the ones that were ready to purchase. As the road curved ahead of me, my gaze shifted up the hill to the large oak tree. I came to a slow stop in front of the gate. It didn't take me long to push it open and walk up through the thick grass.

The stone markers came into view, and I stopped

near the bench, setting down three of the bundles. I pulled a few blooms out of the bouquet I was still holding as I approached the graves on the right, under the low branch, and laid them by Mary's name. Two steps away, I put down a few more for Lizzie. The rest of the bouquet remained whole, tied neatly with twine, and I set it down for Mam.

I moved back a couple paces, my eyes slowly tracing their carved names and the dates below them. Something came over me then in a rush, making my body feel heavy, so I sat on the edge of the grass that had once been dirt over my mother's resting place. With my back to her name, I pulled my legs up, wrapped my arms around my knees, and looked out at the view of our land.

"*Mammy, I've met someone,*" I whispered. "Everything's a horrible mess, and I just keep making it worse, I think. But when I see him, none of it feels so bad." The ever-present wind blew over us there on the hill, exposing my injured forehead. I held my hair back in place with my hand.

Before I met Breck, I would've called my life steady. Two years had provided me with enough time to regain the normalcy any man wished for. And though I was grateful for that, I recognized now that I was also lonely. Despite the closeness of my family and my friends, and the full schedule I kept, I didn't have anyone who gave me something to look forward to. A future to think about. I was set in my ways and living the life that had been cultivated for me, but I hadn't been living for me. Not really.

But what did a life with him in it look like? We

weren't the same. He was more than human. More than the world I lived in. More than just a magical creature, even. He was destined to be a guardian of our land. He was like Fallon and the others, powerful and divine in a way that should've separated us from each other even more.

His arrival into my life had brought so many other things. It brought knowledge of what had really happened to me. He had given me insight on my family's success in our business. He uncovered the truth about Anne's struggles, and why I'd lost Jamie. And, even though I rarely felt that I needed it or deserved it, he'd made me feel protected and looked after in a way that I had never been before.

I struggled to keep in mind that all of this was a part of his job, too. He'd been sent to me to do all these things. Every day, he was tasked with proving to Eabha that he was ready to take his roll beside the others. When he'd earned his place, then what? Would he continue to run the mill? Would he still be allowed to see me? Would he want to see me? Surely, he would be even busier than he already was when that time came, and maybe we would drift apart.

Finna said that dark and light magic couldn't mix. I'd kicked myself several times for allowing the thoughts to stir in my head, but they persisted. It meant we could never be together in any proper way. In my world, the possibility never existed. I had long since accepted that for myself. Even in his world, though, the dark magic living inside my lungs apparently meant the same.

This thought was crushing. Both of our worlds

had reasons why we weren't allowed to be together. I wanted desperately to pretend that I didn't know why this made me so upset, but the truth was hard to ignore. On his mission to help me, and to prove himself worthy of his role as guardian, he'd also swept me off my feet. Heat spread across my chest and face as I finally admitted it to myself, and I closed my eyes as I hung my head.

My eyes popped open as it occurred to me that my thoughts weren't always private. Could he hear them any time he wanted to, or did we have to be nearby? My cheeks grew even hotter as I pushed myself up off the ground, scooped up my remaining bounty, and started down the hill.

***

By the time I arrived home, the sun had shifted more in the sky, and I worried that showing up to train now would anger Wally more than if I just didn't show up at all. I transferred the bouquets into one arm as I pushed the kitchen door open. My luck had run out, apparently, and I was greeted by the stares of all three people I knew would be waiting for me. Lucy gasped and then squealed with delight as she spotted what I was holding. She flitted over to me and wrapped her arms around my waist, hugging me tight. I put my free hand on her back, but kept my eyes trained on Anne, waiting for her reaction.

"These are so beautiful! Where did you get them?" I looked down long enough to hand one of the bundles to my sister, grinning at her.

"I saw them in the village and thought you would like them," I explained. "Those are special, just for you."

Our garden had some flowers, but nothing like the ones I was holding. Lucy hugged me again and announced that she was going to put them in water in her room as she left us in the kitchen.

"What've you done to yourself now?" was the first thing out of Nan's mouth. She pointed at a chair, and I knew better than to argue with her. I pulled it away from the table and sat down as she came over to stand in front of me. She gripped my chin in her crooked fingers and used the other hand to push my curls back. "You need your hair cut." Her wrinkles deepened as she inspected the bandage.

"I fell," I offered, trying the less is more approach. Our eyes met, and she shook her head at me before her gaze fell to the flowers I was still holding.

"And I suppose you're trying to bribe us with pretty things as an apology for being gone a whole day without explanation?" She let go of my face and took one of the bouquets, turning it to see all the types and colors in the mix.

"Is it working?" I asked lightly, which earned me a glare from her and Anne, who was still sitting across the table from me. Nan made her way around the counter and started shuffling things around in one of her cupboards until she found a small vase. I watched as she dipped the vase into her bucket of fresh water and put the bouquet inside, before she slid it to the middle of the counter.

"A word, Peter?" Anne had made it to her feet and was waiting for me by the hallway. I hurried up out of my chair and followed her. She led us to William's study and shut the door. As kids, Dad would bring us there to scold us or have important talks because nobody could hear the conversation from the outside if the door was closed. It was the only room like that in the house, and privacy was rare in a home as full as ours had been.

Anne went directly for the chair behind William's desk and lowered herself into it. That left me to stand awkwardly in the middle of the small room, bouquet in hand, and I had the terrible thought that this must've been how other men felt as suitors, trying to offer a token during courtship when they were still uncertain how it would be received. Thoroughly nerve-wracking.

"Where were you?" she started, getting to the point faster than I had hoped. I sighed and moved myself to one of the chairs along the wall, feeling defeated. How much was I allowed to tell her? She already knew much more than she should, and if I told her anything else, would that force the Unseelie to seek me out again?

"I can't tell you." I knew it was a mistake the moment the words left my mouth. Anne rolled her eyes and shook her head. "I can't. I'm sorry. It'll make more trouble for both of us."

"What could possibly be left to create more trouble?" she demanded, her voice harsh but quiet. "You cannot tell me what you did and then *disappear*, and then expect me to just accept that you're not willing to explain yourself."

"It's not that I'm not willing, Anne, it's... it's that I can't tell you because your safety depends on it. And mine, too. All of us." I gestured to our surroundings, indicating that I was talking about our whole family.

"Well clearly you're not safe anyway," she said, thrusting her hand toward the bandage on my head. "Where did you fall that someone was able to fix you up so cleanly? Is that why you were in the village this morning? Did you visit the apothecary?"

"Never if I can help it," I scoffed under my breath. She gave me a disappointed look. "My friend helped me," I added finally, trying to navigate the fine line between truth and lie in my head.

"The lass you've been seeing?" she guessed casually, though I could hear the intrigue underneath. "It's quite surprising that you're being so secretive about her. It's not like you to hide things."

If only you knew, I thought. "No. It was another friend. The one I told you about, who is also friends with Breck." It felt dangerous to even mention them by name to someone in the unmagical part of my life now. But to Anne, Breck was still our neighbor and the miller. Finna was another story.

I could feel Anne's suspicions from across the room, as if they were reaching out to me because of how badly she wanted to voice them. I got up and crossed the decorative rug to stand in front of the desk and held out the flowers for her to take. After a moment of hesitation, she reached and brought them close to her. She dipped her head to press her nose delicately against one of the rose blooms and inhaled slowly. When she looked up at me again, there was a small smile on her lips.

"Are you courting this girl, Peter, or just fooling around with her? Because you need to be fair. Don't mess with her emotions if she thinks your intentions are good when they're not."

I bit my tongue as she spoke, nodding. I could tell she'd been thinking about this since we spoke last. I knew it came from a good place. She wanted me to be happy, and to have what she had with my brother – a loving relationship and marriage, like Henry was about to have with Sarah, and like my parents had before all of us. I couldn't blame her for not understanding my secrets I'd never shared.

"Nan will be gutted when she finds out it's not Bette O'Clery," she laughed, but then her face fell, and she lowered her voice. "It's not, it is?" I gave her a look of exasperation, and when she laughed again, I did too.

TWENTY

I decided to risk showing my face at the practice field. I managed to get there on foot by the time they were nearly ready to wrap things up. I stood at the low stone wall and watched as Wally drilled them from the saddle of his horse. My eyebrows came together as I realized it was the chestnut mare he was riding. Nobody had ridden her but me since she'd arrived.

She was as spectacular to watch as she was to ride. The way her coat flashed red in the sunlight when she cut hard on her turns, and the relax in her body when she was allowed to run gave me a pang of something akin to jealousy. Wally looked old and stubby on her back. He was a skilled horseman, but he didn't know her like I did, and some of her transitions were choppy because of it. I made my way to the gate and let myself in when they called it for the day. Henry pushed his gelding to reach me faster when he finally saw me.

"What the feck happened to you yesterday?! Was your headache so bad that you forgot about me? I thought you'd at least say somethin' before you left."

"Sorry, I hurt myself," I explained, pushing my hair back to expose the bandage. "Hit my head. I think I passed out. Nan didn't let me back out for the rest of the day. She won't let me ride today, either." I felt bad for how easily this lie slipped out, but Henry seemed to believe it. Probably because he was the one person I didn't lie to very often.

"Will the auld bat still let you ride tomorrow?" Wally asked, appearing beside Henry. The chestnut mare eyed me and tossed her head a little. It was strange to see someone else's bridle on her.

"I'll be fine for the match," I promised them, the mare included. I didn't want to give Wally any excuse to ride her again. He and Thomas rode ahead toward the stables as the sun started to dip in the sky. Henry dismounted and walked beside me, his gelding trailing behind us calmly. I dug myself a little deeper into the untruth so I could deliver Sarah's message. I knew she would bring it up when they met again.

"Nan sent me to the village this morning to collect the messages since I couldn't ride. I ran into Sarah and her sisters," I told him. I forced a serious face. "She wanted me to tell you the wedding is off."

"Oh, that's a gas," he came back, deadpan. "With the money that's been spent already, I don't think we have a choice, boyo. She might tell me she's slept with every man in this village and the next, and we'd still be taking those vows, if our parents have any say."

I chuckled shortly, watching Wally and Thomas disappear from our view along the road. "Well, at least you know it wouldn't be the truth."

Henry reached up to clutch my shoulder with his free hand, giving it a squeeze and a shake before he let go.

"Aye, what a comfort to know me best man would be the last person to bed me new bride."

"I would never," I promised, hand over my heart. We both laughed, and he drew in a deep breath, blowing it out in a rush. "They'd just left the seamstress. They're all very excited about their new dresses." I must've struck a chord, because Henry rolled his eyes dramatically beside me with an *ugh*.

"It's all they've talked about, Pete. For weeks! Sarah's getup cost more than me feckin' horse." He gestured to the gelding for emphasis. Even if he meant purely from a money standpoint, that was more than what some people earned in a year, but I knew his emotional tie to the animal doubled or tripled that sum in his mind.

"Wow," was all I could come up with. The thought of being surrounded by so much finery made me a little nervous. I was expected to play this role of best man for Henry, which meant I would be standing in front of all the wealthiest people both of their families knew. I glanced down at myself as we walked, hopeful that what I planned on wearing would be sufficient.

"Have you decided if you're going to bring the miller along?" he asked.

I wasn't prepared for the question. It made my heart beat a little unevenly in my chest. I gave him a sidelong glance. "You know I can't," I responded quietly. Henry paused only for a moment before he understood.

"Well, I just mean invite him like you did before. He doesn't have to accompany you or anything. He's just another guest," he said, shrugging.

Sure, I could invite him as just another guest. He would blend in with all the others. Maybe he would even

S.O. CALLAHAN

be recognized as a familiar face, though most of the attendees wouldn't be the type to do their own shopping around the village for kitchen goods.

The problem was that I would want to talk to him. And only him. Just like I'd done at the engagement party. How many times would I be allowed to behave that way before someone started to question it? I'd always tried to be as inconspicuous as I could be, just as a general rule – it'd been rather easy as the third son and proverbial middle child in my family. But ever since those dynamics had shifted, I felt more exposed to the scrutiny of others, both inside my home and in the community.

My silence had drawn Henry's attention. "You really like him, don't you?" I brought my hand up to the back of my neck, giving it a few slow squeezes before I nodded, my eyes fixed on the pale dirt road passing under our feet. "*Shite*," he sighed. I knew he meant it as an apology.

"I know," I told him. It came out sadder than I'd meant it to. I dropped my hand back to my side, and we walked in silence for a while. I listened to the sound of our footsteps falling and the horse's gentle breathing, finding comfort in the familiarity of the subtle noises Henry's tack made as it moved with each hoofbeat. "Can I?" I asked finally.

Henry looked at me and my outstretched hand, then passed over the reins. I took them, moving my other hand to pat the gelding's neck a few times. I focused on his calm energy and slowed my breathing to soothe my troubled mind. I could tell Henry was thinking hard, too, and we walked the rest of the way to the

318

stables without talking.

**

I was wrung out before our match even started. My sleep had been plagued with vivid dreams that kept waking me up. In all of them, I saw the face of the Unseelie. I was worried that he would return to ask his question again. What would I do to lift the curse? My human instinct was to tell him I'd do anything. I knew better than that now. He would take it literally. And if I offered something else, he would play tricks with my words or find some loophole. It was a situation I couldn't win.

Anne was still carrying her child. This time was different. That's what I kept telling myself to try and ease the pressure I felt to come up with a solution. Maybe the dark fae was trying to get me to promise something new to him under the pretense that this cycle of loss was going to continue for some time, when it was really coming to an end. I wanted to ask Finna about it, but she'd told me to leave it alone. I didn't want to get Breck in trouble by asking him about it, either. Anne was in too fragile of a state to worry her over it again. I was out of options.

I removed my cap and reached for my helmet, which was sitting on the low stone wall, and I was surprised to find something underneath it as I put it on. I looped the strap to secure it before I picked up the white envelope. The faintest smell of mint crept up to meet my nose as I opened it.

Your breeches are distracting.

Have a drink of water

before the match.

B

A grin instantly spread on my lips as I quickly folded the paper back up to return it to the envelope, trying not to draw the attention of my teammates around me. I stuffed it inside my cap to put with the rest of my belongings.

Our bucket of drinking water was only a few paces away; I dipped the ladle inside and brought it to my lips, draining it in a few swallows. My eyes scanned the crowd of spectators who were taking their seats, ready for the match to begin. I couldn't see him. Maybe that was for my own good. I filled and emptied the ladle once more before I put my foot in the stirrup and swung my other leg over my horse, adjusting in the saddle. Wally handed me my mallet and clapped his hands in an encouraging way as the four of us rode onto the pitch to join the other team.

Henry said some taunting words under his breath so the referee wouldn't hear, but he must've gotten his point across, because the other players now wore fresh scowls on their faces. He turned his horse around and winked at me when his back was to them. I laughed silently, my shoulders shaking as I tried not to encourage his behavior. By the time I hit my first ball, I could feel the effects of whatever Breck had done to the water. My exhaustion started to fade, and my mind grew sharper. A small part of my brain was still begging to locate him in the crowd, but I forced it down. This match was too important to be distracted.

Toward the end of the third chukka, we were

ahead, and the real reason for Breck's absence revealed itself when storm clouds began to gather overhead. If it started to rain, we wouldn't be able to finish the game. My mind went to Fallon's ability to handle the weather. She had proven that she could summon the clouds and rain when she needed to. I wondered if she also had the ability to send them away.

Thomas was busy pushing the ball down the field when I felt a raindrop land on my cheek. I squinted up at the sky and wished hard that no more would fall. Postponing the match wouldn't be the worst thing to ever happen, but our team was in a good rhythm. We just had to make it a little longer to secure our position in the championship game.

A player on the other team hooked Thomas's mallet when he went for another swing, and our direction of play shifted when a second player smashed the ball toward our goal. I urged my gray mare forward, picking up speed. Before I could reach them, Henry executed a nearly flawless bump on the player with the ball, their horses coming shoulder-to-shoulder as he moved the player out of the way so he could gain control. I charged past him, open to receive a pass on my right side, and he sent it to me with a solid hit.

I brought my mallet down and dragged the ball with me as I turned the mare around, keeping it close with a few small taps, before we took off, accelerating to avoid the other players who were gaining on us. Any trace of fatigue I'd been feeling earlier was gone. Adrenaline was pumping through me, and though my lungs were starting to feel like I needed to clear them, I held off long enough to send the ball sailing through the goal.

I released the coughs I'd been holding in and breathed deeper, grateful for the short break we had entered before the final chukka. I trotted my horse over to Wally and dismounted, exchanging her for the chestnut mare to finish the game. Her energy shifted as she realized it was her turn to play. I glanced at my cap and pressed my lips together against the grin that tried to return as I thought of Breck's letter.

When play resumed, I estimated that there was just enough time to finish the game before the clouds gave out above us. The wind had picked up, too, and I noticed many of the spectators had already gathered themselves up to leave. Sarah and her sisters were gone from the seats they'd occupied. I looked toward Henry to see if he'd noticed, but he wasn't paying any attention to the people around us. He never really did. I shook the distractions from my head and focused. Thomas had the ball again after knocking it away from the other team. He took a big swing but missed. I groaned and pushed the chestnut mare faster.

Our fourth man, Fergus, swooped in and hooked the ball away before I got close enough to make a move. He was good at maneuvering in the middle of the heavy action, which he proved by successfully keeping possession of it until he was clear to speed up and take a shot. As he did, a player on the other team cut across the line of the ball. He narrowly avoided smacking the horse with his mallet, and the umpire called a penalty on the other player. It gave us an even bigger advantage with a free goal.

They made us work for it, but when the final

horn sounded, we'd won, and then it was bucketing. The remaining spectators scrambled toward their carriages waiting to take them home. Henry laughed and tossed his head back in the rain, arms stretched up and wide in celebration of our victory. Thomas looked like a cat somebody had thrown into a pond. Wally yelled for us to hurry up and get off the field so we could leave. I moved the chestnut mare over to the stone wall and leaned down so I could grab my things, and I made certain to protect the envelope from the weather inside my cap.

Before I went to collect the rest of my team, I shielded my eyes with my arm and looked up at the sky. *"Thanks, Fallon,"* I whispered.

***

We were all soaked by the time we arrived at the stables. We made quick work of delivering our horses to the hands as thunder boomed over our heads.

"Fellas!" We all turned to look up toward the house, where Anne was standing in the open kitchen doorway, waving a handkerchief to catch our attention. The three of us exchanged glances before we darted back out into the weather and up the hill.

"What is it?" I asked when we were close enough to not have to shout to be heard. I assumed there would be more panic in her voice if something was wrong.

"Nan wants you all out of the weather. She's made supper for everyone. Come in," she said, stepping aside to give us room. Not long after, we were all crowded around the hearth in the sitting room with steaming bowls of stew in our hands and thick blankets around our shoulders. We'd been forced out of our jackets, waistcoats, shirts, and riding boots. They were by the fireplace in the kitchen, set out to drip dry.

Henry was already on his second helping of Nan's stew, which had made her smile bigger than I'd seen in a long time. Thomas and I were moving a little slower. I had a suspicion that Thomas viewed this meal as something his father would feed to their hunting dogs, but he was being polite about it, thankfully. I wasn't above kicking him out of my house into the rain if he offended Nan.

"Are you excited to be playing in the championship?" Anne asked on her brief sweep through the room to make sure we didn't need anything. Even though she hadn't directed the question at anyone in particular, I knew Henry would be the one to answer.

"Aye, but I think I'm going to need to sleep for three days to prepare myself for the upcoming weekend," he said, laughing to himself. "I don't know why I agreed to Sarah planning our wedding for the day after our biggest game of the year." Anne laughed demurely and nodded in agreement.

"At least the game is first so we're able to drink as much as we like the next day," Thomas added. Henry gave him a pointed look and set down the spoonful of food he was about to put in his mouth.

"Thomas, you better not make a feckin' – sorry Anne – an arse of yourself at my wedding," he warned, lowering his voice at the end of his sentence. "Sarah will kill me if anything messes up her big day." He retrieved his spoon out of the bowl and finished the bite he'd started before with a little more force than necessary.

"I didn't say I was going to get *hammered*," he retorted, setting his bowl on the floor in front of his crossed legs and pulling the blanket tighter around his shoulders. "I just meant I'm glad I'll get to enjoy myself." He paused and gave me a cheeky grin after Anne had returned to the kitchen. "Besides, we have Peter to fill that role whenever the booze comes out." Before I had time to react, Henry reached up and slapped Thomas on the back of his head. He looked aghast as he reached back to rub the spot, and then he frowned. "Ow."

"Feck your *ow*, you tool. His Nan is filling your belly and warming your bones. You don't get to say shite like that to a man in his own home. Have a little respect, would you?"

Thomas kept the frown on his features, but his eyes flicked up to me before they fell back to the fire burning near us. "Sorry," he mumbled.

Lightning flashed in the window behind me, but the rain had finally died down as the cool air of the night rolled in. Despite the company sitting in front of me, my mind drifted to Breck. I wondered if he'd made it back home from delivering his letter before the downpour started. I recalled the storm I'd run through to see his shimmering freckles, and the gentler rain that had dripped down our faces as we revealed how we felt about each other.

My thoughts crashed to a stop.

We had done that, hadn't we? We stood out in the rain and held each other and said that we wanted what we both felt coming. Then he'd taken me to his bed, and we'd slept together for the first time. My first time.

I thought I didn't want him to fall for me because of what we couldn't have. We couldn't have a marriage like Henry and Sarah. We couldn't be recognized before Eabha, either. But I wanted him for what we could have. He'd taught me so many things I never knew about. He introduced me to his friends. He took me to breakfast and thoroughly spoiled me just because he wanted to. He cared about me. Despite our differences, and the things about ourselves that we couldn't show the rest of the world, we could show them to each other, and that was okay.

It's enough, I thought. I sucked in a breath that made me cough. Thomas and Henry didn't look at me. They'd also settled into a silence, watching the flames on the hearth.

"I've something I need to do," I announced. I stood up off the floor, letting the blanket fall from my bare shoulders. I went up the steps two at a time, shoved my feet into an old pair of shoes, and grabbed the first shirt I found in my room. I was still pulling it over my head as I ran back down the stairs, blowing past the sitting room and out the front door.

"Pete?" I heard Henry call out as the door shut in my wake.

I pushed my arms through the sleeves of my cloak and started running. I wasn't going to let this happen again. I'd lost Jamie before I could say all that I needed to say, and soon I would probably lose Breck to his responsibilities, too. My lungs started to burn as I kept urging my legs to move.

I felt the rain soaking into the new, dry bandage Nan had put on my temple. I blinked the water out of my eyes, and when I opened them, I thought I saw a shadow of something cross directly in front of me. It was enough to break my momentum; I slowed down, panting hard. Then, I felt a rough shove on the back of my shoulders at the same moment a wave of dizziness hit me. I stumbled forward onto the muddy road. Tiny pieces of gravel pressed uncomfortably into my palms and knees through my breeches.

"Looks like you didn't see that dip in the dirt there," he said, confirming my fear. I turned to look at the member of the Unseelie court standing behind me. His cloak had a hood that was pulled up over his head, protecting him from the rain.

"You pushed me," I argued quietly as I attempted to get up. He set fire to his magic in my lungs, making me cry out and land back on my hands. "What do you want from me?" I asked through gritted teeth when I could breathe enough to speak again.

"I came to see if you'd given any more thought to my proposition."

"I've barely had enough time to recover from your last visit," I told him, which made him laugh. It was deceptively smooth, almost friendly. I was determined to get to my feet in front of him. He finally allowed me to stand up, and I wiped my hands together before I looked at him. He seemed to take this as more of a communication than I'd intended. A challenge. His eyes narrowed.

"Breckabhainn came to us very concerned about you. He told us that you were to be his mate before

I touched you with my magic. Is this true?" I looked down in shame as the words left his mouth, before I remembered that fairies didn't have the same concerns as humans did when it came to intimate relationships. I didn't want to lie, but technically he *had* told them that.

"Yes," I said finally. He hummed in the back of his throat, his eyes shifting back and forth between mine. He was reading me. I tried to think of nothing. I didn't know what he was capable of.

"He's awfully young to have already picked his mate. Most don't for at least fifty years or so. If they ever do." His gaze traveled from my face to my shoes and back again. "Personally, I've always preferred keeping my options open." The last part left a smirk on his face, before it disappeared. "What's so special about you? A simple human who nearly died from a simple human disease. Your young Breck is destined for greatness. Why would he waste time committing himself to someone who will be dead soon anyway?"

I couldn't decide if he was trying to get under my skin, or if he truly believed what he was saying, but I bit back the emotions his words stirred in me. The way his eyes lit up told me that something was betraying my attempt to appear calm. Inside, his words were cutting like a hot blade. In my haste to get to the mill, I'd taken the shorter trail along the river rather than the main road from our house. My eyes shifted to the water running by steadily in the darkness. A shiver went down my spine as I remembered how cold it was when I'd been thrown into it. The Unseelie chuckled.

"Perhaps we should adjust our focus to make the deal a little more enticing for you," he said, taking an easy step toward me. I didn't dare move. I didn't speak, either, for fear of saying too much. A burn developed deep in my lungs, enough to make me wince. I took shallow breaths until he made it stop. "I could change it, you know. The magic in you." He reached out like he meant to touch my chest. Fear welled in me as my eyes followed his pale, bony hand. He stopped short of actually making contact with my cloak, grinning at the reaction I was certain he could see or feel in me.

"Would I die?" I asked, looking at his face again. He was close enough now for me to see that his eyes were dark and sunken underneath.

"Yes. Unless, of course, we'd come to a new agreement." He let his hand fall back to his side and turned, starting to pace around me in a circle that was too small for my comfort.

"Do I have to make a wish? I don't know how this works," I confessed. I saw his eyebrows go up in my peripheral as he came around to my other side.

"Years in bed with the same fairy, and you *don't know how this works*?" he questioned slowly, and I swallowed hard at my mistake.

"We don't discuss things like this." I squeezed my hands in and out of fists at my sides.

"*Ah*," he breathed then, as if something made better sense. "Mouths too busy for talking. I understand." His expression changed to something more suggestive, making me shift uncomfortably on my feet. He began his second pass behind my back as he spoke again. "Since we're discussing it, we can smooth out the details first. But yes, you have to present it to me as a wish."

Something told me that saying no wasn't an option I had any longer. He was going to force this wish out of me one way or another. I was relieved that we were moving away from Anne, at least. I had to take my family out of this completely if I had any hope of keeping them safe. When I remained silent for too long, he stopped his circling and stood in front of me, his expression growing darker. I pushed my hand back through my wet hair and shrugged helplessly.

"Come now," he said, agitated but trying to hide it. "What's your greatest wish? What's the thing you desire most in your short, human life?" He stepped closer, until his face was near enough to mine that he could whisper. "*What had you running through a storm at night like it was the most important thing you'd ever done?*" My heart constricted as I realized what he was trying to get at. He wanted me to make a wish that involved Breck.

Breck. Where are you? I need you. I decided I wasn't above begging for him in my thoughts if it meant I could get out of this somehow. I'd said too much and worked myself into a corner. I didn't know what else to say to stall the conversation. *Please hear me.*

A strong gust of wind blew past us, and then it became even more intense, whipping my cloak open. The Unseelie and I both grimaced against the sudden change in the weather as raindrops met my skin like they'd been shot at me. Lightning flashed overhead as the storm grew even more powerful.

I swallowed hard, weighing my options as the dark fae seemed to grow more distracted. He turned his head as the strongest gale hit us, blowing his hood back off his head to expose his silver hair and long, pointed ears. As quickly as it had started, the wind was gone, and it had taken all the rain with it. I looked up and found stars in the sky above us instead of the clouds that had just been there.

"Orin. Leave him alone."

The dark fae had already taken several steps away from me when she spoke; I took my chance to do the same as Fallon stepped out of the line of trees behind me on the trail. She gave me a once-over with her eyes before turning her attention back to the man staring at her as she came to stand a short distance in front of me. The smooth, confident expression on his face hadn't changed, but I could tell he'd given her space because she demanded his respect.

"This lad has all of you looking after him, I see. I wish I'd known that I planted my magic in such an important human," he said, bringing his hands up to guide his hood back over his damp hair.

"All humans are important," Fallon retorted. Her arms were in their favorite position, crossed over her chest, and she stood as though she was ready to block him from me if she needed to. A short silence settled over us on the trail as they seemed to establish who had the upper hand without needing any words. It was all done with body language and eye contact. The tension around us finally broke as Orin chuckled and looked down, shaking his head with a slight grin on his pallid mouth.

"You know, Fallon, I thought after all these years, you would've given up on them." His gaze shifted to me and lingered before he spoke again. "But I suppose after you've had your taste of human, it's hard to stop. At least that's what I hear. I've never had one myself. Too risky. Too... boring," he concluded. He had taken a few steps as he spoke, but they didn't bring him any closer to us. He was skirting an invisible boundary they had created out of what seemed to be mutual aversion.

Thunder sounded in the distance, and Fallon advanced a few steps toward him. He retreated until the same distance existed between them as it had before. His actions drove him closer to another curve in the narrow trail. Behind him was the river, still running by as fixedly as water could manage. I was busy imagining him falling into it as revenge when another slight breeze picked up. I felt the chill start around my ankles and wrists, before the icy sensation curled up my legs and arms lazily. Despite the shiver it sent through me, I felt my chest and face grow warm at the reaction my body had to Breck's magic on my skin. It was the worst time to have relief and arousal mix within me, but there was no stopping it. He was there, somewhere, and I was safe.

"Peter doesn't want you here, and neither do I. You're not welcome on this land. All you do is bring trouble for the humans," Fallon started, exuding authority. I managed to keep my reaction to a minimum as Breck's magic found its way around the rest of me. The water was pulled from my clothes and my hair, leaving me temporarily cold but dry. I shivered again as the last curls of ice slid away. "You might get away with this where the humans live under different protection, but you will not get away with it here," she continued.

"You think I would *choose* to mess with humans

in your domain?" Orin asked, amused.

"You did choose us. You picked their wishes from the Wishing Tree," I cut in, finding my voice. His eyes cut to mine sharply. "Breck said that you told him the wishes called out to you, and you took them. Both of them." My heart was beating hard in my chest at my newfound confidence to speak to him that way. Fallon didn't seem concerned, though, so I continued. "You didn't have to take them. You didn't have to put this inside of me." I smacked my hand against my chest, brows furrowing. "But you did."

"Are you not grateful to be alive?" he countered nonchalantly, his hands coming up in question. "I can remove it, if you'd like..." he trailed off. I swallowed thickly.

"You can't change a wish unless someone makes a new one to counter it," I said, taking a step forward. I had no idea if this was actually true, but something told me to say it. The vexed look growing on his face told me that I'd been correct. Orin took a few steps toward the side of the path opposite of the river before he looked at me again.

"You're not happy. Living this way." Even with distance between us, I could see his eyes trail over my body for the second time, slow and calculating. "You're a young lad with the lungs of an auld man. You wish you could get through a day, a *moment*, without having to stop and catch your breath." I clamped down on my thoughts, squeezing my eyes shut to make sure any reaction I had to his words wouldn't be taken as me agreeing to what he was saying. "It could be different. You could run again. You could fill your chest with air.

It's been a while since you could do that," he kept on, pausing to chuckle deeply. "You could take your lover to bed and save the gasping for *after* he's fucked you instead of before."

"That's enough," Fallon cut in finally, making him back away with only her words this time.

"Let him speak for himself," he challenged. He was staring at me when I finally opened my eyes again. "Tell us, Peter. Don't you wish for all of those things?"

Truthfully, I had wished for all of it. I had wished for so many things in my life. I'd wished that my family was still with me. I'd wished Jamie was still alive. I'd wished that I was as good at everything as Henry was. I'd wished that I didn't do such a poor job of not worrying Nan all the time. I'd wished that I was a better brother for my siblings, and for Anne. I'd wished that I could be interested in women like all the other lads. I'd wished my curly hair would behave when I needed it to. I'd wished for hundreds of winning shots during our matches, and thousands of other things that I couldn't remember.

I'd wished for my family to be safe. I'd wished to find love again. I'd wished to be happy. "No," I said quietly. "No, I don't wish for anything. I already have everything I want."

Orin made a frustrated, growling sound that wasn't entirely human before he regained his composure. Fallon side-stepped in front of me to stand directly between us, and he laughed, waving his hand dismissively.

"Don't bother with that. He's useless to me. It's

only fun when they're scared." He grabbed the edge of his cloak and extended it out wide before he whipped it across his body and disappeared entirely without a sound. I blinked at the empty spot where he'd been standing as Fallon looked at me. She seemed almost proud as she dipped her head before taking her leave back into the trees. I wasn't sure how she could just set off after all that with nothing to say, but before I could call after her, I felt Breck's brumal touch on me again.

I turned to find him standing a short distance behind me on the narrow trail, hands in his pockets with an unreadable expression on his face. All the other feelings I'd just gone through melted away, and I grinned at him, shivering as he withdrew his magic. I decided to hold on tight to this confidence I'd dredged up from somewhere inside me.

"Are you—"

"Please don't ask if I'm alright," I cut him off, stepping forward to close the gap between us. My hands came to the sides of his face. I slid my thumbs over the freckles on his cheekbones slowly, back and forth. He brought his hands up to hold my wrists as I leaned in to kiss him. Our mouths came together, and he made a small sound of surprise before he kissed me back.

"But are you?" he pressed when we pulled apart, his eyes searching mine. I kissed the frown lines between his eyebrows before I rested our foreheads together.

"I'm more alright than I've ever been, I think," I told him.

"Did you mean what you said?" His voice was

quiet, tone soft.

"Which part?" I asked on an exhale, laughing a little. I'd been so wrapped in my emotions that I'd already forgotten what my responses were to all of the Unseelie's questions. My hands were still trembling as I came back down from my encounter.

"You said you don't wish for anything. That you have everything you want," he reminded me, before he chuckled, almost sadly, and pushed his forehead against mine, making our noses bump together. "That's going to make it hard for me to keep helping you."

Something squeezed in my chest. I leaned back so our eyes could meet again. He looked vulnerable, showing his age for once. I felt my nerves start to buzz to life inside me. They were tempting me, as they always did, to shy away from saying the hard things to say. To keep things hidden the way I'd always done, to protect myself.

I took a shaky breath and let it out before I moved my hands to embrace him, one on his neck and the other on his lower back, pulling him against me. The last boost of confidence I needed came when his arms slid beneath my heavy cloak and wrapped around my waist, holding us close together. He wanted this, too.

"I'm going to need your help every day," I said, my voice barely above a whisper as I rested our foreheads together again, "to show me how to love you the best I can."

TWENTY-ONE

I placed a few pieces of split wood into Breck's small stove after I'd managed to get a flame going. I waited for it to grow a bit before I closed the door and adjusted the damper. We'd opened the window over the bed to get some fresh air, and that combined with his magic curling around me as he slept had woken me up with a chill.

As I returned to the bed, I paused for a moment. I had only seen Breck asleep once before, at Finna's after he'd gotten himself in trouble with the Unseelie. He'd looked pained and exhausted then. I studied his face in the moonlight. Half of it was pressed heavily into the pillow. The other half was relaxed, his forehead and eyebrows covered by his hair. His shoulders rose and fell smoothly. My eyes continued down his bare back to where the bedclothes were resting at his waist, and the dimples there.

Before I got worked up for the second time that night, I eased myself into the empty spot I'd left, trying hard not to disturb him. I was almost able to pull the blankets up over us when he breathed in deeply and turned onto his side, facing away from me. I decided this was an opportunity I couldn't pass up. I wrapped my arm around his chest and pulled him close to me. He relaxed into my embrace.

After the encounter on my way to the mill, Breck and I had struggled to break out of each other's arms long enough to make it across the bridge, up the steps, and into the bed. His touch, his smell, everything about him was a draw that I couldn't ignore.

I moved my head closer to his on the pillow and rested my face against the back of his neck. Before I could stop myself, I started placing gentle, soundless kisses on his shoulder. Our breaths had fallen into the same rhythm. I closed my eyes and focused on it. I was certain I'd never felt this level of contentment in my entire life.

The sound of the water rushing over the falls outside the window brought a grin to my lips. We'd done that. I had all but thrown Breck onto the bed after I got his trousers off, and while I worked on my own, he'd ripped his shirt over his head and reached for the small jar he kept for us. It had been a frenzied mixture of touching mouths and hands and other things as we tried desperately to get enough of one another.

"I can't decide what's louder right now, your thoughts or your emotions." Breck's voice was thick with sleep, but I could hear the smile in it. I wrapped my arm around him tighter and nuzzled against his neck and hair.

"I didn't mean to wake you," I told him, kissing his shoulder again. He chuckled and pressed closer to me, our bodies flush.

"Looks like I'm not the only one you woke up," he teased. My erection was wedged between us. His snuggling back against me wasn't helping. I shifted my hips a bit and hid my face against his shoulder, which made him laugh again. He turned over under my arm to face me, pulling the covers up higher as he did, and found my mouth with his for a slow, tender kiss.

"Did you know," he paused, bringing his hand up to push my hair away from my face with his delicate fingers, "that you are glowing?"

I blinked and looked around us without moving my head from the pillow, eyebrows coming together as I searched for what he was talking about. All I could find was what I'd already been seeing in the soft moonlight. "No," I said skeptically.

He hummed with a grin and moved his hand to my cheek as he kissed me again. "You can't see it. I can only see it a little bit. It's your energy. I've never felt it so strongly before."

"I'm sure I can thank you for that," I guessed. I watched his eyes study my face in the moonlight. My wet bandage had come off at some point. His gaze lingered there, his untroubled expression faltering slightly. I'd looked at it the night before when I applied the salve from Finna. It wasn't so bad, really. Breck leaned up and kissed next to the spot that was sutured, his lips staying on my skin for a beat.

My arms went around his waist so I could hold him closer, and he slid his knee between my legs, which I parted to give him more room. I had to stifle the sound of pleasure that threatened to escape me as his fingers found the back of my head and began playing through my curls.

"What does it mean when they call you Breckabhainn?" I asked finally, hopeful that I was saying it the same way I'd heard Orin say it. Finna had said it before, too.

"That's my name," he said quietly, fingers still threading mindlessly. I breathed heavily against his chest, where he'd pulled my head to. His cheek was against my hair. "Everyone just calls me Breck."

"Do you have a last name?"

"Not really. It's just the one. At least, I think so. I've never seen it written down before."

"You've never written your whole name?" I asked then, surprised. I recalled the hours I spent writing my name again and again in school as a child. I'd been yelled at more times than I could remember over how I formed my e's, so I'd been forced to write *Peter Walshe, Peter Walshe, Peter Walshe* until the string of letters had temporarily lost all meaning to me.

Breck made a small noise in his throat as he began to speak but stopped himself. He was struggling to tell a truth to me. I kissed the freckled skin beneath my lips to let him know it was alright. "I've only written to you," he admitted. I picked my head up at that, forcing my heavy eyelids open to look at him. Embarrassment had his arched brows pinched together.

"But your penmanship is so nice," I argued, recalling each of his letters and the way his handwriting scrolled across the paper so neatly. He gave me a sheepish grin before he looked over his shoulder at the shelves on the wall.

"I copied the letters from my books. It's harder to combine them into new words than I thought it would be. I should've listened to Finna and practiced more." He turned back to me then, his gaze not meeting mine. "But

I'm still learning. I'll get better. I know it's an important skill to have in the human world." Did that mean he was planning on staying after all? My silence as I considered this exciting news must've made him worry that I was still stuck on his shortcoming, so he continued. "Fairies communicate in many other ways that make writing mostly unnecessary. I can read well, though. I—"

I cut him off with a kiss, trying to calm the state he was working himself into. He relaxed immediately, and I pushed him onto his back as I moved over him, pressing our bodies together. Breck moaned softly as his hands trailed down my back. He pulled his legs up on either side of me, bent at the knees. I couldn't have kept my hips still if I tried.

When we finally broke apart so I could breathe – and cough – I supported myself on one forearm so I could push his messy hair to the side off his forehead. "I can teach you. To write," I said in between my stifled breaths. "I was a terrible student. I got lots of extra practice." Breck gave me a full smile at that and pulled me back down to him, our lips and noses colliding.

We stopped again only so Breck could reach for the small jar we'd left on the windowsill. He seemed to have a special way of taking away any fatigue I felt and transforming it into something more useful. I pushed myself up onto my knees and watched him rub his hands together before he grabbed me, coating me with the thick liquid. "What did you do to the water at my match?" I asked, panting. The thin rings on his fingers glinted in the light from the window, each stroke bringing me closer to forgetting that I'd asked a question at all.

"Nothing," he said, the tone of his voice revealing that his thoughts were also far away from this topic. "You just needed to drink some water. You were dehydrated." I dragged my eyes to his face then, my eyebrows raised, and I laughed shortly. I'd been convinced that he'd used his magic to enhance the water somehow. All he did was encourage me to take care of myself.

I leaned down and kissed him before I sat up again, my hands coming to his thighs. He finally looked at me and tilted his head back against the pillow, his throat working on a swallow. In one motion, his legs came up around my hips and back as I pushed into him, slow and deep. He exhaled harshly and angled his hips more for me, closing his eyes. I was several thrusts in before he seemed to remember that he wanted to be an active participant. He looked at me, half-lidded, and moved his hand between his own legs.

I bent forward to hold onto the edge of the windowsill with one hand, my mind still grasping at his magic and what he could do with it. I'd experienced the intense sensations the minty chill of it could provide. He could control water, drawing it from the air and other places at his discretion. The river responded as if it was an extension of him. He could somehow even sense what the water inside my body was doing. These were not small accomplishments, but he made them seem effortless. What was he capable of if he really tried?

Orin had put it most plainly. He was destined for greatness.

"Stop it," Breck said, breathless, pulling me from wherever I'd gone in my head. "I can't focus enough to hear your thoughts, but I can feel them." I gave him a rueful look and realized how pent-up he already was beneath me, edging closer to his release. He reached up with his free hand and wrapped his fingers around my wrist that was supporting my weight against the sill, and then our eyes met again. "Stop thinking and make love to me."

So, I did. I picked up my pace and kissed him as much as my lungs would allow. A shift of my weight on one knee made him gasp; his fingertips digging into my arm. Eventually, his back arched from the bed and his hand worked faster as I could tell what was coiling up inside of him, ready to snap loose, and then he cried out against my mouth as he came. I wasn't prepared for his magic to envelop me as he did, and it pushed me over with him.

TWENTY-TWO

Breck had been called to meet Eabha with the others the following morning. I spent the rest of the week preparing for our final match of the season during the day and thinking of him at night. Two days before the championship game, I'd paid Finna a visit.

The chestnut mare carried us up the slight hill to her cottage, which was busy blooming with new colors as the season began to shift. Reds and oranges and yellows were replacing the pinks, whites, and purples I'd grown accustomed to seeing on my approach to her home. A few of the trees had begun to make the change, too.

"Finna?" I stepped inside and shut the door behind me. The weather had been mild, and the road was dry, so I wasn't worried about tracking mud through her home as I went around the corner into the kitchen. I let my gaze wander around the small space. Even without her bustling around, there was a certain energy about the room that couldn't be ignored. It was like she left traces of herself wherever she went. The door to the garden hung open, revealing where I needed to check next.

I found her along a row of latticework trellises that held vines with large, flat leaves. My feet crunching on the crushed stone walkway announced my arrival the moment I stepped onto it. Finna continued humming a tune to herself as she worked, cutting clusters of fruit from the vines and placing them into her basket.

"It's one of my favorite times of the year, love!" she said, smiling as she turned to look at me. "It's time to make the wine." Her tiny fingers pulled a few deep blue grapes from a cluster and held them out for me. I took them and popped one into my mouth. The sweetness surprised me as I chewed carefully to avoid breaking the bitter seeds inside. "Almost as fun as drinking it."

"Is there anything you can't do?" I asked as I ate the other one. Finna cackled and tucked her hair behind her ear, giving me a clever look.

"Oh, plenty. I'm a terrible seamstress. My spells still fail me sometimes. I cannot ride a horse." She tapped a finger on her chin, thinking. I waved my hand to stop her.

"Alright, alright. Point taken. You can't ride a horse? When was the last time you tried?" This concept was so foreign to me that I couldn't imagine it. Even William could ride a horse if he had to, he just refused.

"Don't get any wild ideas, lad. I know you've got that beautiful chestnut out front." She stuck another cluster of grapes into her basket and moved to the next vine. "My balance and strength were never good enough for it. I just go bouncing along like a rag doll." I felt bad for the laugh that escaped me, but she joined in too, shrugging in an *oh well* type of way.

"I would never trust that mare with an inexperienced rider anyway," I reassured her. She'd been the reason I tried my first healing salve that Finna made. A small silence stretched between us as I tried to decide how to word what I wanted to say next.

"You came to ask me something, aye?" She eyed me as she reached high to trim another bunch of grapes off the vine. I cleared my throat and rubbed my palms on the seams of my riding breeches twice.

"The... em. The jar that you gave Breck. For us," I bumbled, turning away from her and looking out at the rest of her garden. A bird swooped by to land in a nearby tree, singing brightly.

"You've run out already, is that it?" she guessed, her tone teasing but gentle. She brushed her hair over her shoulder as she turned to me fully, a grin creeping across her mouth.

"No," I said a little too fast, though truthfully, I didn't know for sure. Breck was always the one to take out what we used. "My best friend is getting married, you know. To a woman. But I thought... I thought maybe you might have something I could give to him. As a gift. For the wedding night."

Finna giggled and nodded, her eyes falling to her basket as she set her shears inside it with the grapes. "I'm sure I could come up with something they both would like."

"I can pay you for it," I added. She swished her hand at me, bracelets tinkling together.

"Of course, you won't. Let's go look and see what I've got." She slid her basket off her arm and set it on her potting bench when we reached the cottage. I followed her inside and took my spot at her table, watching as she started to sort through the various jars and cannisters that lined her counters and cupboards. "Can you check that the water's boiling in the pot?"

I followed her directions as she cleared a spot beneath the large window that faced the garden. She stood on her tiptoes on her stool to push it open. The breeze coming through made the herbs hanging there sway lazily. She carefully wiped the area down with a rag and reached for the candle in the holder, exchanging it for one that was made of red wax instead of white.

She lit it with a match and watched it burn for a moment before she pinched the flame out with the tip of her thumb and finger. Her hand cupped at the smoke that billowed from the wick, which she pulled toward her and across the space she'd cleared to work in several times. She began to hum again as she used a new match to relight the candle.

"Fill this with three ladles of water from the pot and bring it back. Use the rag to hold it so it won't burn your hands." I did as she asked, successfully delivering the hot water to her without hurting myself. She had collected her hair into a bundle on top of her head in the meantime, though many pieces had already escaped. "Now, the most important part is breathing the right energy into what we're making. This is for your Henry and his new bride to enjoy on a most special night, so we want to focus on positive energy. Loving energy. Can you do that?" she asked.

I nodded, thinking of what Breck had said about my energy and how strong it'd been. I wasn't sure I knew how to do anything with that energy, but I did know how to think good thoughts. I hoped that was enough as Finna breathed in deeply and let it out even slower, her eyes closed and hands resting flat on her work surface.

When her eyes opened, she reached for a jar that held a fine, white powder. She explained that it was made from arrowroot, which could be used for many different things. She handed me a wooden spoon and instructed me to start stirring as she scooped some of the powder out of the jar and leveled it with her finger before she dumped it into the bowl of water. Two more spoonfuls of the powder went in, and I stirred it dutifully, watching as the mixture began to change consistency.

After she replaced the lid of that jar, she picked up a much smaller one that had oil in it. She removed the lid and waved the jar side to side underneath her nose a few times. "Peppermint oil. Yours didn't need any of this," she said with a wink.

A helpless laugh bubbled up and out of me, and I turned my head away from her, grinning despite the warmth of embarrassment spreading across my face. My focus returned to the bowl as she dripped some of the oil into the mixture. The smell of it flourished as I stirred; I swallowed hard as the mint overpowered my senses. I missed Breck. It had been difficult to go without seeing him for several days before, but now that we'd entered a whole new place in our feelings for each other, it felt nearly unbearable.

Finna relieved me from my task as she took the spoon, stirring with a new vigor that I hadn't known I needed to use. Eventually, the mixture became thick and resembled the concoction that I'd grown familiar with. We used a small cup with a long handle to scoop the viscous liquid into a few empty jars that she'd set out.

"This will just need to set for a while to get thicker, and then it'll be ready to use." She asked me to put the lids on the jars as she cleaned up the space we'd occupied. Another puff of air extinguished the red candle before she stepped down from her stool. "I'll put on some tea. Make yourself comfortable in the sitting room."

I wandered to the other room, taking my time to appreciate her small house and all the things she'd managed to fit in it. Breck's home was barely decorated, as was Fallon's. Finna had filled every empty spot with something. Trinkets here, plants there, furniture, and fabrics, and books. So many books. I was certain it would take years to read them all cover to cover.

I sat in my familiar spot on the sofa and rested my head back against it, closing my eyes. The books made me think of how Breck had been so concerned with his inability to write. I'd pictured him several times since he told me that, leaned over some open pages at his small table, copying the letters the way he saw them to make all the notes he'd written for me.

I'd told him that I would teach him, but what I'd really wanted to say was, *don't you dare be perfect.* He was charming, and intelligent, and painfully handsome. He had to have some kind of weakness. I hadn't expected it to be that, but I was grateful for it, because it made me feel like the gap between us was smaller. I was just a simple human, after all, and he was so much more.

"Tired, love?" Finna asked as she joined me, a cup in each hand. I opened my eyes and sat up, taking my tea from her and shaking my head.

"Just thinking," I told her as I took a sip. She sat in the chair by the sleeping hearth and nodded, bringing her cup to her lips.

"They should be back tomorrow, Breck and the others. He will have lots to tell you about, I imagine. I know they were going to be giving him some lessons with his magic."

"Lessons?"

"Aye, he still has much to learn. The power is all there, but he has to figure out how to use it. It's a great responsibility. He takes it very seriously. I've enjoyed my own lessons with him over the years." Her gaze was on something far away as she seemed to be remembering those times.

"How long have you known him?" I asked, taking another pull of my tea.

"He came to me when he was just a wee lad. Of course, he was nearly as tall as I was by then!" She laughed and pulled her gaze to me, a certain twinkle in her eye. "He was my ward until he turned sixteen."

"He lived with you for all those years? Where is his family? His parents?"

"Nobody knows. Breck has no memory of it either. Fallon found him one day in the woods, dirty and hungry. She brought him to me because she thought I would take care of him. Which, of course, I did. I loved every minute of it."

A silence settled over us. My honeyed tea suddenly felt heavy in my stomach. I tried to imagine what it had been like when Fallon found him. Had she been nice to him, at least? Things started to click into place in my brain faster than I could keep up. It was why he had such a love for Finna. It was why the others spoke about him the way they did. They really had known him since he was a child. They'd watched him grow. They'd been there to see him become the man he was now. I didn't trust my uneasy gut to drink any more. I set the cup down and pushed a hand through my hair to the back of my neck.

"That was a lot at once, I'm sorry." Finna's tone had changed. I looked up and met her softened expression. "I guess he hadn't told you any of that." All I could do was shake my head. Question after question flooded my mind. There was one, however, that stood out. It was something I'd wanted to ask many times, but it never felt right.

"The dark fae said something to Fallon the other night. Something about her having a taste for humans. Or maybe having a taste *of* humans?" I wasn't sure how to formulate the rest of what I was asking, so I decided to let Finna make of it what she would. She looked down at the cup in her hands, nodding slightly. She drew in a breath before she spoke.

"Fallon had a mate. A human mate, many years ago. Their love was unlike most. It was the happiest I've ever seen her." Sadness crept into Finna's words as she spoke.

"What happened?" I asked gently. Finna shook her head, her eyes meeting mine again.

"That's not my story to tell."

***

Later that evening was Henry's stag do. Luckily for me, he was easy to please, so we'd gathered at the pub to have a relatively calm night of drinking and lamenting over the ways his life was about to change.

"We're going to leave straight after for her family's estate by the sea. Twenty-four years old and I've never seen the ocean, would you believe it?" Henry was already a few drinks in. Thomas had offered to split the tab with me.

"You think you'll be spending much time looking at the water?" Thomas teased as he lifted his pint. I'd decided to behave myself and have two drinks at the most. I was only halfway through my first and feeling rather proud about it.

"They've packed us enough honey wine to last the entire trip twice over. I'm not sure what I'll be able to see after we crack those bottles open!" He laughed loudly and finished his drink in a long swig. Memories of my night in the woods with Breck and the other fairies flashed in my mind as we laughed with him. He wasn't wrong.

"Steer it between the legs and you should be fine," I told him with a grin over the rim of my glass. This pulled another hearty laugh from him as he clapped me on the shoulder. I'd already given him my gift, which he'd gladly accepted. I didn't tell him that I'd been the one who made it. I just explained that it came highly recommended from a friend.

"And how would you know that? The prig of the

village himself, never even looked at a girl for longer than necessary." Our attention turned to Thomas as he prodded me with his words. Despite the number of times it had happened before, my nerves sparked to life under my skin as someone drew attention to this observation. My gaze fell to the table as Henry came to my rescue.

"Oh, come off it, Thomas. It's not his fault the women you're ogling after are always looking at him instead of you." Thomas sneered at him and slid off his stool to go collect another round. Henry gave me a look, eyes going big for a moment as he shook his head, and muttered, "Melter, he is."

"I didn't know who else to invite. Wally said he was busy. I thought it would be too boring if it was just you and me," I told him apologetically.

"S'alright. We always have a good time though, don't we?" He gave me his quirky smile and I nodded, agreeing. "I'm glad I'll have you to look after me horses while I'm gone. You know I couldn't trust them with anyone else." Henry and Sarah would be gone for a whole month to celebrate their marriage. I was happy to take on the responsibility for him.

Thomas returned and clanked the new pints down on the table. He was barely back on his seat before he was chugging his down. I took another tip of my own drink as my gaze shifted around the room, coming to rest at the bar. It was the spot where I'd had my first real conversation with Breck, back when he was just the miller. It seemed like a lifetime had passed since then.

"My family goes on holiday at the coast every

year, as you both know," Thomas said, returning to where our earlier conversation had left off. "You'll have to try walking along the edge of the water with your feet bare."

"I will, yeah," Henry told him in a dismissive tone. Thomas didn't seem to notice.

My attention continued to waver as I thought about the ocean. Murray was responsible for the life there, but I wondered if he was able to do all the things Breck could do with the water, too. Maybe he could do things Breck hadn't even learned yet. He would learn them all someday, though. I drained the rest of my glass and tried to shake my distraction before I went too far down the rabbit hole of my fantasies.

"Remember when you first started courting Sarah and you were terrified of her?" Thomas goaded with a smirk. I sighed and rubbed my forehead with my fingertips.

"I was not *terrified* of her," Henry drawled, rolling his eyes. "There was enormous pressure on me to make a good impression. I'd say it worked out well, wouldn't you?" he challenged. "Besides, you can't tell me that it doesn't take a good pint or six before you're loose enough to chat up a lass."

"Some liquid confidence never hurt anyone," Thomas reasoned. "And it makes them even more beautiful." We all shared a laugh at that one.

A man who was a friend of Henry's dad came over then, shaking his hand roughly and congratulating him on his impending marriage. The expectation was that when they returned from their trip, Henry would begin taking on more responsibility with his father's affairs. This was one of the men he'd be working with. I was slightly envious of how easily they spoke, as if they'd already been doing business together for ages.

I'd managed to keep my thoughts about it to myself up to that point, but secretly I was terrified of losing my best friend to his new life. He'd been a part of mine for so many years that I couldn't picture it without him. But now, he would be gone for several weeks and return a new man, with a wife, a boost in his career, and a lot less time to spend training with us. I'd spent months trying to comfort him through his own emotions about it. It was my turn for the reality to sink in.

"Alright there, Pete?" he asked after the man returned to his own table. I must've been revealing my worries on my face. "You look like you were thinking about Thomas giving some poor wan the shift." Thomas scoffed across the table as Henry chuckled. "Have you ever kissed a girl, Thomas?" he continued, really pushing his luck.

"I *have*," he insisted. We'd watched him make some valiant efforts over the years. He'd just never found anyone willing. His expression shifted from indignant to self-satisfied as he squared his shoulders and added, "In fact, it was Emma Clare."

Henry gasped loudly and set his pint down hard enough to slosh some of his drink onto the table, adding to the permanent film of stickiness on it. "*What*?!" I watched something like fear flash across his face before he looked at me. "I've changed me mind. You can have all of Sarah's sisters if it'll keep this one away from them."

I chuckled lightly and gave him a sorry look as I got off my stool. I was in need of that second drink. I made my way to the bar and asked for three more pints. It was a quiet night, so the keep served them for me straight away. I laid down my coins and carried the glasses back.

"He said he had no intentions with her! That makes her free game, does it not?"

"No! You've seen what Sarah and I have gone through. The courtship, the chaperones – every bit of this has been calculated. What are her parents going to think when they find out you've feckin' gone and sullied their precious youngest daughter?"

We watched the blood drain from his face as Thomas seemed to consider this for the first time. "All we did was kiss," he said weakly, his eyes darting between us to gauge our expressions. He reached for his drink and gulped it down until it was gone. Henry shook his head and stared at the table, clearly unable to wrap his head around what he'd just learned. My guess was that he was more worried Sarah would find out and come after him for it.

"Well," I started, grinning to myself, "at least you asked me first."

"Don't," Henry groaned, giving me a nauseated look. "Don't encourage him."

"All we did was kiss!" Thomas repeated, as if saying it again would change Henry's opinion of him. I knew the only way Henry could've been more upset was if Thomas had gone after one of his own sisters. I was just glad that Emma Clare had set her lusty green eyes on someone else.

My grin persisted as I thought of telling this whole mess to Breck when he returned. I knew he would find it funny, too. I still hadn't decided if I would invite him to the wedding. Henry said he was welcome to the reception, no questions asked, but all the seats at the actual ceremony were accounted for. It would be easier for us to disappear in the crowd at the party after, anyway.

"Ugh, the poor lass," Henry said finally, before he tipped his glass back.

"It was *one kiss*," Thomas said miserably.

"Don't you know where babies come from?" Henry asked quietly with a serious voice, teasing him. Thomas frowned at him and slumped in his seat, propping his chin on his fist, his elbow resting on the table. He realized too late that he'd set it in Henry's spilled drink. He complained with a groan as he looked at his wet sleeve, which made us laugh again. I hoped our times like this didn't have to end.

TWENTY-THREE

The game was brutal. It was unseasonably warm, with no clouds in the sky to protect us. Unlike the large crowd of spectators, who were sitting comfortably with their hand fans and hats, our only reprieve was the light breeze occasionally blowing across the pitch. Sarah and her sisters were sitting under their decorative lace parasols, sipping the drinks they'd been served.

Tepid water splashed on me as Henry dumped another ladleful over his short hair. His face and arms were an angry red from being in the sun for too long. My lungs felt heavy and uncomfortable in the humid air, but I was grateful that my skin wasn't as fair as his was. "*Oi*, save some for drinking," Wally scolded him before he could do it again.

The match was tied going into the fourth chukka. We'd played within a point of each other the entire game, and the score was low because neither of us was willing to give up ground without a fight. The purse for the season was substantial. I didn't know how much it was exactly – none of us would until we won – but we'd had record turnouts, which meant lots of wealthy people had been forking over their money to watch us play every weekend. I kept thinking of the look on William's face if I could hand over my winnings and show him that I was doing something worthwhile, after all.

Thomas was busy whingeing about the weather

as I mounted the chestnut mare and turned her around toward the field. Wally shoved his mallet into his hand and didn't bother responding to his complaints. I took a deep breath and coughed it out as I shifted my hips forward to get the mare moving, clicking my tongue. It all came down to this. I had my greatest weapon under my control now. I knew she would play as hard as the rest of us. I reached forward and patted her neck a few times as we trotted to the middle of the field.

The minutes ticked by. I felt sweat roll down my back as the sun glared down on us. The other team scored a goal. We answered with our own. It was a whirl of horse legs and mallet swings that could make your head spin if you weren't paying attention. Thomas had come around enough to look alive as he pursued the ball down the field toward the opposing team's goal. Another player smacked it away from him with a back swing, but Fergus was there to pick it up again and sent it sailing across the turf. We all charged forward after it. The ball was nearly through the posts when it was stolen again.

Henry was able to cut them off mid-field and entered an intense game of keep away with the other team's strongest player. He was a fella we'd known for years. When Jamie was alive, we'd joked that if we could trade Thomas for him, we would be unbeatable. Thomas never found that very funny.

The ball got tangled up in between the horses' legs and came to a stop as they circled around it, trying to get a good angle on it to send it back into motion. The other team got a strong hit on it and sent it rolling, but Henry's horse was faster, and he gained control again as the warning horn was blown. There were thirty seconds left to play before we would have to enter overtime to break the tie.

I pushed the chestnut mare faster to stay with the group, but it looked like Henry was going to score on his own. My heart was pounding in my chest as I watched him swing his mallet. An opposing player bumped him, trying to steal the ball away, but instead Henry took another massive hit and struck the ball under his horse's neck directly toward me.

I brought my mallet down, certain that I would miss, but somehow I made contact with the ball and sent it forward again. The chestnut mare bolted under my direction as we went after it. I watched the rest of the players on the field start to close in on us. I looked ahead at the angle of the goal, leaned forward out of the saddle, and whacked the ball with everything I had.

Sounds, sensations, and the world around me slowed as my eyes trailed it through the goal posts. I heard myself gasp, which sent a sharp pain through my chest, and then the final horn registered in my ears. My mouth fell open as I circled the mare back in a wide arc. The crowd was clapping only slightly more enthusiastically than they normally did, but Henry was cheering wildly, shaking his hands in the air in victory.

The members of the rival team began riding past me, offering their congratulations, and I had to get off my horse to feel my feet on the ground so I could make sure it was all real. As my boots hit the turf, I couldn't help the laugh that escaped me. I brought the chestnut mare's reins over her head and rubbed my hand along her neck to her shoulder. Her ear pricked toward me briefly before it pressed back; I turned to look at what was upsetting her with just enough time to see Henry throw himself at me. I yelped and landed hard on my side, coughing as he squished my sore lungs.

"You feckin' did it, boyo! What a bloody perfect shot!" He grabbed the sleeve on my shoulder hard in his fist and shook me before I could push him off.

"Good man, Peter!" Thomas called from the back of his horse as he circled us. Henry slapped my helmet and got to his feet, jumping into the air with a *whoop*. I laughed again and watched as he ran across the grass toward Sarah, who was waving both hands excitedly and leaning over the short fence that separated the crowd from the playing field. I was impressed that she'd been watching closely enough to know how the game ended. I always figured she just showed up to be seen. Henry wrapped his arms around her and picked her clear up off her feet, dragged her over the fence, and spun her around. She screamed and started demanding that he put her down at once. He didn't.

I rolled onto my back and closed my eyes, my chest still heaving from the adrenaline. I reached up to release the strap on my helmet, pulled it off, and scrubbed my gloved fingers through the disaster of sweaty curls I'd unleashed. I couldn't believe it. The last few seconds of the game flashed through my head as I tried to commit it to memory. I never wanted to forget this moment. Henry had trusted me to get it right. I trusted the chestnut mare to get me close enough to score. It hit me then that she'd startled away when Henry ran over to us.

I pushed myself up on my elbows, my eyes shooting to where Wally kept the rest of our horses tied during the game. I didn't see her there. I turned my head to scan the rest of the field. Surely, she hadn't gone too far. A twinge of panic set in when I still couldn't find her, and I sat up, bracing myself on one hand as I turned to look behind me.

There she was, a short distance away, swishing her stubby red tail. Someone had grabbed her for me. As the mare turned her head out of the way, a slow grin spread across my lips. Breck was rubbing his hand down her forehead, calming her. She pushed her muzzle up into his palm, enjoying his touch. When he finally looked at me, he grinned too, his gaze falling for a moment before our eyes met again.

Someone kicked the bucket inside me. My emotions went spilling everywhere, filling every bit of me with a swell of bliss that I'd never imagined. I chuckled to myself and flopped onto my back again, my hands coming to cover my face. To anyone else, I was just a fella on the pitch. But I knew he could see me for my truth. I was flint against steel, sparking and exploding from within, desperate for the chill of his magic to wrap around me and soothe the desire I couldn't contain.

I missed you, I thought. *I love you.*

ABOUT THE AUTHOR

S. O. Callahan

S. O. Callahan has always been fond of sweet things, namely chocolate and love stories. When she's not writing or reading, she enjoys baking, visiting National Parks and Historic Sites, and traveling with her husband. They live in Georgia and have two very spoiled cats named Ozzy and Beau.

Made in the USA
Columbia, SC
22 February 2022

56270561R00219